I0717853

Chronicle of Summer

Book Two of The Chronicle Series

Books by S.J. Garrett

CHRONICLE SERIES
Chronicle of Destiny
Chronicle of Summer

ETERNITY SERIES
Ghost Eyes

DESCENDANTS SERIES
Shadow on the Sea

3RD DISTRICT SERIES
The Shaughnessy File
The Carmichael File
The Dease File

Chronicle of Summer

Book Two of The Chronicle Series

S.J. Garrett

Chronicle of Summer

Copyright © 2016 S.J. Garrett

ALL RIGHTS RESERVED

No part of this book may be reproduced or transmitted in any form or by any means, electronic or mechanical, including photocopying, recording, or by any information storage or retrieval system, without prior written permission from the copyright owner unless such copying is expressly permitted by federal copyright law. The publisher is not authorized to grant permission for further uses of copyrighted selections printed in this book. Permission must be obtained from the individual copyright owners identified herein. Requests for permission should be addressed to the publisher.

Published by Line By Lion Publications, LLC, 318 Louis Coleman Jr. Drive, Louisville, KY 40212

Cover art by Stacy J. Garrett Photography

ISBN 978-1940938844

This is a work of fiction. Names, characters, places and incidents are products of the author's imagination or are used for literary purpose and are not to be construed as real. Any resemblance to actual events, locales, organizations, or persons, living or dead, are entirely coincidental. The names of actual locations and products are used solely for literary effect and should neither be taken as endorsement nor as a challenge to any associated trademarks.

Dedicated with love to all my fans: you guys keep me going.
Thank you.

Part One

~Memory~

Prologue

Dear Reader,

Summer is the best season on Lucksphere. Everything and everyone enters into its growth cycle. Children—be they Magi, Kin, or Dragon—enter into their first or second puberty. If entering first puberty, their birth-given powers evolve and they develop the true elemental powers that define our world. Air, Fire, Water, Soil. The Kin call them secondary powers because they learn Light or Dark from birth. Magi call them primary because they don't develop the secondary powers until second puberty and instead have lightning from birth. Some Magi, though, deviate from the norm.

Some Magi are Chronicles.

Chronicles are hated and feared. If a child becomes a Chronicle, their bodies develop golden lines of Dragon power upon first puberty. Lines that are a map leading them on some great journey. More deaths than births have littered the Chronicle past. Magi law dictates that all Chronicles are to be killed upon discovery.

But, you see, Chronicles are different in another way too. When they enter first puberty, they learn both primary and secondary elements. Air and Thunder, Fire and Smoke, Water and Ice, or Soil and Wood. There are also people known as Master Magi—people like me—who are exactly like Chronicles in their first puberty development. We, too, learn both elements from that time and evolve differently through our lives.

In the summer of my nineteenth year of life, I began my second puberty. This was the time when I would truly become an adult. You see, first puberty defined us as our gender, developing our bodies physically. Second puberty defined us sexually, allowing us to grow in ways that would give us the ability to reproduce.

Second puberty is the most beautiful time of life and makes summers beautiful as well. Growing and blossoming, discovering the beauty in yourself and in others. Discovering how to find pleasure in your entire world, and not just in a sensual manner. Your skin is more sensitive, and your eyes see clearer. You go through the world more conscious of yourself and others. It's like being born a second time. At least, that's what people say.

They don't mention the awkwardness or the shyness or the self-consciousness. They don't mention how wearing covering clothes because you live in a forest will make your sensitive skin itch like it was on fire. They don't mention how even a normally out-going person will feel embarrassed to go swimming when other people are around.

Second puberty is a pain in the ass.

Kelsey Renaire

Chapter One

The city of Verdenture boasted a population of fifty thousand Magi, a handful of Kin, and absolutely no Dragons. It was not unexpected. The Kin, both Sun and Moon, both Faerie and Elf, stuck to their own islands because they didn't always like Magi ways of life. Dragons . . . well, they intensely disliked Magi and stayed on their hidden isle to stifle the desire to start eating them.

Among the cities on the land of Carnelian, Verdenture was one of the biggest. It was also well noted on maps: within the forested city was a young Master Magi by the name of Kelsey Renaire. She was a Fire Magi who also used Smoke powers despite not yet being through second puberty. In fact, she had only recently begun that beautiful development, and every unattached person in town was waiting with their fingers crossed to be noticed.

In addition to her world-renown skills as a Master Weaponsmith, Kelsey was without question the most beautiful girl in her city. Her hair was a thick mane of red curls that varied between shades of red that were more blue and reds that were more orange. It cascaded down her back in a thick mass that she often tied on top of her head in a messy bundle wrapped in ribbon.

While she worked at a forging table, she wore little more than a snug, strapless top and a pair of shorts. She felt no fear of injury; her own fire could not burn her. She *did* worry about material catching flame, though, and cut down on what she wore. It could also get blinding hot, enough that it bothered even her.

When the small MoonKin Faerie approached the stone shed where her friend worked, she was highly disgruntled to see the men peeking inside. Unsurprised, naturally, but disgruntled regardless. She skidded to a stop and propped tiny hands on her hips. Her nearly translucent double wings fluttered to hold her in the air. "Ahem!"

All four males jumped and turned around quickly. The youngest was only just past second puberty, and the oldest was potentially old enough to be Kelsey's father. Etude wasn't sure which was more vexing. "March!" she ordered. She pointed down the road. Her slender arm with its rich mocha colored skin displayed its silver tattoos brightly in the filtered sunlight from the trees.

With distinct reluctance, the men dragged their feet and shuffled down the stone path toward the rest of the buildings. This part of Verdenture was purely residential with the pointed exception of Kelsey's stone shed. Though she was more social than most Master Magi, she was still inclined to retreat for her work.

Etude flew into the shed and landed on a shelf near the door. It was never a hardship to watch Kelsey. To be a Weaponsmith meant that the Fire Magi had to have a precision mastery over wielding her element at the same time that she manipulated her material. Every hammer blow had to have a delicate combination of physical force and Fire power.

Kelsey's skill was evidenced in the way sparks flew with every blow, and her strength was seen in the sleek muscles that lined her arms. Even Etude thought that Kelsey's strength was sexy, and she didn't have a particular preference for Magi. But Kelsey wasn't a normal Magi by any means of the imagination. Etude wasn't sure *how* different Kelsey was, but she had suspicions. Ones she would never speak out loud.

With a final rap of the hammer she held, Kelsey straightened and held up the sword she had been working on. She set the hammer aside before shoving her visor up on top of her head. Her crystalline blue eyes nearly looked green in the light from the fire in front of her. With a contented sigh, she put the sword to the side. It was just a blade right now. She would be smoke-carving the hilt later.

"Cross-eyed yet?" Etude asked.

Kelsey turned with a grin. "Only a little. Ugh." She swiped at her arms and her forehead to remove sweat but only added more soot and ash. "Air!"

Etude obligingly created a soft breeze to flow in the shed and remove the oppressive heat. Even Fire elements could get overheated. Etude, as an Air secondary Kin, was the perfect partner to work with. She was also a master etcher and could use her tertiary Thunder power to make intricate designs on Kelsey's weapons.

While Kelsey lied down on the floor, Etude flew over to look at the blade. It was double edged and both sides were razor sharp. The blade flared at the base where it would eventually be mounted to a hilt, and the entire blade came to a point that was no wider than Etude's hand. "It's beautiful," she said finally. "You just get better every time." She flew over to her friend and peered down at her face. "Can you walk?"

"I'm not sure. How long was I in here? My back says it was about ten hours."

"The sun says it was more like twelve."

"Who am I to argue with the sun?" She pushed herself up to a sitting position with a groan and then gained her feet. "I need a hot bath."

Etude smiled in bemusement as she followed her friend out of the shed. "She goes from a hot forge to a hot bath. I'm surprised you don't sleep in a fireplace, Kel. Really."

"Mom and Dad swear I used to crawl into them, actually. I was always covered in soot to the point that people were thinking I was part MoonKin because my skin was dark."

Etude studied the smudges across her face. "I ought to call you Soot then."

Kelsey stopped walking sharply, a fist emotionally slamming into her chest. Something hurt. Something hurt a lot. She felt as if she should remember something that she couldn't. She had forgotten something. Something important. She had always felt that way, but the missing memory suddenly seemed downright painful.

Etude's smile faded and she flew closer. "Kel?"

She shook her head. "I'm okay." She pushed it aside and walked faster down the road. "Let's get indoors before I get bit." Forested lands were notorious for insects. It was why the dwellers within the trees tended to wear longer clothing.

Because she wasn't an adult yet, she still lived with her mother and father. In deference to her very strong independent nature, though, her parents had made her room on their house to be self-sufficient. She had her own bathing room, kitchen, and work area. If she was in a mood where she didn't want to see anyone at all, it wasn't required.

That didn't mean her parents didn't try to spoil her.

She smiled as she walked into her bathing area and saw that there were already towels stacked neatly beside a special soap that wouldn't make her sensitive skin itch. The large pool was already filled with hot water, courtesy of her father who was a Water Magi. Water made by a person rather than nature itself never changed temperature.

"Your parents really love you," Etude noted.

She stripped off her clothes. "Yeah." She contentedly got into the tub and sank in to her neck. She remembered her hair was still up, and she pulled out the ribbon. The thick mass tumbled down, and she ducked underwater entirely. When she surfaced, she slung her hair out of her eyes and said, "Second puberty is overrated."

Her partner tried not to smile. She was six years old by Magi standards. By Kin Faerie standards, she was closer to her mid-twenties. Faeries grew very fast for their first three years and then grew at a normal rate until the age of one hundred when they stopped growing entirely. On the flipside, Kin Elves grew very slowly until about fifty. At that point they would start aging normally to two hundred when they stopped growing. Kin weren't immortal like Dragons, but their average age span was around five hundred.

As such, second puberty was around three for Faeries and around fifty for Elves. Etude was well past the process. "You're just reacting stronger because *you're* stronger." She gathered up Kelsey's discarded clothes and put them in the basket where they belonged. "You know flesh is secondary to power on Lucksphere. You went to school, didn't you?"

As if from memory, Kelsey obediently recited, "All Magi learn lightning from birth. Around an average age of thirteen, they enter first puberty where their bodies develop and define their gender. Their lightning becomes a tangible primary element. Around an average age of nineteen, they enter second puberty where they become capable of reproducing. Their primary element evolves into their secondary."

"With . . . ?"

She sighed and sank further in the water. "With the noted exception of Master Magi who develop secondary elements from first puberty and tend to grow at a faster rate. They also experience things far more clearly because, like all beings, their bodies are made by their power. The stronger the power, the stronger their bodies and feelings."

"Good girl." Etude flew over and picked up a cloth to help scrub Kelsey's face. Her friend never did manage to get all the soot off. In return, Kelsey always helped Etude get her wings clean. They didn't fold in ways that allowed her to reach all the parts.

There came a loud commotion outside, and Kelsey opened her eyes. "Now what?"

Etude flew over to the window and opened it just enough to hear. Outside, two women were talking with a visitor from Prismatic. "What do you mean you saw one?" one of the women asked.

"I saw one of the Chronicles that saved us nine years ago," the man explained. "It was just in passing, but it was definitely the female! She was riding on the back of a Dragon, and if that isn't a clue, I don't know what is. Dragons can't carry passengers, but Furies can carry their Chronicles."

"Ugh," the other woman said. "I still don't know why we let them live and have to kill all the rest. It's been nine years. The Black Magi Elite are gone. I say it's time to live and let live. If the two we've seen are anything to go by, then I don't believe Chronicles are the terror we've always been led to think."

"You may be right," the man said softly. "The woman I saw didn't look like a monster. If anything . . . I think she looked a little sad."

Etude shut the window and thought swiftly over things. That was a really good thing to hear, especially for the Kin. She flew down to where Kelsey was scrubbing her hair and landed on the edge of the pool. "They were talking about a Chronicle sighting." She watched Kelsey's face as she spoke. "She was seen flying on her Fury's back past the continent of Prismatic."

Kelsey's hands stilled as she felt a fierce pain welling up inside her chest. Her skin burned, and her soul felt as if it was being torn apart. She *needed* something. There was something that was critical to her existence. There was *someone* out there. She felt him at the back of her mind and heart. "What are Furies?" she managed to ask. She hurriedly rinsed her hair free from the soap though her fingers trembled.

Her reaction only confirmed Etude's suspicions. She closed her eyes. "Furies are Dragon Lords. Dragons are

Dragons, as you know, but Dragon Lords are Dragons who can take Magi form. Or Kin form, actually. Dragon Lords aren't always Furies, but Furies are always Dragon Lords. A Fury is the destined lover for a Chronicle. They're always complete opposites. Opposing genders, opposing elements. You know how Chronicles have lines? Well, those lines are a map leading them to their Fury. They say that the love between a Fury and a Chronicle is unlike any other. They become bound in ways that go beyond a Linking union for Magi, or a Binding one for Kin."

"Someone to love them," Kelsey said softly.

"Someone to love them no matter what happens. It's instantaneous, if what I've heard is true. They meet and . . . it just happens. I think part of it is the power exchange." When Kelsey blinked at her, she rubbed the back of her neck. "We call it feeding on power, but it's more complicated than that. You know how Dragons have infinite power and Magi don't? It's flipped in Chronicles and Furies. A Fury feeds on the Chronicle's power and it maintains balance. The Fury doesn't risk destroying his or herself and the Chronicle doesn't risk going out of control."

"It sounds beautiful."

The longing in Kelsey's voice was poignant and clear. It was also completely subconscious. Wanting to distract her, Etude flew over and tickled her ear. "Still ticklish?"

"Gah!" She grabbed Etude and dunked her. "You little fink! Taking advantage of my skin is not fair!" With an annoyed sound, she got to her feet and began wringing out her hair. It tended to dry very quickly because her natural body heat was high. "I hate this part of puberty! Yes, things I like are more enjoyable, but on the other hand, the things I don't like are LESS enjoyable!"

Etude surfaced and flew out of the water. She shook out her wings before grabbing Kelsey's clean clothing. "I think you're just having a double dose because you're a

Master Magi. It should go away in another month or so. I think."

"Think!" She muttered under her breath as she pulled on her underclothes. For women, the two-piece set was called a bikini. It consisted of a pair of underwear, and a top that crossed over a woman's breasts and tied behind her back and neck. The set could be worn with or without clothes over the top. The tighter the top, the better the support. She had seen some desert girls wearing literally nothing more than a bikini and some cloth tied around their hips. She *envied* them.

Because Kelsey's figure was on the lusher side—lush when compared to her average five-six height—she wore her bikini top slightly snugger than usual. She paired with it a pair of snug black leggings and a loose dark red tunic. The tunic had sleeves that went to her wrists, and it belted around her waist. The clothing was standard for a forest dweller.

It was for that reason that she walked into her parents' central room and complained, "Can we move to the desert already?"

Luke Renaire looked up from the book he was reading and smiled. "Hello, Etude."

Etude waved from where she was sitting on Kelsey's shoulder. "Hello!"

"What are you complaining about now?" Mildred Renaire asked in exasperation as she walked in from the kitchen. She moved over to the other seat in the room after stopping long enough to kiss her daughter's cheek. "Hello, Etude." The Faerie had been a common sight in the household for years.

"I'm complaining about this!" Kelsey held out her arms, and the sleeves flopped past her hands. "Long sleeves! Long leggings! I just put them on and already my arms and legs are itching!"

Luke frowned and put down his book. "I think

perhaps it's time you went to the doctor in town. This is going beyond unusual, even for you. If it was just your sensitivity, it wouldn't be isolated. Your whole body ought to be itching."

"It's not my whole body. Just the undersides of my arms and the outsides of my legs." She crossed her arms to keep herself from scratching her skin. It nearly burned in intensity. "No doctor. I'll deal with it."

Neither Luke nor Mildred felt surprised. Kelsey was, indeed, more outgoing than most Master Magi, but she was still highly sensitive emotionally. She wouldn't go to a doctor unless she was dying and, frankly, even that seemed debatable. "Very well," Luke conceded.

A knock came to the front door, sounding as three sharp raps. Mildred's brows rose. "The Militia?" She hurried over to the door and opened it slightly to peer out. On the doorstep she found a young man wearing the uniform of the Magi Militia. "Is there something wrong?"

"Not at all." The man smiled. "Might I enter? This is the home of Kelsey Renaire, is it not?"

"Bye." Kelsey turned to leave, but Etude grabbed her tunic collar and Luke grabbed her tunic bottom. She groaned but stopped trying to get away.

"Yes," Mildred said dryly, "it is. Please come in." She shut the door once he had entered and led the way to the sitting area. "What can we help you with?"

For a moment, Ilian Deepforge couldn't speak as he spotted Kelsey. He had never seen such a strikingly beautiful young woman before. Her thick red hair was like the purest of flames, and the blue eyes glowering at him reminded him of the clearest sky. Stunning was the only word he could think of to describe her.

She covered her face with a hand. "I'm not out of second puberty."

He blinked and then smiled apologetically. "I am

sincerely sorry for my absorption, and also sorry for the people in this town."

"So am I," Luke muttered.

"*Dad.*" Kelsey smacked his hand off her tunic and dislodged Etude as well. That done, she drew her thumb over her cheek and nose in the universal Magi greeting even as Etude folded her wings around herself and bowed in the Faerie greeting. "Nice to meet you. I am Kelsey Renaire, Master Fire Magi. This is my partner, Etude, Air secondary MoonKin."

Ilian returned the gesture. "Argyle Ilian Deepforge, Fire Magi, leader of one of the Militia parties deployed to Carnelian." He repeated the gesture to Mildred and Luke, including them in the respectful greeting.

Mildred and Luke also returned the gesture. "Luke Renaire, Water Magi, and my mate, Mildred, Soil Magi," Luke said. "What brings you to our home, Argyle?" He couldn't quite keep the confusion off his face or out of his voice. Argyles were the highest ranked members of the Militia, answering only to the king himself, and only half a dozen existed across the world. They did not usually show up randomly in cities; that was more a duty for the captains of individual units.

"Ilian, please. I was only recently promoted to Argyle and I'm not used to it." He took a seat when Mildred gestured to it. "I'll make a long story short. I am here to request aid from Kelsey to make new weapons for my unit. Our weapons simply won't hold up to our current duty. We need better, and there is none better than Master Kelsey's weaponry."

Kelsey was intrigued despite herself. "Can you tell me what your duty is?"

"I am afraid I cannot," he admitted. "We have to deploy in a few days, however. I suppose that is not long enough."

"For one or two weapons, perhaps. How many do you

need?"

"Twenty."

She grimaced. "Never happen. I can do it in a week or two, though."

He almost offered to come back for them but changed his mind at the last moment. He couldn't seem to look away from her crystalline eyes. He wanted to be the one she noticed when she was ready to experiment in second puberty. The only way to do that would be to keep her near. "Would you be willing to travel with my unit long enough to make the weapons?"

"Only if I go too," Etude muttered. Her rose-colored eyes told him that she had not missed his interest.

"Naturally you would be invited," he agreed. "I would not expect her to simply travel off with a person you have no reason to trust."

"It's up to you, Kelsey," Mildred said softly. "You are a Master Magi and therefore you exist under rules different from the rest of us. If you wish to go, we won't stop you."

"I'll make the first weapon," she decided. "If it is sufficient for you, I will agree to travel with you long enough to make the rest. What would you like me to work on first?"

Ilian drew the sword he wore at his side and offered it hilt first. Though he had been expecting it, he was still a little nonplussed as she took it with one hand and no effort. There were few women who could swing a sword one handed. "As you can see, this sword has seen much fighting and is stressed to the max."

"Hmph. Looks like it was never high quality to begin with. I could do better in my sleep." She propped the sword on her shoulder. "Let's talk payment."

"I can offer a payment of ten bronze coins for twenty weapons." He smiled when the others stared at him. "It's a payment well made for Master Kelsey's work."

Bronze coins were worth five times the amount of ivory coins, the common currency for the world. A single bronze coin could allow someone to buy food and supplies for an entire month. "*Aiyea,*" Etude breathed.

"Pardon?" Luke asked.

"It has no translation to Magi," she apologized. "It's more an exclamation of surprise than a word. Remember, we have five hundred characters in our language and you only have one hundred."

"Aiyea indeed," murmured Mildred.

Kelsey shrugged one shoulder. She was used to hearing outrageous amounts of money thrown at her. Truth be told, she had a sealed trunk in her room with enough ivory that she would never want for anything again. "Done." She turned to head for the door.

Startled, Ilian said, "You do not need to get started right now."

"Why shouldn't I?" Without another word, she headed back to her rooms to change into her work clothes again.

Luke said softly, "She's more comfortable there. Though she smiles and laughs and makes friends easily, she is more secure in her workshop." He ran a hand through his hair with a sigh. "When she was a child, she was precocious. But when she entered first puberty . . . a part of her retreated. If she didn't have her weaponry, she wouldn't even live in a town."

"You want to see?" Etude asked. Ilian nodded and she flew over to the door. "Follow me." With him close, she headed back down the trail toward the shed. There was already a plume of orange smoke coming from the chimney. "You liked Kelsey, didn't you?"

"I did," the Argyle admitted. "It was a bit surprising. I've never been quite so strongly attracted to anyone before, not since my own second puberty."

"And that was . . .?"

"About ten years ago." Realizing what she was fishing

for, he offered, "I am twenty-eight summers old." He ran a hand through his short black hair. "Her eyes . . . they remind me of the glass I often work with. I've always wanted to make that shade of blue."

"Oh so you work mostly in Smoke?" The element of Smoke allowed a Fire user to create and craft glass. They could also break down glass into sand for Soil users to weave cloth with.

"I do. I have not done it since joining the Militia though. Perhaps I ought to pick it up again." He stopped talking as they reached the door to the shed. As quietly as possible, he opened the door and peered inside. At first, he was distracted by Kelsey's stunningly long legs, and then he focused on her work and his breath really caught.

The sliver of metal she hammered looked like nothing remotely resembling a sword. But as he watched, he could see the beginnings of the shape forming, the metal melting and reforming under master control. His eyes shifted to her face, and he was left spellbound. The color of her eyes . . . he wanted to capture it within glass.

"Don't fall in love with her," Etude warned softly.

"Why?"

"Because she can never love you back." She flew off without another word through the darkening twilight.

Ilian, with nothing else he could do, turned to go to the camp where his party rested while they waited to set off again. Her words confused him highly. In a world where you couldn't *know* how a person's heart would function until after second puberty, how could she know whether or not Kelsey could love him?

Something told him he didn't want to know the answer.

Chapter Two

When Kelsey finished the sword blade, she went immediately into smoke carving. Smoke carving was arduous. It meant making glass and then fire hardening it until it was unbreakable. During that hardening process was a very small window of time where carving could be done without detail being lost. As soon as it hardened completely, it was too late to do additional work without breaking the hilt down entirely and starting over.

The normal course of work wasn't without its mishaps, and there were several piles of discarded glass by the time she deemed the hilt ready to be forged to the blade. That was another several hours of work because the fusion of metal and glass involved excruciating heat and detail to make sure the two halves bonded permanently. She had never had a sword break. She didn't intend to start.

Once the sword was finally done, she dunked it into a spinning barrel of sand to polish up. The spinning barrel was an invention of Air Kin and could spin for as long as needed. She had it set to spin for two hours. The sword was on its last step, and not a minute too soon. She pulled off her visor, curled up near the forge, and fell asleep.

When she woke next, she discovered that someone had draped a blanket over her. Groggy, she pushed the blanket aside and sat up. She rubbed at her eyes blearily. She was *starving* and she wasn't sure what day it was. She had lost track of time again.

"Good morning."

She squinted at the doorway and discovered Ilian standing there. "Good morning," she said automatically. She blinked. "Is it morning? What day is it?"

"Two nights and a day since I asked you to make the sword." He walked in and removed his hat reverently. "I've never known any Weaponsmith who could sustain herself on her power alone for two days while she crafted. I can see why you are a master at your work."

"Uh-huh." She covered a yawn. "I don't like interrupting myself." She got to her feet, then went over to where the barrel had long since stopped spinning. She pulled the sword out and shook the sand off. "Here you are." She held it out to him.

He took the sword from her slowly, and his eyes filled with astonishment. It was twice as long as the original sword, but it was also twice as light, evidence of the master crafted glass hilt. Magi characters for strength and speed had been etched into the hilt. The blade looked sharp enough to split hair, and hair was one of the strongest physical components on any being's body.

"I need a bath and food." Still rubbing her eyes, she walked past him and headed for her home.

He realized belatedly that he was being left behind. He sheathed the sword at his side and hurried to catch up. "Would you be ready to leave within the day? We must move quickly, and for that I apologize. Do you even think you can craft on the move?"

"Please stop talking." She stopped at her door and gave him a disgruntled look. "Please, leave me alone for a while."

He frowned when the door shut in his face. "I did not mean to offend her."

"You didn't." Etude had flown up without his awareness and she circled around in front of him. "She's just sensitive right now. Come back later. She needs to rest now." She entered through a smaller door designed just for her, and the sound of the lock sealing was distinct.

Once inside, she flew over to where Kelsey was staring at a hot bath with a look of consternation on her face. "I saw the sword was done," Etude explained. "We knew you'd be ready to relax soon. I'll get some food for you."

Kelsey stripped down and climbed into the pool gratefully. She still felt groggy and disoriented. She hadn't slept long, but she had slept hard. She had also pushed herself intensely hard and was even more sensitive than usual. The hot water felt delightfully comforting against her skin.

When Etude returned with a basket full of piping hot food, she could only sigh. Kelsey was asleep in the bath. The girl needed a keeper. She worked too hard and too long. The part that frustrated Etude was that she *knew* Kelsey's perfect match was in the world. She just didn't know where he was exactly. "I'll help you find him," she vowed softly. She landed on the edge of the pool to study her friend. "I'll find your Fury. And I'll help you find yourself." She shook it off and gave Kelsey a shake. "Kel. Come on, Kel."

Kelsey's eyes blinked open. "Huh? Oh." She sat up and rubbed her eyes. "I fell asleep again. Sorry." She got to her feet, then got out of the bath. "I guess I was still tired." She got dressed in fresh clothes and took the basket into her kitchen to eat. "I worry you, Etude. I'm sorry."

"It's all right. You wouldn't be my Kelsey if you didn't." Etude took a biscuit from the basket. It was nearly bigger than she was, but Faeries ate a lot compared to their size. "Do you think you'll be able to do the weapons justice while traveling?"

"I think so." Kelsey happily ate the blended rice and fruit she had been given. Her mom could *cook.* "I figure I'll work on the weapons at night while we're camping then sleep during the day while we travel."

As she proceeded to demolish the rest of the food, Etude had to smile. Kelsey could eat on a level comparable to a Kin Faerie.

After eating, Kelsey got out a hipsack to begin packing for the trip, and Etude hurried for her own home to do the same. The hipsacks were another invention of the Kin and could expand in size to hold whatever they needed. The Kin had made a lot of things that way; everything from blankets to furniture. They had even invented portable meals that remained as little bricks until a missing element was added. Kelsey kept a supply of the meals that lacked Fire. Once she added it, she had a full meal ready for eating. She was fond of the fruit ones, personally.

As soon as the hipsack was ready, she tied it to a special loop on her belt. She preferred to wear the sack there rather than using the strap to carry it across her body or on her back. She just preferred the freedom of movement.

Since she didn't know when she would be getting back, she headed to her parents' side of the house. "I'm leaving now," she said as she walked into the room. "I'm not sure when I'll be getting home, though. Probably a week or two. Maybe more."

Mildred hugged her daughter tight. "Be safe."

Luke didn't much like the idea of his baby girl heading off with the Militia for two weeks when she was still in the beginnings of second puberty. He didn't like Ilian's admiration of Kelsey for the same. It was a normal process and no stopping it, but he hated his baby growing up. "Come home soon," was all he finally said.

Kelsey smiled and hugged him tightly. "You can't stop me from growing up. But don't worry. Ilian isn't for me." She tilted her head. "I'm not sure how I'm sure, but I am. So, no worries. Once I find the person for me, you can bet I'll be in a bigger hurry to finish puberty. Until then it can take its time." She scratched at her arm. "Except for the itching!"

He laughed and hugged her again. "That's my girl." His smile faded as she headed out of the house. He had a terrible feeling that he wouldn't see her again for a long time, if ever. There was something important about her that he had forgotten. He was sure of it. He just couldn't call it to mind.

Kelsey found Etude outside and they headed out of the city to where the encampment was set up. The people there were already breaking camp, and Kelsey noticed males and females of all elements present. They wore all manner of weapons, from swords to spears to clubs to gloves with blades in them for slashing. Her mind automatically began cataloguing what she would be making. Some would be easier than others and that would cut down on the time needed.

"Are you feeling better?" Ilian asked as he walked up. "I sincerely apologize for overwhelming you this morning. I wasn't even thinking."

"It's okay," she assured him. "I was just a little . . . raw. If it is all right, I would like to obtain a wagon for the trip. It will allow me to bring my smaller forge, and it will also give me a place to sleep during the day. I can work at night."

"That can be arranged," he agreed. He smiled. "You're doing us an immense favor. It's the least we can do." He turned and gestured to the Militia members. "I'll introduce them as we go along. It might be too much all at once."

Etude saw several people studying Kelsey with interest and pointedly sat on her shoulder with arms crossed. The message was clear: You had to go through the MoonKin to get to her partner. The looks averted.

They set out within an hour and Kelsey rode in the back of the wagon with her forge. The wagon was being pulled by a findral, and the rest of the Militia rode more of the same though theirs had been bred for battle. Studying the large beasts, Kelsey asked Etude, "Were findral a Kin invention gone awry?"

Etude giggled softly. "No, they've always been here. I think the fact that they can climb mountains and swim in water is an adaptability feature. There's much more water than land now, and I think I remember my elders telling me that they used to be just land creatures."

"And the fact that they look like large dogs with a bird's head and fins instead of wings?"

"I'd like to point out that we Kin find you Magi weird because you don't have large ears or wings." Kin Elves were known for their varied ear types. They could be feline ears, canine ears, or any other kind of ear. It was those ears that marked an Elf in the way that wings marked the Faeries.

"You have a good point," Kelsey conceded. She turned to where Ilian rode beside the cart. "Where are we heading? Can you tell me at least that much?"

"I can. We're heading for the center of Carnelian. It's the only plains area that any Magi land has that isn't covered in sand." He studied her intently for a moment. Though he wasn't supposed to divulge details, he felt that she could be trusted. More still, if she was riding into a battle, she had a right to know. "What do you know of the Black Magi Elite?"

Her heart gave a dull thud inside her chest that she tried to ignore. "Nine years ago they tried to destroy the world. They were diverted by the only two living Chronicles who stayed on the lost Isle of the Dragons afterward and have not been seen much since."

"That's the summary of events. The Elite broke off from the original Black Magi, which was a faction led by the male Chronicle to create a haven for Master Magi like you. It was a place for them to grow and develop and adjust to society. I've always thought he was drawn to the duty because he knew how it felt to be different."

Her heart was beating harder and there was again a pain in her head as if she couldn't remember something. "And the Elite?"

He studied her, wondering why her voice seemed strained. "Were led by an insane man named Soh. He was responsible for the death of the former king of the Magi and the upheaval we endured for two years to find a new king. Soh took control of Glacia and was going to instigate war. The Chronicles gathered Dragons and Kin and launched a surprise attack. I'd like to say they won, but it wasn't entirely a win. A rogue Dragon who had been assisting Soh got away. She also translocated the remaining Elite across the world."

"Translocation is an ability of Air elements to send someone to a random location in the world," Etude explained.

"Oh." Kelsey frowned. "I would have been ten. Why don't I remember any of this?"

"That's the problem." Ilian looked again toward the road. "No one remembers anything clearly. We can tell you the events, but we couldn't tell you what the individual players looked like. I remember *distinctly* fighting the Elite during my first year with the Militia. I do not remember their faces or their names. No one in the world remembers."

"We Kin are investigating," Etude said softly, "but even our best scholars cannot determine how or why the entire world would forget something so important. Many don't believe the Elite ever existed or exist now."

"Oh," Ilian's voice sounded grim, "they do. That is where we are heading. An Elite member named Phi has shown up. He is disrupting the flow of the land and causing quakes. The quakes have been traveling underground and reaching even the edges of Prismatic. It needs to be stopped before there is irreparable damage done."

Kelsey lifted a brow. "And that's why you need my weapons."

"Indeed. Phi is a Master Magi as well. If we are to fight him, we need to be prepared." He cursed softly under his breath. "It would be so much better if I knew precisely what he looked like."

When they camped for the night, Kelsey got to work. She completed two weapons over the course of the night.

Upon the morning, she was curled up in the back of the wagon and deeply asleep. The Militia didn't disturb her. They were slightly in awe at the speed and the quality with which she produced weapons.

It was a repeat of the same for two more days. As the third day dawned, they exited the forest and entered into the only open grassy plain that now existed on Magi lands. If it had been flown over, it would have resembled a green bowl surrounded by a rim of dark trees. At only ten miles wide, the valley was considered protected territory. It could be traveled through, but it could not be populated for fear it would go away.

Halfway through the day, Etude woke Kelsey so that she could see the plains during the day. She sleepily rode with her arms draped over the side of the wagon, enjoying the scenery but half wishing for more sleep.

"If you will permit me?" Ilian had ridden closer and was holding out a hand.

She scrubbed at her eyes before reluctantly holding out her hand. His hand closed around her wrist gently, and she hid a flinch as the itching got worse. She focused instead on the feel of his Fire power sliding into her body and helping replenish her. Elements could lend power to one another to bolster strength and reserves.

Even after the exchange, he held onto her wrist. His eyes searched hers but he saw no awareness in her for him as a man. It was frustrating. The more he was around her, the more he liked her. He could very easily lose his heart to this woman. "Will you write me a letter when you're an adult?" he finally asked.

Etude said nothing. Kelsey studied Ilian's face before gently freeing her wrist. "No," she said softly. "I'm sorry. I'm not comfortable enough with you to consider sharing my power with you in that way. Don't take it personally. Etude is the only close friend I've ever had. I just . . . am different from normal Magi."

For the first time, he felt as if he had seen the true Kelsey. The vibrant and fiery exterior hid a deeply vulnerable core. He had always heard that Master Magi tended to be withdrawn and hide from society, but she had seemed different. In that moment, he knew she wasn't. "I hope you find the one whom you are comfortable with," he finally said quietly. "And I wish it would be me."

There came a shout from someone riding at the front. "There's a Dragon flying on the horizon to the right! I can just barely see their scales from here. Do you want us to flag them down and ask if they've seen our target?"

Though Magi and Dragons did not get along in the slightest because of the Chronicle Massacre of a thousand years past, there was a tentative truce between them. Magi didn't ostracize Dragons, and Dragons didn't eat Magi.

Ilian frowned. "Are they going our direction?"

"Seems to be."

"Let them be then. If we need to, we'll flag them down. For now, let us see if we can't find our target on our own. I just hope it takes a little while longer." He looked at Kelsey. "I'd rather see you finish the weapons and be on your way home before the fight. You're not Militia. You don't deserve to be pulled into our fight."

She finished the rest of the weapons three nights later when they were three-quarters of the way through the plains. She was tired and drained to her core but also well pleased with herself. She had done some of her best work. As she curled up in the wagon to get some sleep before dawn for once, her eyes were drawn to the distance where she could see the Dragon landing for sleep. Something stirred in her heart, something fierce and longing. She fell asleep before she could capture the feeling again.

She woke again later when Ilian gently shook her shoulder. Groggily, she said, "Yes?"

"Kelsey." He smiled when her eyes blinked open. "I

just wanted to tell you that we're parting ways here." He desperately tried to ignore how beautiful she looked with her hair falling in her face and her cheeks streaked with soot. "Etude has said she can drive the wagon and findral home for you."

"Oh." She rubbed at her eyes. "Okay. Are the weapons sufficient?"

"Sufficient?" a female repeated in awe. "It's *incredible*." She used dual daggers and was swinging them lightly in the air. "They weigh nothing yet they're stronger than anything I've ever seen. You earned every ounce of your pay."

"And as to that," Ilian handed Kelsey a small bag, "here it is." A trace of longing in his voice, he asked, "Are you sure you won't consider me someday?"

She opened her mouth to respond when the ground suddenly began to shake. The quake was quick and violent and knocked several people off their feet. The findral began to panic, stamping their feet and screeching in fear. The findral attached to the wagon reared so sharply that he jerked the wagon in the air and it sent Kelsey flying.

"Are you all right?" Etude asked urgently as she hurried to her partner's side.

"I'm okay," was the shaky response. "What's going on?" Under her hands, the land felt like it was in a riotous frenzy. "The power in the land is going out of control!"

Grimly, Ilian said, "I think Phi found us before we found him. I am sorry, Kelsey."

She got to her feet and shook her hair back. "Don't be." She looked at her now ruined forge. "I'm a little pissed off right now." Because she was far more sensitive to the fluctuations of power than normal Magi, she felt the rolling power before the land began to shake again. "Brace yourselves!"

That quake was much harder and lasted much longer.

Cracks began to appear in the land. Vents of pure elemental power began to shoot in the air violently. One appeared under Kelsey's feet, but she didn't bother to move. It was the rawest sort of power, and it replenished her in a way that sleep never could.

Seeing her absorb the power, Ilian felt his heart begin to pound in his chest. He had never heard of a Magi, Master or not, who could absorb the surplus power in the world. It was too raw, too concentrated. There *was* a theory he had once heard, however, and it terrified him. He didn't want it to be true.

A fireball erupted in the middle of the area and flung everyone in all directions. Some Militia members didn't immediately get up. Others didn't get up at all. The sheer potency of the power told Ilian that Phi was indeed a Master Magi, despite his hoping it might be just a rumor. That was the last thing they needed. "Air Magi, get a shield up!" he shouted. "Someone try to find out where he's attacking from!"

Things began to get worse. The power in the land disrupted the life of the findral and began to mutate them into monsters. The few Militia who had seemed to have been knocked out by the first blast also began to mutate. It was a terrifying and disgusting sight as the newly made monsters turned on everyone around them, even each other.

Etude grabbed Kelsey's arm. "We need to leave!"

"Go, quickly!" Ilian urged.

Kelsey didn't waste words. She turned and ran. Her target was the line of trees in the distance. Though it was running away from the direction of her home, it would be easier to lose an attacker in the forest; on the plains she was a perfect target.

An eruption of Water power forced her to stop running. Before she could double back and go around it, her skin began to itch violently. She turned sharply and discovered a man standing behind her. He was taller than she was and wore a heavy white cloak etched with a black chalice and dagger. The chalice was the symbol of the Magi. The black chalice was of Black Magi. And the chalice and dagger were the mark of the Black Magi Elite.

Phi couldn't have been more pleased as he slowly approached her. "A Master Magi. How fabulous. Your death will certainly break up this land entirely."

"You've got to kill me first, *poka*!" She hurled a fireball right at his face with all her strength.

The other Magi was a Master Soil Magi. He didn't have the power to neutralize or block her; he had to scramble to the side. As he did, he felt the heat of the fireball scorch his hair and clothes. The fireball proved to be the first of many. She continued to throw fireballs at him until he was scrambling everywhere in his efforts to dodge. "How are you doing that?!" Even Master Magi weren't that strong!

"I can hold him off," she said softly to Etude. "Go get the Dragon! Tell they they can eat this guy with the Magi's thanks!"

Etude didn't want to leave her but knew that it was more important to get the Dragon for more reasons than her friend understood. Without a word, she turned and shot across the sky like a small mocha colored bullet. Phi turned sharply but the vines he sent after her were no match for a Kin's speed. A fireball detonated at his feet and flung him backwards. He landed hard and the ground rippled like water. The fight was only making things worse.

Vines shot out of the ground and struck Kelsey in the chest. She hit the ground and rolled several feet before rolling up to her feet again. Her chest hurt like hell and she could see where she had been cut by thorns. Her skin itched violently again, and it seemed as if her power literally burned in her blood.

Eyes blazing red with power, she hurled another

fireball. "Let's just see which of us is better! I think I'm a little better equipped for battle, don't you?" The next fireball barely missed her enemy.

He snarled at her. "I look forward to ripping you apart!" He gathered his power and broke the land open under her feet. It caused a lethal amount of power to spew in the air. To his shock and horror, she absorbed it as if it was nothing. *It wasn't even her element*! "What in the name of the Underrealm are you?" he demanded sharply.

Fire gathered around her hands. Her eyes burned with the same flames at her fingers. "Very, very angry," she warned softly, her voice crackling like a bonfire. "And congratulations! You're my target."

As he dodged both fireballs, he knew he was not dealing with a normal Master Magi. He didn't know what she was, but he knew damned well that she was not normal by any stretch of the imagination. He should have easily won over any Magi opponent. He just needed to survive long enough to figure her out. Once he did, he would be able to destroy her.

A fireball narrowly missed his head. At the least, he *hoped* he would be able to destroy her.

Chapter Three

Solis T'mer was a Water Fury. He was one of the younger, only slightly over two hundred years in age, but he was by no means the weakest. Just being a Fury made him stronger than any of his regular Dragon brethren, but he always had to be careful of his majiks usage for fear that he would drain himself out. Then again, his brothers and sisters never played too hard with him. They were gentle with him.

They knew he was going to die.

It was the curse of a Fury. They always knew when their Chronicle was born, and they always knew when their Chronicle died. Hundreds of Furies had been mercifully killed over the centuries to save them from eternal suffering. It had become a painful way of life for the Dragons. It was why Solis had never said anything about sensing his Chronicle's birth even ten years after it occurred.

That had been nine years ago. He didn't know how, but his Chronicle still lived somewhere. He had his suspicions, though. When Jazz Eaglewind and Dominic Whisperer had found their Chronicles, both miraculously alive despite all odds, it had given hope to all the other Furies. More still, Morgan Chronis had spoken of the four Chronicle children he had found and sheltered. One in particular had caught Solis' attention: a female Fire Chronicle. Solis was a male Water Fury. The chance of that Chronicle being his was very, very high.

In the nine years since the Chronis siblings had come to the Isle of Dragons, Furies had gone out to live in society. The Magi still killed Chronicles when they were found. Dragons and Furies couldn't track a Chronicle, but they knew them when they were right on top of them. No one had found any Chronicles yet. And some Furies had returned to the Isle to be mercifully killed. In some ways, things had not changed.

Solis didn't mind living among the Magi too much. Because he was Fury—a Dragon Lord—he could take a Magi form and walk among the crowds. He still stood out, though. His thick brown hair was streaked with pale blue as mark of his Dragon origins. He was of average height for Magi males at five-eleven, but he was slightly broader in the shoulder and overall more powerful. It was to be expected. Dragons retained their strength in any form they took.

His intent was to spend a year in every city, long enough to meet every citizen. When that was done, he would go to the next city. It was the only way he could think of to ensure that he found his Chronicle. He *knew* he would know her when he found her. His only fear was that he might miss her in passing.

He had spent three years on Prismatic. He was ready for Carnelian. He decided to start at the southern end, so he flew past the northern end along the outside of the trees. He wasn't allowed to fly directly over cities because it would disrupt the flow of power in the land. He wouldn't have minded taking out a few Magi, but he refused to hurt the world. It had suffered enough. It still suffered.

As he flew slowly along, he could see the Militia party traveling to his left. He was half-tempted to go buzz them just for the humor, but they seemed to be on a mission. Because it was an oddity, he decided to stick around and keep pace with them. He knew Carnelian was having quakes and that was unusual enough.

At twenty feet in length with brown scales and blue streaks across them, he knew they had to have seen him. No signal flares went up, so he camped when they did and flew when they traveled. What *were* they up to?

He got his answer when the land erupted into violent quakes and began spewing power everywhere. He dodged the blasts sharply and found a safe place to land. When his feet touched down, he could feel the riot under the land. Someone was deliberately disrupting the flow. He landed on the plains side of the trees, and his sharp eyes could see the signs of the Militia battling.

Before he could make up his mind whether or not to help, he spotted a streak of brown coming toward him. He hastily caught the small MoonKin Faerie gently before she could tumble past him. "Easy!" He held her on one claw and brought her to eye level. "What's wrong?"

Kin and Dragons were close allies. Etude felt no fear. Trying to catch a breath, she said, "Elite. Fight. Help!"

"Breathe!" His eyes narrowed slightly. "What's this about the Black Magi Elite?"

She closed her eyes and tried to get a steady breath. Flying that fast always drained her to the core. Her euphoria at finding a Water Fury, a *male* Water Fury, couldn't override her breathlessness. Precious time was wasting! After a moment, she was able to say, "My partner! She's in danger! We were traveling with the Militia so Kelsey could make weapons for the Militia to fight Phi, from the Elite. But Phi attacked us! Now Kelsey is fighting him and we need help!"

He closed his claws around her gently to hold her securely and flapped his wings to fly up into the air. "Which way?" he asked.

"Look for the big explosions."

A large fireball blew up even as she finished speaking. He immediately began flying in that direction, and he skirted around the edges of the Militia's battle with many monsters. The Militia was trained to deal with this sort of thing. Etude's partner was not. But as he flew, he felt his heart begin beating harder. Those fireballs didn't look like normal Magi fireballs.

The fireball ripped open a crater in the ground and

dropped Phi into the center where he landed with a bone-jarring thud. He scrambled back out and shot a wave of soil at Kelsey that sent her tumbling backwards. To his frustration, she just rolled to her feet again. They were both lined with wounds and he knew he was reaching the end of his power. She just seemed to keep on going. "No Magi has infinite power!" He hurled vines at her.

She let the vines wrap around her waist and then grabbed onto them. "Try me!" Fire poured down her arms and streaked down the vines toward him. He was flung backwards as the vines evaporated. Reaching for reserves of power she didn't know she had, she went after him directly.

Before she took two steps, the Dragon suddenly passed by right overhead. She felt his power wash over her, and her skin seemed to burst into flame. She fell to her knees on a cry as fire whipped around her wildly. Her head pounded and her body throbbed. Her skin was stretching, stretching, until she thought it would tear apart. Hotter and hotter her power grew until something inside broke.

Golden lines blazed into appearance along the insides of her arms and along the outside of her legs. They were vividly displayed by her working clothes and unmistakable. With little sharp edges and some rounded curls, they looked stark and powerful and like nothing else in the world.

Phi's heart leapt into his throat. "A Chronicle," he managed to say. "Well, that explains that. I guess I won't kill you after all!" He started to lunge forward only to stop sharply as the Dragon landed in front of Kelsey with teeth bared. Terrified, he scrambled back instead. He knew those markings. "A Fury!"

Solis was in a rage he had never felt before. The instant he had laid eyes on Kelsey, he had *known* she was his. His Chronicle. The only being that was his alone and he alone belonged to. He hadn't needed to see her painful awakening to know the truth. Now she was dazed and vulnerable, a far cry from the magnificent fire goddess he had just witnessed. He would protect her when she could not protect herself. "Get away from my Chronicle." The words were little more than a guttural growl.

"*Your* . . .?" Phi kept backing up. The last he needed was to tangle with a Dragoon set! "You win this time, Fury! But I'll be back to take her away! She will be the harbinger of destruction for the Magi!"

Power erupted from the land and momentarily blinded Solis. When the power faded, Phi was gone. Solis dismissed him and turned back to Magi form. He hurried to Kelsey's side and realized she had fallen unconscious in the grass. He knelt and tenderly eased her into his arms. She was *exquisite*! The lines that flowed so sensuously down her body were made from his power. "Finally," he managed to say. He buried his face in her hair. "Finally, I've found you."

Etude started to speak when she heard a sound. "Solis!"

He turned his head sharply, and his brown eyes narrowed. "Who goes?!" The words came as little more than a snarl, clear evidence that he would protect his mate. Water and ice condensed warningly around his feet.

Slowly, Ilian walked forward. The hand holding the sword that Kelsey had forged was trembling. Wounds marked his body from the fight he had just left. Eyes riveted to Kelsey, he was scarcely breathing. "She's . . . she's . . ."

"A Chronicle," Etude confirmed softly. "I warned you that she could never love you."

Solis held Kelsey closer to his chest possessively. "Kelsey belongs to me, Magi." The words were gentler than they might have been otherwise. He could see the heartbreak in Ilian's eyes that said he truly cared for Kelsey. "What are you going to do?"

Ilian closed his eyes. "Magi law states that all

Chronicles are to be killed when found." His eyes opened and he looked at the sword he carried. Slowly he lowered the blade and turned his back. "It would be blasphemy to kill a Weaponsmith with a sword she forged herself, and it is the only weapon I am carrying."

Taking the gift as it was given, Solis gently laid Kelsey down on the ground and stood. He returned to his Dragon form and then picked her up with his claws and cradled her as if she was the most precious thing in the universe. She *was* the most precious thing in his universe. "There was no Chronicle here," he said.

Ilian nodded without turning around. "When I arrived, I saw Phi escaping. I did not see Kelsey. For her sake, it is better that the world think she is dead for now. Take her away." He did turn then and look at Solis. "And love her the way I wanted to."

"You have my vow." With a flap of his wings, Solis rose into the air. He turned to go west, to the Isle of Dragons, and realized in belated dismay that he had forgotten the way. Mentally cursing, he turned instead to head for one of the many islands that dotted the edge of Carnelian. They would be safe enough there.

As they went, Etude flew alongside his head. "Solis," she said apologetically, "Kelsey's only just starting second puberty. I can't even tell you how far along she is. She's felt no attraction to anyone."

A sigh was his answer. "Well, I know Dominic had to suffer Tariah going through second puberty. If he can handle it as a Fire Fury, I can handle it as a Water Fury." He glanced down at Kelsey, enchanted by her delicate features and lush mane of hair. The soot that streaked her face seemed to enhance rather than decrease her appeal. From where he was holding her, he could feel the steady rise in her power. It was matched by a decrease in his majiks. It was curious.

Etude seemed to sense it. "You need to bond as

Dragoons." When he glanced at her, she asked, "I take it you haven't inherited the memories of any older Dragons."

"None that were Furies," he admitted. He angled down toward the small island that he could see approaching. Like most islands around Carnelian, it was covered in trees. He changed into Magi form as he landed, and Kelsey remained gently cradled in his arms.

"It's simple," Etude said as she flew down to join him. "Her power rises automatically and your majiks drain. This is to ensure that the first bonding takes place as soon as possible. Once you've bonded, you'll be Dragoons, tied in ways that surpass even normal Linkings for Magi or Bindings for Kin."

"Or Unities for Dragons." He wasn't entirely listening to her anymore; his eyes were riveted to Kelsey's face. Her name reminded him of the word *kelsin*, a word in Draconic that meant 'storms of fire'.

Sensing the demands of nature, Etude smiled and flew off to give them privacy. He didn't notice. He gently put Kelsey down on the soft grass, and her hair burned against the sun-dappled green. He sat down beside her and lifted her hand with his. She was of average size for a Magi female but her hands looked strong and capable. He could see the tiny scars from working with weapons and he could feel the calluses from the same.

He lost track of the time. He memorized the lines of her face and the supple curves of her body. Every minute made his hunger for her grow. Hunger for her shocking beauty and her deceptive strength. Hunger for the spirit she had revealed as she stood on a battlefield and burned wild. Hunger for the power he felt smoldering under her skin and begging for his attention.

When she began to stir, he moved closer. He framed her face with his free hand and held her other hand to his heart. "Kelsey?" he asked softly. "Wake up, *ishke*. It's all right. You're safe with me."

Her lashes fluttered and lifted. His breath caught. Her eyes were the crystalline blue of the purest glass, framed by thick red lashes, and now shimmering with fires barely held in check. He had never seen eyes like hers before, yet they were somehow achingly familiar. He had waited to see these eyes.

Kelsey woke to raging pain in her body. Her power was out of control. She wanted to burn and ravage the land as a firestorm. She could barely breathe for the heat consuming her. The tender touch on her cheek was disorienting for its familiarity, then she heard *it*. A male voice that her very soul recognized. She recognized it all the way to her cells, to the power that built her. *Hers.* This man was hers.

Her eyes opened and she found herself staring into a somehow familiar face. The shock of his features reverberated through her body. A hunger she had never felt before made her eyes move over him swiftly in an attempt to memorize everything. She felt the lure of his watery power brushing against hers seductively, and the sudden sharp hunger to taste his kiss was stunning. It was nearly as stunning as the sight of her arm when she lifted a hand to touch his face. She had lines.

"It's all right," he said huskily. He could feel the alluring touch of her power to his in a call as ancient as time. She was further in her development than Etude had believed if she was instinctively able to send out such a signal to her mate. "You're a Chronicle, Kelsey. My Chronicle."

Delight brought her smile quickly. "I'm not alone?"

"Never again." He gathered her closer. "I've looked for you for so long . . ."

She went to put her arms around him but her body protested. Her breath caught in pain. "What's wrong with me?"

"We need to bond. I need to feed on your power." He brushed his lips over her shoulder and a soft red aura instantly began to rise as her power emanated in a physical way. It shimmered and danced like flames. "Are you afraid?"

"Not of you." Her eyes closed as his lips sipped delicately along her skin. The little shivers of delight were completely foreign but she wasn't afraid of them either. They felt utterly right.

Unable to resist the temptation, he began to breathe in her power and drink it from her tender skin. He followed the trail as it went down her arm. His lips teased the lines along the inside of her arm and traced their shape. Her power tasted wild and spicy, stinging his tongue lightly but exploding with flavor after. His free hand smoothed compulsively over her side and shaped the curve of her hip.

He slowly traced his lips back up to her shoulder and then brushed them over her face. He moved steadily toward her lips. "I'm going to kiss you," he warned, his lips a breath from hers. "Do you mind?"

She didn't answer with words. She simply wrapped her arms around his shoulders and pressed upward to take his lips with hers. She had never kissed anyone before. She had never wanted to. This man . . . she wanted. She wanted to kiss him with a vengeance that was as much emotional as it was physical.

The kiss deepened further as he fed from her power there. It was hotter and sweeter, still spicy but now flavored. He was instantly addicted and knew he would never have enough. And even when he felt the last of her power enter him, he couldn't make himself release her lips. He nipped lightly at her lower lip and felt her shock as if it was inside his own heart.

It wasn't the only thing he could feel. As the bonds between them cemented fully, he could see all the way inside her soul and her mind. He could see and feel her every emotion and her every thought. She saw into him the same way, and he could sense her wariness for the volatile emotions inside him. Love, desire, and more. A third emotion that encompassed the others and was yet stronger.

"What is that?" she asked softly, her voice smoky with a desire she had only just discovered. Inside her heart and body, she could see the stirrings of the same emotion, as yet growing, but sure to be an inferno before long. The love . . . that already consumed her. She didn't question it. She simply accepted it.

"Dragons call it *ishke*." He smoothed her hair from her face. "It's a word meaning all the needs, wants, and desires of the world." He lifted her onto his lap as he sat up properly and hoped she was as yet innocent enough to miss his body's unmistakable reaction to her mere presence—he didn't want to scare her away.

She still noticed, but she ignored it. She wasn't ready for that much exploration of her Fury's body, no matter how incredibly beautiful he was to her eyes and no matter how much her body ached now. "I'll try to be nice to you," she finally said. "Because I'm not the type to wait around for things to happen."

His eyes half closed. "Try your best not to throw me on the floor and ravage me until you're absolutely sure that you're ready for me to return the favor." His breath hissed out as her power curled around his temptingly. It wasn't done with the intent to seduce so much as it was done to see if it *could* seduce. Her curiosity in second puberty would be the death of him, but he would die a happy man.

"It won't kill you!" Oddly content, she curled against his chest and then pulled back in surprise as she felt an odd heat. His power was . . . changing. Being the type of person she was, she immediately untied the laces of his tunic and opened the front.

A bit dryly, he asked, "Are you further along than I

presumed?"

"You have lines." In wonder, she traced them with a fingertip. They looked just like her lines as they flowed across his muscular chest and down toward the edge of his pants. It was her power that made the lines on his skin, and the knowledge was heady. She wanted him to be marked. She wanted him to be visibly claimed. One tiny little detail eluded her though.

He eyed her warily as he sensed the steady rise of her ire. "Yes?"

She grabbed the open edges of his shirt and shook him quickly. "How am I Chronicle?!" she demanded in aggravation. "How did I not know?! Where were my lines? Why didn't I know until you went by overhead?! And why didn't you eat Phi?!" She broke off as he wrapped his arms around her and cuddled her close. The fight went out of her body, and she sighed as she relaxed against him. "You won't win all fights like that," she muttered against his shoulder.

He just smiled. "For now I will. You'll have other weapons to use against me later." He slowly smoothed his hands over her back and curled his power around her comfortingly. "I didn't eat Phi because he got away. As to how you didn't know you were a Chronicle . . . that would be Morgan's doing."

She frowned as something hurt fiercely inside her heart. "Morgan?" She shook her head as she felt again that disturbing empty place. She felt Solis probing gently at her mind and said nothing.

As he examined her mind, he said softly, "Morgan Chronis. Nine years ago, he was the leader of the Black Magi. He found four secret Chronicle children and kept them hidden from Magi eyes under the disguise of being Master Magi. When the fight went down, he erased their memories of him and sent them away via translocation."

She began to tremble and pressed closer against his

chest, desperately needing him to ground her. "But I grew up in Carnelian! Didn't I?" She shook her head. "I can't remember. Why can't I remember?" She lifted her head in new annoyance as a thought occurred. "What's your name, damn it? I can't just go around calling you 'my Fury' no matter how much I might want to!"

"Come back here." He pulled her close once more. "My name is Solis T'mer." He continued to examine her mind until he found the gaping hole. It was nearly five years' worth of memories that had been taken away. There were 'filler' memories inserted in their place, illusions based on the memories of her first five years so that neither she nor her parents suspected anything. "There it is."

"I want them back."

"I know, *ishke*." He shook his head. "But I'm not sure if I can do anything. This is an Air Chronicle's work, and Morgan is a Chronis. He and Tariah are stronger than anything anyone has ever known, even our only Fury Elder, and he lived back when Chronicles were not killed outright."

"Well *try*." Her lips moved into a pout that instantly drew his attention. She sensed it and grumbled, "Don't kiss me! Fix my memories *then* you can kiss me. Better yet, I'll kiss you. Fair enough?"

With incentive like that, who was he to not try? He began to gather the fragmented portions of her mind by using his Water power to sweep them together. The more he looked, the more sure he was that Morgan hadn't *erased* the memories. They had been broken into dozens of tiny fragments that only a Fury could mend. "What he can do with his power is astonishing."

"Fix it!"

"Don't be so impatient, Kel." He swirled the pieces together and put them into the empty place in her mind. Once reassembled, they naturally refused together. Even as the completed memories punched into his mind, they punched into hers.

As the memories swamped her, pain mushroomed inside her chest. She doubled over against Solis with a low cry and a sob tore out of her chest. She beat at his shoulder with a fist. "*He sent me away!!*"

Heart breaking, he could only rock her back and forth. He could see the love inside her heart and mind yet felt no jealousy. It was a love entirely different from the one she felt for him. "He wanted to protect you."

"I'm going to fry him to a crisp!" She straightened and swiped at her eyes. "He *promised* to come get us!" A hiccup caught in her chest as she remembered her surrogate brothers and sister. "Roman and C.J. and Jayda." She wiped her eyes with the edge of his tunic. "We have to go find them."

"Right now?"

"Yes, right now!"

"No."

Her eyes went wide as she stared at him. "What?"

"*Some*one owes someone else a kiss."

Blue eyes blinked at him for long moments before beginning to spark with a distinct challenge. Defiantly, she grabbed his hands and held them at his sides. "You can't touch me," she ordered. "Because it's the first time I've ever instigated a kiss like this." Despite her bravado, her heart pounded in her chest.

Sensing it, his power curled around her softly and comfortingly but with a distinct lure to her own. It was as instinctive as breathing. "I'm waiting." Try as he might, his voice came out deeper and richer, evidence of his hunger for her.

Before she could change her mind, she leaned in and kissed him. She had intended to keep it quick, but he tasted like the purest of spring waters. Tempted, she went back for a second kiss and softly teased his lips with her tongue.

When his lips parted, she couldn't resist the offering. She deepened the kiss slowly and savored the way he tasted. Heat began to rise in her body as ripples of pleasure spread outward.

This time when he nipped at her lower lip, the little sting wasn't alarming. She returned the gesture and the rumble in his chest was wonderful. She moved to press closer and her breasts flattened against his chest. The lash of pleasure shocked her, and she jerked back. Her eyes were wide as she carefully took a breath. "Uhm."

He mentally counted all one thousand characters in the Draconic language and aimed for maintaining control. He wanted nothing more than to yank her back into his arms. Instead, he contented himself with tugging her closer and nuzzling his nose into her hair.

"Why do you keep nuzzling me like that?"

"It's how Dragons show affection." He rubbed his nose against hers and made her smile. "See?"

"I like it." She let out a breath. "So. Leaving now?"

"Best to wait until tomorrow," he disagreed. "We don't know what is going on with Carnelian or Phi." His eyes narrowed sharply. "And I assure you, if I get my hands on him, he will become the main dish at a roasting."

She barely stifled a giggle as she saw bubbles coming out of his nose. Quirks of Dragons; they tended to breathe their element when they reached a certain level of anger. And though it was a sign of temper, it was still funny to see Solis breathing bubbles. Her humor faded, however, as another thought entered her mind. "What about Etude?"

"You mean me?" Etude flew down from out of the sky and hugged Kelsey around the neck tightly. "I'm right here."

"You scared me!" Kelsey grabbed her friend and glared at her. "And why didn't you tell me? You had to know! You're a Kin! It's why you told me about Furies and Chronicles, isn't it? Damn it, Etude!"

"She gets cranky easily," Etude told Solis gravely.

"I'd noticed," was the dry response.

Smiling because she liked him for Kelsey, Etude turned back to her partner. "I didn't tell you because you didn't know. Someone had gone to great pains to hide your identity and I was the last person who would reveal it." When Kelsey released her, she flew over to land on Solis' shoulder. "We should go to Kindred."

"Really?" Kelsey frowned. "For shelter?"

"For one, yes. But we can contact Daylar there."

"Who is Daylar?"

Solis smiled. "He is the Kin brother to Tariah. You remember the wing in her lines? That was the mark of it. She is considered honorary Kin, and she and Daylar claim each other as brother and sister. His Bonded mate was Tariah's partner for a while."

"Oh." Kelsey frowned thoughtfully. "Okay, we can go there." Belatedly, she realized how bossy she was being. Slightly chagrined, she looked down. "That is, if you're all right with that, Solis."

"Don't be demure." He smiled. "It doesn't suit you. I am perfectly content to let you lead as you see fit, and if you ever try to push me into something I don't want, you'll know instantly. You'll feel it from inside me." He skimmed his knuckles across her cheek and brushed her hair back. Tenderly, he wiped away a smudge of soot. "You need a bath."

"There's a little basin not far away where you could make one," Etude offered.

"Good idea." He stood and scooped an astonished Kelsey up in his arms. "Let's go take a bath."

"With Etude?!"

Etude giggled as she followed. "Don't worry! I'm not interested in Dragons or Magi. If he isn't offended, I'm not." She grinned when Kelsey glowered at her. "Are you jealous, Kel?"

"Yes!" Kelsey crossed her arms indignantly. "He's *my* Fury."

Solis decided he liked the possession in her voice and emotions. "Yes, I am. And therefore you should know there's no reason to be concerned." He spotted the basin that Etude had mentioned and put Kelsey down on her feet. "Stay here."

She obligingly waited while he went to the edge of the basin. It looked like a portion of the land underneath had given way from a collapsed cave. The top was covered with smooth grass. At its deepest point, it would go up to Solis' chest. At the widest point, it was ten feet across.

Solis first used ice to cover the bottom with a smooth and clean surface. Once done, he began filling the basin with fresh water. Because both the ice and the water were of his power, he could maintain the ice and use hot water at the same time. He brought it to a point where it began to waft steam in the air. "There we go."

Etude dove in, clothes and all. Kelsey, for the first time in her life, found herself immensely shy. She hesitated in taking off her clothes, and Solis sensed it. He walked over and tugged her into his arms. "Never found this part before, did you?" he asked lovingly. He nuzzled her hair softly. "For some, the self-consciousness never quite goes away. Based on your personality, I imagine you'll be one to get over it quickly."

She frowned. "I don't like being worried about how people think I look. I know I'm beautiful." It was said without conceit because it was a statement of fact. And, being Kelsey, she decided to get to the point. She stepped back out of his arms and stripped off her clothes. "There. Now tell me I'm beautiful so I can get past your first reaction and get used to being naked around you."

Speech literally beyond his capabilities, he could only stare at her. His eyes devoured every perfect curve of her body. Her lines burned gold against her pale skin where they traversed her arms and legs. Her body was lush compared to most other females but she looked like perfection to his eyes.

The wordless absorption was exactly what she needed to restore her confidence. She could feel his power boiling as it swirled around her, and she felt her own power turning to steam. In fact, steam was lifting from both their bodies as power and desire merged. Her breath hitched.

He averted his gaze. "I should have made the water glacial," he managed to say at last. "And I think it would be best if I kept at least some of my clothes on for the time being."

Her gaze lowered and red color climbed her cheeks to match her hair. "Yes, please." She hastily hurried into the water and ducked under the surface. Why was it so much more unnerving to see the reality of what she had learned in school? The combination of trepidation and anticipation was vexing. Curiosity gnawed at her but couldn't override her nerves. "Why does growing up take so long?" she asked when she surfaced.

Floating on her back, Etude said, "You wouldn't appreciate it so much if it didn't. And I'd like to note that you're going through something in a short time that normally takes people months."

Kelsey's eyes met Solis' and fresh steam that had nothing to do with the pool rose from their skin. "Not fast enough," she said softly. "Not nearly fast enough." She sighed and turned toward the setting sun in the distance. "Where do you suppose Roman and the others are?" she asked.

"I don't know." Solis tugged her back against his chest. "But if they're like you, they're living a normal life as Master Magi. Once we reach Kindred, we'll see what we can do to find them." He pressed his lips to her hair. "I'm sorry I can't take you to the Isle right now."

"It's okay." She covered his hands with hers and smiled. "We'll appreciate it more because it takes longer."

He laughed outright and hugged her closer. He wouldn't have traded her for any other Chronicle in the world. She was the perfect one for him.

Chapter Four

To the northeast beyond Carnelian was the mainland of the Magi. It was a large continent called Spectrum. A handful of medium sized cities were sparsely scattered across the vast deserts, and tinier little towns sat even farther apart. The two cities with the most traffic were the capitol known as Prismatic and the port town to the south known as Mirah. Very few boats ever docked on the northern end of Spectrum. Most sailed all the way to the south. Boats from the northernmost icy land of Glacia couldn't sail south at all; violent storms always barred the way.

Mirah was a decent sized town of many thousand Magi and half a dozen Kin or so. They were mostly SunKin, though, since they survived in the desert sun better than the MoonKin did. Spreading out from city central were dozens of farms where Soil and Water Magi made the desert land fertile enough to grow food. Air Magi owned windmills that provided fresh breezes to the farms in the surrounding areas when the sun reached its most unbearable points. The windmills also ground assorted crops into a state that could be used for cooking.

One windmill in particular was located closest to Mirah and provided heat relief to the people. The windmill was owned by a young Master Air Magi by the name of Roman Arequo. His parents lived in the city proper and owned a market where they sold fresh fruit. Even they didn't see Roman very often; as with other Master Magi, he kept to himself.

It was to the regret of all the available women in the town. Roman was one of the most attractive males around. At the age of eighteen, he was an early bloomer and already partway through second puberty. Only one girl could verify it was true. She had been the lucky recipient of his first kiss. Most assumed he had to be nearing the experimental stage, but he had made no signs of being interested in anyone that way.

At six feet tall, he was of average height for a Magi male. His hair was yellow blond, and his eyes were dark ocean blue. His shoulders were strong, and his skin golden from exposure to the sun. Like other desert men, he wore loose pants, boots, and a vest. Very little else could be worn without fear of passing out.

When he went into town for supplies, his path was almost always inundated with females. It was to the amusement of the older Magi that he simply never seemed to notice! Either he was exceptionally innocent for someone in second puberty, or he was being selectively blind.

As Roman stood watching his mother load up a hipsack with fresh fruit, he saw one of the village girls approaching. He barely stifled a sigh. Seeing it, Liza Arequo murmured, "Roman . . . be nice."

The girl had reached the counter, and she leaned on the top of it. As she did, the curves of her breasts were clearly displayed within the sturdy bikini top she wore. "You're such a stranger!" she scolded Roman. She smiled, her lashes fluttering slightly. "When are you going to write me a letter?"

He pretended as if he had only just noticed her. "Oh. Melody. Did you say something?"

She sighed. "No, nothing. Nice seeing you, Roman." She crossed her arms and sulked as he slung the sack over his shoulder and headed out of the building. "Why is he so blind?" she complained to Liza.

"He's a Master Magi," Liza said simply. "We're lucky that he even comes into town, Melody. Ever since he was a child, he's been isolated from others because of his power. How many Master Magi do you know of existing in this world?"

Melody frowned. "Four. There's that Weaponsmith in Carnelian, some doctor on Glacia, a weaver on Choral, and Roman."

"The sheer fact that there are four currently in this world at once is astonishing enough," Tomas Arequo explained as he walked up. He absently rested a hand on Liza's back. "Master Magi are born one in a few thousand. It seems much rarer than that because they simply . . . go away. Their power is so strong that they are unable to handle society."

"But Roman . . ." She trailed off slowly as she realized that Roman never came into town unless it was for supplies. He never came to festivals and never celebrated the harvests. "Is it because we treat him differently?" she asked softly.

"He feels different." Because she liked Melody, Liza offered, "You could go visit him. He might like that. I think his father and I are the only ones who bother. Perhaps having someone reach out to him might do some good."

"Then I'll go out there tomorrow!" Melody smiled. "He might never write me a letter, but I still like him."

Roman kept a findral for the brief trip in and out of town. He actually had a small herd of the beasts and they wandered all over his property. He couldn't help but relax as he entered onto his land. He *hated* going to town. The people were always talking and moving and putting off energy that rubbed him raw.

He went into his small house and put the sack down on the kitchen counter. Absently, he scratched at his face and his right arm. Ever since he had begun second puberty, they had been itching like mad. Combined with his overall increased skin sensitivity, it was vexing.

As he was putting things away, he saw a small fire flare in the air over Mirah. He smiled wryly and went to the base of the largest windmill. His power welled up as a whisper of wind, and he poured the Air element into the machine. The top began to turn and a steady breeze began blowing toward Mirah. It could spin for a few hours without more power added.

Because it was his favorite way to pass time, he headed into the small area he used as a workroom. He had a partnership with a Fire Magi in town. She made glass art that he etched for her. They split the profits though he had often tried to turn down his share. He just liked the work.

He lost track of the time as he worked. All his concentration was on using his Thunder powers to make precision details without shattering the glass. He hadn't shattered anything for all the four years he had been doing it, but he was always careful.

The rising moons surprised him and he looked out the window. There were two visible in the sky and it was definitely nighttime. There were no more signals over Mirah; he didn't need to regenerate the windmill. Content with his day, he headed for a bath and then for bed. This plain and simple life was his favorite.

He was in the fields the next afternoon tending to the findral when he saw several Magi approaching. He frowned and headed toward the fence to meet them. One Magi was the Elder in the village. Others were Soil Magi. It looked like a search party. "Is something wrong?" he asked. He automatically drew his thumb over his nose and cheek.

The Elder returned the gesture. "Has Melody Brenik been out this way?"

Roman's brows went up in surprise. "She hasn't. Was she supposed to be?"

"She set out this morning to visit you, or so she said. She hasn't come back and we're worried." The Magi who had spoken blew out a breath. "If you were anyone else, we'd have assumed that you and she were 'together.'"

Roman rolled his eyes. "I'm eighteen. You can use the

phrase 'sleeping together' just as well as anyone. I won't be offended. And, no, she's not here, nor are we 'together.' I'm not interested in her that way. Or in anyone." He shrugged one shoulder. "It's uncomfortable around other people."

"And that's why we're worried," the Elder confirmed.

Roman's eyes studied his face. "What aren't you telling me?" At the surprised look, he crossed his arms. "I'm not an idiot. I'm also an Air Magi. I can sense the fluctuation in your minds. So, what's going on?"

"There have been a series of disappearances around the town," one woman said. "We're almost positive the people who are disappearing have been murdered. The power in the land under Mirah is steadily going out of control. Waves are starting to spread and are connecting with ones from Carnelian. Storms have started to form and are cutting off trade."

"That's why the ports have been quiet," he murmured mostly to himself. "Has anyone contacted the Militia?"

"The king is sending out a party as soon as he can. He dispatched one to Carnelian as well. There is some fear that the Black Magi Elite are returning." When Roman frowned, the Elder explained, "You would have been too young nine years ago to remember. It was during the war when the two Chronicles and their Furies joined with Kin and Dragon to protect us Magi from the Elite. It was an . . . eye opening time for us all."

His heart began to beat hard inside his chest, and a pain grew inside his soul and mind. His skin began itching as if it were burning. "A Fury?" he asked softly. "What's a Fury? I think I know what a Chronicle is."

Wondering why he sounded so odd, one man offered, "A Fury is a Dragon Lord that doesn't have infinite power. He or she has to feed on the power of a Chronicle who, unlike Magi, does have infinite power. We used to think it was some sort of evil pact but it really isn't. Some of the last people to see the two Dragoon pairs said they looked beautiful together."

"I see." Roman pushed down the throbbing inside his soul. He wanted . . . something. Someone. He didn't know what. He just knew there was someone in the world who needed him and that he needed in return. "Well, I didn't see Melody. I hope she's okay."

"So do we," the Elder said. "Sorry to disturb you, Roman."

"No, it's fine." He leaned on the fence and watched as they headed back toward the city. He looked almost blindly at the desert sand under his feet. Hearing about the Elite had made him somehow afraid. Hearing about Furies had made his heart and soul hurt. Something in his mind was blank as if he had forgotten something important. Nothing seemed to make sense.

By evening, he could feel the faint tremors under the land that meant that things were getting worse. There had been no word about Melody. His concern grew, and he headed for the town in the morning. When he reached his parents' store, he made a beeline for the back where Tomas was sorting wares. "Has anyone found Melody?"

Tomas looked up sadly. "They combed a five-mile area around the town and found no sign of her power. It went to a dune past the city, where it then disappeared. It's just like the other disappearances. We have to assume the worst."

Roman sat down on one of the wooden crates in the area. "I liked her," he said softly. "Not like she wanted, but she was nice. She didn't judge me." When his mother came up behind him, he leaned back against her. "It doesn't seem right."

"The Elder is preparing to issue rules about traveling alone. We can only prepare for the worst." Liza sighed as she heard the bell over the door. "Already? We're not fully set up yet."

"I'll go." He got to his feet and headed out to the front of the store. "Can I help you? They're not quite open yet."

The woman standing at the bins where some of the fruits were just being stacked was of average female Magi height and wore the comfortable clothes of the desert. He had thought he knew everyone in town by then, but she was new. She had pale brown hair and matching eyes. There was nothing unremarkable about her, yet he felt wary.

The woman turned to smile at him, and her eyes widened slightly. She stared at him in genuine surprise. She hadn't expected him to be *that* attractive. Other women had seriously underestimated his good looks. "I'm sorry," she apologized. "I just wanted out of the heat. I don't mind waiting."

"Mm-hmm." He began to edge toward the doors. He didn't trust the double take she had made. "In that case, you can just wait a few minutes and my parents will be right out."

"Oh, your parents own the shop?" She moved and blocked the door by casually leaning against the frame. She made the Magi sign of respect. "Beta, Air Magi."

He automatically returned the gesture. "Roman Arequo, Air Magi."

The name registered and her eyes widened. "You're the Master Magi that owns the windmill near here, aren't you? You're much younger than I had been thinking. In fact, aren't you a glass etcher? I've seen some of your work. It's beautiful."

"Thank you." He longingly eyed the exit behind her. He hated small talk. "You're new in town?"

"Just got in a few days ago," she confirmed. "Been meeting people and learning names." She pointedly blocked the door more firmly. "Are you an adult?" It wasn't a rude question, not when he was only eighteen. Second puberty could hit at any time after sixteen.

"Not quite yet. Could you let me out?"

"Depends on if you agree to come have dinner with me."

Tired of the games, he reached out, grabbed her around the waist, and bodily lifted her out of the doorway. As he set her aside, he said, "No, thank you. Nice meeting you." With more haste than grace, he hurried out the door and toward his findral.

Mouth hanging to her knees, she couldn't find a single word. When Tomas cleared his throat, she turned and gestured at the door. "Did you *see* that?!"

"Yes," he said dryly. "I did."

"I don't take no for an answer." She tossed her hair and stalked out of the building. Under other circumstances, she would have just kidnapped Roman or lured him away from the village. This, however, was personal. She could break his stubborn Master Magi isolation and *then* get around to killing him. His death would surely break the land. The boy had a lot of power. She had felt it when he had touched her. It just didn't entirely feel . . . normal.

When Beta showed up at the windmill the next day, Roman was cleaning out the shed that served as a shelter for his findral. He nearly groaned when he saw her. Why were women in the town determined to 'make' him see them? If he was going to be attracted to them, it would have already happened! Without looking at her, he said, "You're too old for me."

Her eyes narrowed and she planted her hands on her hips. "And what makes you think so?" she challenged. "Are you saying I look old?"

"You have three lines at the corner of your eyes," he noted. He raked down fresh dunegrass from the bin and began to spread it out. "Those lines don't appear on Magi until at least the age of thirty. Even at that, you're too old for me."

"It's actually better." She moved closer and leaned on the edge of a stall, trying to ignore the findral inside. She hated those things. "Wouldn't it be better to finish second puberty with an older woman who knows her way around things? No strings attached."

"Anyone who attaches strings to anything said or done during second puberty is an idiot to begin with." He hefted a bag and began pouring out grain. "And maybe I'm not ready for experimenting. Ever think of that?"

"You kissed Terina in town," was the retort. "She's quite proud to be your first kiss."

"As she ought to be. I'm proud to be her first as well."

Frustrated, she threw her hands in the air. "All I'm asking is for you to give me a chance! Let me hang around and maybe you'll be attracted to me. Are you saying I'm not attractive?"

"Not to me." He kicked the stall door as he added some fruit to the grain.

She opened her mouth to retort when the findral in the stall snorted and grabbed a mouthful of her hair. "Let go!" she yelped. "Let go of me!" She smacked the findral and it released her with a squawk. She backed up quickly. "Yick, I hate these beasts!"

As she turned and fled out of the barn, Roman patted the findral on the neck. "I owe you one, friend." To his amusement, the findral made a point of eating the fruit first to get rid of the taste of Beta's hair. Sometimes animals called it just right.

He was in the fields the next day when she showed up again. "Either be helpful or go away," he said bluntly as he cut down long stalks of dunegrass. It was the only crop he grew simply because it was cheaper to grow it than buy it. "There are spare gloves in the wagon."

Reluctantly, she put on the gloves and moved over to help. She held the grasses while he cut them and then helped tie them into bundles. "I can't believe you run this place by yourself. I rode the edges of your land. It's very big. Very isolated."

"It's isolated because it's big and it's big because I want to be isolated." He hefted the bundle into the wagon and began to cut the next. "And I enjoy the work. It keeps me busy. If I wasn't busy, I wouldn't even live near the town." His eyes flicked to hers. "Do you know what it's like to be a Master Magi?"

Softly, she said, "Yes, I think I do. I knew some Master Magi once. They walked the edge of madness sometimes. Maybe they needed a desert farm like this." She studied his face. "Don't you dislike the Magi? They've committed genocide of the Chronicles for a thousand years, and only a few centuries ago, they tried to erase the Kin. They've made our world more sea than land."

"They're collectively stupid." He grabbed a strip of cloth and tied it around his head to keep his bangs out of his eyes. "Does that mean that we need to get rid of them instead? No."

She let the subject shelve. Instead, she blew her hair out of her eyes as she continued to help with the dunegrass. Manual labor wasn't her favorite but she couldn't deny the benefits of getting to see sunlight ripple across Roman's muscular chest and arms. That was worth the aches she would have later.

As Roman was getting a bucket of water for them, he saw a flare over Mirah. He instantly diverted and went into the windmill. Beta followed him curiously. She had never been inside a windmill before.

He wound up the base of the windmill and then added his power to make it start. Once it was running, he also added power to the system of pipes that went around the house to keep the heat out. As he did, her eyes narrowed slightly. He was using a lot of power, even for a Master Magi. How could he maintain two separate systems without draining himself?

"Drink some water before you pass out." He handed her a cup.

"Oh. Right." She gratefully drank the water, only belatedly realizing she was thirsty. It was deceptively easy to forget to drink anything while in the desert, especially for Air Magi. Their power automatically cooled their bodies and they never knew they were overheating. "When did you come to Mirah?"

Why wasn't she leaving yet? He rubbed his forehead. "About nine years ago. I grew up in a much smaller town but it wasn't comfortable for me so we came out here. Where are you from?"

"Prismatic."

"Long way to move."

"Felt like a change." Beginning to sense that he was at the edges of his patience, she headed for the door. "Well, I'll see you tomorrow."

As she disappeared out the door, he considered digging a basement and hiding in it. Why wouldn't she take 'no' for an answer? The sad part was that he couldn't even say that he was starting to like her more now that they had spent time together. The opposite was true. He did not trust her and he did not like the sense of her power. It smelled bad.

She showed up again the next day as promised. This time he waited for her at the door. He pointedly blocked the opening. "Listen," he started, "I'm flattered. But you're wasting your time and mine. I'm not interested in you, and I won't be interested in you. Please stop coming out here. It's really getting on my nerves."

"Can I watch you etch for a while at the least? Then I'll leave." It took effort to remain cheerful and pleasant. How *dare* he dismiss her like that?

He debated with himself for long moments and then

reluctantly stepped back to let her in. "For a very short while," he said. "And when I tell you to leave, you have to leave." He absently scratched at his arm as he headed for the workroom. His skin was more sensitive than usual that day. It felt like something inside burned.

He didn't bother to offer a chair to Beta. If she wanted to stay, she could stand. He put her out of his mind entirely and went over to his worktable. His favorite current project was a figurine made of glass that looked like a MoonKin Faerie. It had been specially requested by a SunKin on Kindred; he wanted a statue of his mate. Roman's job was to add the little silver tattoos that marked a MoonKin and to add detail to the wings.

Etching involved first filling the inside of the glass with air to keep it from shattering. That alone was tricky because you had to be very precise in how you put the air in, else you shatter it anyway. It took him long minutes to fill every corner since there was a lot of shape and form to the statue.

Once it was secure from the inside, he made several bolts of lightning of different sizes and potencies. He wielded them like a pen and began the process of carving into the glass. After the first few marks, he entirely forgot Beta was there. The project was a challenge of him artistically and he loved it.

Beta forgot her real reasons for being there as she watched him work. She was caught between fascination for his precision and skill, and desire to see how nimble his hands would be on her body. She couldn't believe he was only eighteen. He looked and acted much older, as if he was already an adult. But that was to be expected. He was a Master Magi. His power had fully developed before his body even started first puberty. Power made you what you were. It was the curse of exceptionally powerful people, of all races, to be exceptionally intelligent and mature.

Under his hands, the glass began to really look like a

Faerie. The silver tattoos went down the outside of the arms and then along the legs. He made the wings thin and translucent to allow the veins underneath to show and reflect light. He added detail to the skirt and tunic and made them light and airy.

By the time the sun was high in the sky and starting a downward descent, he had finished his work. He put the statue on the desk and studied it contently. It was not much smaller than the Kin it was modeled after, and it looked real enough to take flight.

He jolted when Beta's hands suddenly came down on his shoulders and began to rub away tension. He tensed up further. "Don't touch me." Because he couldn't move his chair back, he pushed the table forward until he could stand. "Leave." It wasn't a request.

She eyed him, then suddenly sprang forward and threw herself against him. It caught him off guard and he fell on the floor. As she pinned him bodily, his eyes narrowed sharply. The air began to spark and sizzle. "I'm tired of playing nice," she said. "And it's time you grew up!"

"Not with you." The sparks became lightning bolts as thick as her arms. "I will not hesitate to hit you so hard that you'll be lighting up houses for a month. Don't think that your power will protect you." The blue of his eyes flickered with white. "I'm stronger."

The silence stretched. She felt one of the lightning bolts jab her in the side and the pain was blinding. Realizing he was serious, she scrambled off him and got to her feet. Her rage welled, and she grabbed the glass statue from the table. She hurled it to the floor where it shattered into bits. "You'll regret it!" she snarled as she stormed from the room.

The door slammed behind her. Roman sat up and looked at the remains of all the hard work he and Terina had done. Anger began to simmer inside his heart. "Not as much as you will." There were laws against destroying the work of master craftspeople.

Chapter Five

The next morning, Roman went directly into town with the broken statue in a bag. His first stop was at Terina's shop. Though he had never been attracted to her beyond their mutual first kiss, he considered her to be his only real friend. She was the only one who didn't expect more from him than he wanted to give. She had already finished second puberty but had let him know that if he ever wanted to become an adult with her, she would be interested. One statement, made once, and made sincerely. For that, he liked her all the more.

When he walked into the back of the shop where she was working, he waited for her to notice him. She was concentrating on molding the liquid glass in her hands. Like all Fire elements who worked with glass, she worked bare handed for precision crafting. She couldn't burn herself on her own glass.

Under her skilled hands, the glob of glass formed into a tall vase with scalloped edges. His mind automatically began to catalogue the detailing he would need to do. When she finally straightened and shoved her visor up, he said, "This is beneath your mighty skill."

She grinned at him. "Hi, Roman." She studied the vase. "Sometimes it's nice to do something easy." She stuck the vase in a spinning barrel of smoke and sand to set and smooth the surface and then swiped an arm across her forehead. "Did you finish the statue?" she asked eagerly. "It was the best thing we've ever done."

He set the bag on the counter and condemned Beta to the Underrealm as Terina's face fell and despair filled her eyes. "I had finished it," he said evenly, "but then that new woman, Beta, decided to smash it because I wouldn't let her seduce me. She's been after me for days despite me telling her no."

Terina's black eyes began to smolder with a fiery anger. "Who does she think she is?" Furious, she grabbed the bag with one hand and his wrist with her other. "We're going to the Elder and she is getting kicked out of the town. Comes in here acting like she knows everything then tries to ruin our lives!"

He followed obediently. There was no swaying her when her mind was set. She reminded him of someone, but he couldn't remember who. It was another blank space in his mind. He tried to ignore his forgotten memories, but it wasn't always easy when he felt as if they were important.

The Elder lived in a small house in the center of town. Four different dirt streets led to the house, ensuring that anyone who wanted to find him could. Every couple of years, there was a town vote to see who among the oldest in town would be Elder. For the last three votes, it had been Elder Rynic. At close to eighty, however, he was considering retiring and letting someone else take over.

He had seen Terina approaching with Roman in her wake, so he was standing on the front step waiting for them. "Come in, young ones." He held the door for them and his eyes studied the bag Terina carried. "What is wrong?" He sat down behind his desk with a sigh.

Terina put the bag down and the broken shards jangled together. "Beta." Her hands hit the top of the desk with a thump. "She destroyed something I made and that Roman etched just because Roman rebuffed her! *I want her hide*!"

"Calm down," he soothed. He looked at Roman. "Kindly be more levelheaded than your partner and tell me what's going on."

"Beta made offers that I was not interested in," Roman explained. "Repeatedly. When I finally told her to get out of my life, she smashed Terina's statue in anger. It was probably the best thing we've ever made."

Rynic began to frown deeply. "I see. She will, naturally, be brought in and questioned. She's committed a grave crime and may need to be turned over to the Militia when they arrive today."

Terina and Roman exchanged a quick glance. "The Militia will be arriving today?" Terina asked.

"Indeed. Word reached us that the Militia party in Glacia and the one in Carnelian have cross-confirmed the presence of the Elite causing trouble. As the end results are much the same as what is happening here—namely the disrupted land flow—we can only assume there is someone here as well."

Roman began to have an ugly suspicion. "At the risk of jumping to conclusions, did the first person disappear from Mirah about the time Beta showed up?"

Carefully, Rynic said, "There are some . . . coincidences about her appearance, yes."

"That's it. I'm setting her hair on fire."

Roman caught Terina around the waist and held tight despite her mad wiggles. "You're saying that no one can prove she had anything to do with the disappearances?" He firmly put Terina down on a chair and ignored the glare she leveled at him.

"I'm afraid so, Roman."

Three short raps sounded on the front door before it opened to admit a man wearing the uniform of the Militia. "I apologize for the intrusion, but I was told I could directly enter, Elder Rynic."

"Indeed." Rynic stood. "You are Argyle Vinhri, are you not?"

"I am." Vinhri drew his thumb over his nose and cheek. "Water Magi."

Rynic returned the gesture. "Elder Rynic, Soil Magi. The two present are Terina Faturi and Roman Arequo. Terina is a Fire Magi and Roman is a Master Air Magi.

You've likely heard their names before."

"I have!" Vinhri gave both a warm smile. "I am a fan as well. It's an honor to meet both of you." He looked to Rynic. "May I speak freely, or should I wait until later?"

"Speak freely. Roman and Terina can be trusted."

"Very well." He linked his hands behind his back. "My party is currently examining the town and outlying areas. Just entering town, we picked up traces of the Elite."

"How do you know?" Terina asked curiously.

"The Elite carry tainted power in their bodies," he explained. "Therefore they leave a smell behind that the more attuned power can catch." He saw a flicker across Roman's eyes and was instantly intrigued. "You have witnessed a bad smell around someone, Master Roman?"

Roman hesitated and Terina's eyes went wide. "It was Beta, wasn't it?" A low sound rumbled in her chest as she crossed her arms. "Now can I set her on fire?"

Vinhri lifted a brow. "Perhaps an explanation is in order." He listened to the events as they were outlined, and his eyes went to the bag sitting on the desk. As a Militia member as well as a fan, he was doubly outraged that anyone could destroy someone else's craft. "I see," he finally said. "Well, that certainly puts this Beta at the top of the suspect list. Is she still in town?"

"That is a very good question," Rynic murmured. He went over to the door and stepped outside. "Has anyone seen Beta lately?" he asked those going by on the street.

"No, Elder," one man said.

A woman offered, "I last saw her yesterday."

One of the children came running up to Rynic and tugged on his pant leg. "I saw her this morning! She had a hipsack packed. When I asked where she was going, she said she was just taking a trip. She was lying though."

Children could always tell when someone was lying or telling the truth. The ability went away with first puberty but was restored between couples when they became

Linked mates. Rynic, therefore, took the little girl's word as absolute that Beta had lied.

Vinhri had overheard the exchange. "I will send out a team to begin searching," he decided. "If she was innocent, then she would have no reason to flee on the day the Militia arrived. Warn everyone to remain in town and not wander off alone."

"Done."

Vinhri left to begin issuing orders to his party, and Rynic sent Terina and Roman home. As he was leaving Terina at her shop, Roman found himself with a stubborn Fire Magi attached to his arm. He sighed. "Terina, let me go."

"He said to stay in town."

"He said to go home as far as I'm concerned."

"You're in the most danger!" She released his arm but promptly smacked him instead. "She already set her eye on you, and killing you might destroy this entire city! The land here is so accustomed to your power that it would go *insane!*"

"So be it." He shrugged one shoulder. "I'll die if I stay in town anyway."

As he walked away, she wiped fiercely at the tears in her eyes. "Stupid stubborn man!" she whispered. She was *not* going to break her heart over him. She refused to. If she did, then she would lose his friendship and that was more important than anything.

He was halfway home when he sensed a familiar power. Shocked, he stopped his findral and looked around. He could feel Melody's power. He was sure it was hers. He quickly turned toward the direction the power had emanated. If he felt her power, then she was still alive. It was worth the risk of trying to find her if she could be saved.

A mile beyond the city, he found a dune that looked

like it had been recently disturbed. He swiftly dismounted and began gathering his power in brisk winds that swept the sand away from the dune in ways that were far faster than he could dig. His first hope came when he saw a flash of dark hair. "Hang on, Melody!"

Using his hands and his power, he shortly uncovered her body. She began choking and coughing, and his hopes rose. He braced her over his arm and began a rhythmic beating on her back that forced her lungs to keep expelling the sand she had inhaled. He kept a flow of wind directly at her face, allowing her to cough out the sand through her mouth and breathe fresh air through her nose.

It didn't take long before the coughs faded to faint whimpers. "Roman?" she managed to whisper. Her entire body began to shake violently. He turned her over and lifted her, and she slumped weakly against him. "I thought I was going to die."

"Not yet, I promise." He got onto the findral's back and held her tight as he rushed back toward town. As he went, he fired multiple lightning bolts in the air in a repeated four-one-three pattern. It was the signal for medical aid that was used by all races and cities across the world.

Because of it, the three town doctors were waiting for him at the edge of the city. Many others had gathered as well, and a cry rose on the air as they saw Melody. "She's alive!" Roman said quickly. He bent and handed her gently to one of the men standing near. "She was buried alive in a dune. If she wasn't a Soil Magi, she'd be dead."

"I'll have the head of whoever did this!" her father almost roared. "Where's Beta?!"

Word spread fast in towns. Everyone knew Beta was under suspicion. But because the Militia was already out searching, there was nothing anyone in town could do. Roman watched long enough to see Melody taken to the Healing Shelter and then immediately headed for the edges of town. He was going to go looking himself, and he would have a few 'words' with Beta, Elite or not.

He caught the distinct smell of tainted power a few miles beyond the town. It was stronger than ever. Eyes narrowed, he left his findral and began walking. He didn't want the poor beast to be caught in the crossfire of the inevitable fight.

Another mile out, he was brought to an abrupt halt as a dust storm suddenly surged up and blocked his route. His eyes narrowed further and he slapped at the storm with his own wind to kill it. Even without turning around, he knew Beta stood behind him. "You really went too far."

"You mean you actually care about someone or something? I'm shocked."

He turned around and studied her white cloak. There was something almost blasphemous about it to him. He felt as if something that should have been cherished was being insulted instead. "Don't mistake disinterest for a lack of feeling. Just because I'd sooner sleep with a findral than with you is no reason to think I'm emotionless."

She very nearly shot a lightning bolt at him but restrained herself. He was clearly braced for battle. She needed him off guard if she was to have any chance of taking him out. "My apologies," she said with a touch of bitter humor. She cocked her head. "How'd you find me out here?"

"Your power reeks. Tell me, did you leave town when you heard the Militia was to arrive?"

"Naturally. What made you come after me?"

"You want the whole list? Where do I start? The part where you tried to force yourself on me or the part where you destroyed Terina's statue? How about the part where you've been kidnapping and murdering townspeople to try to destroy the city? Or maybe where you attempted to kill Melody as well."

"*Attempted*?" She sighed. "I should have buried her deeper. Damned Soil Magi."

If there was anything more disgusting than such a careless regard for life, he didn't know of it. If this was what evil was like, then he hoped he never saw it again. "What's the game?" he asked. "You've got to have a reason for this."

"It's simple." She flashed him a smile. "Magi need to die. Once they die, the world will have a chance to heal and start over."

He blinked. "Pardon me?"

"You heard me well enough. It's like I said: Magi are the cause of all the suffering of the world. Genocide of Chronicles, war with Kin . . . if they could find the Dragons, they'd probably try to steal their lands as well! They're nothing but land hoarding, narrow minded, uptight fools."

"And are you really that much better than they are?" He began to gather invisible power at his hand. "Right now I don't see you as any sort of miraculous savior of the world. You're nothing but a murderess. If you were doing such a great thing for Lucksphere, your power wouldn't reek like day old findral droppings."

She snarled and hurled a lightning bolt with all her strength. He had been prepared for it and snapped up a shield of wind that deflected the attack. His other hand shot forward and released the power it held. A rapid fire of small bolts began flying at her. The tiny bits of lighting were far more deadly than a single blast and had the potential to tear flesh to pieces.

She shielded herself as fast as she could, but bolts still tore through the shield and slashed at her clothes. Fear began to edge into her heart for the first time. He was even more powerful than she had suspected. She turned and began running across the sand to have the time to make a bigger blast.

Much to her dismay, Roman was as fast on his feet as he was with his power. He was able to navigate the dunes better and with more skill than she had. It didn't take him long to catch up. Shortly after that, he passed her. He skidded around in front of her and fired a tornado right into her chest that sent her flying back the way she had come.

She skidded across the top of a dune, then rolled down the side. Aching all the way through her body, she painfully rolled to her feet. She fiercely whipped up a dust storm and hurled it at him.

He waited until the storm was close before taking forceful command and reversing it back toward her. As he did, he wrapped the storm within lightning bolts. It grew larger and larger until it was twice his size. The Elite Magi was caught off guard by the change, and she scrambled out of the way. The lightning ripped open the back of her cloak.

She swung around to attack, and then she ducked hastily before a fireball took off her head. She turned sharply and saw Terina standing less than fifty feet away. Fire swirled around the younger woman's feet. "You!"

"Me, *poka*!" Terina hurled another fireball. "Back away from Roman!"

"Get out of here!" Roman snapped at her.

"Well, since you're here, you'll be first!" Beta hurled a massive lightning bolt at Terina. Glee that was both professional and personal filled her. Roman liked Terina, and Beta knew she would never forgive the other female for taking his attention.

Roman hit the ground running and tackled Terina down onto the sand at the last second. The bolt narrowly missed them both. He returned the blast with his free hand and sent Beta scrambling. "You idiot!" he snarled at Terina. "Get out of here!"

"Was I supposed to let you fight alone!?" was the counter snarl.

Beta began to laugh maniacally. "How cute you are!" Ugly yellow wind began to swirl around her and the smell of tainted power rose on the air. "You should have stayed safely at home!"

"What is she doing?" Terina asked in horror.

"I don't think we're going to like the answer." Roman released her and rolled up to his feet. When she stood as well, he held an arm in front of her defensively. The land under their feet had begun to rock and ripple like water when pebbles were dropped inside.

The yellow power suddenly whipped into a tornado and came flying at them. Roman shoved Terina to the side and went the other direction. The attack missed them by inches but the flying sand struck them both in the arm and rose large welts. "That's not possible!" Terina said fiercely.

Roman didn't bother with words. He summoned up an even larger tornado. It consumed the yellow one and something popped loudly as the power was purified. The pure tornado whirled and went after Beta. She shielded herself from the hardest hit, but the sand scored her face and arms where her cloak couldn't protect her.

"That shouldn't be possible either," Terina managed to say. It was in reference to both Beta's shield and Roman's tornado. Roman, even as a Master Magi, shouldn't have been able to absorb the power. And Beta, not being a Master Magi, shouldn't have been able to protect herself from the blast.

From the corner of his eye, Roman saw a distant shape on the skyline. His hopes soared. There was a Dragon crossing the desert. "Terina!" He ducked a lightning bolt. "Go and get help!"

She looked and saw the shape. Dragons may have hated Magi, but it was a sure bet that they hated the Elite more. She scrambled to her feet without hesitation and took off running. When it came to running on sand, no one could outrun a desert dweller.

Beta didn't notice the Dragon but she did notice Terina running. She turned to fire after her, but Roman came up firing instead. The rapid bursts of lightning forced her to dodge as fast as she could. It was getting harder for both of them to move with the land rolling like the sea.

Bursts of elemental power began to geyser into the air. Beta dodged one. Roman didn't. As she watched him absorb the power, she began to have an ugly suspicion she might know why the blue-eyed farmer was so very different even from the Master Magi she had known.

She whipped up another yellow tornado and hurled it at him. This time she opened fire with the same lightning bolts he had used on her. It was a calculated risk. Every ability she used forced her to draw more power from the land. If she didn't destroy herself by using all her power, she might destroy herself by taking in too much external power. Her Magi body was not meant to be infinite.

He shielded from the lightning bolts and then rushed forward swiftly. Before she could dodge, his fist cracked across her jaw and sent her sprawling. "There's a rule about not hitting someone smaller," he said through his teeth, "but I'm really getting tired of this!" He began to say more when he saw the blood welling on her lip. Shocked, he backed up slowly.

Her blood was yellow.

Only tainted blood was yellow. Pure Magi blood was red in color. Kin had silver or gold blood, and supposedly Dragons had green blood. No blood was ever yellow unless the owner's power had been corrupted and made to be an aberration of nature itself.

She wiped her fingers over her lip and studied the smear on her fingers. With a shrug, she wiped her fingers on her cloak. If anything, her callous disregard for the reality of the monster she was made him all the more disturbed.

As she began to advance toward him, yellow lightning flickering around her, he backed up slightly. For the first time, he was beginning to question whether or not he would actually win this fight.

Terina had better hurry or the Dragon wouldn't have to worry about protecting Mirah. It would detonate in Roman's death, just like Beta wanted.

Chapter Six

Grecia Laluna was a Soil Fury. She was over six hundred years in age, older than many Dragons and certainly one of the older Furies. She was the second oldest, in fact. The only Fury older than her six centuries was Fury Elder Xander Journe. Xander was nearly twenty-five hundred years old. The gap between their ages had a simple explanation but a heartbreaking one.

No other Furies born after Xander but before Grecia had lived longer than a few hundred years before losing their Chronicle and needing to be mercifully put out of their misery. Grecia, herself, had inherited the memories of another Fury, as was the Dragon way. Newborn Dragons were always given the memories of other Dragons who passed in the same moment, thus ensuring no knowledge was ever lost.

She was one of the most beautiful among her kind. In Dragon form, she was slightly over seventeen feet in length, but she was all slender lines and graceful curves. Her scales were pale lavender with gold and green patches to denote her Soil element. Her slenderness, however, hid a deceptive strength. She was very, very strong. Even the males were wary to wrestle with her.

Thinking about that made her smile as she wandered the shops in Prismatic. She was in Magi form, naturally, and it was a form no less beautiful than her Dragon one. She was five-eight, slender and willowy, and her long hair shimmered pale gold streaked with distinct lavender color. Her eyes were also lavender and tilted at the corner. Even though she was obviously a Dragon, many Magi watched her wistfully.

She had been living in Prismatic for the last nine years. It had been the last known location of the Chronicle children, and her hope was that eventually one might return. It was a desperate hope. Though she had never spoken of it to anyone, she had felt her Chronicle's birth just over eighteen years earlier. The timing was coincidental enough to make her nearly positive that the young male Air Chronicle that Morgan Chronis had spoken of was *her* Chronicle.

When word of the trouble in Mirah reached Prismatic, she had the sneaking feeling she knew who was behind it. Removing the Elite was as important as finding the missing Chronicles, and she headed to the 'airport.' It was thusly named because Air Magi used wind to keep people safe while Dragons were taking off and landing. The port had been there for millennia, and though largely unused for the last thousand years, it was still maintained.

She took to the skies and skirted around the outside of the city; she didn't dare fly over it for fear of disturbing the land. It was just as well. She needed to head south anyway. By flying along the shoreline, she was able to fly at her natural speed. It was a speed that would let her cover as much ground in a single day as a findral could in a few. However, it was also a speed slower than other Dragons because she was a Fury and her power was not infinite. Not without her Chronicle.

She began to notice the signs of trouble on the third day of flying. She could see the land rolling like waves. A flicker in the corner of her gaze indicated there was a fight of some kind but she paid no heed to it until she saw a sudden staccato of fireballs in the air in the familiar four-one-three pattern. Someone needed help.

She instantly stopped flying and angled down toward the sand. She landed carefully to keep from disrupting the land further. Her sharp eyes saw a small figure rushing toward her, and it moved with a speed over the dunes that meant this person (likely Magi) was a desert dweller. To keep from alarming him or her, Grecia used her Soil power to create a willow tree that was the universal symbol of peace.

Terina slowed her run as she realized the Dragon had landed. Try as she might, she couldn't keep out the fear. Her heart pounded wildly as she slowed to a walk. The Dragon was more than three times her height and at least twice her size. It was, however, standing next to a willow tree. Things were perfectly safe.

She didn't *feel* safe! There was no way to feel safe next to a beast as magnificently powerful as a Dragon. This one seemed oddly feminine though her face was fierce and powerful. Terina was tempted to call it a beautiful face, but it was hard to think of something that potentially dangerous as beautiful.

She stopped when she was feet in front of Grecia and struggled to catch a breath. As she gasped for air, a gentle claw was laid on her back. Cool Soil power slid into her body and healed the restrictions on her lungs. It allowed her to take deep breaths. Startled, she straightened. "Thank you."

"I will assume that is not why you were signaling me for help," Grecia said. Her slanted eyes tilted even more as they narrowed. "You are wounded." She lowered her head to touch the wound on Terina's arm with her nose. The smell of tainted power was sharp, and she lifted her head. "The Elite."

"Yes!" Terina forgot her fear and put her hands on Grecia's leg pleadingly. "My friend . . . he's fighting Beta! I jumped in like an idiot, but we should have been able to win! Roman is a Master Air Magi! But Beta . . . she did something. It's not natural! You need to save Roman! If he dies . . . Mirah is doomed!" She gave a squeal as a large claw closed around her body. "Don't eat me!"

"Don't be silly. You can't ride on my back, but I can carry you." Grecia flew up into the air. "We're going to save your friend."

Heart in her throat, Terina held onto her claw. "They're where the explosions are!" She closed her eyes. Worry choked her painfully. "I don't want him to die! He's my best friend! He was my first kiss!"

Second puberty was a strange and wonderful time. Grecia had gone through it over five hundred years earlier. She still remembered her first kiss and her first lover. "Then we will save him." Her teeth bared as she smiled. "I'll teach this Beta what a real quake is like."

At the fight, Roman blocked the next attack and countered with a series of larger lightning bolts that forced Beta to dodge. He knew exactly which direction she would go, and he sent a tornado whipping at her from the side. It caught her and flung her high in the air. When she landed, something broke audibly. She got to her feet and her left arm hung uselessly at her side.

As she started to gather her power together for another attack, a Dragon shadow passed by overhead. The power washed over the field, and it seemed to arrow in directly on Roman. His skin burst into riotous pain and electric shocks flooded the air. His skin stretched violently and felt as if it would split open. Wind whipped around him and sent sand flying wildly. He fell to his knees as something inside swelled larger and larger, pushing against what felt like unnatural binds. Then, with a shockwave of air, the tension broke.

Golden lines suddenly appeared on the right side of his face and blazed a trail down his neck and shoulder all the way to his right hand and fingers. As they covered the entirety of his arm, they appeared as straight lines with little curls at the end. His soul was throbbing but he felt oddly more peaceful than he had in his entire life. He slowly lifted his hand and stared distantly at the lines. He was a Chronicle?

Beta felt no less shaken. Her suspicions had in no way prepared her for reality. It was disorienting, to say the least. She shook it off and started to step forward when a powerful roar ripped through the air over her head. It chilled her to the bone and she scrambled back instead.

Grecia landed on the ground in front of Roman with her wings arched and her teeth bared. Her scales fully lifted to reveal sharp edges in a battle-ready pose. "Stay away from my Chronicle!" she snarled. She had known it the instant she saw Roman. With or without his awakening, she had known.

Beta's eyes slowly widened as she saw the markings on Grecia's body. "You're a Fury?"

The answer came in the form of deadly thorn covered vines bursting out of the sand. As they advanced toward Beta, she knew she was outmatched. Even her stolen power was not enough. Not against a Fury this old and powerful. A ball of lightning filled her hand and she threw it to the ground where it detonated with a blinding light. When it faded, she was gone.

Grecia looked around, but she neither saw nor smelled her enemy any longer. A soft thump had her head swinging around, and she saw Roman lying unconscious on the sand. Her heart broke.

Lavender light flared around her body, and she transformed into her Magi shape. She walked over to his side and knelt beside him. Tenderly, she eased him into her arms. Tears burned the back of her eyes as she buried her face in his hair. Finally. After six centuries of waiting, she had finally found the one man who completed her. The one being that was hers alone.

Wonder filled her as she studied his beautiful face. She softly trailed a finger across the lines on his face. It was wildly seductive to know that it was her power that made his lines. Without lifting her gaze from his face, she said, "I am sorry."

Visibly trembling, Terina walked forward from where she had been hiding behind a dune. "I always knew he would never be mine," she whispered, "but never why. I can see the why now."

"You don't fear and hate him?"

"Why should I? He's still Roman." She took a long breath. "I am going home, and I'm telling everyone that I saw Beta and Roman fighting. Roman overpowered her and she fled. In doing so, he realized that he was a threat to the city and decided to leave entirely."

Grecia studied Terina's face. "It is not entirely a lie. This is the ideal time for Roman to leave. The land is already in fluctuation and his returning there now after awakening will make things worse. But by the time the land settles, he will be gone. It will accept his leaving." In a very soft voice, she added, "I will love him in a way you can't."

Their eyes met in a moment of understanding. "I want you to," was the soft response. "He needs someone to love him. Just . . ." her voice broke for a moment, "just send me a message somehow when he's happy. If I could know that . . ."

"Consider it done."

"Then I will leave now." She turned, then paused for a moment. "Will you have a Linking ceremony?"

"There will be a bonding, but it will not require a ceremony. If we do have a ceremony, you will surely be invited."

"Thank you."

Grecia watched Terina until she disappeared on the horizon and then turned her attention back to her mate. She could feel his power rising steadily even as her own majiks began to drain. The sun was devilishly hot overhead and she didn't want to remain out in the open. They were along a common land route between cities.

She gently put him back down on the ground and got

to her feet. Soil power welled inside her and flowed down into the land. It stilled its soft tremors and fell quiet. She waited a moment, then focused her power. It surged from her as a swirl of summer leaves and the top of a dune lifted entirely.

Under her expert control, the land began to shape and form into a cave deep under the surface. Because she might have been slightly smaller than Roman in her Magi form but she was still as strong as her Dragon one, she bent and wrapped an arm around his waist to lift him off the ground.

She lowered the dune back into place once they were inside the cave. It was pitch black but she always carried lamps in her hipsack. She pulled out several and set them up. It took a minute but eventually they realized it was dark and obediently began giving off a strong light.

She felt no worries for using her majiks now that she had her Chronicle. She took the effort to cover the cave ground with soft and lush grass and even scattered around flowers for visual appeal. She made every effort to make the area comfortable before returning to Roman's side. She sat down beside him and studied his form. There were wounds marking his body and she began the task of healing them all.

Technically, all elements could heal though MoonKin with their Dark power were the most potent. It really depended on whether or not the owner's power could be used in that way. Grecia's could, and it was also her specialty. She took great delight in removing the blemishes from her mate's perfect beauty.

Perfect wasn't even the word for him. She had never seen such a stunningly handsome man before. Hunger churned inside her body. She wanted him. Had, in fact, never wanted anyone or anything more in her long life. It was a physical hunger for his strong muscles and rich golden skin. It was an emotional hunger to see him smiling at her and loving her. It was an elemental hunger to feed on the power she felt beckoning to her even then.

Time slipped past. She didn't know how long it was until he finally began to stir. She moved closer and leaned over him, her hand seeking his and lacing their fingers together. "Open your eyes," she pleaded huskily. "Please."

He woke to agonizing pain in his body. His Air was going out of control. He wanted to sweep across the land and become a tornado across the skies. He wanted to unleash storms of lightning and tear open clouds. When he tried to move, every muscle protested. A tender touch on his hand was shocking, and it reverberated all the way to the power that made him. He *knew* that touch. And he knew the beautiful voice calling to him. This woman was *his*.

He forced his eyes open and found himself staring into the lavender eyes of the most beautiful woman he had ever seen. His breath caught as a sudden searing desire consumed him. For the last few months, his second puberty curiosity had been little more than a passing thing that was easily ignored. There was no ignoring it in that moment. He ached from head to toe in a way that had nothing to do with his rampant power and yet had everything to do with it.

When he tried to reach for her, his body protested. She instantly brought his hand to her cheek. "We need to bond as Dragoons," she said softly. "I need to feed on your power." Her eyes searched his. "Do you understand what has happened and is happening?"

"Acknowledge and accept it? Yes. Understand? No." He found a smile for her. "I don't care that much, oddly, that I don't understand anything about what has happened. You're here and that seems to make everything else not matter."

Her heart clenched wildly for a moment as she slowly eased him off the floor. She softly nuzzled her nose into his shoulder. He smelled like desert winds and rich desert storms. It was addicting. Unable to resist, she lightly tasted his skin. A soft white aura instantly lifted and covered his body in response. Who was she to resist the offer?

As her lips sipped delicately along his shoulder, he felt a shiver from his head to his toes that was pure delight. As instinctive as breathing, he curled his power around her. It vividly underlined a more physical desire to make them one.

She followed his power as it lured her into trailing soft kisses over his face. He tasted as wonderful as he smelled. She would never have enough. As she teased his lips with hers, she asked softly, "Tell me you're through second puberty."

"I'm," his voice caught as he felt her fingers kneading his muscles like a cat, "I'm in the third phase."

Experimentation phase. It was, without question, the best and most frustrating part for a pair of lovers. Bodies and powers more than ready and willing for the final step but emotions and minds still catching up. Feeling his power swirling around her seductively, she knew at the least that she could take the kiss she craved.

Her lips softly covered his, and he freed his hand to bury his fingers in her long hair. He couldn't tell where the greatest pleasure originated. The softness of her lips, the richness of her taste, the silk of her hair, the scent of her skin . . . it all tangled together inside him and merged with a matching hunger to feel her mind and soul, to bind her as tightly to him as he could.

And as the last of his power flowed into her, just that happened. He could feel her breathing inside his lungs, feel her thoughts inside his mind. Her emotions burned hot and wild inside his heart. He could see everything she was and had been. Centuries of memories fluttered across his mind and broke his heart as he saw how long she had waited.

She felt his heart, breathed his breath, and felt his love burning inside her. The volatile three emotions that marked Dragoons rioted inside him as they did inside her. Her heart soared as she realized that the third emotion, the one that could only be at its peak when the Dragoons were lovers, was nearly as great inside him as it was inside her. He was nearly ready for her.

But as his memories fluttered across his mind, she immediately saw that there was something missing. There was a large blank space present. She touched it lightly and felt the lingering traces of Morgan Chronis' power. Roman was, without question, one of the missing Chronicle children.

They slowly parted but she couldn't move very far with his fingers tangled in her hair. She tried to free herself, her control shaky enough, but as she pulled back, he sat up and pulled her closer again. Startled, she let her head rest on his shoulder. She felt . . . small suddenly. It was an odd feeling. She had never felt small around any male that wasn't a Dragon.

She decided she liked it and nuzzled his shoulder. He promptly set her away, and she began to frown. "What? I was comfortable!"

"And I want to see you." He held her at arms' length and eagerly looked her over. Her figure seemed sturdy rather than generous, and her legs looked almost outrageously long. She wore a desert bikini under snug shorts and a top that wasn't much more than a bikini itself. She looked like any other desert girl, but at the same time, she looked far better. And, before his delighted eyes, a flare of light made lines identical to his surge across her slender stomach and down her legs to her knees. It was *his* power that made her lines.

Her eyes closed helplessly as he tugged her onto his lap and she felt his heated intent. "That's not fair!" The last word was almost a gasp as his nose buried between her breasts. "Really not fair!" She shivered in wonderful delight as his lips teased her skin. "I hate this part."

"Liar." He really wanted to peel the offending clothes from her body to see more but knew it wouldn't be fair to either of them. He knew he wasn't ready for more than a simple exploration of his lover's body.

"*Simple*?" She wound her arms around his shoulders. "Simple is staring at me. *This* is torture!" She let out a long breath. "Say something to distract me. Fast. Else I'm having my wicked way with you."

The threat of ravishment from his Fury was *vastly* more appealing than the threat of being ravished by Beta. A sudden surge of violent emotion from Grecia had his eyes widening, and they widened further when her lavender eyes turned dark green with rage. "What's wrong?"

"She tried to *what?!*" The words came out as a soft snarl. "I'm going to roast her alive!"

"Tried," he stressed. "And failed. No, you don't." He wrapped his arms around her waist and held her firmly on his lap when she tried to get up. Wanting to distract her, he smiled at her. "What's your name?"

She opened her mouth, then closed it. Bemused, she offered, "Grecia Laluna."

"Roman Arequo. And now that that is out of the way, I don't suppose you can fill in some of the details of what the hell is going on. I went from a Master Magi to a Chronicle who seems to have one hell of a beautiful Fury."

"Stop complimenting me so that I can get my thoughts organized," she grumbled. Her breath hitched in her chest. "And stop petting me with your power! You're just being mean!"

"I'm just experimenting, Grecia." His smile was half innocence and half masculine amusement.

"I'm doomed." She blew out a breath, firmly removed his arms, and got off his lap. She sat beside him instead and curled their fingers together. When he leaned closer, she felt herself surrounded by his heat and presence. It soothed her all the way to her soul. "You seem to know something of Chronicles and Furies."

"A little. Just what I was told. I can see the rest inside your mind. I just want to know how I never knew what I was." He held up the arm with his lines. "Is this why my skin has been itching like mad ever since I started second puberty?"

"I'd have to guess it is. This is an, uhm, unusual circumstance. I have nothing to base it on." She sighed. "Does the name Morgan sound at all familiar? Or Tariah?"

He began to frown. "It feels . . . it feels a little familiar." Pain seemed to flash in his head and he pressed his fingers to his forehead. "There's something missing in my memories. I've always thought that but . . . damn, it hurts."

She framed his face with her hands and swirled her power around his mind. Looking at his mind was like looking at a puzzle missing a piece in the very center. "Nine years ago, you lived in Prismatic with three other Chronicle children, your parents and theirs, and a young man named Morgan Chronis. He and his sister, Tariah, are the two most powerful Chronicles this world has ever seen. They can do things that even the Elders of the Kin and Dragons have never heard of being done.

"When the war with the Elite started, Morgan erased the memories of his Black Magi and sent them—you—away via translocation. He put a lock on your powers by using his own to create a barrier under your skin to hide your lines. It would not break unless you were in the presence of a Chronis or a Fury."

A flash flickered across his eyes of a young man with auburn hair and silver eyes. Eyes that were almost always sad but unwilling to give in. Someone he had idolized. "He .. . his eyes are silver."

She sensed movement in his mind and began to see fragments of memories in all corners. "So that's what he did." She used her power to begin gathering the fragments, connecting them by tiny vines that she could pull together. "He didn't *erase* them. He just fragmented them. I think . . . I think I can put them back."

The fragmented memories came together in the empty space in his mind. Silently they fused together. The lost memories punched into both their minds at the same time, but seeing them brought blinding pain to him. He doubled with it and she caught him close. She wrapped her arms around him tightly. "How could I forget?" he asked in despair. "I forgot Morgan. I forgot Kelsey, and C.J., and Jayda."

"It was better that you did." She rocked him gently. Her heart broke for him. "I don't know where the other three are, but I know where Morgan is. He's on the Isle of Dragons. It's . . ." She slowly trailed off as she realized she didn't remember where the Isle was located. She groaned and closed her eyes. "Your journey isn't done."

"You forgot how to get to your own home?"

"It's your fault! It happened to Dominic and Jazz too! Because a Chronicle *has* to finish their journey, the Fury forgets how to get home." She released him when he straightened. Tenderly, she wiped the traces of tears from his eyes. "We will get there, *ishke*," she promised softly.

"Is that a Dragon word?"

"It is. It's the greatest word we have. It encompasses all the wants, desires, and needs of the world." She smiled. "It's what we call that third emotion inside Dragoons." Sensing the next question, she said, "We're Dragoons. When a Fury and Chronicle bond, they become Dragoons. It won't be long until we start developing tertiary skills that only Dragoons can use. I'm not sure I want you to have Telekinesis, though. I hope it's Telepathy."

"I wouldn't move you anywhere against your will," he promised. He sighed and fell over onto his back on the grass. When she curled up against him, he realized he was happier than he ever had been in his life. "So, what do we do next? We can't just sit here forever."

West.

The throbbing in his lines was shocking. He sat up sharply and looked around. The strongest compulsion was inside him as if he heard a voice in his mind. *West.* He had to go west. He shook his head but the urgency commanded him. "I have to go west."

She sat up as well and studied him. "To the west beyond Spectrum is the land of Kindred where the Kin live. That might be an ideal location, actually. The Kin will offer shelter, and Tariah's Kin brother is there. He can contact her. It might be the only way to contact the Isle since I've forgotten how to get there. I can't even put a finger on anyone's energy signal either."

"I guess we go there then." There was a long silence and then he asked achingly, "I can't contact my parents, can I?"

"Not yet." She scooted closer and pulled him into her arms. His arms wrapped around her in turn, and she rubbed her cheek against his hair softly. "I am sorry, Roman. It just isn't safe. Though Magi mindset is changing, there are still many who hate what you are. Your parents would be in danger."

"I know." He straightened and tugged her onto his lap. "You know," he decided, "I forget that you're a Dragon. You're much smaller than I am right now. You're so slender! Do you weigh anything?"

"Yes, thank you." She sniffed disdainfully and then laughed. "Actually, even among Dragons, I am considered slender. Not small, mind you. Sadly, Jazz holds the distinction of being the smallest, but that's only fitting. Morgan is really short for a Magi male, and he is a very 'protect everyone he loves' type person, so her shorter stature makes him feel as if she needs protecting—even if she probably doesn't. It's adorable how she lets him think so."

He grinned a bit. "I'm not necessarily a type to need to protect everyone, but I apologize in advance if you being a healer and smaller than me makes me forget you're not exactly helpless."

She had to grin as well. "Furies and Chronicles always give each other something they need. Tariah is *very* short and petite, and that tends to send both her brother and her Fury into overprotective mode. Which works, really, because she needs that—even when she chafes at it sometimes." She thought about it. "Tariah is smaller than Jazz, actually, so I guess, technically, Tariah is the smallest Dragon when she is borrowing Dominic's Dragon form."

"Borrowing his form?" His eyes went wide.

"Oh, yes. A quirk of Dragoons. The majiks are what let Dragon Lords change shape. It's technically what defines us as Lords. *But* with you . . . we can do entirely new things. By my feeding on your power, I am given the ability to use my majiks in ways that are wholly different from the ways Dragons normally do. And in return, you can use them too."

"Amazing," he said softly. "And feeding on my power means your power is now infinite as well?"

"Kind of. It means I can use my full potential as a Fury without risk. Without you, I've had to be *very* careful not to drain myself." Her smile came slow and sensual. "Now I don't mind being a little . . . reckless. The reward is well worth it." She eased in and brushed a teasing kiss over his lips. "We are one in a way that no other being will ever understand. Everything about us is made to be together. The power that flows back and forth between us will go on for infinity. Living as one . . . breathing as one . . . forever. Never alone, never doubting each other's love . . . It is our destiny as Dragoons."

If that was the destiny of a Dragoon, he thought he had a good idea why Magi had always been so jealous of

Chronicles. The way he felt for Grecia and the way he felt when he could feel her emotions for him . . . he would kill to protect that feeling.

And something told him he might have to. The Elite were still lurking in the world. The next time he saw Beta, he wouldn't hesitate to destroy her. She had to be stopped once and for all.

Chapter Seven

The small continent of Choral was the land to the furthest southwest on the world of Lucksphere. Only three cities existed on its harsh desert landscape. One was a port town to the north, another was a port to the south, and in the very center was the city of Symphony. Choral had the hottest lands in the entire world with temperatures soaring to the near boiling during summer. Only those with the highest durability lived on Choral.

Once, nine years before, Symphony had been home to a Chronicle. Tariah Chronis had fled from her hometown after discovery by the Militia, and her abrupt departure had caused disturbance in the lands for two years before settling. Animals and Magi alike had been mutated into monsters until the land calmed.

Now, seven years later, the city had recovered. Many owed the stability to the presence of a young Master Magi who had arrived seven years earlier. At the age of nineteen, C.J. Daragon was the best weaver in the world. The tapestries and banners he wove with his Soil powers were amongst the greatest any had ever seen.

He lived on the outskirts of Symphony in a shelter built beneath the harsh desert sands. He was slightly anti-social when it came to his interactions with others, but he could be coaxed into coming into town for the occasional festival. His empathy for others and his ability to provide comfort to those who were lost far surpassed his short years. He wasn't even an adult yet and only barely beginning second puberty.

Everyone in town who was single was hoping that his less-than-anti-social personality would allow him to find one of them attractive enough to become an adult with. C.J. was downright beautiful. He had short ash brown hair that seemed to glow with silvery highlights under the sun. His eyes were a stunning iridescent black, and they reflected rainbows in the right light.

Only one person in town knew C.J.'s ways of thinking. That distinction belonged to a young SunKin Elf named Cole. He was sixty in age (or twenty-five by Magi reckoning) and had been C.J.'s friend and confidant since the younger male had arrived in town. Cole was a Soil secondary Kin, and he had been the one to help C.J. master his unpredictable power in a body that wasn't fully developed.

Cole wasn't precisely unattractive himself with his long feline ears and lively brown eyes. He was shorter than his friend—five-six to C.J.'s five-eleven—but every inch had been well used. When the two of them walked through town together, most people were compelled to stop what they were doing to watch.

C.J.'s parents were Ferris and Alline Daragon. They lived in the town proper. They had never tried to force him to stay with them, understanding that he needed his space. They still tried to baby him though. Ferris owned a restaurant and took advantage of it to feed her son.

When Cole arrived at C.J.'s home under the sand one day, he was, as usual, carrying a basket. "I need to stop going by your mother's restaurant."

C.J. didn't look up from the cloth he was weaving from the bag of sand near his feet. "After these years, one would think you'd learned that."

Cole put the basket down and stepped over to watch. Though he did the same kind of work, every weaver was different. Watching C.J. was an art in and of itself. Some weavers could only make cloth of the most simple color and designs. C.J. could use every color imaginable and had created complex tapestries that were even then hanging in the palace of the Magi's king. Cole had personally delivered special banners to the Elders of the Sun and MoonKin as well.

After a few minutes, C.J. finished the cloth he was working on. It was a thick blanket of soft yellow hues. Cole fingered an edge and felt the extra fluffiness inside the material. "Going to Glacia, is it?"

"It is." He removed the blanket from the frame and folded it up neatly. "It will decorate the bed of a newly Linked couple."

Cole wigged his brows. "In other words, it will be broken in fairly shortly."

He grinned at that. "I would hope so." He rolled his shoulders. "I think I've been standing for a couple hours. Where's the moon?"

"Set. The sun is currently right over your dune."

"Okay, more than a couple then. Explains why I'm starving." He picked up the basket and began pulling out the still steaming breads and the assorted chilled foods in their own special containers. "I shouldn't let her spoil me."

Cole took a big bite of sweetbread. "If you have a parent that cooks like this, you don't argue. You just smile and say thank you. And anyway, your mom scares me."

"Me too." C.J. didn't have many chairs in his house. He just sat down on a rug on the floor. When Cole joined him, they divvied up the remaining food. Cole got a slightly larger share but he consumed more food because his body housed three elements: Light, Soil, and Wood.

As C.J. absently scratched at his chest and his hand, Cole asked, "Is it getting worse?"

"Well, it isn't getting better! Are you sure this is normal for second puberty?"

"Skin sensitivity is, but I'm not so sure about the itching. I didn't think anyone could be allergic to puberty, but you might be a new case." Under his lashes, he watched C.J. He had some . . . *suspicions* about his friend. Ones that he was too afraid to say out loud. Instead, all he offered was, "We could see the new doctor in town. Maybe she has some herbs or something."

"The last time you convinced me to take herbs for a problem, my skin turned blue. I looked like your cousin."

"Hey, I warned you not to take them with water, but did you listen to me? No, you did not." He tilted his head and one ear cocked at a curious angle. "Let's hit the library first. Maybe there's something in a book there."

"Oh all right." C.J. reluctantly got to his feet. "At least the library is quiet."

"Careful. Keep up talk like that and I might think you were turning into a normal Master Magi. I hear the one near Mirah almost never goes into town."

"I've heard he's also an Air Magi and Air elements are notoriously aloof to begin with. He has my sympathies." He opened the dune for his friend and then followed him out into the hot sun. He closed the dune behind them and began heading toward town. Like all males of the desert, neither wore more than pants, boots, and vests.

The library in town was one of four on the world. There was one on each main Magi land in the central city location. Books were traded back and forth across the world and copied at each location. Choral, however, housed the best. It had once been owned by the parents of Tariah Chronis. Now it was owned by the entire town.

Contemplating things as they went inside, C.J. asked Cole, "Why don't Kin have a library?"

"We don't use books." He began to look for the books on Magi physiology. "Our stories are passed on by word of mouth. I've probably got half this library worth of tales in my head."

"Is that why there's no room for anything else?"

He flicked his ears in the Kin version of a rude gesture. C.J. just grinned. Ignoring his smart-mouthed friend, Cole began flipping through the pages of the book he had found. "I'm not sure what scares me more. That someone took the effort to detail the potential effects of second puberty, or the fact that the book is this big." It was almost as thick as his forearm, and Cole was unusually strong for a Kin. They usually ran to slender or pudgy physical types rather than muscular.

C.J. sat down on the side of the table. "Anything about allergic reactions?"

"No . . . not that I'm seeing. But this is interesting. I didn't expect to find a section about Chronicles in here." He thumbed past a few pages. "Guess they have their own set of problems if they're ever allowed to reach second puberty."

"Like what?"

"It's called a journey. I guess it was the Chronicle equivalent of second puberty. They'd start things the normal way but would be compelled by the lines on their bodies to go seeking their Fury." He watched C.J. from the corner of his eye. "It's pure speculation based on the fact that only two Chronicles are known to have survived to second puberty and most other records have been erased over the last thousand years. But the thought is that since Chronicles develop so fast to begin with, they might hit a slow growth until meeting their Fury which then propels them at their normal excessive speed."

C.J. felt a sudden pain inside his chest that seemed to consume everything. He needed something. Someone. There was someone out there that was looking for him. She needed him. He pressed a hand to his heart and stared almost blindly at the floor. How did you hunger for someone you didn't know? "A Fury?" he asked softly, not even conscious of asking.

Cole closed the book. "The destined lover of a Chronicle. A Fury is a Dragon Lord who doesn't have infinite power. The Chronicle does, and by feeding on their power, the Fury can use their majiks safely. Elder Juniper of the SunKin says that the tales of the things a Dragoon pair can do are pretty amazing." A little wistfully, he said, "I envy Chronicles a little. A love like that must be wonderful."

C.J. forcefully shook off the feelings. "Okay, so that's a Chronicle and Magi. What about Master Magi? We're that odd gray area between the two."

"Why don't you ask a doctor?" a feminine voice asked behind them.

Both males blinked, then turned. Behind them they found a stunningly beautiful Magi with thick cream-colored hair and matching eyes. She was tanned from the sun and wore the casual bikini and shorts of most desert women. The only pointed difference between her and most other women was that she had a tattoo around her lower right arm. It was an entwined chain of water drops that marked her as a doctor.

Cole's ears quirked with interest as he looked her over. "And who says Kin don't appreciate lovely Magi," he said under his breath.

Even C.J. thought the woman was beautiful, but he didn't feel the slightest bit attracted to her. Sadly, he couldn't even say if it was because he wasn't through second puberty or simply that she wasn't his type. He didn't even really know what his type was yet. His curiosity was, thus far, more general and less specific.

The woman walked forward and drew her thumb over her nose and cheek. "Kappa, Air Magi."

C.J. returned the gesture with a smile. "C.J. Daragon, Master Soil Magi."

Cole lightly touched his ears and bowed slightly in the Elf equivalent of the Magi greeting. "Cole, Soil secondary SunKin." His smile was decidedly warmer than C.J.'s. "It's a pleasure to meet you, Kappa. You're the new doctor in town?"

She wasn't sure which was more amusing: that the Kin was flirting with her or that the Magi wasn't. They were both outrageously attractive and she wasn't entirely sure which she preferred. She felt oddly drawn to both of them. That, of course, might have been simply because she was of the element of Air and both were of Soil. They were natural opposites to her. "I am indeed," she said after a moment. She walked closer a step. "I overhead a bit of the conversation. You're having some odd problems with second puberty? What stage are you in?"

"Second."

"Starting or ending?"

"I don't know. I'm curious, but it's more general. I haven't really been attracted to anyone specific. I'll say the beginning though it's possible I'm further along. I'm not entirely comfortable with people. It might simply be that I'm not at all compatible with anyone around here."

"Hmm." She tapped a finger on her chin. "What exactly is the trouble?"

"My sensitivity is making my skin itch in places."

"I think he's allergic to puberty."

C.J. made a quick gesture with his left hand that was as rude as Cole's from earlier. Kappa hid a smile. "Now, boys." She stepped closer and lifted a hand. "May I?" When C.J. nodded, she lightly put a hand on his chest. Her power lifted to surround him in the only surefire method of evaluating his health. After a moment the power dissipated and she stepped back. "I don't sense anything unusual. Your skin *does* seem to be acting oddly, though. The best way to describe it is to say that it's acting like the land does when the power fluctuates."

"Ah, I see." Cole tucked his hands in his pockets. "That's causing the irritation. Well, he is a Master Magi. We'll need to contact the author of the book and have them come examine you. Make a new chapter."

"Be nice," she scolded. "As for you, C.J., if you'd like, you can come by my Shelter tomorrow and I'll see if I can find something for you to bring down the itching. I doubt I can stop it though."

"I can do that."

"What about me?" With a distinctly flirtatious smile, Cole leaned closer. Kappa stood an inch taller, and he rather liked it. "Want to make sure I'm healthy too?"

She turned toward the door with a smile. "Maybe another time. You're probably too old for me anyway, being a Kin and all."

"That's not fair," he complained. "It's only a technical age gap." He studied the lines at the corner of her eyes. "Besides, you have to be at least thirty. Technically, you're older than me."

"I'm not interested in Kin, even attractive ones," was her laughing retort as she headed out the door.

There was a moment of silence and then he said, "I like her."

"You need to be committed to a Healing Shelter for mental health." C.J. got to his feet. "But in a purely unphysical way, I liked her too. I felt strangely comfortable near her, and that's not something I can say about a lot of people."

From where she was listening outside the door, Kappa couldn't have been more pleased. She had plans for C.J. and having him comfortable with her presence was crucial. She had come to Choral with the intent of taking advantage of the disturbed land, but it was oddly stable.

Asking around had told her that it was his presence that kept things steady. It puzzled her. How did a Master Magi manage to calm the wake of a Chronicle's departure? Master Magi were more like Chronicles than they were like Magi, but there were still distinct differences between levels and scope of power. A lack of infinite power in Master Magi was first and foremost.

She headed back to her Shelter and thought about her plan of action. There was no set time limit for what she needed to do. Her best bet was to win his (and Cole's) trust, and hope that he was eventually attracted to her. If she could become his lover, she would have a better chance at understanding why he was vastly different compared to others. Once she understood that, she would be able to kill him. Choral would be decimated in his death.

Being in town meant an obligatory visit to his parents. C.J. headed to the restaurant and Cole tagged along. He peeked in the front door and said, "Full house." Even before he finished speaking, C.J. was heading toward the back as if his boots were on fire. Bemused, Cole followed him. "You sometimes move as fast as my sister and she's a Faerie."

"When I have reason." He barely hid a shudder. "I refuse to walk into a room full of that many people. If I'm allergic to anything, it's crowds." He blinked as a slender woman suddenly grabbed him in a hug. "And my mother, but don't tell her that. In fact, I feel itchy already."

"Oh stop!" Ferris Daragon tweaked his nose. "Nineteen or ninety, you should be nicer to your mother." She propped her hands on her hips and studied him. She didn't see him very often, and whenever she did, she looked closely to make sure that he was healthy. He looked just fine. "Did you eat?"

"I force fed him," Cole offered. "Do you have any sweetbread left?"

"Bottomless pit." It was said affectionately. "There's a day-old loaf on the counter. Feel free to have some." As he went to cut a piece, she tugged C.J. into the kitchen and out of the sun. "What brings you by? I wasn't expecting a visit this soon."

"We came into town to go to the library. My skin still itches. The books didn't have any answers so I'll be talking to the doctor tomorrow. She's fairly sure she can say what's wrong, but not how to fix it. She's going to try to find something to make it itch less."

"Did you find her lovely?" Ferris asked hopefully.

Cole's ears perked. "I did."

"You hush and eat your sweetbread."

"Yes'm."

Ferris sighed and C.J. just laughed. "I did; it just wasn't personal. I'm not attracted to her. Cole is, but she countered all his advances. If he tried to write a letter, it'd be returned to sender."

"We don't write letters, exactly," Cole explained. "We usually offer to read someone's energy. It's kind of the same pick up line, but different because we write letters to each other by writing with another person's energy."

"Convenient," Alline Daragon said as he walked into the kitchen with an empty tray of dishes. "It must be much faster too."

"Sometimes it is. Other times it's slower. I sent my sister a letter once that didn't arrive for weeks. She was ill. Her energy was diluted and couldn't receive any letters." He brightened as Ferris handed him a cup of sweetened tea. "Thanks!" He happily dunked the bread in the tea. Like other Kin, he had an incurable sweet tooth. Yet somehow, he didn't get overweight. It puzzled most who met him.

"I hear things are getting worse," Alline told Ferris. "They're saying that the Militia has been dispatched to Carnelian, Mirah, and Glacia."

She frowned deeply. "And yet nothing has happened here. How very odd."

"It's still affecting the northern port," he disagreed. "We're getting bad waves from Carnelian. Most ships are grounded now. It's even worse, though, because our ships that do leave can't make it to Mirah. The waves between Spectrum and Carnelian are making storms. Bad ones, I might add. At this rate, all lands will be isolated."

"Wait a minute." C.J. frowned. "What are we talking about?"

"Members of the Black Magi Elite have shown up."

Just saying it made something inside Ferris viciously angry. She had always felt as if the Elite were an offense to someone or something. "They've been upsetting the power in the land on Carnelian and making quakes. On Mirah, it's causing waves near the shoreline. In Glacia, it's been avalanches."

Cole put down his tea. "If they keep that kind of thing up, they'll break something."

"That's their known intent. Though the world forgot their faces, we remember their deeds." Ferris rubbed at her forehead. "The Militia has been sent to confront them and to try and get rid of them, but we can't be sure it will work. Nine years ago, it took the Kin and the Dragons to get rid of the majority of the Elite."

"And the Chronicles," Cole murmured.

"Well, of course them! And they're better people than I ever will be," Alline said, "to willingly save the people trying to destroy them. I sincerely hope they are living happily now on the Isle of Dragons."

"Kin still keep in touch with them," Cole offered. "I can tell you that last I heard, they were very happy." There was more to the tale, but he wasn't going to speak of it right then. It was a closely held secret.

"We'll take each day as it comes." C.J. straightened from where he had been leaning against the wall. "I'm heading for home now." Suiting action to words, he headed out the back of the restaurant.

The following morning, he returned to town. He met up with Cole halfway and they headed together toward the Healing Shelter. It had once been owned by a Kin, but he had been murdered by the Militia because he had kept Tariah's origins a secret. It had taken a few years for the truth to come out, but now that it had, the Militia had to step lightly in town. Those who remembered had still not forgiven.

The Shelter was located among the main street through the center of town. A large white water drop was on a sign hanging outside the door. It had never been especially cheerful before, but now it seemed much livelier. The outside had gotten a fresh white color and the windows in the front were filled with desert flowers.

The steps were swept meticulously clean and a comfortable set of chairs sat outside the open doors. Cole started to climb the steps but stopped to let a little girl go past. She had come running out the door at top speeds. "Thanks, Doctor!" she shouted back over her shoulder. "Hi Cole! Hi C.J.!"

As she disappeared into the distance, the two males exchanged a smile before continuing up the steps and into the Shelter. "Anyone home?" C.J. asked.

"If you're not bleeding, please give me a moment."

"I *really* like her," Cole murmured.

After a few moments, Kappa walked out of the back room, wiping her hands on a towel. "My apologies, boys." She sighed fondly. "Magi should not learn lightning until they're ten. Five-year-olds frighten me."

Cole leaned on the counter with a smile. "You seem to be fitting in just fine."

Something in his blue eyes made her heart flutter but she ignored it. "Everyone has been very welcoming. It's not hard to be equally accepting in return. Now, then. C.J." She went over to a cabinet and began to sort through the medicines and herbs that were inside. "Normally I'd give these herbs to someone with an allergy, but they ought to have a similar effect."

"They won't turn my skin blue, will they?"

"Blue?" She blinked, then hid a smile. "No, they won't, I promise. You might be a little more sensitive to the sun though, so take care not to get a burn." She put the herbs in a bowl and began to expertly grind them into a fine powder.

"I'll make it into a lotion you can rub into your skin. It's more effective than eating them. And anyway, they might make your stomach upset."

"I've eaten Cole's cooking and survived."

When Cole didn't say anything, Kappa lifted a brow. "No witty comeback?"

"I can't argue with the truth," was the dry response. "If they really want to get rid of the Elite, they should feed them my attempt at sweetbread. It's probably more lethal than a fireball from a Master Fire Magi."

She bit her lip to hide a smile. Without another word, she finished grinding the herbs. She then added a liquid serum from some desert flowers to make it into a spreadable condition. "The only side effect other than the sensitivity to the sun will be that you might smell like flowers."

"I'm a Soil Magi," C.J. pointed out. "I frequently smell like anything that has to do with growth, and flowers often fall out of my hair. Spring is the worst. The findral keep trying to chew on my flowery hair."

"That's why it's so short," Cole offered. "We couldn't get the findral away fast enough."

"Are you sure you're not brothers?"

The males grinned at each other. "Well, in a way we are," C.J. admitted. "We've been best friends ever since I was twelve. No one knows me as well as Cole does. Actually, I've never been comfortable around anyone but Cole, so that's part of it as well." Honesty made him admit, "I'm fairly comfortable around you as well."

She started to ask if that meant he would write her a letter someday, but she saw Cole watching her. Something in his eyes made the words go away. Averting her gaze from his oddly piercing blue one, she said instead, "Well, if you'd like another friend, I wouldn't mind. I've never had that many friends either."

"You do seem fairly strong for a Magi," Cole noted. "You're probably a little more sensitive yourself."

She looked at him quickly. "I always forget that Kin can sense the power in other people. But you're right." She poured the medicine into a jar and sealed the lid tightly. When she was sure it wouldn't leak, she handed it to C.J. "One use in the morning should make the rest of the day better. If you find yourself waking because of the itching, use it before you go to bed."

"Yes'm." He thought for a few moments and then made his decision. "Would you like to come see where Cole and I weave? We work together sometimes and he uses my workroom. I'm supposed to make a tapestry for someone in Carnelian and it needs five different colors. It might be interesting to you."

"*Five* colors? Very interesting indeed." She smiled. "I'll even bring lunch with me, how's that?" Her smile turned into a laughing grin. "I promise it's far less lethal than anything that Cole might produce."

"Sweetbread?" Cole asked hopefully, his ears perking up.

Knowing Kin and their notorious sweet tooth, she sighed fondly. "Yes, including sweetbread. I might even bring some pudding to go with it. But you have to share!" she scolded Cole as he and C.J. headed for the door.

Cole paused in the doorway as C.J. went down the steps to the street. Softly, his eyes warm, he said, "It's the only thing I'll share, Kappa. C.J. won't notice you, no matter how you might hope. When you accept that, my shoulder will be there for you to cry on."

She felt as if she wasn't breathing as he went down the steps toward the street. Why was she so breathless? Because a handsome Kin was flirting with her? She was thirty-two. She had been flirted with before. She'd had lovers before. She couldn't afford to be distracted by Cole when it was C.J. she needed. She couldn't afford to get her heart involved else she would never have her revenge on the Magi.

But why did it hurt so much?

Chapter Eight

The next morning, Kappa headed out of town and across the dunes to where she had been assured that C.J. lived. To her puzzlement, she didn't see any buildings or structures at all. There was nothing, as far as her eyes could see, that even remotely looked like a house. And more specifically, how would anything survive? There were cliffs nearby, though. Maybe he had dug out a home there.

"What's a pretty Magi like you doing lost in the desert?"

She stifled a yelp and a jump as she whirled around. Cole just grinned at her and her shoulders relaxed. "That was not very nice!" she scolded. "I thought Kin were supposed to be gentle and kind."

"Oh, we are." Power welled up around him and flowed across the ground to climb up her body. It focused near her ear and became a lovely desert flower the same color as her eyes. "Is that sufficiently gentle?"

Ignoring the smile he was giving her as hard as she was ignoring her rapid heartbeat, she found a breezy smile. "Indeed. Now be a gentleman and tell me where I'm going. I think I'm lost."

"Actually, you're not. You're standing on his roof."

"His roof?"

The dune lifted under her feet and sent her tumbling forwards. She landed safely in Cole's arms and stared wide-eyed as the dune lifted to reveal a cave. C.J. peeked out of the opening, laughter in his black eyes. "Did someone knock?"

"You two are *horrible*." She straightened and refused to be charmed by either of them. She held up the basket she carried. "That's a fine way to treat someone who came bearing gifts." She reached in the basket to find the sweetbread but it didn't come to hand. Puzzled, she peeked inside. "Where did the sweetbread go?"

"Ahem."

She turned and her eyes went wide as she saw Cole holding the loaf. "How did you do that?"

"I'm good with my hands." He handed her the loaf and then headed down into the cave with a merry whistle.

She wasted no time in following him and watched in fascination as the dune was put back in place. You could hardly tell that it was a cavern under the land. The walls were covered with sturdy wooden planks and the floor had thick woven rugs. The ceiling was more wooden planks, and lanterns hung on all the walls. Except for the absence of windows, it felt like any other home. "This is incredible."

"It gives me as much quiet as I want. Only people who know where my dune is can find it. And even better, they can't get in unless they have Soil power *and* I let them." C.J. poured a glass of tea and offered it to Kappa. "It's not big, though. The main room where we are, my bedroom, a washroom, and my workroom. I never bothered with a kitchen. My mom is driven to feed me."

"She's driven to feed everyone," was Cole's dry opinion.

"That too." He headed to the workroom. "Over here."

Kappa followed him curiously. She had never been in a weaver's workroom before. It looked like a normal room with a couple of tables covered in bags of sand. The predominant object, however, was a large wooden frame in the center of the room. "What's this for?" she asked.

"It's the frame that holds whatever I'm working on. For clothing, I don't need a frame. But for banners and the like where I need to see the entire piece at once, I use this." He grabbed a bag of sand and dropped it on the floor near the base of the frame. In the back of his mind, he could already see what he wanted.

Cole tugged Kappa back a step and offered her a chair. Fascinated, she watched as C.J. began gathering the sand with his power and forming it into threads and cloth. Under his skillful hands, the tapestry began to take form. It was a sea of color formed to depict a sunset on the ocean. The colors were so vivid that she half thought the imagery was real.

When he finished the first section, he put a temporary seam on the frayed edges. "Well?" he asked. "What do you think so far?"

"You're showing off."

"Am not."

Kappa shook her head. "It doesn't look like he's showing off at all. It's really beautiful, C.J." She got to her feet, beginning to feel the first stirrings of unease. What right did she have to destroy someone who made such beauty? "Let's have some food."

They all sat down in the main room and divided up the food. Kappa had indeed brought pudding, and Cole was more than happy to take a large portion. Much to her surprise, Kappa found herself enjoying the visit immensely. Cole and C.J.'s verbal banter kept her laughing, and she was oddly touched when they listened to her talk of living in Prismatic for a while.

"Why become a doctor?" C.J. asked curiously.

"It was a decision I made about nine years ago. I just .. . felt driven to heal people. My Air powers are best applied to healing arts, so it seemed logical. Until that point, I'd never really been sure where I belonged."

"I know how that feels," C.J. said softly. "It's hard to fit in when you not only *are* different but you *feel* different." He smiled. "But you can visit with us any time, Kappa. Just ask Cole to bring you for a visit."

"Or you can visit me at my home in town." Cole's smile was warm in a way that meant she was welcome in any way at any time. "I wouldn't mind."

The message went over C.J.'s head if the look on his face was any clue. For that, Kappa was glad he was still not an adult. "Maybe I'll visit you both," she made sure to the stress the 'both' part, "or you can come visit me. I've never really had that many friends."

"Well, we'll change that." C.J. bumped her foot with his. "You're a good person, Kappa."

She abruptly got to her feet. "I need to be going."

"I'll escort you back," Cole offered. He also stood and opened the dune above their heads. He held it long enough for her to scramble out and then followed her and closed it behind him. She moved very quickly across the dunes, but so did he. He shortly caught up. "That combination of childhood astuteness and not-yet-an-adult maturity is vexing, isn't it?"

She crossed her arms tightly. "Neither of you know anything about me. You probably shouldn't even want to be my friend."

He caught her arm and swung her around. Her eyes were instantly drawn to the gold tattoos on his strong arms. They glimmered in the sun, oddly beautiful, and the strength in his body was a lure. If she wanted, he would hold her. She hadn't been held in years.

"I know enough," he said softly, "to know that C.J. is right. You're a good person. Maybe it's time you learned that too." He ran his fingers through her hair tenderly and then released her entirely. "You'll fall a little in love with him. It can't be helped. I'm a little in love with him too. But he'll never belong to you, and you'll never belong to him."

"No one's ever wanted me to belong to them."

He smiled a little whimsically. "I wasn't there." He turned her around and nudged her toward the city in the distance. "Go home. We'll come visit tomorrow. Have you been to the oasis inside the town?"

"No, I haven't had time."

"Make time." With that, he turned and headed back toward the dune where C.J. lived.

C.J. went to town by himself the next morning. He was going to be meeting Cole and Kappa at the central oasis. The oasis had been built by Soil and Water Magi to provide a place where the people of the city could escape the harsh desert and enjoy lush green scenery. The oasis was half a mile long and half a mile wide, big enough for a lake and for lots of trees. Kin Faeries who flew over it claimed it looked like a tiny blue and green dot in a sea of brown.

He got to the lake area first and sat down on one of the stone benches. The lotion was working wonders, and his skin didn't seem to be itching quite as badly. He also wasn't getting a sunburn; he seemed to be weathering the side effects just fine. He sensed Kappa before he saw her and smiled as he turned. "Good morning."

"Good morning." Relieved that he was alone, she walked over and sat down beside him. "Out of curiosity, what brought you to Symphony? Considering the problems that the city has had, it seems strange that anyone would voluntarily move here during the worst of it."

"By the time we arrived, it was centered mostly in town. And I've always lived in the desert, though for a while I and my parents lived in a very small town on Prismatic. Mom had a falling out with her family, and we moved here. I've just really liked it here so I haven't bothered to leave. I probably never will. Well, I might go to Kindred someday. Cole is nagging me to visit with him one year."

"The out of control power didn't frighten you when you got here?"

He tilted his head. "Oddly, it didn't. Because my power is strong, I thought I might be able to help a little bit. I tried to grow something directly in the sand, you know, giving back when something had been taken away. It worked." He pointed to where a large cactus was in full bloom. "That's what I planted."

"My goodness." Her eyes widened. "It's huge!" She walked over to it and discovered it stood bigger than she was tall. "I've never seen a cactus get this tall!"

"It was an accident. Every time the land had an aftershock, I added more power." He smiled sheepishly. "By the time the shocks stopped, my cactus was a little, erm, distinctive. We built the oasis around it."

"You were twelve," she murmured. Most twelve-year-olds weren't even in first puberty yet. "You must have started first puberty early."

"I did. I'd started it about a month earlier to our move. I was trying to deal with my Soil powers and my Wood ones at the same time. It was actually helpful to me too. I didn't have to worry about excess power." He winced. "I only once put a tree through the roof of our house."

She walked over and sat down next to him. Conspiratorially, she said, "I set my neighbor's barn on fire when I was learning my Thunder powers. It didn't help my cause any that I happened to be in the middle of the curiosity phase of second puberty and *really* liked my neighbor's son."

"How did that end?"

She grinned. "Well, he was a Fire Magi. He accidentally filled his house with smoke and had to ask me to help clear it. We were even at that point. He kissed me before the wind was fully gone." With a fond sigh for the memory, she said, "You never forget your first kiss." She quirked a brow as he shrugged at her. "You're not even at the curiosity for a kiss yet?"

"Well, I think I am, but I haven't met anyone I wanted *to* kiss. I'll sit and think about what kissing someone must be like, but at the same time, not have anyone I'm inclined to kiss. It's really frustrating."

"Frustration is another name for second puberty," she

countered dryly, warmed by his honesty. "Wait until you get to the exploration phase. It's *murder* on hormones. Both yours and your lover's." She lightly put a hand on his. "I wouldn't mind being your first kiss," she offered.

"I don't know if I'm attracted to you," he admitted.

"The offer stands if you decide you are." She knew better than to push things and looked around instead. "Where is Cole, anyway? I half expected him to just appear from out of thin air. He startled me something fierce yesterday."

"You called?" There was a swirl of gold light, and Cole appeared right in front of them.

C.J. grabbed Kappa before she could fall off the bench. Desperately trying not to laugh, he helped her sit back up. "Actually, Kin can travel via land current, so they are invisible to the average eyesight until they stop moving."

"And we can move *really* fast." Cole pointedly sat down on the bench next to Kappa. "Good morning. Sleep well?"

Cursing the faint heat she could feel in her cheeks, she found her bravado and looked him dead in the eye. "I did, thank you." She pointedly turned back to C.J. "How did you meet Cole?"

"Mom fed him and we haven't gotten rid of him since." He grinned a little as Cole flicked his ears at him. "Truthfully, I got lost in the desert. He was coming back from the northern port and found me. By the time we got back to Symphony, we were friends. We just seemed to hit it off."

"It's clear there's a special bond there," she agreed. She got to her feet. "I need to go back to my Shelter now. I'll see you both later. Maybe we can spend more time together. This is a nice place to take a break."

"Anytime." As she disappeared out of the oasis, he said to Cole, "I don't want to be in the middle."

"I don't think it can be avoided," Cole admitted. "She's

. . . conflicted."

"Why?"

"Reasons you wouldn't understand." He stood. "Don't worry about my feelings. I know you won't suddenly fall for her." Hands linked behind his back, he headed out of the oasis as well.

Over the next few days, the town got used to seeing Kappa with Cole and C.J. They spent time in the oasis together when Kappa was taking a break, or the males would visit her at the Healing Shelter. Other times she visited them at C.J.'s place, or even Cole's home. No one could even be sure which of the two males Kappa liked more. The only thing the people were sure of was that Cole was falling for Kappa and C.J. wasn't.

Even Kappa didn't know which male she was drawn to more. She was attracted to Cole, *badly*, and her heart ached around him. At the same time, she really cared for C.J. as well. She was attracted to him, but it was a gentle attraction. She couldn't even sort out her own feelings. It felt like second puberty all over again and it was disheartening.

She was goofing off and slacking off. She wasn't even doing what she was supposed to be doing. Her job was to find the reason why Symphony was balanced, and she had. The part where she was supposed to remove the balance was what held her up. How did you bring yourself to kill someone you loved?

A knock on the door jarred her out of her thoughts and she got to her feet. "Coming!" As she entered into the front area, she went very still. The man standing inside the doorway was very familiar, and at that moment, very unwelcome. "Hello, Delta."

When C.J. got to the Healing Shelter a few minutes later, he had to move aside as an older man went down the steps. "Pardon me," he said politely. "Is Kappa in?"

"Yes."

A little puzzled at the abrupt answer—and the fact that the man dressed like someone from a forest while in the middle of a desert—he went up the stairs and into the Shelter. "Hey, Kappa!" he started to say cheerfully. He broke off as he saw her sitting and staring out the window. His smile faded and he hurried to her side. "Are you okay? Did he hurt you?"

"No." She closed her eyes. "He just told me some . . . unpleasant truths." At a touch, she looked down in surprise to see his hand covering hers. "Don't be nice to me."

"Why not?"

"I don't deserve it." Her smile turned a little crooked. "I'm a little in love with you, C.J., but I'm doomed to hurt you. Pathetic, isn't it?"

He stood quickly. "That's ridiculous!" he said sharply. "You always have a choice! And anyway, I don't think you care for me the way you care for Cole!" Her eyes swung toward him and he raked a hand through his hair. "I'm not *that* naïve! And I refuse to get in the middle of this!" He swung toward the door. "I'm getting Cole. We're going to all have a talk. I'm not watching you two suffer when it's just you both being stupid!"

As the door slammed behind him, she winced. Her gentle and innocent Master Magi wasn't always so gentle, and he certainly wasn't entirely innocent. He was definitely further in second puberty than they all thought. Hating herself for what she had to do, she got to her feet to go into her room. She would change clothes, and then she would follow him. The sooner it was done, the better.

Cole wasn't at his home so C.J. headed toward his own. If Cole wasn't at one location, then he was assuredly at the other. And, sure enough, halfway between town and his dune, he saw Cole walking through the sand. He hurried to catch up. "Cole!"

Cole stopped and turned around with a smile. "Hey,

C.J." The smile faded as he saw the seriousness of his friend's face. "What's wrong?"

"Well, for starters, some forest dweller just upset Kappa." He caught Cole's arm to keep him from running off. "Hang on, there's more." He let out a quick breath. "Kappa said she's a little in love with me."

"As she should be. I knew she would be."

"That's not the point!" He released Cole's arm and walked a step away. "She said she was doomed to hurt me! What is wrong with her? She was fine until that mainlander showed up! And you!" He turned and poked Cole in the chest. "You've clearly been hiding something from me! You always say that you *know* things are going to happen or won't happen. How do you know these things? I'm not saying I think I'll fall in love with her, but how can you be sure I won't? I don't want to hurt you two!"

Cole closed his eyes. "Your destiny is different, C.J." His eyes opened, and they were intense and nearly grief-stricken. "You're a Chronicle."

Silence fell. C.J. shook his head a little as he backed up a step. "Th-that's impossible! I don't have any lines!"

"That we can see. If my hunch is right, they're hidden right now. That's why your power is causing your skin to itch badly. And that's why you seemed to be 'stuck' in second phase of second puberty. Why do you think you calmed the land when you got here? What was taken by a Chronicle was returned by one. Your power is *not* Magi in origin. I always suspected, but I was sure when I saw your reaction to being told about Furies."

The painful longing welled up again and this time it made utter sense. Barely breathing, he lifted his hands and stared at them as if they belonged to a stranger. "But how is any of this possible? Who could have locked my power?"

"Nine years ago," came Kappa's voice behind them, "there was a man named Morgan Chronis living in

Prismatic. He is a Chronicle. He had four Chronicle children hiding in secret. He sent them away and we've been hunting them ever since."

Both males turned and C.J. went very still as he saw that Kappa wore the long white cloak with the black chalice and dagger that meant she was a member of the Black Magi Elite. How he knew what the cloak stood for, he couldn't say, but he was utterly sure. He was also not very happy, or surprised, to recognize the forest dweller standing beside her in the same cloak.

"Well done, Kappa," the man said. "I commend you for finding one of the Chronicle children."

Kappa said nothing. Cole, pointedly, stepped in front of C.J. "And who are you?" he asked.

"Delta." He gave a tight smile. "We are from the Elite, Kin. And if you value your ears, you'll leave now. This matter does not concern you."

"I'm afraid it does." Something powerful swirled through Cole's eyes. "You're threatening my friend, and you seem to be hurting someone else I care for." His eyes met Kappa's startled gaze. "Why do you stay there?"

She said nothing. What could she say? She didn't have an answer for him. All the things she had thought she knew were completely false. It broke her heart. She didn't want C.J. to be a Chronicle. She wanted even less for him to be a Master Magi and need to be killed. "I . . ."

"Don't be swayed," Delta ordered her. A little madness gleamed in his eyes as he slowly advanced toward the males. "If you won't leave, Kin, then you'll just die here. I'm sure your death will disrupt the land as nicely as your friend's would have. As for him, we have other needs for him."

The land began to tremble softly. Eyes narrowed, C.J. said, "Maybe you should ask me if I'm interested." He shot a look at Kappa. "I thought better of you than this." She flinched and he began to gather his power. "I'm not going anywhere with the Elite."

Pulsing white light surrounded Cole's hands, burning as brightly as the sun. "If that's his wish, then I'll help him."

Delta sighed. "Must you make things so difficult?" Fire began to gather around his hand. "I'm a Master Fire Magi, Kin. You won't find this battle easy. Kappa, you subdue the Chronicle." She said nothing and he looked at her sharply. He turned away in disgust. "You would have affection for these two. Very well. I'll kill the Kin first and that should clear your mind."

C.J. stepped up beside Cole. "You're not touching him."

The land under Delta cracked and surged upward, flinging him high in the air. He twisted around to get his feet under himself and began shooting fireballs at C.J. and Cole. They ducked and dove two different directions. When Cole rolled to his feet, he threw a ball of light directly at Delta. Vines covered in thorns shot out of the ground and threatened a painful landing for Delta.

He barely managed to dodge the light and then surrounded himself with fire as he landed. It burned away the vines. He drew a dagger and ran directly at Cole, but the land rocked violently and tossed him back the way he had come. As he landed, he had to roll swiftly across the sand to avoid the vines shooting up from the land.

As the fight began to progress, Kappa realized that the land was shaking and quivering in ways that had nothing to do with the quakes that C.J. used. She knelt and touched the sand and felt the violent churning under the surface. Symphony was balanced, but it was still recovering. Her head jerked up. "Cole! C.J.! Don't use quakes!"

"You little . . . !" Delta swung around and shot a fireball directly at her. "You can die with them!"

At the last second, Cole appeared in front of her and shot a ball of light at the fireball. The two met and exploded together and tore out a large crater. The land went mad.

Rolling waves of sand lifted and swelled like the ocean. They rippled as far as the city, and from even that far they could hear the people beginning to scream in terror.

Cole grabbed Kappa's wrist and pulled her along behind him as he began running across the sand. "C.J.!"

C.J. wasted no time in following. Putting as much space between them and the city as possible was critical. He didn't bother to look back over his shoulder. He knew Delta was following them.

When they were at least a mile out from the city, they stopped running to catch their breath. Cole released Kappa and she sank down onto her knees. She was trembling as hard as the land. "What is going on in your head?" he almost shouted. He knelt and gave her a shake.

"You wouldn't understand." She shook her head and her hair flew. "A few years ago . . . I had nothing to live for. The Magi . . . they destroyed my life. Joining the Elite was all I could do. I needed to do something!"

"That wasn't the thing to do!" C.J. snapped at her.

Cole caught Kappa's face in his hands. "You're not alone! Not now."

Tears burned her eyes. "You're not the one I'm supposed to love. You're breaking my heart."

Before Cole could respond to that, he sensed a familiar power. His head lifted sharply and he saw Delta approaching with fire coalescing around his body in a deadly inferno. At the last moment, Cole and Kappa disappeared from where they were kneeling. A fireball shattered the land at their location and they reappeared closer to C.J.

Laughing a little maniacally, Delta began shooting fireball after fireball at them. "You can all die! It doesn't matter anymore!"

A solid wall of wood appeared and the fireballs splashed off harmlessly. Before Cole could say anything, the wall splintered and became wicked shrapnel that fired directly at Delta. C.J. ran toward the older man and Soil power swirled around his body.

The rioting land was spreading and had reached them again. Geysers of elements shot up through the surface. Delta had to dodge. Cole made a protective shield of light around him and Kappa. C.J. either didn't notice or didn't care, and it was evidenced when a geyser broke under his feet and fired raw elemental power directly into his body. He absorbed it instantly.

Kappa's eyes went wide. "I thought that was a myth!"

"That Chronicles can absorb any power excess?" Cole shook his head. "The Kin call it the reason for their existence."

Delta was so startled by the sight of C.J. absorbing the blast that he didn't know the Chronicle was on him until too late. C.J.'s fist connected with his chin and sent him flying. He had to hurriedly get to his feet to avoid another geyser and shot rapid-fire balls of flames at his enemy. C.J. blocked but ended up singed. Almost as if something had snapped, he lifted the land as high as he was tall and hurled the wave at Delta.

Cole's eyes fixed on the city in the far distance. He could see an oddly familiar shadow approaching it on the horizon. "I'm going to get help," he told Kappa. "C.J. can't do this alone." His eyes glittered as he looked at her. "If you're not here when I return, I'll look for you until I find you."

Before she could respond, he had disappeared. Shivering despite the heat, she looked at the bloody war that was being fought. Delta was outmatched. C.J. was stronger than one would expect for an unawakened Chronicle. He was still at a disadvantage though. His powers hadn't been intended for battle and Delta's were. Kappa knew she could jump in the fight on C.J.'s side and give him an advantage.

She just didn't know if she dared risk it.

Chapter Nine

Dahlia Stalker was over four hundred years old. She had been friends with Jazz Eaglewind since they were both hatched. When Jazz had found her Chronicle, Dahlia had been happier than anyone else. Behind her happiness, however, she had hidden a great secret. Everyone knew Dahlia was a Fury; it wasn't something one could simply ignore. No one had known, however, that she had felt her Chronicle's birth ten years prior.

Now, nine years later, she still felt him.

That feeling, that longing and aching in her heart, told her he was alive. In knowing he was alive, she was fairly sure he was one of Morgan's hidden Chronicle children. For nine years she had been looking, crossing from city to city. Examining every face, bumping shoulders with every Magi. Looking for that one person that would complete her.

She had always been a loner. It wasn't as painful for her as it was for the other Furies searching the world. They were caught between the hunger for their lover and the longing for home. She called the Isle of Dragons home, but she didn't entirely miss it. Even her own kind didn't realize how solitary she felt inside.

She laughed, she smiled, and she spent time with the others. But inside . . . she felt alone. She was honestly surprised no one had realized sooner just how alone. She was well past second puberty, but she had never taken a lover.

Never.

Though she had gone through the curiosity and the exploration and the readiness to become an adult, she had never found someone she was fully comfortable enough with to have as her lover. Dragons had offered, and so had Magi. In fact, a few Kin had offered. She had turned them all down. Her heart had been unmoved by them. If her heart wasn't moved, why should her body be?

As she stood in the southern port on the land of Choral, she was aware of the interested gazes of Magi as they went past. It was to be expected. She was unusually lovely and surprisingly tall with her curvy six-one height and her knee length blonde hair. Her hair was streaked with stark white, courtesy of her Dragon blood, and her eyes were the creamy color of milk soaked sweetbread (a delicacy unto itself).

She had to suppose that another reason she was different was that she had never truly hated the Magi. Oh, she disliked many of them intently, and she had met a few she wouldn't have minded eating for a snack, but as a general rule . . . she didn't mind them that much.

She had seen their mindset change over the last nine years. The new Magi king was more open-minded and had expressed a desire for change. He was working with the land of Kindred, with both Elders of the Kin, to more firmly cement the treaty. He wanted to offer them some additional land on islands the Magi didn't use to help them spread and grow.

She didn't know where he stood on the issue of Chronicles, though. He hadn't changed the law, but he didn't seem to be *enforcing* it either. By her reckoning, if the Elite were gone, perhaps the law would change. The general feeling was that killing Chronicles kept them out of Elite hands. Stupid, perhaps, but far easier to deal with than the horror and hate.

She was startled out of her thoughts when she saw a little girl trying to peer onto the counter where a vendor sold candy. She smiled and knelt next to her. "Hi."

The girl looked at her in surprise but didn't initially see anything unusual about the pretty lady with cream-colored eyes. She was wearing the same bikini and cloth skirt that most older females wore, and she was wearing sturdy dune-walking boots. The girl finally spotted the streaks in her hair and felt the tickle of strong power. Delight filled her face. "You're a Dragon!"

"Mm." Dahlia inclined her head at the table. "You want to see the sweets?" When the girl nodded, Dahlia picked her up so she could look. She couldn't help but be warmed by the way the girl's eyes went wide with wonder. She loved children of all races. "Which is your favorite?"

"That one!" The girl pointed to a round candy covered in spots. "Cactear bites!"

Holding the girl with one arm, Dahlia grabbed a few coins from the bag on her hip and handed it to the vendor. She then plucked up the bite and handed it to the girl. "My treat." She set the girl down gently. "Now don't ruin your dinner."

A woman came hurrying through the crowd and skidded to a stop near the girl. Wariness filled her eyes as she pulled her daughter close. "Was she bothering you?"

"Not at all. I was just being indulgent." Dahlia smiled. "I don't eat children. They get stuck in my teeth."

The girl giggled and the woman's shoulders relaxed. "I apologize for my wariness," she offered. "Dragons and Magi aren't known to be that friendly to one another." She made the Magi sign of respect. "If your race is all like you, perhaps we might find peace."

"Only if yours is like you," Dahlia agreed with a graceful bow. It was the Dragon sign of respect. "Warm winds, as we say."

The woman smiled. "Always in the desert."

Appreciating the humor, Dahlia waved to the little girl and walked away. It was time to leave the city. She had met every person and seen every child. There were no Chronicles there, neither child nor adult. Her Chronicle wasn't there.

She went half a mile beyond the city before turning

into her Dragon form. As a Dragon, she was a slightly taller than average twenty-one feet in length, and her scales were cream and white. Ironic though it was, in Magi form she was considered lovely, and in Dragon, she was often termed cute. She had no idea where the distinction occurred. She supposed it was a cultural thing.

She sensed the trouble long before she reached Symphony. She could see the waves of the land rolling back and forth. Startled, she stopped in mid-air a mile out of the city. She had thought the land was said to be calm now. Alarmed, she hurried faster toward the city where she could hear the rising panic.

Normally Dragons were not allowed to fly directly over or near towns because that too could cause ripples in the power under the land. Since the land was not likely to notice her presence right then, she flew directly over the city and landed on the northern side. A particularly vicious wave of land was rolling directly at her, and she knew it might destroy the city.

Her wings arched and Air power swirled around her. It connected with the wave of land and sent it back the way it had come. Other waves rolled into her barrier and then bounced back away. After a moment, the shaking stilled in the area. She could still see waves in the distance, but they weren't reaching the city.

She turned and looked at the city just as several people on shaking legs walked forward. "Is everyone all right?" she asked. Her voice was no different from her Magi one, but it carried a stronger echo of power.

"We are," one woman managed to say. "We'll have to check to be sure. You . . . you may well have saved all our lives." She drew a long breath. "We owe you."

She shook her head. "No, you don't." Her eyes moved to the distance where she could see a battle being raged. "Have you been dealing with the Elite?"

"No . . . not that we know of," a man spoke up. His eyes were on the horizon as well. He could just faintly see the lights and sparks.

"Where's my son?" Ferris pushed her way through the crowd gathering. "Where's C.J.?"

Something about the name sounded very familiar to Dahlia and she frowned. "Is he missing?"

"He lives in a dune home outside of town." Ferris went up to Dahlia without fear and touched her leg pleadingly. "Please! Go make sure the waves didn't hurt him! He's a Master Soil Magi and might have ridden out the storm, but I can't be sure!"

"I'll go and check," Dahlia promised. As she turned to look at the distance, she not only saw the more distinct signs of Soil power being used, but an unusual light flare in a two-one-one pattern. A Kin was signaling her. "Everyone stay here."

Everyone backed up and she lifted into the air to fly swiftly toward the signal. When she reached it, she found a SunKin Elf waiting for her. He looked healthy enough, but he showed the signs of recent fighting. "Is something wrong?"

Cole couldn't have been more delighted to discover himself talking to a female Air Fury. "My partner is in danger!" He pointed toward the fight. "He's a Soil Chronicle and unawakened! Everyone thought he was a Master Magi though!"

Shock reverberated through her. "How old?"

"Nineteen!"

Too afraid to hope yet too afraid not to, she shot across the land in a white colored streak. It was too coincidental to be true, but it was too likely not to be. "Please," she said over and over again as she flew. "Please!"

At the fight, C.J. was wounded. He had taken a fireball across the arm and was burned from elbow to wrist. It was also hard to breathe now that Delta was using smoke to obscure the air. Kappa had run away. C.J. didn't blame her at all, but he knew Cole would be furious.

Reaching for reserves of power he hadn't known he had, he grabbed up a handful of sand and hurled it at Delta. It formed into a thick piece of cloth that stuck to the other man's face like tar. Choking and wheezing, Delta clawed at the cloth. He couldn't see or breathe. Small boulders began to pelt his chest, and he felt the stings that meant he was being wounded.

He was at the last dredges of his power. C.J. was a Chronicle. His power was infinite, and every geyser under his feet just seemed to heal and refresh him. Finally tearing the cloth off, Delta gathered all his power for an immense fireball. "Cursed Chronicle!"

A furious roar ripped across the land and sky, and a Dragon's shadow passed directly overhead. C.J.'s power went out of control. The land broke into riotous bloom of flowers and immense trees burst hundreds of feet upward into the sky. With a surge of golden light, lines appeared across his chest, over the backs of his hands, and across the top of his feet.

Dazed and shaken by the near detonation of power inside his body, he fell to his knees amid the flowers. Dahlia landed gracefully in front of him, and her wings spread wide to make a more imposing sight. Every last one of her teeth bared as she snarled, "Get away from my Chronicle!"

Delta backed up slowly and then turned to run. Before he could take more than a step, he found himself face to face with an immense ball of light power. The heat scorched his skin. He had just enough time to meet Cole's eyes before the ball consumed him. It burned so hot and fast that in seconds there was nothing left. Only a tiny ripple in the land was all that marked his passing.

Cole lowered his hand and looked around. Kappa was nowhere in sight. He could only curse mentally as he crossed to C.J. "Are you okay?" he asked softly as he knelt next to his friend.

C.J. barely noticed. His eyes were fixed on Dahlia. He had never seen anything as magnificent or beautiful as this cream-colored Dragon. "Mine," he whispered. It was all he could say. It was all that was important. Still suffering his own internal aftershocks, his eyes closed and he fell to the sand without another sound.

Dahlia turned and went into her Magi form. Wonder filled her eyes as she knelt beside him and eased him into her arms. He was more beautiful than she had dared dream. She had known the instant she laid eyes on him that he was hers. Dormant emotions, unawakened emotions, rose to the forefront with a hunger and desire she had yearned to experience.

If there was anything more beautiful than seeing the face of a Fury who had found their destined Chronicle, Cole had never heard of it. He got to his feet and looked around for evidence of the direction Kappa had fled. "Damn her," he said softly. "Always so willingly blind."

Dahlia looked up in surprise. "Someone is missing?"

"Yes." He glanced at her. "Someone as important to me as C.J. is to you."

"C.J." She found she liked the name immensely. "What does it stand for?"

"He won't say, and he threatened his parents with bodily harm if they blabbed. You'll have to tell me what it is when you two bond." He let out a little breath. "I won't ask you to love and protect him. You cannot do anything less. But I will ask that you eventually contact me when he finishes his journey."

"You have my word," she promised softly. "And when you find your lover, please let me know." Softer, she added, "Thank you, for protecting him for me."

"C.J. and I are much alike. And he's easy to love."

As he disappeared, she returned her attention to C.J.

In wonder, she brushed his hair out of his eyes. He wasn't a warrior. She had noticed that instantly when she had approached the fight. He had thrown *cloth* at his enemy. On the other hand, she *was* a warrior, and her Air power was suited for battle. She would protect him.

She tenderly put him down on the grass and backed up. She changed to her Dragon shape and picked him up with her claws as gently as she could. She didn't bother to determine the way home. It had been her guess years before that suggested Jazz and Dominic had forgotten their way home because of their Chronicle. Now she was sure of it.

As she flew into the air and began looking for a safe place for them to rest, she reflected back on the memories in her mind. She had inherited the memories of another Fury at her birth and she knew precisely the steps needed for the bonding. She already felt the drain on her majiks even as she felt C.J.'s power rising.

She flew to the east beyond the desert and to the scattered islands that dotted the ocean. They were the only remnants of other great lands. Though the Magi had not wanted to, they now had to accept that Kin were crucial to the world. They represented the land. And the Magi, too, could never be removed. They were the sea. The Dragons, infinite in power, were the sky.

One island looked like a floating oasis and she angled down that direction. There was just enough room in a small clearing for her to land. She put C.J. down and turned back to Magi form. Her senses told her there was nothing dangerous on the tiny isle, but she sent out a probe of Air power regardless. It also told her it was safe.

She walked over to a tiny spring sitting nearby and filled a flask from her hipsack with fresh water. It broke her heart to see burns on C.J.'s arm, and while she couldn't heal them, she could at least tend to them.

Her heart fluttered as she wiped away blood and dirt. Something low in her belly tightened with pure desire. Unable to resist, she ran her fingers over the supple muscles of his arm. She couldn't believe such a magnificent creature was hers. "If I had to wait to finish second puberty," she said softly, stroking his hair from his face, "then you were well worth the wait."

She curled up beside him and tugged him into her arms where he could rest. She couldn't bear to leave his side. There was nothing more comforting than the sound of his breath feathering over her skin. The rise and fall of his chest was almost hypnotic. Softly, she ran a finger over the lines on his chest. They almost looked like vines and leaves as they ran across his golden skin. Knowing it was her power that made every curl was a potent thing on her senses.

A little laugh caught in her throat. He was only nineteen. She could only pray that he was part of the way, if not all of the way, through second puberty. Things would be very interesting if he wasn't.

C.J. woke to raging pain in his body. His power was wild and out of control. He wanted to shake the land and tear it apart in quakes. He wanted to create mighty trees that stood taller than the sky. There was a presence nearby that he violently wanted to bind to him. He wanted to curl his vines around it and keep it close for all time.

A soft hand touched his cheek and the touch reverberated through to his very soul and power. He knew that touch. He knew the power curling alluringly around him. *His*. He was sure of it. He gathered his strength and forced his eyes open and found himself staring up into a lovely face he knew he would never forget until the day he died. She was . . . breathtaking. Wonder filled his eyes as he reached up to cup her cheek. "You," he breathed. "You're my Fury."

Dahlia turned her face into his hand and her eyes

burned with tears. "Yes," she said softly. "I've waited for you for so long." She felt the soft swirl of his power surrounding her in a call as old as love itself, and she felt some of her nerves ease. He was, at the least, old enough to send out the signal. She softly rubbed her power against his in return and saw the faintest of pink color climb his cheeks. "Don't be embarrassed. There's nothing to be embarrassed by."

He tried to lift his other hand and pain ripped through his blood. She instantly moved closer and leaned in protectively. Her fingers kneaded almost compulsively at his chest. "We need to bond," she said huskily. "I need to feed on your power."

"Like sweetbread?"

It made her smile. "So to speak." She nuzzled at his chest softly. A soft green aura immediately lifted and covered his body, just begging for her attention. He smelled like flowers and rich summer. A time of growth and learning; a time when the world, for a moment, was utterly perfect. Half drunk, she softly brushed her lips over his skin and tasted his power. It was as thick and wonderful as it smelled.

As her lips softly trailed over his chest and up over his shoulders, he wasn't breathing. Nerves and curiosity tangled inside him. The pleasure of her touch was more like an ache and it was spreading. He wanted . . . he didn't know what he wanted. He wanted *something*. He shivered in delight as her lips found a sensitive place on his neck. His lips had begun to tingle. "What's wrong with me?"

She smiled as she nuzzled his cheek. "You're not an adult yet."

"Second phase." His eyes dipped to the lush curves barely held by a bikini top. He *really* wanted to touch her. "Potentially entering third. I never found anyone to be curious with." His eyes met hers. "Until now." The pain in his body faded rapidly to be replaced by a wholly different ache. He propped himself up on an elbow and tangled his fingers in her hair. "Forgive my curiosity."

"Forgiven." Her lashes lowered as his warm breath washed over her lips. She wanted his kiss with a vengeance she had never felt before. The first touch of his lips was almost shy. The second was teasing. She made a frustrated sound. "Tease later." Her arms wound around his neck and she fused their lips together in a way she longed to fuse the rest of their bodies.

He proved to be a quick leaner. The kiss deepened further as he willingly followed her lead. She fed on his power the entire time. It flowed from his mouth to hers with a wild and rich flavor more potent than she had thus far encountered. She was going to be addicted. She was never going to be able to look at flowers the same way again. He had ruined her entirely. And she was happier than she ever had been in her life.

She found herself sprawled against his chest when he sat up fully. Her fingers ran down his body with a possessive touch, and she simply couldn't resist gliding her hands over his back and down his butt. It was a *really* nice one. He promptly broke the kiss with an odd look on his face, and she bit her lip to hide a smile. "Should I apologize?"

He wasn't really sure which the stranger feeling was for him. That she had actually grabbed his ass or that he hadn't really minded it in the first place. "There's a lot more to things than they teach you in school."

"Some things can only be learned by trying." She nuzzled his shoulder where she could see some lingering power. Far be it for her to stop mid-meal. As the last of the power flowed into her, it seemed to ricochet back out of her body and into him. Their power swirled together, fused together, and bonded them in ways that no other being besides another Dragoon might understand.

She could see everything in his heart and mind, could see the generous and feeling heart that ached for the entire world. She could see the mischievous boy that had never truly given sway to correct behavior for an adult. She also saw something else, a close held secret that made her lips curve. She saw why he hated his name.

He could see no less fully into her. He saw the carefully guarded heart that would protect and defend her loved ones to the death. He saw a careful veneer of outgoingness hiding a shy side. He saw a love of the absurd and a hunger for someone to hold. He saw four centuries of lonely waiting for her own death, expecting that she would never be complete. And he saw something else, something that stunned him to his very depths.

She felt her cheeks slowly heating as he stared at her. Feeling suddenly shy, she looked away. "I just . . . wasn't comfortable. I don't deny being curious. And I don't deny one or two kisses getting a little interesting. But . . . even when I was with someone, I felt alone. What was the point?"

He smiled. "The same point that has likely kept me from acting on my curiosity." He ran his fingers slowly through her hair. The sensitivity of his skin seemed to be in overdrive because the soft glide of her hair over his fingers was sensual and wonderful. "If you'll help me satisfy my curiosity and my eventual exploration . . . Then I'll satisfy yours."

She almost wasn't breathing as she watched him lift a handful of her hair and rub his cheek against it. His tactile delight in everything about her was exhilarating. His power softly caressed hers not with the intent to seduce, but simply to see what would happen. His curiosity, now unleashed, seemed to make him want to catch up for lost time. "C.J.?"

"Hmm?" He ran a finger down her arm and enjoyed

the feel of her skin. Delight filled him as a wave of lines followed his finger. They were identical to his and he knew they were made of his power. She was marked as his. She was also struggling for control, and he lifted his hands quickly when he felt her stifle an urge to touch him in return. Nerves made his heart trip over itself. He wasn't sure he was ready for her to return the favor. Chagrined, he looked away. "I'm sorry."

"Never be sorry, *ishke*." She looked to where her new lines went down the side of her neck and right arm. They had also appeared around her left ankle. She had been expecting their presence, though she hadn't expected to feel that wonderfully claimed. It made it hard to keep reign on the emotions inside her.

He felt their volatile presence but wasn't alarmed. He could see the three distinct emotions inside her, and he could see where her love matched his. Her desire was greater than his, but he could see the awakenings of it inside himself. The third emotion . . . it was deeper, wilder, and more powerful than the other two combined. He felt the start of it inside his heart. "What is that?"

"Our gift as Dragoons." She let out a little breath and laced their fingers together. "My name is Dahlia Stalker. I'm saying it because I don't consciously think of my name so you shouldn't pick up on it in my mind."

"C.J. Daragon." He narrowed his eyes when she smiled. "You know my full name. How'd you get that?"

"Unfortunately, *you* think about your name consciously, potentially because you hate it. Me, I find nothing wrong with it." She squeezed his hands tightly and took a deep breath. "How did you know you were a Chronicle?"

"Cole told me." He frowned. "Kappa mentioned something about a man named Morgan." Even saying it made something hurt inside. He had forgotten something. He had often felt there was something missing, but he had never really been sure what. He tried to reach for the memory and encountered a large blank space in his mind.

Dahlia's presence was instantly there and she probed at the empty place gently. She curled her mind around his and soothed his rising distress as she looked for the signs of what had been done. As an Air element, she was more adept at mind searching than other elements. She had still never seen anything like Morgan Chronis' powers. She had a deep hunch that Tariah could do nearly all of the same things, but she hadn't seen her demonstrate the power.

She found the empty place within moments. While she searched for the remaining fragments, she explained, "Morgan is a Chronicle. He and his sister were the ones who fought the Elite nine years ago. Prior to that, Morgan ran the Black Magi; the *real* Black Magi. He gathered four secret Chronicle children with the intent of nurturing them in a safe environment."

As the fragments began to gather, C.J. saw flashes in his mind. "He's short."

She smiled. "Compared to Magi men, yes. He makes up for it in personality." She had routed the fragments and was slowly gathering them toward the blank spot. "When the trouble went down, he erased—fragmented actually—the memories of the children and their parents. He then sent them away via translocation so that no one could find them."

"But what about my lines being hidden?"

"He did that too." She hesitated for a moment and then swept the pieces together.

They fused to the blank space and the memories pounded into his head. He doubled over in agony. She caught him and held tight as the memories brought searing waves of emotional pain. His tears burned her skin and broke her heart. "I'm so sorry," she whispered. "He did it because he loved you."

"I'm *killing* him!" was the fierce mutter against her breast. "He sent us away!" His breath caught with a new wave of pain. "My friends. My sisters and my brother. We were family! How did I ever forget them? I should have remembered!" He straightened and swiped an arm across his eyes. "I'm not a crybaby," he muttered.

She rose up slightly and tenderly kissed the tears away. "Never that," she said softly. "You just willingly feel more than most."

"Willingly? I have a *choice*?"

She laughed. "There's my C.J." When his arms went around her and he buried his face in her hair, she slid her arms around his waist. How she would keep someone with such a tender heart safe and happy was beyond her, but she looked forward to the challenge. She had waited her entire life for this person, and it had been worth every moment.

Her lover sniffed. "You're making me cry more," he grumbled.

"I know. I'm sorry. But these are happy tears, right?"

"Yes." He let out a little breath. "I need to find him. I want to find him. You can't find your way to the Isle, so we'll have to do something else." He eased back. "I want to go to Kindred. Please. Cole might be there. I have to see that he's okay. And I have to thank him."

"He won't be there," she disagreed. "He went to follow Kappa and you can bet she won't go there herself." Half to herself, she added, "There was something oddly familiar about her. I can't put my finger on it. But that's probably because she's a member of the Elite. I was there at the last battle, and my memories were tampered with too."

"I don't see any blank places in your mind, though."

"That's what has everyone confused. Our memories weren't removed unnaturally." She looked up toward the sky where the sun was distinctly setting. Twilight was coming in and she could already see two of the four moons in the sky. "We ought to camp here tonight and set for

Kindred tomorrow."

"Will Symphony be all right if I leave?" Sadness filled his face. "What about my parents?"

"We can ask a Kin to deliver a message to them," she promised. "As for Symphony, I don't know. I was able to calm the land, so it might be all right. But there's no way of knowing for sure. We can find that out on Kindred as well."

"Okay." He looked down at his clothes and saw that they were muddy and torn. He looked longingly at the spring. It was just big enough to swim in. The only thing that kept him in place was an unexpected shyness at the idea of taking his clothes off around Dahlia.

"Why?" She smiled slowly. "I can already see a fair amount of your body, and it's an amount well worth seeing." She tugged him up to his feet. "Let's go. Clothes off, *ishke*. You're just feeling self-conscious because you're attracted to me. And I'd like to point out that even though I've never had a lover, I've seen many naked men in my long life. I can be fair."

He grabbed for his courage and removed his vest and boots. He would dissolve them back to sand and recreate them once he was clean. It took all of his bravado, but he also removed his pants and stood naked. It took a lot of willpower not to cover himself with his hands; his body was making it *very* obvious that the physical signals of desire were going through *just* fine.

Her eyes slowly widened as she stared at him, and she hastily put her hands behind her back before she gave in to an urge to start petting him from head to heels. He somehow seemed even more beautiful with the evidence of his desire for her surrounded by his perfect strength. It made her realize just how much of a woman she was, and just how perfectly they were made to be one. She closed her eyes to remove temptation from sight. "Spring. For the moons' sake, get in the spring before I scare you to death."

He could feel her emotions. He wasted no time in getting into the spring. He didn't feel embarrassed though. Not anymore. Feeling the hot caress of her emotions had removed all self-consciousness. How could he be embarrassed when he knew precisely how his Fury felt about him? Once more at ease, he tilted his head. "Can I watch you undress?"

She really wished his curiosity was stemming from pure attraction. Sadly, it wasn't. Oh, there was attraction there, but she knew it wasn't wholly focused directly on her. Not yet at the least. If it was, he wouldn't have asked. He was the type to have taken her clothes off for her.

He grinned a little. "Eventually I will."

She sighed, then laughed. She really hoped his mischievous side never went away. With only a little hesitation, she untied the cloth around her hips. She removed her shoes and then swiftly removed her bikini as well. Naked except for her exceptionally long hair, she propped her hands on her hips. "Well?"

His eyes studied her in fascination. "You're a lot curvier than Magi females. I like it."

"Thank you." She walked over and sat on the edge of the spring. His enjoyment of her body had removed her nerves. She was glad; she liked the feel of air on her skin without clothes to impede her. "I'd hate for you to dislike it. I can't change it."

"Why would you want to?"

Bemused, she explained, "In my Dragon form, I'm very rounded and curved too. But to the Dragons, that makes me really cute instead of pretty. My friend Jazz is really curvy too, but somehow she's beautiful. I don't know how she does it. It's vexing."

His eyes met hers. "I saw you in Dragon form. I thought you were beautiful." He felt her surprise and tugged her into the spring with him. "Sorry, but cute isn't a word that comes to mind when I'm around you."

Her smile spread across her face and came from the very depths of her soul. She had never been happier in her life. "If it ever does, we'll ask Morgan to erase it."

"Deal." No less happy, he hugged her fiercely and spun her around in the water. He was worried about Cole, and Kappa, and he was definitely worried about his missing childhood friends. But right then, it didn't matter that much. Having his Fury made everything right in the world.

He could only hope for his friends to experience the same. Nothing would be better.

Chapter Ten

On the world of Lucksphere, there was only one land mass that had ice and snow: Glacia, the land to the far north. Despite its place on the world, it was also considered the far south since ships could not actually sail north from Prismatic to reach the port. Natural storms barred the way between the two lands with such fury that none could pass. Ships wanting to go to Prismatic had to take a much longer route by sailing around Glacia's land mass.

There was a town to the far south—Stalagmite—and a town to the far north. Partway between the two was a town on the western shore called Arctica. A range of mountains wrapped around the back of the city and cut it off from the fiercest central storms.

Across the face of the continent were dozens of tiny farms. As a rule, Glacia was very spread out. The people liked it that way. There had once been a capital city called Bergia, but it had been the site of the war nine years before and had not yet recovered. The people were scattered across the land for the time being and the city leader who oversaw Glacia as a whole lived in Stalagmite.

Summers were always cold on Glacia. The only thing that made them different from winters was that there were no storms. At least, that had been the norm. For the last few months, avalanches had been occurring in the mountains near Arctica. It had been assumed at first that they were the byproduct of a still settling land, but now people were surer that it was deliberate.

The Black Magi Elite had arrived.

Expeditions that went into the mountains to mine and to harvest snow plants were now in danger. Many people had been injured or killed in the avalanches. One survivor remembered seeing someone in a white cloak running away. It was enough evidence to request Militia presence. They were, even then, on their way.

It was common knowledge that Carnelian and Spectrum were experiencing much the same problems. It kept everyone in a state of alarm and constantly on the lookout. They couldn't just stop going into the mountains; their livelihood rested there. All they could do was increase security as much as possible.

Despite the increased security, Jayda Lakemore found herself with more than a double in injured patients. She was a Master Water Magi and worked as a doctor in town. Or rather, she helped the people from town, but she didn't live in town. She lived outside the town in a small house that she never left.

She was exceptionally powerful as a healer, and she paid the price for her strength. She was painfully sensitive to people and society. She could barely stand having two people in her home at once, but she made a pointed exception because she couldn't fight the need to heal those who were hurt.

Arctica loved Jayda. They had loved her since she had arrived nine years before. It hadn't been hard. Abut then, at thirteen, she had entered first puberty and revealed she was a Master Magi by learning both Water and Ice, and almost overnight, the spunky child had become a softer and more withdrawn young woman.

Now, at nineteen, the town couldn't even be sure she had started second puberty. She could even have been done with it, but they had no way of knowing. No one minded. You couldn't help but love Jayda. The children of the town took turns taking supplies to her home every week. Sometimes, if they were the lucky one, she left a basket of sweets on the doorstep for them.

It was especially frustrating for the men of the town. With shoulder length seagreen hair that hung straight as a pin, opaque black eyes, and a lovely, delicate figure distributed over a slightly taller than average height of five-ten, she was the reigning beauty of the town, and likely Glacia as a whole.

The sound of findral feet on the snow brought Jayda to her front window. She gave a little sigh and contemplated locking the door and hiding in her room. She couldn't bring herself to be that rude though and instead went to the front door. She didn't open it very far as the male in her yard got off his findral and approached. "Good day."

"Hello, Jayda." He smiled. "I was wondering if you would like to have dinner with me."

"No, thank you."

She stepped back a little and tried to shut the door. It was stopped as he reached out and grabbed the edge. Impatience filled his eyes. "Look, Jayda, you can't just live out here like this. You have to grow up eventually. Have you just not started second puberty?"

"I'm a late bloomer," she lied. Truth be told, she was fairly sure she was all the way through, short of having a lover. Thoughts of having a lover didn't alarm her in the slightest, and for a while they had.

"Maybe you're just not being exposed to the right people."

A delicate seagreen brow lifted ever so slightly. "You come knocking on my door every week. Clearly, you are not the right person either."

A flash of anger lit his eyes and he let go of the door. "Are all Master Magi so stuck up?"

An icicle fell from the roof and landed an inch from his foot. It landed hard enough that it imbedded itself several inches into the wood of the porch, and it was still as high as his knee. He went very still. Softly, Jayda said, "It is not being stuck up to know the difference between affection and self-gratification."

She shut the door and locked it. She stood where she was for long moments and listened to the man as he got on his findral and left. She shivered and went down the hall to her washroom. The pool was always filled with hot water, and she knelt to thrust her arms inside. After a few moments, the heat finally sank into her body. The weather didn't make her cold. Being around other people did. Sometimes she felt as if she would break apart from the inside out from her own Ice power.

Warm once more, she went back to her kitchen where she had been before she was interrupted. The dough still sat on the counter and she resumed kneading and pressing it. Once it started to get flaky, she rolled it into the twisted loop shape of sweetbread. She moved quickly and competently and shortly had several loaves in the oven.

Because she always did her baking every five days, she began to put together the makings for other things she would need. She loved to bake. It was a calming process that let her mind wander without thinking about anything specific. If she stopped and let herself think too much, she would be tempted by the urge to escape into the mountains. Here, at any time, someone might come to her home. It was stressful to say the least.

As if called for, she sensed someone new approaching. She moved quicker and put the tray of mini cakes into the oven as well. She dusted her hands on her apron, and then removed it to go find her cloak. Once it had been wrapped securely around her shoulders and the attached shawl was snug around her neck, she stepped out onto her porch. She would be warm enough between the cloak and her long sleeved tunic and slacks.

Riding toward her was a wagon pulled by two findral. The woman who drove the wagon looked as if she had recently been in an accident. Wounds marked her arms and face, but Jayda didn't see anything life threatening. In contrast, the two men lying in the wagon looked to be in terrible shape. "Doctor!" the woman said in relief as she saw Jayda. "I'm so sorry! We need you!"

Jayda moved down to the wagon and climbed up onto the step beside it. She flinched as she saw the state of the two men. Both were alive, but their power was at a critically low point and escaping their bodies from their wounds as quickly as their blood did. "What happened?" she asked as she rolled up her sleeves.

"An avalanche collapsed a cave," the woman explained. "We were the deepest in and got hit the hardest. Everyone else seemed to make it out safely. Assorted bruises and cuts, but nothing severe."

Jayda formed a needle from ice and drew a thin thread of water through it. Swiftly and expertly, she began to stitch the worst of the wounds closed. The thread would dissolve into the wound and aid in healing it. There wouldn't even be a scar left. "What caused the avalanche?"

"We can't be sure. We . . . we think it might be the Elite. We always feel the mountain's power shake before the avalanche occurs. We've never felt that with normal events." She made a sound of frustration. "Why do they hate us so much? What did we ever do to them?"

Jayda switched to the other male. "That's a question I am sure that another race has asked for a millennia."

There was a long silence. Then, finally, "I never looked at it from that perspective. I suppose we have been doing to Chronicles what the Elite are doing to us."

"It bears a strong resemblance." She finished the stitching and began using her power to find internal injuries. One man had three broken ribs. She wrapped bands of water around his chest, and they sank into his body to begin setting the ribs in their proper place. The power would remain to hold the bones together until they healed.

"How are you so wise, Jay?" The woman watched her

work with fascination. "You're only just nineteen and you have the skill of someone twice your age. It's as if the uncanny clarity of childhood never left you."

"Sometimes I'm not sure I was ever a child." She shifted attention to the other man and discovered internal bleeding from his stomach. She removed several herbs from the small bag she wore on her hip and ground them between her fingers. She lifted his head and put the herbs in his mouth. He reflexively swallowed them but he winced when he did. "I know, they taste horrible," she apologized softly.

Both were breathing far easier, and the bloody wounds had closed. The constellation of bruises could only heal with time. The woman let out a little breath of relief. "Will they be all right now?"

"They should be. Watch them both closely, though. If they expend any power, my work will be wasted. Half the problem was that their bodies couldn't naturally heal." She hopped down from the wagon. "Make them drink tea mixed with *femi* herbs. The tea will negate the taste and the herbs will help with swelling."

"Thank you, Jayda." The woman lifted the reigns and studied Jayda. It was a damned shame that a young woman this amazing would be cursed to hide away from a town and a society that loved her. She deserved to find the perfect mate and to live a normal life.

As the wagon left, Jayda hurried back into the house. Shaking, she sat down in the main room and wrapped her arms around herself until the trembling stopped. She seemed to be shaking apart from the inside. Dizzy and ill, she sat there until she smelled her bread finish baking. She was still shaky as she went into the kitchen and took the loaf and the cakes from the oven.

The comfortable rhythm of the baking again helped erase the lingering pain and discomfort, and she focused solely on making the tiny candies the kids from town loved. She couldn't hug them or play with them the way they wanted, but she could show she cared in some way. When you were a child, it was critical to know you were loved. She remembered little of her childhood thanks to large spaces in her memory, but she remembered being loved. That was all that was important to her.

As she begam to get ready for dinner, she heard again the sound of a wagon. This time she recognized the wheels. She went to the door and smiled. "Will you ever get that wheel fixed?" she asked.

Eli Lakemore also smiled as he hopped down from the wagon. "If I did, you wouldn't know it was us." He walked over and hugged her tightly. He was one of only two people whom she felt comfortable around. The other was her mother, Serenity.

Ren tied the findral at the fence and then walked over to hug her daughter tightly. "Let's look at you." She held Jayda at arm's length and looked her over intently. She looked as lovely and peaceful as always. If living so far from others made Jayda happy, Ren would gladly make the hour ride every week if not every day. "You look lovely."

"I look like my mother."

"You do indeed," Eli agreed.

"Oh hush." Ren followed Jayda into the house and sniffed the air appreciatively. "What are you making now?"

"It's just a mush," Jayda said as she went into the kitchen. "Rice and cactear from Choral. It was a gift from one of the people I healed recently. I've added some crater clam as well."

"Do your loving parents get any scraps?" Eli asked.

She smacked his hand when he went to steal a taste. "Yes, if you keep your fingers out." She was smiling as she said it. Just being with her family could make her feel better. "Can you get the bowls?"

"Of course." Ren opened a cupboard and burst into

laughter as she saw the three misshapen bowls. "Oh my." She pulled them down to see them better. They were sturdy and big enough to use, but they were crooked and lopsided with a very interesting combination of pink and orange.

Eli lifted a brow the same color as his daughter's hair. "Have we been experimenting with clay in our spare time?"

"If I was, they wouldn't even hold water. No, they were a gift from the kids. Liaon only just entered first puberty, and he has Soil power. He was practicing." Jayda smiled at the bowls. "They're lovely for a first try."

"Colorful," Ren decided. "I'm not sure about the lovely."

They were durable, though. When Jayda served the mush in them, they held up just fine. They also didn't get hot from the food, which showed the maker had some natural talent in crafting.

They sat together at the small table in her kitchen. "Someone mentioned things getting worse," Jayda noted. "I tended to two people who were wounded in an avalanche. They were badly beaten up."

Ren sighed. "It's a reciprocating trouble. The first few deaths caused the first instability. The instability causes more avalanches . . ."

"And that causes more deaths." Eli ripped a piece of sweetbread from the loaf with a carefully controlled motion. "The Militia is due to arrive in a day or two. They're positive we've got an Elite member behind things. Apparently it's so bad in Carnelian that the land is sending out waves into the ocean. Mirah is also in fluctuation and the waves are meeting the ones from Carnelian. Trade is being cut off."

"It makes me so mad," Ren muttered, stabbing at her food with her spoon. "I don't know why. But every time I hear about the Black Magi Elite, it just makes me furious! I'm sure it has to do with those blank spots in my memory, but I just can't get those memories back."

"Maybe they're gone for a good reason." Jayda took her empty bowl to the basin for washing. "Maybe we're not supposed to remember those things, whatever they are." She turned around and linked her hands inside her sleeves.

"Stop scratching," Eli scolded.

She sighed and stopped scratching at her arm. Her left arm had been itching something fierce ever since the time she presumed she had started second puberty. Her right leg itched as well, the skin sensitive in a way that was frustrating because of her long clothes. "I forgot to put on my lotion earlier, sorry."

"I'd say it was all right, but it isn't." Ren frowned. "It's not normal."

Jayda had to smile at that. "Am I normal in any other way?"

"I believe she wins that," Eli told Ren.

"Indeed she does." She smiled. "She wouldn't be our Jayda if she was normal."

As Jayda prepared for bed much later, she thought about that. People who were normal wanted to be different. People who were different wanted to be normal. Was one or the other truly better? She sat on the side of her bed and studied her arm. It looked perfectly normal, but she knew her power rolled under the surface of her skin. She couldn't say why it did any more than she could explain why contact, verbal or physical, with other people hurt her. She couldn't say that she minded though. She didn't want to change.

She was awakened in the early hours by the sound of rumbling in the land. Startled, she pulled on her robe and hurried over to a window. She could see the mountains from there. They looked as if they were actually swaying in the moonlight. A chill went down her back. When thousands of feet of mountain could dance like a piece of string in the wind, things were truly bad.

Unable to get back to sleep, she got dressed and made herself some sweet tea. The sun was just peeking over the horizon when she heard the sound of a findral approaching very quickly. By the time she got to the front door, the beast was skidding to a stop and sending snow flying. "Dad!" She stared at Eli in astonishment. "What's wrong?"

"There was a massive avalanche." His handsome face was very grim. "It's bad, baby. Over a hundred people have been injured. Some are too wounded to move. The two doctors from town are on their way but they have nowhere near your power and skill. We need you. I'm so sorry."

She shook her head. "I'll deal with it. If someone died because I stayed here, I'd never forgive myself." She hurried into the house and pulled on her heaviest boots. She added a second tunic over her regular one before pulling on gloves and her hooded cloak. She grabbed her hipsack with emergency supplies and slung it across her body.

When she joined Eli, he lifted her onto the findral's back before swinging up behind her. Time was of the essence and he urged the findral to run as fast as it could. He hated having to ask her to enter into a large crowd of people, but there was no other choice. The fewer people who died, the less the impact on the land would be.

Halfway up the mountain, she knew they were getting close. Her stomach rolled, and her skin seemed to burn as if tiny bugs crawled all over her. The anxiety rose in waves, and she closed her eyes. She gulped the cold air to keep from begging her father to take her home.

Then, softly, she felt the faintest caress of a power. It stirred something inside her heart and soul. Something seemed to rumble as if waking from a long sleep. Her arm and leg throbbed almost painfully and her power swelled sharply. It ebbed without breaking free and the throbbing went away. Something had almost happened, but she wasn't sure what.

She was sure, however, that her anxiety had gone away. She was calm suddenly as her stomach settled and her pulse slowed down. She was safe. "Were there any Kin there?" she asked her father over the wind. Only a Kin or possibly a Dragon could have had a power strong enough to reach her from a distance.

"No Kin that we know of," he answered. "But there was a Dragon seen flying past the mountain last night."

"That must be what I sensed then." Odd that he would leave a power signature even after leaving, but perhaps he was an Elder.

The site of the avalanche was a bloody horror. Jayda, for all her exposure to wounds and injuries of all shapes and sizes, winced. Nearly a hundred men and women were injured to varying degrees. People from the town wrapped and bound as many wounds as they could to stop bleeding. Others handed out hot tea and blankets. Fire Magi worked with Air Magi to keep the temperature of the area from being cold enough to cause frostbite but not so warm that the snow melted.

Even before the findral stopped, Jayda jumped down. She rushed over to the closest severe injury and knelt beside the wounded woman. Her leg was twisted at an odd angle and lacerations were visible through her ripped clothes. "I need scented air!" she shouted to a nearby Soil Magi.

He didn't look up from the wound he was tying off but he let the air fill with the scent of flowers. The scent was comforting as it drifted over to her. "Just breathe," she said softly. "Breathe and stop thinking. It doesn't hurt. It's not really painful. It's not cold. You're somewhere the sun is shining."

The soft, melodic words were as effective as the scented air. The woman was lulled into the place between sleep and consciousness, unaware of the outside world. When another woman knelt beside her, Jayda made motions with her hands to show what she needed. The other woman nodded and carefully untangled the broken limb so that it laid properly. The patient didn't notice; she was drifting in the place where Jayda had sent her.

Jayda wasted no time in setting the bones and stitching wounds closed. As soon as they were closed, her aide began binding them to keep out the cold air. Jayda also put a splint on the broken leg and bound it tightly. "Wagon!" she called. It was the medical shorthand for saying a patient was ready for transport.

With the woman aiding her and assorted Magi lending their powers as needed, she moved quickly between the worst injuries. The other two doctors worked with the lesser injuries, and everyone moved as fast as they could. The land still trembled softly under their feet in a warning that all was not safe or secure. Water Magi watched the mountain intently, ready to use their Ice power to stop new danger for as long as they could.

People were still being dug out of the rubble. Some didn't come out alive. The city Elder was on hand and keeping track of those who were alive and dead. He knew everyone in town by name. Only he could be sure who was safe and who wasn't. He was also able to keep track of who was still trapped.

As Jayda was setting another broken bone, she saw movement from the corner of her eye. She looked up sharply and saw the figure of a man fleeing up a mountain path. He was wearing a white cloak that looked oddly, and disturbingly, familiar.

A commotion behind her had her turning to see that the Militia had arrived. There were twenty soldiers in total. Most of them saw the scene and immediately began helping with the transporting of the injured. Others began to help gather the dead. The two healers among the Militia joined the doctors in making the rounds.

The young woman in charge immediately focused on Jayda as being the head doctor and hurried over to her. She swiftly made the sign of respect. "Argyle Quinn Flyer, Water Magi."

Jayda's hands were full with stitching a wound closed and she couldn't return the gesture. She inclined her head instead. "Jayda Lakemore, Master Water Magi. Warm greetings."

"If only." Quinn knelt beside her. "Can you explain what has happened here? When we got to the town, we were told there was a catastrophe in the mountains. They seemed to have understated the case."

"An avalanche." She looked around and spotted her aide. "Wagon!" She got to her feet and hurried to the next patient with Quinn close behind. "I was wakened in the early morning by a quake. It made the entire mountain dance. An hour ago, my father fetched me to come help heal. I'm the strongest in the Arctica area."

"Glacia too." Quinn watched Jayda's speed and competency. She could also sense the rolling turmoil in the younger woman's emotions. Gentler, she said, "You're a good woman to come out when it is painful for you." When Jayda looked at her in surprise, the Argyle admitted, "My little sister was a Master Magi. She never left her home. If she lives, we don't know it. No one can approach."

"I've considered barring my home," Jayda had to admit. "But I am driven to heal. It is a painful combination. I am only enduring now because the Dragon in the area seems to have calmed me."

"I've heard that Dragon Elders are quite sensitive themselves," Quinn concurred. "If he sensed your distress, racial tensions aside, he'd be inclined to help." She cursed softly under her breath as she saw more bodies brought from the rubble. "Curse those Elite to the Underrealm!"

"What do they look like?"

She sighed. "We don't know. We can only identify

them by the cloaks they wear. White cloaks with a black chalice and dagger. They make a mockery of the Magi symbol. Our chalice is a sign of justice, not murder!"

In the hours that passed, two more avalanches shook the mountain. Both were stopped by the Water Magi. As the last people were being loaded into wagons, Jayda began to feel the nagging sensation that there was still someone injured. It had been there all along, but she had been ignoring it because it had been very obvious that people were hurt.

Everyone had been tended to, and she still felt the urgency in her body. "Are we sure we got everyone?" she called to her father.

He shook his head. "We're still combing the mountain to be sure. Do you feel someone injured?"

"I think so. I'll help look." She headed for the mountain path. "If there's someone out there without help, we have to find them!" Without waiting for consent, she hurried down the path and began to climb higher in the mountain.

The sun was bright, and she could see clearly even though a light snow fell. The further she went, the more she felt the sharp pull and compulsion of a power sending out a subconscious distress signal. It was a *strong* power, not Magi in origin, and seemed to whisper along her soul with a voice she knew.

She rounded one bend and suddenly caught sight of a man lying face down in the snow. Alarmed, she rushed to his side. "Are you okay?" There was no response, but she could sense his power still moved and he was still alive.

She fell to her knees beside him and turned him over onto his back. Shock stole her voice and her breath all at the same time. She had never seen such a shockingly handsome man before. He looked roughed up from an avalanche and there was a large bump on the side of his head. It called to her healer side, and it called to something more. Her sudden attraction to him went to a place inside her that lurked beyond her power.

With a roar, that something awoke inside her. Her power rose and surged wildly under her skin to make it burn fiercely. It broke free, and water and ice swirled through the air in a short but strong cataract. It finally died down, and she felt her arm and leg throbbing.

Almost fatalistically, she reached out with trembling fingers and pulled up her sleeve. There were golden lines shaped like little waves on her arm. Based on the throbbing in her skin, she had to assume they went from shoulder to wrist and hip to ankle on the two limbs that had itched so hard.

She was a Chronicle.

The man stirred slightly and startled her out of her shock. She tugged her sleeve down to cover the marks and got a grip on herself. This was not the time to be thinking about things that she couldn't understand.

She swiftly began to check her patient for severe injury. He had definitely been banged up, but she didn't find anything too terrible. Only the bump on his head looked like it needed closer attention. Terror and anguish churned in her stomach. A living fear that she might lose him before knowing him stole her breath.

Her eyes went to his thick black hair and the bright streaks of red through it. She tenderly ran her fingers through the vibrant locks. He was a Dragon. Now that she was close, she knew his was the power she had felt. He was a Dragon Elder. Whatever was inside him felt like a hot caress of fire against her soul. "Mine," she said softly. She was sure of it. Somehow she knew this man was hers alone.

She heard a footstep and turned her head to see Quinn approaching. Quinn spotted her in return and let out a breath of relief. "There you are!" She came to a stop beside Jayda and took a sharp breath. "A Dragon!" She knelt quickly. "He looks pretty bad! He must've been caught while camping!" Chills rippled down her skin. "He's *powerful.*"

"An Elder is my guess," Jayda said. Her eyes watched as Quinn lightly touched the lump on the man's head. It took considerable willpower to resist telling her to keep her hands off. "He deserves care as much as the next person. We need to get him off the mountain."

"Agreed." Quinn felt a soft warning of power from Jayda and lifted her hand. The menacing feeling immediately faded. Pondering it, she got to her feet. "I'll, er, go get a wagon." Suiting actions to words, she turned and hurried back down the path.

Jayda didn't wait for the wagon before beginning to tend to the wounds she could see. It broke her heart to see injuries on such a magnificent creature. In a distant part of her mind, she was a little amused and a little confused. If the feelings churning inside her body were any clue, then she was definitely near to the end of second puberty. Desire, never before felt, was nonetheless oddly familiar as it swirled through her blood.

Quinn returned shortly with Eli and a wagon. Jayda watched intently as they carefully lifted her Dragon into the wagon. "Be careful!" she ordered sharply as she saw them jostle his head.

Eli looked at her in surprise. He had never heard her sound that way before. A nameless fear clenched his heart as he looked at the streaks in the wounded man's hair. It wasn't possible . . . was it? The moons only knew that nothing else had made sense of Jayda in her life.

"Should we take him to town?" Quinn asked as she helped Jayda into the wagon and then climbed up beside Eli.

"No." Jayda's fingers almost compulsively stroked the man's arm. "I will tend to him."

Quinn began to frown. "Jayda, Dragons are not friends with Magi."

"He wouldn't hurt me." She felt sure of it.

Not liking it, but accepting it, Eli aimed the wagon for her home. He and Quinn carried the man inside and settled him onto the guest bed that Jayda kept for when her parents visited overnight. Quinn left to begin the hunt for the Elite, and Eli stayed to watch as Jayda began to bind wounds and stitch others. "I never thought I'd be near a Dragon, let alone an Elder," he finally said.

"Me neither." She pressed ice against the head injury to bring down the swelling. "But perhaps that is why I am so comfortable with him. I feel . . . safe. I've never felt safe near Magi. And . . ." she admitted, "well, I'm attracted to him." She sighed as she saw her father grimace. "I'm sorry, but it's true. If he wants to be, I would have him for my first lover."

He would have much preferred her to set her eye on a Magi, if only for the lesser danger, but he could not deny she had taste. "Because you would be that contrary."

She had to smile. "I take after my father."

"Well, I can't argue with that." He straightened. "It's odd but . . . I feel that you're safe with him. I trust him. It's curious." He ran a hand over her hair. "I'm proud of you," he said softly. "Never forget that." Unable to shake the feeling that it might be goodbye, he turned and left.

She finished healing her unwitting visitor and covered him with a thick blanket to keep him warm. His was a face that looked stark and beautiful, yet it was a face that spoke of living alone for too long. She felt the loneliness inside him as if it was inside herself. Perhaps it was. She gently pressed her lips to his cheek. "We don't have to be alone anymore," she promised softly.

Wanting to be ready when he woke, she got to her feet and headed for the kitchen. She wasn't going to think about being a Chronicle. Not yet. She wasn't even sure what it meant. But she knew, somehow, that it was connected to the Dragon in her home. Everything about her connected to him.

He might very well be the piece that would complete her.

Chapter Eleven

Among the race of Dragons, there were ten who were Elders. There were the four who belonged on the Council of Elders—one Dragon representing each element clan—then there were five others scattered among the tens of thousands of Dragons that called the Isle of Dragons home. There was only one other Elder, but he wasn't often considered a Dragon Elder.

He was the only living Fury Elder.

For over two thousand five hundred years, Xander Journe had endured day after day, week after week, year after year of painful waiting. He had waited fifteen hundred years to find his Chronicle, only to witness the massacre of the entire race. From that day on, for a millennia, he had waited with his breath held for the day his world would end.

Then, one day, he had felt *her*. He had felt the birth of the only being that could end his loneliness. The only person who would love him as completely as he loved her. Because he was a Fire Fury, he knew she would be a Water Chronicle. He knew because he was older and more mature, so would she be. And he knew that because he was increasingly more sensitive to those around him, so would she be.

For ten years, he had thought that his hope was groundless. All that had changed the day he met Tariah and Morgan Chronis. They had survived. They had found their Furies. And Morgan had told the Dragons of the secret Chronicle children he had found. Four children, two boys and two girls, each of a different element. It hadn't been until after the war with the Elite that Morgan had gently told Xander that one of the girls showed signs of being a Water element.

Now, nine years later, Xander had not felt the death of his Chronicle. He knew that she had to be the one Morgan had found. For nearly a decade, he had spent his every waking minute searching the face of Lucksphere. Even when asleep, he thought of her. He wouldn't let himself think of what she might look like. He wanted to feel that first punch of shock and recognition all rolled together.

He had already spent time on the other lands and now he was working his way through Glacia. He *hated* Glacia. It was all ice and snow and *cold* but he went anyway. In truth, Glacia was the best place to visit if you were a Dragon or Fury. In Stalagmite to the south, all Dragons were welcome. It was in this city that Morgan had grown up, and his parents still lived there. Furies who were even then in the world seeking their Chronicle would periodically stop to say hi or pick up and deliver messages.

Xander couldn't land in the city, unfortunately. He stretched fifty feet long from nose to tail and was greatly larger than average. Luckily for him, he was nimble in his age and able to change into Magi form in midair before landing safely on the docks. He had perfected it so well that barely a ripple touched the land despite his power.

The Magi females of town never minded when he came for a visit. In Magi form, he was one of the most gorgeous men they had ever seen. He stood much taller than average at six-five and his shoulders looked broad and powerful. His black hair had streaks of red, courtesy of his Dragon blood, and his eyes glowed the same ruby red.

No one knew of his Fury status, though. Truth be told, there really was no way for Magi to tell the difference between a Dragon and a Fury without their Chronicle. Only the Kin knew because they could sense different powers in other beings. They could sense the lack of infinite power yet infinite potential inside a Fury.

One Kin had described it like seeing a raging river

that had been blocked. Until the block was removed, the power was restrained. Once freed, it would be far more potent than anything else. Of course, that same Kin had teasingly told Xander that that made him *really* scary because he was so powerful even without his Chronicle. Xander didn't mind. He liked the Kin Faerie that Tariah called a brother.

The city was the same bustling port as always. He made his way through the crowds to the restaurant that fed most of the tourists who came through. Cruises from Spectrum to Glacia were often used by newly Linked couples as a celebratory trip. He didn't see the point, personally, but that was a cultural difference.

He stepped over a child and then stopped to let a wagon go past. Once clear, he entered the restaurant through the back door. "Hello?"

Persia Chronis looked up from the bread dough in front of her and her face brightened. "I wasn't expecting to see you! It's good to see you, Xander." If she was at all uncomfortable with a Fury Elder in her kitchen, she didn't act or show it. "Are Morgan and Jazz well?"

"Last I saw of them, yes. That was about two years ago though." He sniffed at a basket holding fruit. He had a weakness for fresh fruit.

She offered him one with a smile. "When are they giving me grandchildren?"

"That is harder to say," he admitted, nibbling on the fruit. "Dragons have large families, but the Dragoon couples I remember only had one or two children. With them being immortal . . ."

She wrinkled up her nose. "I want grandchildren. You tell Morgan that he had better not wait one hundred years to have a child!" She huffed out a breath. "What about Tariah?"

"She *suspects* she might be pregnant." He smiled as he said it. "If she is, it happened too recently for even our most accomplished healers to detect the new life. Dominic is as sure as she is. I think I've seen him walking a few feet off the ground."

"Ah, then I have at least *one* grandbaby in my future!" She was appeased with that. Tariah was, at most, a distant cousin by blood, but she and Morgan acted and felt like twins and so his parents had adopted her.

"How is London doing?" Xander asked.

"The limp is only really bad during the coldest days, but he's overall much better." Her gaze lowered. "How we let ourselves believe that foolishness . . ."

"The Elite fooled many," he said quietly. "You're not at fault. At least you survived." He straightened from the counter he had been leaning against. "Any message to pass on, short of the 'give me grandkids' one?"

"Visit!"

He laughed. "I'll tell him that, and in just that way." With a little bow, he left the restaurant. He enjoyed the entirety of the Chronis family. He himself felt confident in Tariah's knowledge of her own body and couldn't wait to see what sort of child came from her and her Fury. There would be no knowing what race it might be until further in her development when the power coalesced and could be sensed by healers.

He spent a couple days in Stalagmite, long enough to be sure that his Chronicle was not present. As he was preparing to leave town, a tremor shook the land. He caught his balance and helped a young woman walking past keep from falling as well. "I didn't think there were quakes in Glacia."

"There aren't, usually." The woman shook her head. "Haven't you heard about the Black Magi Elite? They're causing much chaos in Carnelian and Mirah. We've been suspicious that they were here as well. Arctica to the north has been having terrible avalanches in the mountains."

His frown deepened. "I see."

"It's spiraling around itself too. The Militia who came through yesterday on their way there said that the more people who were killed, the worse the land shook. I heard there's an immensely powerful Master Water Magi living near Arctica, but I don't know if even she can help. She's only nineteen."

He went very still. Chronicles appeared nearly indistinguishable from Master Magi to the average person. "A Master Magi? I thought they were almost never seen."

"They're never seen because they can't handle society," the woman explained. "We actually have four on the world right now. They keep to themselves to varying degrees, but they don't hide away entirely. I think there's an Air one near Mirah, a Fire one on Carnelian, a Soil one near Symphony, and then the Water one near Arctica." She sighed. "All nineteen or eighteen. Such heavy burdens on such young shoulders."

He had never believed in coincidence. Four Master Magi, one of each element, of the eighteen to nineteen age bracket. They had to be the missing Chronicle children. "Indeed," he agreed softly. "Perhaps I will head north and see if they need help."

"I thought Dragons didn't like the Magi."

His smile showed several sharp teeth. "We like the Elite even less."

"Oh." More fascinated than alarmed, she waved as he headed out of town to find a place large enough for him to go back into Dragon form.

Once he had changed back, he flew into the air and began heading north. His heart pounded hard in his chest. He had tried to teach himself not to hope, but it got harder and harder every minute. Maybe it *was* just a Master Magi living in Arctica. Maybe his Chronicle was somewhere else entirely and he just kept missing her arrival as he left.

His attention diverted the closer he got to the

mountains around Arctica. He could smell and sense the fear and pain that climbed the snow covered cliffs. And as he entered the mountains and began to make his way through them, he smelled something else.

He smelled tainted power.

His eyes narrowed. He flew closer to the surface to track the scent to the best of his ability, and the land rippled harder in warning. The state of fluctuation was in no way aided by his presence. He stopped flying and changed form as he landed. Though he was no less powerful in Magi form, it dispersed over a smaller area. The tremors lessoned without going away entirely.

Grateful for his heavy cloak (he *loathed* snow), he worked his way through the mountains on foot. He didn't bother to camp when night came. He could see just as well in the dark as he could in the light, and he wasn't tired. Tariah had accused him of existing on pure stubbornness and the occasional fruit. He sometimes wondered if she was right.

Halfway through the night, he caught the sharp and acrid scent of power that had been corrupted. He also caught the scent of a pure power. They were close together, and he hit the ground running as he rushed toward the scents. He skidded around a corner just in time to see two figures struggling near the edge of a cliff. One was a scrawny man in a white cloak. The other looked like a miner. "Stop!" He ran toward them. "Get away from the cliff!"

The man in the cloak gave a nearly insane cackle and shoved hard. The miner went flying over the edge of the cliff with a terrified scream. The Elite member turned to flee when he realized that Xander stood right behind him. The color drained from his face. He had been there at the final fight nine years before. He knew this Dragon. "You!"

"How nice to be remembered." Xander walked

steadily closer, fire swirling around his hand. "I'd threaten to eat you, but I'd get indigestion and we both know it." His eyes glowed as red as his power as he lifted his hand. "Don't think you'll be able to escape. I've been on this world a lot longer than you can imagine."

Gamma knew he stared death in the eye. He was only a slightly stronger than average Soil Magi. He held no chance against a Dragon Elder, let alone one this powerful. He had seen Xander in battle. He had ripped apart entire groups of his enemy and shrugged off blasts as if they were bugs.

Before Xander could throw the fireball, and before Gamma could think of a way to escape, the entire mountain quivered. The land lifted and rolled so fast that both men found themselves standing on air for a second before dropping down. The tremors started coming faster and faster, and the mountain swayed violently.

Great waves of snow began to roll down the side of the mountain. Distantly, Xander heard the screams of many people. Gamma began to cackle. "Crush them!" he crowed. "Crush them all!" His eyes gleamed with madness as he looked at Xander. "The people mine at all hours. How bad for them!"

Xander turned with a snarl but the next wave of the land sent him rolling one way and Gamma the other. Snow had begun to fall, and even with the moons overhead, it was hard to see. He found himself trying to find something to grab onto as the mountain rocked and shook and sent him tumbling further down the side.

He cracked his head against a tree and stars exploded behind his eyes. By the time he finally stopped rolling, he had no strength or energy to move. He could only lay face down in the snow, aching and disoriented and dimly grateful that his heated breath melted the snow enough for him to breathe. He couldn't move, couldn't quite think. The pain in his head was excruciating. It swelled more and more until he finally, blessedly, blacked out.

He only had one lucid moment after that. He could vaguely sense the distress of dozens of people. Pain and fear ran rampant. Yet through the chaos, he felt one person clearly. Her anxiety rose and rose until it made his throat ache. He knew that pain. He lived with it every day. He instinctively reached out for her, wanting only to comfort. His power brushed hers . . . and he recognized it.

Wild triumph and elation swelled on two millennia worth of loneliness. It was *her.* He had found his Chronicle. He tried to will his body to move but it wouldn't respond. Even when the blackness took him again, he was desperately trying to shake off the cold and the pain. She needed him. She needed him as badly as he needed her.

The next time he woke, it was all at once. His eyes opened and his senses sharpened. He was dry and warm, and his wounds were gone. The bump on his head seemed nearly non-existent. He had been tucked securely into a soft bed, and the tender scent of fresh snow lightly filled the air. It stung his lungs wonderfully.

He felt cushioned and surrounded by the scent and feel of a power that was utterly feminine and utterly familiar. *His.* The savage joy was only dimly shocking. He probed the house with his power to find her and encountered nothing. She had been there recently because the signature she had left was still fresh, but she was not there at the immediate moment.

He swiftly got out of bed and made a physical exploration of the house, restlessly prowling through the small space with the hope that he was wrong. He wasn't. He was alone.

As he entered into what he assumed was her bedroom, he realized why she had left. He could feel the unsteady and arching swell of her power lingering in the air. Her body and her power were trying to prepare for the natural bonding demanded between Dragoons, and she didn't know what was going on. All she would know was that her power was going out of control.

Her reaction came as no surprise. He could feel the sharper drain on his majiks as indication of the same need. A lack of consciousness was not a viable excuse for nature to take a temporary hiatus.

He cursed softly and hurried through the house to the exit. He could still feel her. He could still smell the scent of her skin. Once outside of the house, he changed to his Dragon form and took to the sky. He was going to find her and then he was never going to let her go again.

~*~

Jayda didn't know there was anything wrong at first. She felt a little shaky, and her power seemed slightly riotous. Her only assumption was that because she had become a Chronicle, she was a little unstable. She ignored the trembling in her fingers and went about her daily business.

The influx of people to her home had increased by triple as injured miners kept coming by for her more advanced healing skills. After she sent the tenth person on their way, it dawned on her that she wasn't feeling as raw around others as she always had. When she finally had a free moment, she went into the guest room where her visitor still slept. "It's you, isn't it?" she murmured.

She smoothed his hair from his eyes and felt his power stirring under her fingers. He was drawing closer to waking. Her eyes went wide and she dashed down the hall to her room. She began to quickly brush her hair to remove the tangles, and only belatedly did it dawn on her what she was doing. She sat down on her bed with a sigh. She had always wondered what self-consciousness felt like. She didn't like it.

The Dragon didn't wake even an hour later. It was a stressful hour. Jayda just felt more and more out of sorts. She started contemplating a hot bath to soak away the stress but heard footsteps in the snow outside. She peeked out the window, saw Quinn, and opened the door. "Hello." She drew her thumb over her cheek and nose. "What brings you out here?"

"Many things." Quinn took a deep breath. "I'll start with some hot tea."

"Come in." She shut the door and led the way to the kitchen. As she poured two cups, she asked, "What's next? I'm sure you didn't make the ride just for the tea."

"Naturally not." Quinn wrapped her hands around the cup. "How is the Dragon?"

"Better. He's healing quickly. I sensed his power move not long ago so he should be preparing to wake."

"That's good. He was as much a victim of the incident as the town was. Then, of course, it would look bad on the Magi if we didn't take care of him. The Dragons would be glad for an excuse, I'm sure."

Jayda tugged her sleeve down further defensively. "I imagine they would. And on that same note, I don't suppose you know anything about Chronicles, do you?"

"Chronicles?" Quinn blinked. "Well, no more or less than others. They're hyper-powered Magi, I guess. They look and act like you Master Magi do, but they have infinite power. They also develop lines on their bodies at first puberty. Those lines lead them to a Dragon Lord known as a Fury. Based on what we've been learning over the last few years, it's not quite the parasitic relationship we all thought. The Kin said the closest word we could understand would be 'love.'"

"Parasitic?"

"Apparently, Furies *don't* have infinite power. They're limited. They're more powerful than regular Dragons, but they have limits. If they feed on their Chronicle's power though, then they can be all but infinite. The recent hypothesis from scholars is that Chronicles might be taking in the excess power of the land and filtering it through their Furies. In other words, they might be a naturally occurring phenomena."

"Then why kill them?"

Quinn lowered her gaze. "Nine years ago, I'd have said that they were a horrible aberration and a disgusting perversion of nature. Now . . . I don't know." She shook it off and smiled. "You distracted me."

"My apologies. I get curious sometimes and it seemed like a time to ask. Now what did you need from me?"

"I was hoping you might have seen or sensed anyone at the site. I've had conflicting reports from various miners that they might have seen someone lurking around that didn't belong. My party is combing the mountainside, but we're coming up blank."

Jayda frowned. "When I was working with someone, I saw a man in a white cloak running around the side of the mountain path. I didn't really think much of it. I just assumed he was looking for more survivors."

"I see." Quinn drummed her fingers lightly on the table. "That's encouraging at the least. The Elite smell of tainted power. We should be able to track him if he's the one we're after." She tilted her head. "You seem . . . odd. Are you all right? I keep feeling like waves of your power are lapping over the edges, so to speak."

"I'm still recovering from being around so many people, I think." She tugged her sleeve down again. "I've also had a steady stream of patients today. People with smaller injuries who know I can remove them entirely where the other doctors cannot."

"Understandable. You're one of the best healers I've ever seen." Quinn got to her feet. "I will be joining my party in the mountains. For the time being, the mountains seem to be stable. Perhaps your internal fluctuations helped with that. I've seen it before where the correct element can help calm the land. It might be worth gathering many Water Magi like us and trying to calm the mountain entirely."

"That's a very good idea." Jayda followed her to the door. "Be safe."

"You too." Quinn headed down toward where she had left her findral and glanced back only once to see Jayda tugging on her sleeve again. What was she trying to hide?

Once she was alone again, Jayda headed into her washroom and pulled off her clothes. She stepped in front of her full-length mirror and looked at her body with a thoughtful frown. The lines started at her left shoulder and wrapped around her arm to her wrist, and then they started at her right hip and wrapped around her leg to her ankle. They shimmered gold against her pale skin, and she thought they were unexpectedly attractive.

Shrugging it off, she put up her hair and got into the pool. She felt a little bemused at herself. There was a perfect stranger in her home, and he could wake and walk in on her at any time. She felt neither fear nor concern for it if it happened. She was safe with him. She knew it.

Quinn's words danced in her mind. Was her Dragon guest a Fury? If he was . . . was he hers? Her heart said yes. Nothing else made sense of the situation.

Her power began to rumble warningly and pain blossomed under her skin. Alarmed, she sat up and got out of the tub. She dried off and got dressed, but by the time she was brushing her hair in her room, she felt surer than ever that something had to be wrong. Her power was rising too fast, and it was getting more and more painful.

Rather than worry about it, she got dressed in her warmest clothes and left her home. If she was going to go out of control, then she might as well be in the mountains. The land needed power from a Water element to help settle, and she was going to settle it for a *long* time. She had a feeling she had power to spare.

She went by foot and covered ground much quicker than most people because of her Ice power. She was climbing the mountains within an hour and made her way steadily higher. It was snowing lightly and she still felt the tremors under the surface of the land. It grew harder and harder to walk as the pain slowly became blinding. The clouds far overhead responded to her power, and the snow began to fall heavier.

Just as she reached a cliff where there was shelter, she couldn't walk anymore. She fell to her knees and carefully crawled under one of the trees. Maybe this hadn't been the brightest idea.

She heard footsteps crunching on snow at the same time she smelled the unmistakable whiff of spoiled power. Alarmed, she looked up sharply. The man from before approached her, and his white cloak fluttered in the wind. "Who are you?" she asked warily.

"My name is Gamma." He stopped in front of her with a pleasant smile on his face. "I'm a member of the Black Magi Elite." When her eyes widened, he waved a hand in the air. "Oh don't worry! I'm not here to kill you. That'd be such a waste!" He knelt and shoved her sleeve up her arm. "You're a Chronicle, after all."

She tried to pull her arm free, but his grip was strong and her body hurt. "How did you know?"

"I was going to kill that Fury when you arrived. I saw your little awakening. Imagine that. A little Chronicle, hiding as a Master Magi." His grip tightened on her wrist. "What are you doing out here all alone, anyway? It's dangerous. You never know who you might run into."

"Let go of me!"

"The Elite have plans for you, little girl. We need you to help us find the key to destroying the Magi." His brown eyes were wild and more than a little mad. "Doesn't that sound delightful?"

She jerked at her arm again, but he countered and dragged her up off the ground. She went stumbling past and fell to the snow, and her sleeve ripped off her tunic entirely to reveal the full length of her lines. She painfully turned her head to see him approaching. "Why do you hate Magi?"

"They keep trying to destroy the world! They put it in the state it's in now. We'll erase all Magi, and Chronicles will take their place. But we can't do it without you." He walked toward her, a hand held out. "You hurt, don't you? Well, come with me and you can use that power for destruction, just like you should."

An immense icicle formed from the sky and landed sharply at his feet. He backed up quickly and turned to see Quinn standing nearby with more ice swirling around her hands. "Back away from Jayda," she warned. "She's not going anywhere with you."

He laughed wildly. "She's a Chronicle! Don't you want to kill her? Why would you protect her?" He whirled toward Jayda. "She saves you only to murder you! You know it!"

Jayda pushed herself painfully to her feet. "No, she doesn't. And even if I'm wrong, I trust her more than I trust you." Her lines rippled as if alive and water flowed around her body. Shards of ice formed in the water, and she hurled the blast with all her strength.

Halfway toward Gamma, it was joined by a blast from Quinn and they sent him flying backwards through the snow. He scrambled up with a snarl. "If that's how you want to play, then let's play!" He flung out his hands and vines shot through the air at the two females.

Quinn was able to dodge. Jayda wasn't. The vines slammed into her chest and sent her tumbling back across the snow. Winded, she rolled to a stop at the edge of the cliff. She couldn't think or move. Quinn scrambled over to her side. "Jayda!" She lifted the other female into her arms slightly and felt the rioting power under her skin. It was barely held in check. "Jayda!"

Gamma staggered toward them as if drunk, weaving back and forth across the snow, nearly stumbling over his own feet. "She will be the catalyst of destruction! You better kill her yourself if you want to save her from me! Isn't that what you Magi have been deluding yourself into thinking?"

A terrifying roar ripped through the air. It reverberated off the mountains and made them tremble in fear. It echoed and doubled time and again, and it rang in everyone's ears. Gamma went deathly white. Quinn couldn't breathe as she felt a fierce and deadly power behind her. Gamma slowly started to back up, stark terror on his face.

Slowly Quinn looked over her shoulder and saw the biggest Dragon she had ever seen in her life. He was fifty feet long, at least a third of that wide, and covered in pitch black scales with flicks of flame red. His teeth were as long as her arm and his face looked somehow frightening and beautiful all at once.

Xander had never been more furious in his life. He landed on the cliff and then whirled and swung his tail sharply. The end slammed into Gamma and flung him straight into the air and into the distance so hard that he shortly disappeared from sight. Slowly, Xander turned to look at the Militia member holding his Chronicle.

"Are you a Fury?" she managed to ask.

"I am a Fire Fury Elder," he confirmed. He lowered his head to be closer on eye level. "You are holding my Chronicle. For saving her life, you have my thanks."

"What's wrong with her?"

"She and I need to bond as Dragoons. Nature makes its demands known. Her powers rise and my majiks drain. I woke and found her gone before I could tell her. Will you give her to me?"

Quinn looked down at Jayda. She wasn't fully

conscious, but her gaze fixed on Xander with something akin to wonder in her eyes. There was also something more, some powerful emotion that Quinn wasn't sure could be called love. "Yes," she said softly. "Magi law for killing Chronicles is made with the idea that we do it to keep them from the Elite. If you have her, then she will not be with the Elite. The law is upheld."

He reached out and picked up Jayda with his claw. A tremor went through his mighty body. She was smaller than his entire claw. She was taller than average, but she was slender and graceful and as elegant as her element. Beautiful. She was beauty incarnate. He drew her closer possessively and slowly rose into the air. He had enough power to get them to shelter. "Does she have family?"

"She does. I will think of something to tell them." Quinn got to her feet and smiled a little. "I had wondered what she was hiding. But I can't say I'm surprised. Be well, Elder." She stepped back to give him more room and watched as he flew across the sky. Under her feet, she could feel that the mountain had stabilized and become secure because of Jayda's spent power.

At least *something* the Magi believed had turned out to be right.

Chapter Twelve

By the time Xander saw a small island off the coast that *didn't* have more snow than land, he was flying low to the surface of the ocean because he didn't have the power to remain aloft. He angled down to the island and gave it a cursory look with his eyes and senses. The only signs of life came from plants.

Relieved, he landed and looked around. The land felt much warmer than Glacia but there wasn't much by way of shelter. There were only a handful of trees scattered across the scenery. There were, however, a couple standing together not far away. He walked over there and gently put Jayda down on the ground.

He grabbed the tops of the trees and carefully bent them down until they formed a canopy. Using the smallest amount of his power as possible, he created ropes of glass and bound the treetops in their bent position to ensure they would stay as good cover. He added more leaves on the top for additional protection before going back into Magi form.

He stumbled a step before he caught his balance. He waited for his head to stop spinning, and then carefully sat beside Jayda. He lifted her into his arms and onto his lap. His fingers trembled as he smoothed her hair out of her face. Had he ever tried to imagine what his Chronicle might look like, he would have fallen far short of reality.

Her thick hair smelled like fresh snow and glacial flowers, and her body was lithe and graceful. She was taller than average, but so was he, and he loved every inch on her body. He buried his nose in her hair for a moment. His throat closed tightly and his eyes burned. He had waited. Even in the face of despair, he had waited. And he had been rewarded.

He lifted her left arm and studied the lines wrapping

around her soft flesh. Hunger tightened his body in a searing wave. It was *his* power making her lines. He lifted her wrist to his lips and felt her pulse beat strong. His fingers had begun to shake. He couldn't separate the hungers inside him. Hunger for her power, hunger for her impossibly perfect beauty. Hunger for her smile and her gentle nature.

Her power steadily gained strength and grew wilder. As it did, he felt his desire growing. All he could do was close his eyes and pray with all his might that he would not be suffering Dominic's fate. If his Chronicle wasn't nearly done with second puberty, he didn't know if he had the control to wait.

Jayda woke to raging pain. It was worse than it had been before. A low whimper echoed in her throat. She wanted to go out of control, to unleash floods and hurricanes, to raise the seas and consume the land. It *hurt*. She felt a hand holding hers and curled her fingers around it tightly, knowing at her deepest level who held her.

"Open your eyes," he urged huskily. "Please."

She forced her lashes up and found herself staring into a familiar face. His eyes stole her breath. Ruby red, fiery red, they consumed her and brought warmth to the coldest parts of her soul. Her lips trembled as she smiled. "I'm Jayda Lakemore."

"Xander Journe." He framed her face with his free hand. "It hurts, I know. It's just something to force us to bond." He softly brushed his lips over her cheek and eyes. "Are you afraid of me?"

"If I was afraid of you, I'd have never taken you into my home." She shivered in delight as his lips stirred nerves and senses that had been in suspension. A different ache entirely settled into her body. As instinctive as breathing, her power reached for him and curled around him seductively.

His breath caught. Was he that lucky? He softly returned the touch, and her power rose to cover her in a soft blue aura. It was more beautiful than anything. Unbearably tempted, he lowered his head and pressed his lips to her neck. Her power was fresh and pure, and her skin was cool. It made him feel as if he tasted the purest glacial water. "I might change my mind about snow," he said huskily, drinking her power as he ran his lips down her neck.

"You don't like it?" Her eyes closed in pleasure as his lips teased her collar.

"I'm changing my mind." He hit the edge of the tunic she wore, and it was the one with the torn sleeve. Seeing that torn material made rage churn inside him that someone had threatened his mate. Before she could guess his intent, he literally ripped the tunic from her body.

Her mouth fell open in shock, but her words became a soft gasp as he promptly buried his lips at the opening in the under-tunic. It was like any other tunic except sleeveless and lower cut. It was more for warmth than appearance. One of his hands caressed her from shoulder to hip and then back again, spreading fire as he went.

Eagerly, half drunk, he followed her power back up to her lips. Without waiting for permission, he took her lips with his and deepened the kiss instantly with a demanding thrust of his tongue. Her power tasted even purer there, and the euphoria at finally knowing her presence was as tangled as the other emotions inside him.

A low moan vibrated in her throat, and she freed her arms to bury her fingers in his hair. The pain had disappeared. In its place was a storm of hunger. Hunger for everything he was. She craved his power and his presence, to feel his arms tight around her. She wanted to be his lover, to become an adult in his heated embrace. She wanted to take away the loneliness she felt eating away at him. She wanted his love to match the love in her heart.

When her body arched to press against his, he went light headed with relief. Half-wild, he continued to feed from her power at her mouth until it stopped flowing free. He felt better than refreshed. He felt ready to take on the world and exist for another millennia. He felt more, though. He felt *her.*

The bonds between them formed as naturally as the sun set. He could see everything in her heart and mind, could feel her every emotion and breathe her every breath. And because he could, his heart soared as he saw that the three emotions inside her, the ones marking Dragoons, were as fierce and untamed as the ones inside him. "*Ishke.*"

She couldn't speak around her tight throat. She could see the thousands of years of memories and emotions inside her Fury. She saw everything he was and could be. And she saw her own presence inside him erasing the loneliness. His violent emotions, the three turbulent sides, surged and snapped at the bounds of his flesh. She didn't fear them. She felt the same untamed feelings inside herself and craved the feelings in him.

She wanted to say that she loved him, but the words weren't enough. There weren't even words to describe that other feeling. "Xander." She pressed upward to kiss him, longing for his taste as if it had been centuries rather than seconds since she had last had it.

His hands buried in her hair, and he kissed her as she wanted: long, and deep, and hungry. He wrapped his power around her, unable to release her, and curled his mind around hers as well. He needed to feel her everywhere.

Without warning, he came into direct contact with the blank space in her mind. Startled, he broke the kiss and lifted his head. He was nearly distracted as he looked at her. Her cheeks were flushed and her lips swollen. He went back for a quick kiss, then a second. As he teased her lips for a third, he said thickly, "Distract me. Hit me. Do something."

Her power fluttered against his teasingly and he groaned. "Anything but that, Jayda! I'm trying to find some semblance of control! I need to see what's in your mind."

With a little sigh, she stopped teasing him. Instead, she dropped a ball of snow down the back of his shirt. He yelped and she bit her lip to hide a smile. "Does that work?"

He grimaced at the cold snow sliding down his back. "Yes, quite." Grateful that she hadn't decided to drop it down his pants instead, he framed her face with his hands and softly probed at her mind. Now looking for the blank space deliberately, he found it quickly. It was as if a large chunk of her memory had been fragmented away.

She began to frown. "I've always felt that there," she admitted. A little more fretfully, she grabbed onto his arms. "It's important, isn't it? Who did this to me and my parents? Why were our memories taken away?"

"It's all right, *ishke*," he soothed softly. He stroked his thumbs over her cheeks even as he softly wrapped his presence around her. "I can see who did this, and I was expecting it." He began to search through her mind for the tiny fragments that remained. "Nine years ago, you lived in Prismatic with your parents as members of the original Black Magi, the faction formed by Morgan Chronis as a secret hiding place for Chronicle children."

She almost stopped breathing. "That's why we always felt angered by the Elite."

"It is. And this will hurt you, to remember your friends and Morgan. You were like a family. He's suffered for nine years knowing he sent you away." His Fire power fused the fragments into a single mass as he swept through her mind. When he brought the pieces together at the blank space, they instantly melted together and reformed.

The memories punched into both their minds equally. He wrapped his arms around her and pulled her fiercely close. He pressed her face to his shoulder as a low cry tore from her chest. It broke his heart. "He loved you enough to protect you the only way he could," he said softly.

"When I find him, I'm kicking him!" was the fierce counter. She took a ragged breath that ended with a hiccup. "I miss Kelsey and C.J. and Roman! I always felt so safe with them. If I'd been with them when I went into first puberty, maybe it wouldn't have hurt so badly."

"I'm afraid it would have." He rubbed his thumb under her eyes to remove the tears as she looked up at him and. When more fell, he lowered his head to softly kiss them away. "I'm an Elder. Every year I live, I become more sensitive. Where we are not perfect opposites, we are perfectly alike. We would not understand one another this well if we hadn't experienced similar."

"Is that why when I felt you on the mountain, I felt suddenly safe?"

"I'll *never* let anything hurt you." A little flicker of fire came and went from his eyes. "It's just as well I wasn't in the area when your weekly visitor came by. I'd have eaten him."

"You didn't eat Gamma." Her lips trembled as she tried not to smile. "You punted him like kids kicking snowballs." She let out a little breath and relaxed against his chest, comforted by having him close. "I never imagined this happening to me. Maybe I remembered Morgan a little when I awoke after finding you. I felt a little confused but a little relieved."

"I think I lost my mind a bit," he admitted, "when I woke and you were gone. I had felt your presence when I tried to comfort you. But I was so badly injured that I couldn't do anything about it."

"Oh!" She sat upright. "Your head!" She scooted off his lap and then knelt beside him. She threaded her fingers into his hair to examine the bump on his head. "I completely forgot! You distracted me!"

He admired the curve of her breasts. They currently

rested on perfect eye level for him. "I suspect I will often be distracted by you too."

Ignoring that to the best of her ability, she gently examined the injury. It was all but gone. "It's a good thing you have a hard head. You must have tumbled clear down the mountain!" His memories were hers, and she could see the confrontation with Gamma. Her eyes narrowed ever so slightly. "I suppose it's just as well that I wasn't in the best shape. I might have killed him myself."

"Your gentleness hides a fierce side." Unable to resist, he nuzzled his nose between her breasts just for the delight of hearing her breath break.

"I'm not a pushover." The words came out breathless. The heat in her body had been silent but suddenly awoke with a vengeance. When his tongue lightly tasted her skin, her sensitive flesh sent messages of pleasure to every corner of her body.

"I should wait," he said huskily, "until we have a better shelter." Even as he said it, he slowly untied her tunic to reveal supple pale skin and wonderfully curved breasts hidden behind bikini the same hue as her flesh.

"How long have you already waited?" Her fingers slid down to his shoulders and began to knead lightly. Her fingers tingled, wanting to feel his hot skin. She wanted to explore every inch of her Fury's body, to assuage the curiosity inside. What had seemed impersonal before was suddenly very personal.

His eyes closed. "My whole life," he managed to say. He caught her closer and buried his face against her heart. "I've waited. I waited no matter how terrible it felt at times. No matter how it cut me to see Dominic and Jazz happy with their Chronicles. I've waited centuries, millennia, to find you."

"Then don't wait anymore. My wait wasn't as long, but it hurt just as bad. I was so *alone* without you." When he looked up at her, she smiled tremulously. "We're not alone now. Why wait?"

On a low sound of need, he caught her around the waist and tumbled her down onto the grass. Against the green color, her hair seemed more blue than green, just as against the sky it had seemed more green than blue. It shifted and flowed like the icy ocean. "Be gentle with me. Your curiosity might kill me."

She nimbly began to untie the laces of his tunic. "You'll be okay. You know a good doctor." His laugh warmed her all the way through, and as his tunic opened to reveal the incredible expanse of his chest, her sigh came soft and happy. "You have lines like mine."

They flowed across the left side of his chest in the same pattern as on her body. They were gold against his tanned skin and rippled with every movement of his muscles. Seeing them brought a fierce wave of possessiveness. He was hers. He was marked as hers. "We need to live in the desert," she decided huskily as she ran a finger across his chest.

He shrugged out of the tunic and then lifted her enough to remove the one she wore. "Why? So I go shirtless?"

"Mmm." She ran her hands slowly over his chest and shoulders, memorizing the feel of his body. Her hands burned and tingled to send waves of delight through her body. Desire slid through her blood as surely as her power did. She felt hot and hungry in a way she had never felt before.

His power rubbed against hers and there something sizzled softly. When her eyes went wide, he drew one of her hands to his lips. Steam softly curled from both their bodies. "What did you expect when water met fire?" He was holding her left arm so he was able to trail his lips down her arm and taste every one of her lines. He slowly climbed toward her slender shoulder.

She moved restlessly under him, her fingers flexing in his grip. "Not yet," he said softly, enthralled with learning her body and her pleasure. "Let me memorize you. I've waited too long for this." His lips teased hers softly until she strained up to deepen the kiss. "You'll have your turn."

"I'd better!" The words turned into a soft gasp as his fingers brushed over the curves of her breasts. Before she could take a breath, he had untied the knot holding the bikini together. Now half-naked in his arms, she waited for nerves. There were none.

Their eyes met and held as he softly trailed a finger over her bare breast. Steam curled behind his touch as she arched slowly to follow his caress. He curled his presence around her to feel her emotions and rubbed his thumb over her nipple. The jolt of pleasure that ricocheted through her body rippled to him, and he did it again just to make her voice break on a soft whimper.

She was going out of her mind. He knew exactly how sensitive her skin was and knew that even the barest touch was dizzying. A sense of pressure built inside her muscles, the pleasure circling and coiling. Her pulse throbbed everywhere at once, and heat burned her. If the lines on her body hadn't branded her, then this would. An ache began to build between her legs and she shifted restlessly. Her remaining clothes felt too tight and too confining. "Xander."

He lifted his head and took a deep breath. "Hold on." He ran trembling fingers over her side. "I might rip something."

"And?"

He gave a half-laugh, half-groan. "You'd have nothing at all to wear." He grabbed for as much control as he could and began to work the pants down her legs. It was a struggle; she was softly curling her power and presence around him, deliberately trying to undermine his control. "I'll tear them off you later. Stop teasing me!"

"Never." As she found herself fully naked, she savored

the freedom to be there in his arms. "Where's the self-consciousness part? I only had a little bit much earlier."

"You can't be self-conscious with someone who wants you as badly as I do." He felt fascinated with everything he saw. She was utterly perfect. Unable to resist the lure, he bent his head and closed his mouth hotly over her nipple. Her back arched on a soft cry, and her fingers clenched into his shoulders.

Her entire body began to vibrate like a plucked string. Barely able to breathe, she grabbed his shoulders as her anchor in a world she had never dared dream existed. The ache was growing and spreading. She *wanted*. She had no name for what she wanted. She only knew she did. "Do something," she pleaded breathlessly.

"Like what?" The words were as teasing as his breath as he slowly trailed kisses over her flat stomach. He burned to take her, to bury his aching flesh deep inside her, but he couldn't seem to assuage his heart's hunger to know everything about her. "I am doing something." Her scent, crisp arctic oceans, tempted him to move lower, and his lips trailed over her inner thigh.

She opened her mouth to retort when she felt his breath on her sensitive flesh. She took a sharp breath that came back out on a moan as his tongue found some secret spot, something unbearably sensitive, and teased it mercilessly. The ache grew, the pressure built, the pleasure drowned her, and she couldn't *breathe*, ready to cry and beg him to stop . . . when he did. He shifted back up her body to memorize her face with his lips, and his fingertips scraped over her flesh teasingly.

Shocked, she couldn't find her voice or her thoughts. His feelings lightly fluttered against hers and determination filled her. Two could play *that* game! She slid her hands up to caress his face and then pinched his ear. He yelped, and in that moment of distraction, she was able to get the leverage to tumble him over onto his back. She sat across his hips triumphantly. "Serves you right!"

She looked wild and sultry. Her hair no longer fell straight as it tumbled around her shoulders in disarray. A flush to her skin made her radiantly beautiful. Unable to help himself, he curled his hands around her waist. He could nearly span it with his fingers. How could so much power fit into that slim body? "And what are you going to do with me?"

"I'm not sure yet." She smoothed a hand across his chest, loving the difference in their skin tone. "I'm still learning." She slid off him but he made no move to take control. Instead, he linked his hands behind his head. Delight filled her. "Are you at my mercy?"

"You have to ask?" He laced his fingers together tightly. He didn't know how much he could take, but he was willing to find out. A low groan rumbled in his chest as she bent her head to tease a nipple with her lips. "Quick learner."

"Always." Savoring the freedom, she trailed her lips and fingers over his chest and shoulders, tracing the lines and the curves of his muscles. She wasn't afraid. She should have been. He was so powerful, even in Magi form, but he trembled under her touch and his red eyes burned as they watched her.

When her explorations brought her to the edge of his pants, and the fascinating bulge beneath, she didn't hesitate to tug the pants down his legs. He had to help remove his boots first, and both were amused he had forgotten them, but he was shortly naked as well. She stared at his arousal in a combination of fascination, trepidation, and anticipation.

He couldn't resist teasing, "Surely a doctor has seen a naked man before."

She shook her head a little. "Not one who wanted her."

"Then you've been around idiots." His eyes all but crossed as her hand curled around him to memorize his length and shape. "By the moons." His knuckles turned white as he fought to control himself. He stopped breathing entirely as he felt her hot breath. "Don't . . ." The words stopped as she teasingly kissed him. "That's it!"

She gave a startled gasp as he sat upright and grabbed her. Before she could blink, she was flat on her back with his wonderful weight pressed along her body. She opened her mouth to ask a formless question, but his hungry kiss took the words. Words became unimportant and she buried her fingers in his hair to hold him closer. Restlessly, instinctively, she curled a leg over his hip.

"Do you know what you're asking for?" He got his answer when her emotions fluttered against his like the tide on the shore. She knew. Not consciously, not yet, but she knew. He caught her other leg and pressed it against his other hip, opening her entirely to him. His eyes met and held hers, and his throat closed as he saw the look in her eyes. "*Ishke.*"

Her eyes fluttered closed and her breath caught as she felt him slowly sinking into her body. Ripples spread outward, the ache easing and doubling all at the same time, building the hunger in her body until it was all she could feel. Tears burned her eyes as she felt, for the first time, as if she was whole. She had claimed her Fury. Finally. She felt as if she had been waiting millennia too.

She didn't get long to savor the feeling. He pulled back, then thrust deep again, stealing a gasp. The gasp became a whimper, then a moan, as he moved faster, building the pleasure once more. This time she knew he wouldn't stop. She prayed he wouldn't stop. She was going to go out of her mind if he did. She couldn't breathe anymore. Her fingers clenched in his hair as her body went out of control, tension stretched to the point of bursting.

He did something then. His mind and his power seemed to meld into hers just as his body did. The tension broke and ecstasy shuddered through her body and mind in a burning wave of water that was so hot it flashed to steam. She held onto him even tighter, only dimly aware a world existed beyond them and that moment. And as she felt the searing heat of his pleasure deep inside, she lifted her head to meet his kiss and finally felt as if she was home.

He tucked a hand under her head for support, but that was the extent of what he had any energy to do. Moving was far beyond his reach. *His.* His Chronicle. Every torturous minute of waiting had been worth it to finally feel complete. Her heart seemed to beat inside him, and he curled his presence around her to anchor her close.

Her power stilled its soft pulsing, and he found the strength to lift his head. Tenderness swamped him as he saw she had slipped asleep. He couldn't be surprised. She had gone far too long with uncontrolled power before their bonding. Adding in their energetic mating would be enough to tire anyone out. He was on the tired side himself.

He sighed and forced himself to release her. He sat up and grabbed his hipsack from where it sat nearby. He pulled out a blanket and shook it out. It was Kin made and automatically grew to accommodate his size. When he wrapped it around himself and Jayda, it promptly got big enough for them both.

He tucked her possessively into his arms and buried his face in her hair. He wanted her again. Even after what had just happened, he wanted her again. He softly stroked his fingers over her arm and side. A certainty in his heart told him that he would never stop wanting her. She was just going to have to get used to his hands being on her at every opportunity.

She murmured against his shoulder, "Is that supposed to be alarming? It fell short of the mark."

He smiled and lifted his head. She was smiling up at

him, her eyes sleepy and satiated. "More of a statement of fact."

"Mmm." She smoothed a hand over his chest, marveling at how her skin still felt so sensitive. Or perhaps it was just because of him. "I don't mind. I suspect I might have the same problem. I can't seem to keep my hands to myself."

"I don't mind," he said, returning her words with a smile. He smoothed her tangled hair from her face. "Did I hurt you?"

"If you did, I didn't notice. Was it supposed to hurt the first time?"

"Not if your lover knows what he's doing."

Her smile turned slightly smug. "Mine certainly does. Of course, I'm sure I'm not near to his skill. I'll have to practice."

"I stand ready and willing to help you practice as much as you like. I would like to note, however, that I think you had it right the first time." He stole a tender kiss and lingered until she relaxed wholly. Only then did he release her. "Want to tell me what's really on your mind?"

"Where do we go?" she asked simply.

"Kindred."

Her brows shot up. "Kindred?"

"It will be safe, for one thing. For another, there is a Kin there who is Tariah's brother. He can contact her on the Isle. It will be the only way we can get in touch with her and Morgan. I've forgotten the way to the Isle now that you're here. You need to finish your journey." He trailed a finger down her lines, a good portion of which were now even darker. Light rippled through them as if showing the power flowing inside. "But you're a step closer."

"Do you suppose the rest of my journey has to do with the Elite, or that we'll ever find my brothers and sister?" She felt no hesitation in claiming Kelsey, C.J., and Roman.

They were, in every way that counted, her siblings.

He sighed softly as he thought of the things he had seen and experienced. "I think that it's somehow inevitable. We all have a reason for being. We just need to find yours."

"And after that?"

He smiled. "We'll make a home on the Isle of Dragons and have many children to torment your parents with. You can patch up foolhardy whelps, and I'll give in and actually take my rightful place on the Elder Council."

If that was her reason for being, then she could find no fault with it. "It's a promise."

Part Two

~Journey~

Chapter Thirteen

The Isle of Dragons was located in the middle of the Deepest Ocean, a place of turbulent waters that no ship ever dared sail through. In size, the Isle was bigger than Glacia and Choral, but not quite as big as Spectrum. Its landscape consisted of mountains, deserts, valleys, and rivers. Every manner of scenery existed there. The oldest of Dragons remembered when the rest of the world had been just as beautiful. The younger simply sensed something amiss.

The largest concentration of Dragons lived on the Plateau, a series of cliff steppes that offered caves to live and work in. There was no currency on the Isle. Everything was done through barter and trade. Though their mountains were rich in ivory and bronze, no one mined. What was there could stay there.

When she had arrived at the Isle nine years before, Tariah Chronis had been at the end of her Chronicle journey. She had been pursued across the entire world by people who wanted to kill her and people who needed her to save them. At her lowest point, she had been on the cusp of mental breakdown, ready to detonate her own power and leave the world entirely.

But she hadn't.

From where she stood on the sunny cliff just outside her home, she turned to see her Fury sleeping in a swinging bed suspended between two desert trees. It had been Dominic's unconditional love and presence that had brought her back from the brink.

She smiled and walked over to look down at him. "Lazy."

One eye opened ever so slightly to reveal smoke colored amusement. "You fed me. I'm ready for a nap." He sighed contentedly and reached out to tug her down onto the bed with him. She was quite small, even for Magi, but he loved it. She was perfectly sized for him to cuddle. "I can't seem to get rid of my family when you're cooking."

"That's because you're all bottomless pits." She stretched slowly and the sunlight glimmered across her lines. They covered a fair portion of her body, including the side of her face, across her chest, and down an arm and leg. They were often clearly revealed because she was a desert girl and stuck to the clothing she was most comfortable with.

"Tariah!"

Disgruntled, she lifted her head to see her brother coming down the path toward them. "I was comfortable," she complained. She got to her feet. "And why didn't you just tap my mind?"

Though there was a five-year age difference, Morgan and Tariah had bonds like twins. Most people didn't even know there was an age gap at all except for the fact that Morgan had the three little lines at the corner of his eyes and Tariah didn't. They both had Telepathy skills as Dragoons, and they could communicate with their minds across even large distances.

Morgan Chronis came to a stop and smiled. In height, he was only a few inches taller than Tariah and quite short for Magi males. Both Chronis twins had the same thick auburn hair and glimmering silver eyes. Morgan's lines went across his chest and arms, and they were also often seen because he lived in the higher mountains and wore sleeveless tunics. "I figured this was worth a real visit." He reached out to pat her tummy. "Rumor reaches my ears."

She grinned happily. "What sort of rumors?"

"Oh, I don't know. Dominic strutting around like he owned the world, that sort of thing." The words were said teasingly as he looked toward Dominic, still lazily swinging on the bed. "And I believe a bet has begun about the child being Dragon or Magi."

"No Dragon!" She shook her head vehemently. "I am not laying eggs!"

"Well, not technically," Dominic soothed her. "The egg would be removed from you at the right time." He rolled lithely to his feet and walked over to tug her into his arms. His hands spread warmly across her stomach even as his presence curled around her mind and heart comfortingly. "Stop worrying about it. In a month or two, we'll know definitively which you're carrying and can make plans for it."

Morgan grinned a little. "Mom and Dad are going to be over the moons with happiness. The last few messages that have been delivered to me pretty much sang the same refrain. They want us to visit, and they want grandchildren."

"We flew past Spectrum a week ago," Tariah offered. "Just to see if I could sense anything. I saw some Furies, but didn't sense our children." She smiled. "Well, not children anymore, I'm sure. They're all eighteen or nineteen now."

His eyes lowered. It still cut at his heart every day to remember the necessity of sending away the four Chronicle children he had found. He had only had them for five years, but he had loved them deeply. Kelsey had been his favorite. He had been wrapped around her finger from day one.

A shadow passed overhead as a Dragon came in for landing. She changed to Magi form as she walked over and wrapped her arms around his waist. "Stop," Jazz Eaglewind said softly. She was only fractionally taller than Tariah though distinctly curvier. Tariah had stopped resenting her for it. Jazz gently reached up to frame Morgan's face. "You did what was needed."

Without words, he buried his face in his Fury's hair and drew on her ready support. He too wouldn't have survived nine years before if he hadn't found her.

"Sometimes I need to be reminded."

"Tariaaaaaaah!"

The shout was followed by a small figure tumbling through the air on a gust of wind. Dominic hastily reached out and grabbed the tiny yellow Dragon by the base of her wings and held her steady. She had the potential to be a Dragon Lord, but at only twenty-five years of age, she was the equivalent to a six-year-old Magi. She wouldn't be able to practice an alternate form until she hit first puberty around the age of fifty.

Tariah smiled. "Good morning, Saffron." She held out her arms and took the small Dragon for a cuddle. She was little more than a foot and a half in size. "You know better than to fly that fast," she scolded. "The currents are strong up here."

Saffron's golden eyes sparkled happily. Tariah was her favorite person *ever*. "I heard you're having a baby!"

"That's what I strongly believe." It was said with a smile. "I'm certain of it."

Saffron's tail wagged happily. "I'm glad!" Her nose wrinkled up. "I had something to tell you, but I got distracted. I don't remember."

Almost automatically, both Chronis reached out mentally and nudged her mind as if nudging a door open. Jazz and Dominic exchanged a grin. Jazz had Ultravision—the ability to see the history of objects she touched—and Dominic had Telekinesis. They were special, unique, gifts that only Dragoons could learn. Though Morgan and Tariah came by their Telepathy through their Dragoon gift, they had strange and wonderful other mental gifts that were wholly their own.

Saffron brightened and sat up straight in Tariah's arms. "Now I remember! We're getting reports from Furies out in the Magi lands! It sounds like the Chronicle children have been found!"

Shock stole Morgan's voice and Tariah fared little better. Dominic put an arm tightly around his mate's shoulders to anchor her as he sensed the wild response of her heart and mind. "How did they find them?" he asked. "The four weren't to awaken without Morgan or Tariah or a Fury present."

"They sensed them from other cities. An' the Elders have been conferring. Four Furies haven't reported in yet; the assumption is that they are the Fury with the correct Chronicle. The four who haven't reported in are Solis, Grecia, Dahlia, and Elder Xander!"

"That sounds about right," Jazz said softly. "Because each child was of a different element."

Morgan grimaced. "Solis has my pity for it is a surety he has Kelsey. On the other hand," he added softer, "I am glad that Jayda was the one for Xander. He was alone for far too long." He let out a little breath. "Now what do we do?" he asked Tariah.

She frowned. "We will want to try to meet up with them. We can't bring them here, obviously. They need to finish their journeys. But having us there might be helpful because you can be sure the Elite will be aiming for them."

"They might have already made movements," Jazz noted. "We can't be sure."

"So then let's go to Kindred."

"Why Kindred?" Morgan asked.

"Because I'm fairly sure that at least Xander will think to go there to see Daylar to try to contact me." Tariah smiled. "And anyway, I haven't seen him and Sparkle in a year. This will give me a chance to tell them that I'm pregnant. They're going to be thrilled."

Saffron's face fell. "You're going to leave?"

"Just for a little while." Tariah put her down gently on the ground. "We'll be back as soon as we can, and you'll have four new Chronicles to be friends with." She straightened back up and the sunlight glimmered across her lines. "Let's pack some supplies and get going. The sooner we find them, the better. I have a bad feeling I can't shake."

Chapter Fourteen

Kelsey awoke to soft kisses being feathered over her shoulder. Not even half-awake, she swatted at Solis. "Too early." His soft laugh teased her sensitive skin, and his presence swirled around her temptingly. He was lying along her back with his arm snug around her waist. She had never felt more secure and loved in her life.

As her power fluttered against his, he knew she was finally actually waking. He had been trying to bring her around for the last several minutes. His Chronicle slept like the dead. "There you are." He teased her ear with his lips. His intent wasn't to seduce. All he wanted was to make her gradually more accustomed to his touch. Having everything of second puberty happen at once would only alarm her more.

She turned over and snuggled against his chest. "You know," she murmured softly, "I was half expecting to wake and be disoriented. I'm naked and sleeping in the arms of a man I've known only less than a day."

"Is there *anything* that disorients you?" His fingers moved unconsciously over her back. Her skin seemed outrageously soft considering the work she did. He nuzzled her hair softly, savoring the scent of spicy fires and thick smoke.

Her breath caught. "I'm not sure." Her hands smoothed over the supple muscles of his arms, then linked behind his neck. "I want a good morning kiss."

"Have I mentioned that I love you?" He tilted her chin up and feathered his lips over her face before settling on her lips. As her sigh breathed into his mouth, he deepened the kiss slowly, his tongue teasing hers. Her power rose in a soft red glow, and he happily drank it as he kissed her. If all he could have of her physically for the time being was her mouth, then he was still a very happy man.

She shivered in delight. She didn't know if he was drinking her or her power. Her entire body was beginning to feel flushed, and her breasts were swelling in a foreign way that still seemed oddly natural. When he released her lips and buried his against her neck, she could only manage, "Solis."

His entire body quivered. He would live every one of his two hundred plus years all over again just to hear her call his name. "Yes?" He brushed against her emotions and elation filled him. Just to be sure, he lifted a hand and lightly skimmed his knuckles over the outside of her breast.

Her breath hitched and she arched a little toward him. Drawn back to her lips once more, he sank into the kiss as he pressed a hand against her back and pulled her closer. Her breasts flattened against his chest and made them both quiver with barely leashed hunger.

It was only when he began to softly trail kisses down her collar that her nerves reappeared. As he reached the curve of her breast, the bolt of pleasure went from breast to toes. It was shocking enough that she instantly tried to jerk back.

He immediately gathered her close in his arms. "Easy," he said softly. "Now that I know your limit, I'll stop."

Feeling her body sending out aching frustrated signals at complete odds with the anxiety in her heart and mind, she blew out a breath. "I'm not enjoying this yet," she complained.

"Yes you are, and that's the real problem." His smile looked tender and sensual all at the same time. "It'll get worse before it gets better. There will come a day in the not so far future where you're going to feel like you're on the verge of self-combustion but your mind won't let you take the final step yet." He stole a brief kiss, taking the last of her power waiting for him. "You'll likely be ready to tackle me down, and I'm going to be just as miserable."

"As long as it's mutual!" was her grumpy counter.

He smiled. "When it's second puberty, both lovers suffer equally whether they're both going through it or just one is." He sat up and shoved down the blanket that still mostly covered them. "We need food."

Etude came flying up, and her wings fluttered madly as she carried a hipsack filled to the brim with fruit. "I have some if you'll help me!" She was barely aloft; the sack weighed more than she did.

Kelsey scrambled up heedless of her nudity and grabbed the sack. Solis watched the morning light dapple across her pale skin and covered his face with a hand. He had lied. He was already miserable.

"Patience is rewarded," she reminded him. It warmed her that he wanted her so much. She *needed* him to want her, in ways that had nothing to do with her body.

He cracked one eye open. "When have you ever been patient, *ishke*?"

Defiantly, she took a bite of fruit. She wasn't going to credit that with an answer.

He relented with a sigh and got up. He shook out the blanket and it obligingly shrank back down to its default size. He tucked it safely into the shoulder pack he usually wore and got out a fresh tunic.

She had been mostly ignoring him while she happily ate her fruit, but when the tunic was dropped on her head, she was diverted. "What's this for?" She pulled it off her head and eyed it in distaste. "It has sleeves."

"Desert girl at heart," Etude informed Solis.

"So I can tell." He got out another tunic and pulled it on over his head. "We're going to Kindred. It's another wooded land." Kelsey's disgruntlement made him smile. "When we get to the Isle, I promise we'll live in a desert area. Actually, I have many desert relatives."

"How many is 'many'?" his mate asked suspiciously.

"Hmm. I have about fifteen older brothers and sisters and four younger ones. Between them, I have more than a hundred nieces and nephews." When her eyes went wide, he grinned. "We like big families."

"And your Isle hasn't fallen apart under the weight?!"

Enjoying her, he sat down and tugged her onto his lap. Her crystalline blue eyes looked skeptical, and mentally she was sure he was teasing her. "We don't live only on the surface of the land. Some live under it, others live in mountains. A lot of Water Dragons even live in homes on or under the ocean around the Isle. There's plenty of room."

"Oh." She thought about that for several moments. "Well, as long as I get to live in the desert, I don't care how many of you there are." When he opened his mouth, she shoved a piece of fruit in and got to her feet. "Eat your breakfast."

He obediently ate the fruit. While he did, he watched under his lashes as she pulled on her bikini. She moved as wildly and freely as a flame burned. He wanted her more than he wanted air. More than life.

She pulled on the tunic with trembling fingers. "Stop that."

His smile came slow and lethal. "Why?"

"It's making me jittery!" The sleeves flopped past her fingers, and she eyed them in consternation. "It's too big."

"It'll have to do. None of us is a Soil element." He hungrily eyed the opening in the tunic where he could see the curves of her breasts. "Etude, can you help her lace that? If I try, I might take it off her."

"Is that supposed to alarm me?" Kelsey asked dryly. She felt the sudden searing backwash of his emotions and her eyes went wide. He had only given her a glimpse of what was in his mind, but she saw enough to bring her nerves back to life. "Never mind. Etude can help me."

Smiling, Etude flew over and helped tie the laces on

the tunic to keep it closed. "What about her legs?" she asked.

Solis eyed the long length of Kelsey's legs. "They're stunning."

"Yes, but they need to be covered as well."

Kelsey looked down. The tunic went further down her legs than the edge of her shorts. The tunic, in fact, almost went to her knees. "If I tried to wear anything else of his, it'd never fit. I'll just wrap the blanket around my waist until we find other clothes."

"My friend is a Soil secondary," Etude offered. "I can ask him to help."

"That would be great."

Solis got to his feet. "I guess we're ready to leave then." He skimmed a thumb across Kelsey's cheek as excitement began to hum inside him. When she tilted her head, he said softly, "Dragons can't carry people on their backs, Kin or Magi, because the powers always clash and it makes the Dragon uncomfortable. But Dragoons . . . We Furies can carry our Chronicles on our backs."

Her breath caught. "Because our power is made to be one." The idea of flying was exhilarating, and so was the idea of finally seeing her Fury in his natural form. His lips softly brushed against hers in a tender kiss that brought tears to her eyes. "What was that for?" she asked softly.

"Being you." He rubbed his thumb across her cheek. "Back up and give me room."

Kelsey and Etude both moved back so that there was plenty of space, and fog and ice rolled in around Solis as he began to glow with blue light. There was a flash, and when it faded, he was once more in Dragon form. He shook out his wings with a quick stretch before unfurling them entirely.

Kelsey had never seen anything more magnificent. He was almost four times her size but she felt absolutely no fear. His scales were the same rich brown as his hair and marked with the blue streaks of his Water element. His wings were thin enough in some places that she could see the veins beneath and they formed a beautiful pattern. His face should have been frightening with its sharp lines and wicked teeth . . . but it wasn't. He was beautiful.

She walked over to look up at him, and his beautiful brown eyes looked down at her. He lowered his head until they were on eye level, and then very gently he nuzzled her with his nose. "You seem tiny," he said in awe. "It's hard to believe so much personality is packed into that tiny form."

"I'd take offense if it wasn't true." She softly put her hands on his face and delight filled her. His scales felt as soft as fur rather than the tough skin she had been expecting. She stroked lightly along his beloved face and he gave a contented sigh that almost sent her tumbling. A strong claw instantly closed gently around her and kept her close. She felt . . . safe. She felt as safe as when he had held her in his arms.

She smiled and leaned forward to nuzzle his cheek. He laughed and lifted her up high. "Grab onto my ear fin, but gently please. Then climb over onto my shoulders."

She did as told and then gave a little yelp as she almost slipped off his back. Etude grabbed her by her tunic, however, and held her steady until she could find a secure place to sit. Curiously, the way the bones along his back were shaped provided a perfect perch for her. Was that also because he was a Fury?

"Hang on tight!" He gave no more warning than that before flapping his wings and shooting up into the air. Her shriek of laughter tickled him, and the euphoria of having her on his back made him do a quick loop in the air. There was no discomfort. No sense of something wrong. Only a sense of something right, and the power that flowed between them swirled like infinity.

Etude flew up to join them, and he grasped her gently

with a claw. "Point the direction. The flight's on me."

She looked down. Way down. Hastily she said, "Please free my wings. I believe I have a fear of falling if they're not open." He obligingly changed his grip, and she let out a soft breath. "Faeries can fly without their wings by using their power, but it's never as secure as using my wings."

"A Faerie afraid of falling." Kelsey pondered that. "That'd be like me being afraid of fire." Etude flicked her wings at her, and Kelsey grinned. Despite all events lately, she felt wildly happy. She stretched her arms high over her head to enjoy the wind whipping past. They went through a cloud, and she found herself with an armful of Flutterlies. "Well."

She studied the little puffs of white curiously. No one was really sure what to classify them as. They weren't really animals, but they weren't really plants either. They would often just appear in the sky and gather together. When they did, they formed clouds. When they pulled in Air or Water power, they became rain clouds. Too much Thunder power and they became storms.

Something seemed . . . odd about this batch. She couldn't put her finger on it. She opened her arms and let them go, and watched as they flew off into the distance. They seemed to be heading somewhere with a purpose. "I wonder if they're heading to the storms around Mirah."

"I hope not." Solis frowned. "Things are getting worse around Spectrum last I heard."

"So how far from Kindred are we?"

"About three hours of normal flight speed. I can go faster if you like."

"Won't that be taxing for you?"

His smile, though it revealed many sharp teeth, was anticipatory rather than predatory. She felt a flutter of heat in her body. "I have good incentive to use my power now," he almost purred.

She blew out a breath. She was beginning to think

second puberty was the planet's idea of a practical joke.

~*~

When Roman awoke the morning after he had discovered what he was, he woke to find himself curled up in the middle of a cave covered in flowers. Grecia was contentedly sleeping with him wrapped in her arms. The incongruity of things hit him, and he studied his Fury in consternation. Lives weren't supposed to change that fast.

It was mostly dark in the cave. The balls of lightning he had made for additional light had started fading away; the lanterns had long since been dead. Rather than recreate them, he carefully used his Air power to bore a hole up through the roof to the surface. Light immediately flooded in and he winced in the brightness.

When his eyes finally cleared, he was able to see much better than before. He was also able to see Grecia more clearly, much to his delight. His eyes eagerly ran over every curve of her body. Desire for her, only dormant and not truly gone, roared once more to life. He softly smoothed his hand over her hip and leg and savored her skin. He caught a handful of her hair and brought it to his cheek. It was as soft as fur and carried a strength hidden behind deceptive delicacy.

He gently brushed his power against hers, trying to coax her awake. She only made a grumpy noise and tugged him closer. He smiled and began to rub the back of his knuckles over the outside curve of her breast. Her power stirred and fluttered against his and then he felt her fully awaken. "Good morning," he said softly.

"I guess it is." Her eyes didn't open as she slowly twisted against his fingers. He shifted upward and she released him so he could move. His lips lightly trailed over her face and neck, and she slid her arms around his shoulders once more. Half awake, half dreaming still, she had never felt so utterly cherished.

His fingers framed her face so he could tug her up for a tender kiss. Her entire body felt hot and heavy, her hunger for him stealing every ounce of her strength. She had no will or ability to resist as he tumbled her onto her back and began to explore her face with his lips. As his lips moved lower, she shivered helplessly. "Wake me this way every morning."

"I'll do my best." He smiled as he felt a rumble from her power. "That sounded like the sound my stomach makes when I'm hungry for sweetbread pie."

She opened her eyes and saw the soft white aura covering him. It beckoned to her in a way that was vastly more tempting than any pie could hope to be. "If I start calling you 'sweet pie' it's because you've now gotten yourself associated with it in my mind." She curled a leg over his to keep him close and leaned up to press her lips to his collar. His power flowed into her, cool and refreshing and delightfully sweet.

When she tumbled him over, he didn't argue. His eyes all but crossed as she began to softly trail kisses across his chest. The ache grew and spread, and he wanted her so badly that it was physical pain. His arousal throbbed in time to his heartbeat and it beat only for her.

Heat flushed his skin and hitched his breath as she continued her teasing little kisses. He wasn't entirely sure he wanted her to ever stop. Her lips teased his stomach while her fingers temptingly danced their way up his leg. When she was only inches from her goal, his stomach suddenly let out a loud rumble not dissimilar to the one her power had made.

She blinked and straightened with a smile. He looked horribly embarrassed and it was wonderfully sweet. "Well," she said. "I suppose other hungers must be tended to first." She eased up his body and kissed him lingeringly. His fingers tangled in her hair and she loved it. Softly she curled her presence around him and felt him curl around her in return. The powers merged and flowed endlessly.

As they eased apart, he said huskily, "I'm not going to be willing to stop next time."

A little thrill rippled through her body on a wave of lust. "Are you going to have your wicked way with me?"

"I'm going to have you any way I can. Wicked might be part of it eventually." He caught her in his arms for a fierce hug, simply wanting to have her close. "Mine," he breathed in wonder. "You're mine. I still can't quite bring myself to believe it."

She hoped he never did. She loved the breathless wonder in his eyes every time he looked at her. It was the way she felt when she looked at him. "Maybe in a thousand years you'll believe it." His eyes widened with shock and her smile softened. "You're immortal now, Roman. Our power is infinite between us and it makes us both infinite as well. As long as we choose not to age, so long as no one kills us, we will live forever. Together, forever. Until time ends."

"How do Furies live so long if their power isn't infinite?" he wondered.

She opened her mouth only to close it again quickly. Thoughtfully, she said, "I am not sure, to tell the truth. It's not something we ever asked. But it is a very good question. We'll have to ask Tariah when we find her. She's got an amazing intelligence. She should be a scholar."

"What does she do?"

She grinned. "Feed many hungry Dragons. She's an outstanding cook." She got to her feet and brushed off her clothes. Both hers and his alike were dusty from sleeping on the bed of flowers, but both sets of clothes were sturdy and made for the desert. Dusty and sandy were just part of the choice of living there.

She opened the ceiling with her power and then formed steps leading out. As they got into the sunlight, Roman stretched largely. He loved the desert. Watching him and the way the sun rippled over his stunningly beautiful body, she decided she was becoming a fan of it herself. There was much to be said for the way the desert sun defined muscles on a man like hers.

"What do we do about breakfast?" he asked her. "Unless you're carrying supplies in that hipsack of yours."

"None that are edible." She frowned thoughtfully. "We can't wait until we get to Kindred. It's a good five-hour flight from where we are. And we can't go into a city safely." She skimmed her knuckles across the lines on his face. "The world is changing, but it has not changed enough to make you safe, *ishke*."

"Fruit is out of question because I doubt any oases are near here." He snapped his fingers suddenly. "Let's see if we can hunt up some dune crabs. There are bound to be some around here. I can probably cook them with some lightning and we'll be good to go."

"How do we hunt them?"

He glanced toward her feet. The sand had turned an odd color. "Oddly, they always seem to be drawn to Soil power."

She blinked. "Pardon?" He suddenly snatched her off her feet, and she barely stifled a yelp as she grabbed his shoulders for balance. Eyes wide, she stared at the giant pincers that now stuck out of the sand, trying to grab any and everything they could. "Well then."

A lightning bolt cracked down from the sky and struck the top of the dune. Sand flew and the large crab popped out with a distinctly angered clattering noise. It was as high as Roman's hip, and its pincers were almost as big as its body.

Still holding Grecia, Roman backed up a few steps. His eyes flashed white and another lightning bolt dropped from the sky. It hit the crab in the middle of its back and it flipped up into the air. When it landed, it didn't move. Steam rose from its shell.

"Well," Grecia said again. Belatedly, she realized she was being carried. "You can put me down now."

He slowly put her on her feet, taking care that his hands slid warmly over her bare skin wonderfully displayed in her desert clothing. Breathless, she watched as he walked over to where their breakfast waited. He cracked the shell open, and she got a look at what was inside. She instantly closed her eyes. "Yuck."

He said nothing though he did smile. Using some of the water she had been carrying, he cleaned out the inside of the crab. Expertly, he began to break the shell away from the meat. Sweat rolled down his back and he realized he was sitting in the direct sun. A moment later, a large fern tree sprouted behind him. Its giant fan shaped leaves shaded him from the sun and immediately brought relief. He smiled at Grecia. "Thanks."

Looking anywhere but at the crab, she said, "You're welcome."

"Because of it, I'll refrain from teasing my big, terrifying *Dragon* that she's squeamish at seeing the inside of a crab. And you call yourself a healer."

"I'm fine with blood. Guts are another story entirely." She closed her eyes. "Just hurry up, please. I'm losing my appetite."

He wasted no time in finishing preparing the crab. He washed his hands clean and then went over to Grecia to tug her into his arms. "It's done," he told her gravely. "You're safe now."

She lightly punched him in the arm but still took advantage to cuddle against him. She softly nuzzled his shoulder. "You are incorrigible. But I love you anyway." She eased up for a brief but tender kiss and then released him.

"Let's eat."

Much to her relief, the crab tasted far better than it looked like it would. The taste was also familiar. "I've had this before, but didn't know it," she decided. "They must clean it up a lot before it's served at a restaurant."

"They do. Most people don't realize what they're eating unless they're told. And even then, they don't recognize the crabs when they encounter them. They're normally harder to find, but I suspect the waves from Mirah came out this way." His gaze lowered slightly. "How bad is the rest of the world?"

"It's bad." She smoothed his hair out of his face. "I've only seen parts of it, but it's going to get worse as long as we can't catch the Elite. But, hopefully, the storms between Carnelian and Mirah will die down now that Mirah is no longer sending out waves." She stretched largely. "We need to get going toward Kindred. We'll have to fly south, then west and cross over the ocean rather than the land."

"I heard Dragons weren't able to fly over cities."

"It's true. We cause ripples in the power in the land not too dissimilar from flying too low over water. But the ripples in the land can be worse because of the presence of so many Magi. Unfortunately, as a Dragoon pair, you and I need to keep at an even greater range from cities if we're flying because we put out just that much more a large signal. If we were trying to go between Magi cities, we would have to walk most of it. Since we're cutting across the land and avoiding them, we should be safe in flight—especially with the already disturbed land. I suppose that's the only positive in this."

"Do the rules apply for Kin cities?" he asked curiously.

"Actually, curiously, we seem to be fine flying over our own cities and over Kin cities."

"Then maybe it's just the concentration of Magi power being unbalanced. Another one for Tariah to ponder." He got to his feet when she did. "Are you going to carry me?" he asked.

She smiled at him, her eyes dancing and breathless anticipation swirling inside her. "You're going to ride on my back." She slid her hands into his and brought his hands to her cheeks. "That, more than anything, as much as our lines, proclaims we are a Dragoon pair."

A matching excitement began to rise inside him. He had always wanted to see what flying was like. Beyond that was a hunger to see her in her natural form. He had never seen a Dragon up close, and he wanted to know everything about the woman he loved.

"You're distracting me," she said softly.

"I like distracting you." As if to prove it, he eased in and kissed her softly. He whispered against her lips, "You're the one who is tempting me. I'm just some poor helpless male almost done with second puberty. I'm at your mercy."

Her breath caught. "Promise?" His power fluttered against hers and her pulse pounded. That was as good an answer as any. She freed her hands with great reluctance and took several steps backward. When she had enough room, she let the power rise inside her. Summer leaves and swirls of gold and green power surrounded her. The power flared brightly, momentarily blinding Roman, and when the light faded, she had transformed.

In a sort of stunned wonder, he stared at his Fury. She was . . . breathtaking. She was close to seventeen feet in length judging by how high over him she stood, but she looked overall slender. She seemed as graceful and willowy in this form as she did in her Magi one. She was covered in shimmering gold scales that glimmered with lavender highlights when she moved. Her face was more rounded than angular, and the fins extending from her head were nearly see-through in their translucence.

He held his breath as he walked closer until he stood in the shade of her body. The lavender eyes watching him were the same. "You're beautiful," he said softly. "In any form."

She lowered her head and nuzzled him gently. Her heart quivered. She could feel it from him and it rocked her somehow. She had been worried that he might be afraid of her true form. Softly, she said, "I suppose the idea of beauty being racially subjective is no longer valid."

He smiled and smoothed his fingers over her soft scales. "We're a race unto ourselves, aren't we? And it would entirely defeat the idea of us being mates if I didn't find you attractive in any form. I can't love you in one form but not your natural one. Intimidating though you may be."

"Oh, I'm not intimidating. *Xander* is intimidating. He's fifty feet tall!" She lifted him gently with her claw. "You can ride on my shoulders. You shouldn't slide up there."

He looked, realized that her shoulder bones had been made in such a way that he had a proper place to sit, and pondered the coincidence. It would be another thing to have Tariah examine. He put it out of his mind for the time being. He didn't care for the whys. He was simply enjoying the results. Secure in his perch, he said, "I'm ready."

He stopped breathing for a moment as she literally shot straight up into the air before spreading her wings and catching herself. She was so graceful! Despite her size, she was as nimble as a bird. And before he could say a word, they were flying across the sky with the ocean passing like a blur beneath them. "I can't believe it!"

She did a barrel roll just to make him laugh. "Me neither," she admitted. "I've never gotten to fly this fast before! I always had to restrain myself because of my power."

He smoothed a hand across her scales. "Well, now you have me."

Hungry anticipation colored her voice as she countered, "It would seem I do. And soon I'll claim you entirely as is my right of birth."

His entire body heated happily. "Who am I to stop you?" he asked huskily. "I'd hate to infringe on any rights." Enjoying her low laughter, he ducked down to avoid a cloud. "How far from Kindred are we?"

"A couple hours. By boat, it'd be a few days."

"It's amazing the Magi haven't tried to find a way to fly."

"The few Elders we have who are old enough to remember before the Chronicle War say that Dragons used to carry baskets with people across the oceans. It was back when we had open trade with the Magi. And like everything else, it too fell apart with the War." Her eyes closed briefly. "I long for a day where no one wars with anyone else."

"I think we all do." He wrapped his arms around her neck as much as he could. "If anything, perhaps the Elite will finally show everyone what is truly important. And if not, and I can't walk in Magi lands, we can stay on the Isle. You have a desert, right?"

"A large one, in fact." She smiled. "I might have to fight with a brother or two for the best part, but I think we could find ourselves a home."

Warily, he asked, "How many brothers do you have?"

"Mmm . . . ten? I think. I also have ten sisters." Feeling his shock, she said, "We like big families. Just as a forewarning. But if all I was blessed to have was one child with you, I'd still be happy."

"We can have children together?"

"Furies and Chronicles are the only cross-compatible species in the world. The child is usually determined by the mother's species, but it's always possible I might carry a Magi child." She smiled softly. "I'll be happy with whatever we're given."

He lost his breath. "Me too," he said softly. It was tantalizing to picture his Fury carrying his child. It, like everything else, would be an inescapable bond between them. And daunting as it was to consider raising Dragon children, he found himself looking forward to it. He would never be bored, that was for certain.

Chapter Fifteen

After a breakfast consisting of fruit from a nearby tree, C.J. and Dahlia were ready to leave for Kindred. Well, they were almost ready.

"It's a forested land," Dahlia explained. She was sitting on the edge of the spring with her feet in the water. "We really ought to have slightly better coverage for clothing because of the bugs. I mean, not that I don't love how you look, but I'm the only one who can nibble on you."

Remembering how she had taken distinct delight in nibbling on his skin while feeding that morning, he felt his cheeks flush. Ignoring it, and the smiling sidelong look she gave him, he said, "I can make us some new clothes. I just need sand."

"Hmm. Where can we get some?"

"Normally I get sand from Fire elements. They can make and break glass down for the best kind. But I can also use natural sand." He got to his feet and began to look around closely. "Since this is an oasis, we're lucky that the landscape is born from sand. I just need to find the right kind."

She braced herself back on her hands and watched him without shame. He hadn't bothered to put his vest on. She could see the full expanse of his broad shoulders and muscular chest. She especially loved the way his lines moved across his body. Wherever his lines rested, his skin was hotter. His hands always seemed to burn wonderfully. Her smile spread as she saw the red color on his cheeks. "Am I distracting you?"

"Yes!"

She just laughed. She fell over onto her back, linked her hands behind her head, and closed her eyes. "There. Now I won't keep staring at you. I'm afraid I can't help it. If my eyes are open, I'm going to stare at you."

"That should make me less self-conscious, not more," he grumbled. "Why does it make me nervous?"

"Because you can sense and feel that I want something from you that you're not quite ready to give me. It's a nervous excitement, isn't it?" She softly brushed against his emotions. They were as pink as his cheeks but underneath was a sort of giddiness. "You somehow want to give me what I want, but you don't know what it is nor do you feel ready."

"I don't like it." He began to scoop up the darker sand near a tree. It felt rich and vibrant with Soil power. "I dislike being nervous. When will it go away?"

"That I could not say. But I don't expect it to be long." She turned over onto her stomach and opened her eyes to smile at him. "You've already taken a large leap, *ishke*. And having waited for you as long as I have, I can find patience."

"I can't!" Distinctly sulky, he began to shake up the sand in his hand. "It feels like I waited a long time to start second puberty and now it feels like it'll be too long until it's done. I want it done and over with, so that I can stop being such a source of amusement for you."

"But it's a loving amusement," she countered. Her smile turned soft. "You're so sweet to me. You're unlike anyone else. You're a man who never let the little boy inside grow up. I need that. I get serious too much. So when you're officially an adult, I still want to see you sulking and playing pranks and driving me nuts."

He grinned a little. She seemed to know just how to lift his mood. "I'll endeavor to make you always entertained and tickle you mercilessly until you actually giggle."

Her eyes widened. "I don't giggle." She hastily scrambled up as he gave her a speculative look. "Don't you dare!" She ducked behind a tree. "Just make us some clothes! Keep your fingers to yourself unless they have intentions other than tickling me! I don't giggle. I refuse to giggle!"

That was a challenge worth revisiting. But feeling suitably equal to her once more, he began to concentrate on the sand. It swirled up over his hands, and he began to weave with expert precision. Dahlia was golden skinned with pale hair and beautiful creamy eyes. He wanted to set everything off and display her beauty as it deserved.

With her mentally feeding him the concept of forest clothing, he wove together a pair of dark green leggings, a snug black tunic with long sleeves, and a creamy colored cloak to go around her shoulders. He edged everything with gold color and made sure the tunic laces went from neck to hem so that she could choose how to fasten them.

She took the clothes and stared at them in astonishment. "Amazing," she breathed. She smoothed a hand across the silky material. "I've never seen anyone with this talent before." Never one to turn down beautiful gifts, she swiftly removed her cloth skirt and left herself in her bikini. She pulled her new clothes on over the top and began to lace the tunic. Everything fit perfectly, and she left the top laces undone so that it flattered her bust better.

His eyes dropped to the distinct shadow between her breasts that was teasingly hidden and revealed behind the laces. His fingers began to tingle. He hastily began to weave his own clothing. "You did that on purpose."

"I like being found beautiful," she admitted simply. "You make me feel that way, and I've always felt cute, no matter what Kin or Magi said. I can't forget that I'm a cute Dragon. But *you* make me forget."

"Good." He wove for himself a pair of sturdy slacks, a long sleeved tunic, and a cloak. He chose the same colors for his clothing that he had for Dahlia's because he liked the idea of them matching. Unlike her clothing, however, he chose to add gloves to his set to cover his hands.

She covered a smile as he watched her from the

corner of his eye. "I'm not turning around."

With only a little reluctance, he changed clothes. He was discovering that he liked the way she looked at him. It was just those darn nerves that made him feel awkward! He also discovered something else when he was fully dressed. "I don't like clothes."

"You can't run around naked," was his lover's exasperated response.

"If I could, I would!" He wrapped his arms around her waist when she moved closer. "I can't feel the air. I also can't feel you. It's itchy. And stuffy."

"Desert boy." She leaned down to kiss him softly. He only stood two inches shorter, but they both enjoyed it. It encouraged her protective nature in a way they both needed. "We'll live in the desert or the lower mountains on the isle. Both are warm and both are wonderful for running around in less clothing than the valley or the forest demand."

"Deal." He tangled his fingers in her hair and loved the feel of it sliding over his fingers. Anticipation was beginning to rise inside him. "We're going to fly to Kindred?" When she smiled, he swung her around in a quick circle. "I've always wanted to do that! It's okay because we're Dragoons, right? That's what's in your mind." He could see it there and her eagerness was becoming his as well.

"You're making me giddy." She held onto his shoulders as he swung her around again. "And how you can swing me around like this is beyond me. I could lift you up!"

He stopped, startled. "Really?"

"Really. We retain our strength in any form. If you ever see a Kin Faerie lifting someone off the floor, it's probably actually a Dragon or Fury in Faerie form." She smiled angelically. "Not that I've ever done that, of course."

"Oh, of course." He grinned. "It's doesn't bother me that you're stronger than me." He snorted softly. "You're a *Fury*. Of course you're stronger! I just need to find another way to have an advantage."

She contemplated all his mouth watering beauty and the way she had felt when she had woken with him in her arms. "I think you've got one. You just need to learn how to use it." She reluctantly released him. "Back up to give me room. I'm on the taller side of average for a Dragon, as my height might imply. You should be able to ride comfortably on my back."

Swirls of fog and white power swirled around her and began to rise as the wind blew. A flash of light momentarily blinded C.J., and when he could see again, his beautiful lover had become a Dragon. He had seen her in this form once before, when she had saved him, but it was a fresh and wonderful shock all over again. She was as rounded and curvy in this form as in her Magi one, as she had said, but he took one good look at her and decided that Dragons were either blind or crazy. There was nothing cute about her at all.

He walked over to her without fear. "You know," he said, "I think Dragons are out of their mind." When she cocked her head, he smiled. "You're beautiful."

Cream-colored eyes widened and then closed. She lowered her head and nuzzled him softly, curling her presence around him fiercely. She loved him so much. "*Ishke.*" She curled her wings down to pull him closer in a Dragon's hug.

His throat closed as he felt the emotion pouring out of her. "Are you trying to make me cry again?" His eyes were damp anyway, and he pressed closer. He rubbed his cheek against her soft scales. In some ways, he couldn't be mad at the Magi for their jealousy. This was well worth being jealous over. "I pity them."

"As do I." She released him from her wings then lay down. "Climb up. You can sit right in front of my wings and ride comfortably. I promise not to drop you." When he had climbed onto her back, she straightened up. "Comfortable?"

"Yes." He yelped and grabbed onto her neck as she suddenly shot into the air so fast that sand flew. As she laughed at him, he managed to say, "That's not funny!" His heart flipped into his throat as she did a loop de loop in the sky. "*Dahlia*! Have mercy!"

"Relax!" she scolded him gently. "Enjoy yourself! Do you realize we're flying?"

He closed his mouth and fiercely ignored how high they were from the ground. As he did, he became aware of the wind rushing past and the sensation of moving fast. Delight replaced nerves and he straightened up. "Amazing," he breathed. He looked around quickly, trying to take everything in at once. It wasn't just the flight. He felt *her*. He felt her power inside him as his was inside her, and the endless loop was as exhilarating as the flight.

Several minutes passed in easy silence as they both enjoyed the flight and then he asked, "How long until we get there?"

"Several hours."

"Isn't it normally a few days by boat?"

She smiled. "I fly far faster than any boat ever made. And I can fly much faster than other Dragons now that I have you. It'll drain me, certainly, but . . ."

He smiled. "But you have me." He laid down and rested comfortably on her neck. "That works for me."

Chapter Sixteen

Xander and Jayda awoke to rumbling stomachs and surprisingly warm air. The former was more important to Jayda, but Xander was quite grateful for the decreased chill. She could only shake her head at him. "I suppose I should have expected it since you are a Fire element. Few like the cold." She shot him a teasing smile. "Although, I do believe someone said he was developing a fondness for snow thanks to me."

"It's almost a fetish now." He nibbled at her ear playfully and made her laugh. He smiled and lifted his head to smooth a finger down the lines on her arm. "You're so fair," he said in wonder. "We'll have to live in the valley so the sun won't burn you."

"I won't burn," she promised. "I lived the first few years of my life in a desert, remember?"

His mind immediately pictured her in desert clothing, and he stopped breathing. "Well."

She hid a smile. "Are we distracted?"

"Quite."

She leaned up and nipped at his chin just hard enough to sting. "Better?"

"You're learning Dragon habits." He couldn't have been more pleased. He gave her a quick kiss and then rolled to the side and sat up. He sighed as he surveyed their clothing. "I look forward to a bath and a change of clothes." He tugged on his clothes and started digging in his hipsack for his supplies. A loaf of bread and a handful of fruit emerged, and so did a packet of rare tea. He brightened as he looked at Jayda. "Can you brew this for me?"

Her heart melted at the hopeful look he gave her. He looked just like a little boy asking for treats. Her thoughts collided with his abruptly as they were both suddenly diverted. In both their minds, they saw a little boy with her hair and his eyes running around. Her breath caught. "We can have children? How?"

"This from a doctor." He smoothed trembling fingers through her hair. "Chronicles and Furies are able to cross-breed. Odds are that our children would be Magi because that's your normal form, but you might possibly carry a Dragon egg."

"I don't mind either," she decided as she finished dressing.

His grin widened. "You're one better than Tariah. She's dead terrified of carrying a Dragon egg."

She smiled. "I'll study with the Dragon doctors and tend to her myself so she won't be so scared." She took the packet of tea and nimbly created a cup of ice that she could keep heated without melting. Some hot water turned the tea leaves into a sweet scented brew that she handed over with a smile. "Here you go."

They demolished the meal in short order, and she laughed at him when he munched the ice of the cup as well, just to get the last flavor of his beloved tea. He then took down the shelter of the trees he had made and soon everything was the same as when they had found it.

"If we go west, it'll take longer." He was mostly talking to himself. "From here we could catch a current and head southeast and reach Kindred by afternoon." He smiled at her. "You ready to learn to fly?" Excitement began to hum inside his heart. "In twenty-five hundred years, I've never had anyone ride on my back. I've waited for this moment."

"Then wait no more." She leaned up to frame his face and then rose up to kiss him softly. His excitement was becoming her own. Or maybe she was equally excited. She couldn't tell and didn't particularly care. "I've been wondering when I'd get to see you in Dragon form."

"Don't be alarmed." His thumb skimmed over her cheek. "I'm not exactly a small Dragon."

"Nothing about you alarms me." She rubbed her cheek against his hand and then slipped free and moved well out of the way. She had the vaguest memory from when he had rescued her, but it was more of a lucid dream than anything else. She remembered his pitch-black color and glimmering eyes, and that was it.

Fire and smoke swirled around his body and a bright red glow began to rise. The fire detonated into a storm and momentarily blinded her. When her eyes cleared, the fire burned around the immense fifty-foot length of her Fury's Dragon form. Not breathing at all, she watched as he stretched and shook out his wings. She was *miniscule* in comparison to him yet she felt no fear.

Unlike other Dragons she had heard of, Xander had two horns. They were long and curving and extended from his head near his ear fins. The way they glowed and glimmered, she thought they might well have been glass themselves. His face was sharp and angular, and his teeth were almost as big as she was tall. His body was stark and powerful, pure muscle shifting under onyx scales. He was *beautiful*. It seemed a paltry word for such a magnificent creature, but it was the only one she could find.

He waited for her to say or do something. When all she did was stare at him, he reached for her emotions to know what was inside her mind and heart. The breathless wonder stole his own breath and his heart tightened fiercely. He laid down until he was more on ground level. She seemed small and fragile suddenly, and he wanted nothing more than to hide her away where no one else could discover her.

She walked forward, pulled by a compulsion she couldn't fight. His head was bigger than she was! Without fear, she wrapped her arms around as much of him as she could and pressed her cheek to his soft scales. "It's a wonder Gamma didn't run screaming before you punted him," she said teasingly.

"No one has ever run screaming from me," he mused. "But I believe that a few have passed out. I try not to fly close enough to any city that they notice how big I am. Stalagmite is a pointed exception, but everyone there welcomes me. It's Morgan's hometown." He curled a claw around her gently, and his heart quivered as he realized again that she was smaller than his entire hand. "I think I'm the one terrified."

"I trust you." She pressed her lips to his skin softly. "Now how am I ever going to keep from falling off your back?"

"You can ride near my head. If you sit right near my horns, you should be plenty secure." He lifted her carefully until she could climb onto his neck and then onto his head. He smiled. He wouldn't even know she was there if it wasn't for her power. She weighed next to nothing. "Are you comfortable?"

She sat down next to his right horn and let it be a brace for her. "Comfortable, but not entirely secure. I have nothing to hold onto." Before she finished speaking, smoke curled around her and anchored her securely. "That works perfectly."

He rose up to a sitting position and then stood. His power flowed to her and then back again in a never-ending loop. He rose into the air with a flap of his wings that rippled the trees. Then, like a red comet, he shot across the sky. As he felt Jayda's power pulsing inside him, he felt nearly giddy with happiness. So much so that he did several loops in the air until she was breathless with laughter.

"When was the last time you had so much fun while flying?" She wrapped her arms around his horn since she lacked anything else to hold. Much to her delight, it was as soft and warm as the rest of him.

"I don't remember," he admitted. "There's a lot I'm rediscovering with you, *ishke*." He softly rubbed his power against hers and was contented when she returned the soft caress. "Relax and rest. If you feel compelled for a nap, feel free."

"And leave you alone again?" She snuggled in more securely. "I'll just enjoy the flight too. And anyway," warm feminine laughter filled her voice, "I'll need to be awake when we get to our destination so that I can feed you."

His soft laugh rumbled through her entire body. "Waking you might be equally enjoyable, though." He flew down closer toward the ocean to duck under a cloud. The Flutterlies were flying with distinct purpose, and he didn't want them to siphon her power. "Unusual."

She looked up. "I've never seen a cloud moving that fast. Or in that direction, I might add. I thought Flutterlies couldn't fly in a western or northern pattern."

"Normally they can't." His voice sounded grim. "I get the feeling it's important, yet I can't seem to recall why. It must be from the time that the War occurred. I remember many things of that time, but there are other things that have been taken from my mind." He felt her probing at his mind and sighed. "You won't find anything. They simply do not exist. The only reason I know they are gone is because I encounter impressions that indicate I've seen something before."

"We'll ask Morgan," she said firmly. "He can help. I'm sure of it."

"Possibly he and Tariah together could do something." He was thoughtful. "I do not know the extent of Tariah's mental skills, but they ought to be quite strong considering her brother. They're two halves of a whole in a way not too dissimilar from the way Dragoons are. I suspect they couldn't exist without each other either."

She tilted her head slightly. "That brings up all sorts of new questions, doesn't it?"

"Questions I've pondered for nine years," her lover

admitted. "I suppose we will find the answers eventually." He angled back up into the sky again. "We'll have to get you some new clothes on Kindred. Long sleeves are also best for forested lands." He smiled. "Perhaps you will develop a fondness for trees."

"As opposed to my fondness for snow?"

"A man can hope." Warmed when she laughed, he flew faster. The sooner they got there, the sooner he could have her in his arms again. Draining his majiks had never seemed so delightful before. And if he was really lucky, maybe his Chronicle really would like trees more than snow.

It was mid-afternoon by the time Xander was circling Kindred and looking for a place he could safely land. Kindred consisted of one larger island and many smaller ones. Over the last few years, long bridges had been built between the islands to allow easier travel. From the air, it looked like a string of stones on a necklace. Nearly every inch of the islands were covered in trees except for strips of beaches.

There was one on the larger island where he saw enough room to land. He circled in slowly to give the Kin enough time to recognize he was landing. He touched down gracefully and then lay down so that Jayda could slide down off his back. He had to help her, though, as her legs were slightly rubbery. "Are you all right?"

"I'm new to flight," she admitted. She took a few shaky steps. "The land feels like it's moving and I know it's not." She turned around to say something more but ended up turning into his arms. As they closed around her, everything stabilized. She sighed happily and burrowed closer. "Never mind then. Are *you* all right?"

"Just a little tired," he admitted. "I'll be fine once I feed." He looked up suddenly, his nose flaring. Not ten feet away stood a familiar SunKin Elf. "Rumidia, it's good to see you again. How are you?"

Rumidia smiled as she walked forward. "I'm doing well, and I can see you're doing wonderfully!" She included Jayda in her warm and welcoming smile. "Welcome to Kindred, young Dragoon." She touched her ears and bowed. "I am Rumidia, Fire secondary SunKin."

Jayda drew her thumb over her cheek and nose. "Jayda Lakemore, Water Chronicle." Softer she added, "Former Black Magi, under the leadership of Morgan Chronis."

"Naturally. We Kin knew of the Chronicle children from the moment Morgan and Tariah met. You are very welcome here, as is Elder Xander." Her eyes twinkled merrily. "I run the inn. If you'd like to follow me, there's a room ready for you. Word is spreading and we knew we might be seeing at least one Chronicle."

Xander's brows lifted. "Others have been found?"

"According to the letter Tariah wrote to Daylar, potentially yes. You are among four Furies who have not reported in lately, and other Furies have reported sensing Chronicles in and around other cities and lands. The belief is that all four children have awakened." She began heading down the beach toward a path leading into the trees. "The Chronis twins are on their way here as we speak."

"Twins!" Jayda's brows came together. "I don't remember them being twins. Wasn't Morgan about five years older than Tariah?"

"Physically, yes," Xander said softly. "Their souls are another matter entirely. The way they act and behave, we've all started calling them twins. And . . . there is more as well." In his mind flashed a vivid memory from over a thousand years prior.

Her breath caught as she saw what he had. Two nearly identical Chronicles that bore eerie resemblance to Morgan and Tariah but certainly weren't them for they had blond hair and blue eyes. "Who are they?" she asked softly.

"The first Chronis twins. Morgan and Tariah are direct descendants and . . . possibly more." He smoothed a hand down her hair. "It can be talked about later, *ishke*. It is not important at the immediate moment."

When they reached the inn, Rumidia led them to a room near the back for privacy. "I will let Daylar know you're here," she offered. "He will want to come see you to hear everything before he writes to Tariah." She laughed. "And knowing Tariah, she will want to know everything as well! She has a hunger to learn."

"The amount of knowledge in her mind is indeed amazing," Xander agreed dryly. "Thank you again, Rumidia." He opened the door and ushered Jayda inside, and when the door was shut behind him, he let out a breath. "Peace and quiet."

"Mm." She stretched largely and then laughed as he caught her around the waist and lifted her high in his arms. "Xander! Put me down!" As she found herself tumbled onto the bed and pinned by all his wonderful weight, she had to say, "Not what I meant, but I'm happy with it." His red eyes seemed to smolder as they looked down at her, and her breath caught as her entire body heated. Unconsciously, she curled her power around him seductively.

"You certainly know how to tempt me," he said huskily. He lowered his head, and even before he reached her lips, a soft blue aura lifted to cover her. His stomach tightened with hunger of many kinds. Almost reverently, he took her lips with his, drawing the kiss deeper and deeper, unable to determine if it was her power or her desire that replenished him.

By the time he lifted his head and began to trail soft kisses over her neck, she couldn't move. Her entire body was weak and aching with need. "You are entirely too good at that," she managed to protest weakly.

His lips curved. "I aim to please."

"You succeed, I assure you."

Rumidia was humming happily to herself when she sensed another Dragon power approaching. Brows lifted, she hurried to the window and looked down toward the beach. A large blue Fury was slowly circling for a landing and there was distinctly a young woman riding on his back. Delighted, she headed for the door.

Solis touched down on the sand and his eyes instantly flared wide. He could feel Xander's presence. "Even better," he told Kelsey. "I can sense Elder Xander here. He can surely contact the Isle for us!"

"Oh good." She slid off his side and landed on her feet. Her knees gave out and she promptly sat down hard on the sand. "Oof!" Mutinous and annoyed, she crossed her arms to glower at her mate as he knelt beside her in Magi form, a smile on his lips. "Not a word," she warned him.

"I wouldn't say a thing," he assured her warmly.

Etude flew down with a giggle to land on Kelsey's shoulder. "You'll get used to it, promise." She brightened as she saw a familiar Elf approaching. "Rumidia!" She flew over and happily hugged her cousin around the neck. "It's been a long time!"

"Etude, what a wonderful surprise!" Rumidia hugged her back and then regarded Kelsey and Solis. She smiled warmly. "Welcome to Kindred, Dragoons. I am Rumidia, Fire secondary SunKin."

"Solis T'mer, Water Fury." Solis bowed gracefully.

"Kelsey Renaire." She hesitated and then straightened her back, her blue eyes almost defiant. "Fire Chronicle. Former Black Magi, following Morgan Chronis." She opened her mouth to say more when a shadow passed by overhead. Startled, she looked up to see a large cream-colored Dragon flying in. Her breath caught as she saw the figure of someone on the Dragon's back. "Impossible!"

Solis looked up and his smile spread. "Dahlia!"

Dahlia angled in and landed with precision grace on the sand. She blinked rapidly as she saw Solis and Kelsey. "Well then." As C.J. slid off her back, she changed to Magi form. She was quick, thankfully, and caught her Chronicle as he stumbled. "This is unexpected."

"Why is the sand moving?" C.J. complained. He shook off the sensations and straightened. "I hope I get used to that. Gah!" The last was added as he found himself tackled by a slender redheaded female and sent flying to the sand. "Kelsey!"

"C.J.!" She wrapped her arms around his neck and hugged him tightly. "I missed you!" She straightened up, her arms crossed on a scowl, and was entirely unconcerned that she was sitting on her friend. "Well, if I've found you, I need to find Roman and Jayda!"

He propped himself up on his elbows with a wry smile to Solis. "Hi. I'm C.J Daragon, Soil Chronicle."

"Solis T'mer." He reached down and lifted Kelsey off C.J. "Water Fury, obviously." He smiled at Dahlia. "You look happy."

"I am happy." Dahlia helped C.J. stand. To Kelsey, she said, "I am Dahlia Stalker, Air Fury."

"Kelsey Renaire, Fire Chronicle." The redhead tapped a foot impatiently on the ground. "The Faerie is Etude, my best friend." She saw the flash of pain that went across C.J.'s face and reached out to take his hand. "What's wrong?"

"My best friend Cole." He looked at Etude and Rumidia. "Do either of you know Cole? Soil secondary SunKin Elf."

Rumidia shook her head. "I am sorry but I do not. You will have to ask Elder Juniper." She smiled. "If you'd all like to come with me to the inn, you can rest after your journey. Another of your kind is here."

"Xander Journe, right?" Dahlia asked. "I can sense he has been through."

"Indeed. And he was not alone."

It didn't take long for everyone to understand. C.J. brightened. "It must be Jayda! It *has* to be!" He enthusiastically caught Dahlia in his arms and swung her around. "That's wonderful, isn't it? For Xander and for us!"

Kelsey found herself envious of her friend. She couldn't budge Solis if she tried. His arms curled around her and he murmured softly in her ear, "You have other ways of making me weak, *ishke*. You're only just learning them, though." To add emphasis, his teeth teased the edge of her ear and made her breath catch.

C.J. saw the pink on her cheeks and felt immensely better. "Which phase?"

"First and a half," was the mutter.

"Second and a half."

She brightened. "That makes me feel better, thank you." She leaned back against Solis and drew his arms tighter around her. She could feel weakness inside him and knew he needed her power. Looking at Dahlia, she could see the paleness to her cheeks that meant she needed C.J. "We should rest."

"Indeed." Rumidia smiled. "You would not want to disturb Elder Xander right now. He's . . . indisposed." The two Chronicles blinked at her and her heart melted. Those in second puberty were wonderfully innocent in many ways. Their blend of both child and adult made others feel young again. "Their flight was a long one as well."

"Oh." It was the best Kelsey could come up with.

"Er, right." C.J. coughed. "Okay, we'll see him and Jayda later." He caught Dahlia closer and steadied her when he felt her sudden unbalance. "Lead the way, please?" he asked Rumidia.

"Certainly." She headed down the pathway once more, and her eyes met Etude's as they went. Both were thinking that it was no doubt a matter of time before the fourth Chronicle arrived as well. It was impossible that he not make it to Kindred as well. There was no such thing as a coincidence.

While Etude went to see the Elders and find out where Daylar was located, Rumidia got the other two Chronicle couples settled into rooms. She spaced all of them far enough apart that their powers wouldn't clash and distract each other. Much to her delight, within the next hour, she saw the familiar shadow of another Dragon approaching outside.

As Grecia was coming in for a landing, Roman sighed wistfully. "We're there already?" He had been enjoying the flight too much for it to end already.

"Unfortunately, yes." She angled down and landed lightly on the sand. She waited for him to slide off her back and then hastily turned to Magi form to catch him. She staggered a step but smiled. "Are your legs tired?"

"I have legs?" It was said with a smile. He gathered himself as he felt the feeling return to his legs and he straightened up. "I will get used to it."

"I'll fly you everywhere I can until you do," she assured him. Sensing an approaching power, she turned and automatically put herself in front of Roman protectively. When she saw Rumidia, her shoulders relaxed. "Greetings, Kin." She bowed. "Grecia Laluna, Soil Fury."

Roman drew his thumb over his nose and cheek. "Roman Arequo, Air Chronicle, following the path of Black Magi leader Morgan Chronis."

Rumidia touched her ears and bowed slightly with a smile. "Greetings, Dragoons. I am Rumidia, Fire secondary Kin." Her eyes sparkled merrily. "You're late."

"Late?" Roman lifted a brow.

Grecia suddenly realized that the tingling in her feet had nothing to do with hot sand. Familiar power, three familiar powers, had touched this land and recently. "Oh!" She brightened, a smile spreading across her face. She turned to Roman and took his hands with hers. "*Ishke*, three other Furies are here. Elder Xander, Solis, and Dahlia. I recognize their powers."

"And they were not alone," Rumidia confirmed. She smiled. "Follow me to my inn. They're there, resting up. I'm sure you would like to do the same." She tucked her tongue in her cheek as she saw the smoldering look that passed between the two Dragoons. "Solis and Dahlia will be quite envious of you, Grecia."

Grecia tilted her head and then winced as she realized. "Oh." She bit her lower lip. "Oh my." The smile fought to get free as she glanced at Roman. The idea of having to wait longer than she already had was frustrating and intimidating. A thought occurred to her and she turned back quickly. "Xander didn't . . . he doesn't have to wait, does he?"

"No," Rumidia said softly. Her eyes were warm. "He and his Chronicle are true Dragoons."

Roman let out the breath he was holding. He could see Grecia's memories of Xander, and it had hurt him as well to think someone who had waited so long would be forced to wait more. Over two thousand years. A Fury's dedication could be a little overwhelming.

"But worth it," Grecia murmured. "And he'd be the first to say it."

It was close to dinnertime when Kelsey woke from her nap. She had been wrapped around Solis, and he had been a wonderfully comfortable pillow. She hadn't felt compelled to move, but the distinct feeling of someone jumping on her shoulder brought her around. On a groan, she tucked her face more firmly against Solis. "No."

Etude rolled her eyes. "Kelsey! Wake up! I brought proper clothes for you."

Kelsey cracked one eye open. "Proper by whose definition?"

"The forest."

"No, thank you." She rolled over and pulled her pillow over her head.

By that point, Solis was awake too. He propped himself up on an elbow with a wry smile. "Kelsey," he said warmly, "we will eventually be in a desert. For now, we have to make do. Now, it's dinnertime and we should go to the dining room. Perhaps Xander and Jayda will be there." His nose flared slightly. "And I sense that another Fury has arrived."

She peeked out at him. "Who?"

"It feels like Grecia." He smiled. "She is the closest thing to another Fury Elder that we have. Since she is a Soil Fury, she may be in the company of your Roman."

"She is," Etude assured them. She smiled. "I saw them when they arrived. And," she added, "I talked to Daylar and Sparkle. They said they were going to come meet us for dinner. They have news and they need to hear our news to send to Tariah."

"Oh, all right," Kelsey muttered as she sat up. She blew out a breath so hard that the hair falling in her face stirred. She raked it out of her eyes and caught a breath as Solis' soft finger slowly trailed down the line of her back. A shiver rippled through her body as every nerve seemed to finally awaken as well. Even the feel of the soft sheets sliding over her skin was sensual. "Uhm. Etude."

He tugged on her long hair until she fell back against him. His lips trailed over her ear and cheek. "She was going somewhere."

Desperately trying not to smile, Etude flew backwards toward the door. "Mm. I guess I was." Hiding a giggle, she shrank even smaller and flew out through the keyhole.

Kelsey barely noticed. She was drowning in Solis' tender caresses. She could feel his presence wrapped firmly around her, their emotions meshed, and knew that he knew exactly how he made her feel. She was glad that at least he knew what was going on. She didn't. She could only feel without understanding, accept without knowing. As he turned her and his lips sought hers, her sigh was long and contented and unknowingly sensual.

A quiver rippled through his body as he fought for control. He had never been in this predicament before. He had never been the one to initiate a lover to the wonder of second puberty. His first lover had known more than he had, which had probably been to both their advantage. But if he had done to her what Kelsey was doing to him, it was a wonder they had both survived.

She made a soft sound of protest as he left the kiss and his lips began to slowly glide down the line of her neck. As instinctive as breathing, her power rose to greet him as a shimmery red veil of Fire power. Breath held, she grabbed his arms for balance as his wandering lips set off riots of delight under her skin. Her breasts began to ache and swell, begging for his attention. "Solis." It was little more than a whispered plea.

He buried his nose between her breasts. One hand curved around her waist to hold her and the other slowly skimmed up her body. Giving her plenty of time for nerves, his fingers trailed over the top of her breast. Her heart began to beat harder under his lips but not with fear. Unable to bear it, he turned his head and captured one taut nipple between his lips. Her power there was wild, spicy, and more potent.

The wave of pleasure went from breast to toe and back again before gathering low in her body. When his free hand covered her other breast, she couldn't stifle a soft moan. She would have melted bonelessly to the bed without his strong arm around her waist. Was she finally past that horrible nervousness? Could she finally give herself to the man she loved?

She got her answer when his fingers slid down her

body to her leg. He brushed the inside of her thigh and it shocked her so much that she jerked away, her eyes wide with fear. She instantly covered her face with her hands. "Solis. I'm sorry."

"For what?" He drank the last of the power from her slender and yet beautifully strong arm and then straightened and brushed her hair out of her eyes. He tugged her hands away from her face and kissed her softly. "I have patience, *ishke*. It's not as if we will never be there." He let out a rough breath as his aching body seemed to protest everywhere at once. "I need to go find a glacier."

"Stop tormenting yourself," she muttered.

"And therefore stop touching you? Ha. I'm frustrated, not suicidal." Easily, he continued, "But if you want to return the favor, let me know."

She blinked, then looked at him. It hadn't even crossed her mind. Yet as she watched him get out of bed, the way his strong figure moved fluidly made something inside her body flutter with sheer hunger. He was . . . gorgeous. Had she really noticed before? The urge to run her hands over him was so strong and fierce that she was on her feet before she was conscious of it.

Solis, keeping his emotions from hers for his own sanity, didn't know her intent until he heard her move. He looked over his shoulder and stopped breathing. The way she walked . . . the way she moved . . . she was as fiery and sultry as the flames of her power. "Kel."

She softly pressed her hands to his chest and her fingers kneaded softly. Wonder filled her eyes. "Mine." The word was softly breathed as she leaned in to lightly touch his skin with the tip of her tongue.

He firmly grabbed her wrists and held her away. "Mercy," he begged roughly. "You can be curious later tonight. But, right now, please have mercy on your poor, aching Fury."

Her lips curved slightly with a smug femininity that

was older than her power. "Okay. I'll hold you to that." She freed her wrists and walked over to where her clothes waited. With a long-suffering sigh, she reluctantly pulled the leggings and long sleeved tunic on over her bikini. She gathered her hair up and tied it haphazardly on the top of her head with a ribbon to match.

His clothes were not dissimilar from her own, and she eyed them in distaste. She liked seeing her Fury's lethal beauty and the golden lines marking him as her own. "I hate forests," she grumbled.

He just smiled and wrapped an arm around her shoulders. "I know."

When they walked into the dining room, and Kelsey spotted the slender young woman with seagreen hair, she brightened visibly. "Jayda!" She gave a happy cry and rushed across the room to throw her arms around the taller female.

Jayda felt tears well in her eyes as she held Kelsey just as tightly. "Oh, Kelsey!" She eased her friend back and smiled tremulously. "I can't believe it's you! When Xander said he had sensed the arrival of three other Furies and Chronicles, I was so afraid to hope! But here you are!"

Xander smiled at Solis. "Warm greetings, young Solis."

"Warm greetings, Elder." Solis bowed respectfully. "I am happy for you, Xander." He smiled at Jayda. "I am Solis T'mer, Water Fury."

"Jayda Lakemore, Water Chronicle." Her fingers laced tightly with Kelsey's as if neither could bear to let go just yet. "It's an honor."

Kelsey, showing the same lack of fear and nerve that all those who knew her loved, smiled at Xander cheekily. "I'm Kelsey Renaire, Fire Chronicle." She made the gesture of respect, but it came out sassy. "Nice to meet you. Solis says you're old."

Jayda bit her lip. Hard. Solis groaned. "Kelsey."

Xander just grinned and gave Kelsey a gentle cuff in the chin. "You suit Solis well, fledgling." His grin was almost a taunt as he looked at the other Fury. "Putting his vaunted patience to the test too, I see. It does him good."

"Someone have a party and not invite me?" C.J. complained from the doorway.

"C.J.!" Jayda brightened as she saw one of her brothers. "Over here!"

"Ah ha!" He swooped down and scooped her up, never mind that she was very nearly his height. He hugged her fiercely for a moment. "Missed you," he said into her hair. When she held on just as tight, he felt tears sting the back of his eyes. He had missed his family and never even known it until the holes in his mind had filled.

"Dahlia." Xander smiled as the younger Fury crossed the room as well. "Warm greetings."

"Warm greetings, Elder."

"So," came Roman's voice from the doorway, "I don't suppose there's room for two more?"

"Roman!" Kelsey happily tackled him straight to the floor. In moments, she had been joined by C.J. and Jayda, and all four clung on tightly.

Grecia carefully stepped over and around the tangle and crossed to her fellow Furies. A wry smile was on her lips. "Well. Greetings." She realized that Solis and Dahlia were eyeing her, and she felt her cheeks slowly heat. "What?" It wasn't *that* obvious that she and her Chronicle were full Dragoons, was it?

Xander cleared his throat and then lightly tapped his neck. She blinked in confusion and then warily touched her neck. She felt the little abrasion instantly and went pink. She remembered Roman's mouth being there, but she hadn't realized that he had marked her. "Oh." She cleared her throat as well.

Solis smiled at her. "You've waited longer, Grecia. You're entitled." He walked over to where the Chronicles were now standing and tugged Kelsey into his arms. He loved seeing her happy.

It was only a few moments before the Dragoon pairs were once more grouped up. "Okay," Kelsey said with a smile. "From the top. I'm Kelsey Renaire, Fire Chronicle following the path of Morgan Chronis."

"Roman Arequo, Air Chronicle, on the same path."

"Jayda Lakemore, Water Chronicle, same."

"C.J. Daragon, Soil Chronicle, same."

"Solis T'mer, Water Fury."

"Grecia Laluna, Soil Fury."

"Xander Journe, Elder Fire Fury."

"Dahlia Stalker, Air Fury."

"I'm Etude, Air secondary Kin!"

"Gah!" Kelsey nearly jumped out of her boots as her friend seemed to materialize at her shoulder. "Etude, don't DO that!" She grabbed the small Faerie and scowled at her. "That wasn't very nice!" On an indignant huff, she put Etude on her shoulder.

Seeing the look on C.J.'s face, Grecia asked softly, "C.J.? Is something wrong?"

"My friend." He closed his eyes. "My best friend is a SunKin Elf named Cole. Soil secondary." He took a deep breath and rested his cheek against Dahlia's hair when she wrapped her arms around him. "We fought against the Elite together. I passed out at the end, when I awakened as a Chronicle. Dahlia says he left to find Kappa but ..."

"I think you had best start at the top," Xander suggested. "And let's sit down before we fall down. We're awaiting Daylar and Sparkle still."

They found a table, and each recounted the events that had led to their awakening near their Fury and the encounters they'd had with the Elite. Gamma was surely dead; no one could survive the flight he had taken. Delta was dead at Cole's hands. Kappa was not a threat; if anything, she was better suited as an ally. Phi was still on the loose. Beta was also still free. "But, and I stress this," Grecia noted, "we can't be sure they're the only two left."

"Well," came a dry male voice from the doorway, "no wonder the land is almost purring in contentment! Four sets of Dragoons in our inn!"

They all turned and found a handsome SunKin Faerie hovering in the doorway. Beside him was a lovely female SunKin Faerie. Both had matching sets of wings, which was curious to all except Xander. He knew the story. Both looked much as they had the last time he has seen them, except for Sparkle. The naturally curvy little Faerie was decidedly getting pudgier, and with good reason. He began to slowly smile. "Well."

"Would that be the news they had?" Solis asked Etude dryly.

"It is!" Etude's smile looked happy.

"We don't know what we're having yet," Sparkle admitted, "but we're just happy to have a baby!" She flew over and landed on Xander's shoulder. She folded her wings and bowed with more grace than her expanding waistline should have allowed. "I am Sparkle, Soil secondary SunKin."

Daylar flew over and landed on Xander's other shoulder. He mimicked the bow with just as much grace. "Daylar, Air secondary. I'm very happy to meet all of you." He smiled at Xander. "And happy especially that you have your Chronicle, Elder Xander. Was it worth the wait?"

The way Xander smiled at Jayda made more than one pair of eyes sting with tears. Solis, being the youngest, knew how it felt after just his short time of waiting. He could barely imagine how Xander felt. "It was well worth it," Xander said softly, bringing Jayda's hand to his cheek for a moment. He smiled at Daylar. "Have you written to Tariah?"

"Not yet. I wanted to confirm just who you all were." He sat down on Xander's shoulder and began to trace intricate characters into the air as if writing with energy.

This particular energy was actually familiar to those present for all had met Tariah at some point in their lives. As he wrote the letter, the energy was cool as water but held a hint of the lines that marked the older Chronicle.

While he did, C.J. looked at Sparkle. "Tell me, do you know a SunKin Elf by the name of Cole?"

She cocked her head slightly. "The name is familiar, though I'm not sure from where. Why do you ask?"

"He's my best friend. He left to pursue Kappa from the Elite to convince her to join our side. I just need to know that he's all right." C.J.'s hands clenched together in his lap. "I think I would feel if he was hurt. I just need to know for sure that he's fine."

Etude began to frown thoughtfully to herself. It was very odd indeed that so many Kin would not be certain of Cole's identity. Most Kin knew each other in some way or another. Either he was a Second Born Kin, and that was rather odd in and of itself, or he was the Kin equivalent of a Master Magi, which did exist rarely. She was going to have to start asking around to figure out which it was. If he was Second Born, then they needed to find out who he was fused from so they could easier track him.

Daylar finished writing the letter and sent it off. "I don't know how long it will take her to write back," he said, "so we might as well rest today and meet with Elder Juniper tomorrow morning. The Kin will want to offer you sanctuary, and he may have more answers about what is occurring with the Elite."

"And why we can't remember anything about that time?" Grecia asked quietly.

"That I cannot say," he apologized. "Sparkle and I were there as well, and we do not remember a great many details either." He flew up into the air and hovered gracefully. "Enjoy your dinner. I'll let you know as soon as Tariah writes back."

"Thank you, Daylar," Grecia said warmly. "And you as well, Sparkle."

"Of course!"

The couple flew out of the dining room, and Rumidia began to serve dinner. She had been standing by for a few minutes, not wanting to interrupt the conversation. She too was beginning to think along Etude's lines, and she gestured for her cousin to follow her out so they could talk.

The Chronicles didn't notice and began to talk cheerfully about the lives they had been living. The Furies didn't say anything; they just listened with smiles. The four Chronicles looked nothing alike. They were completely different personalities. But anyone who looked at them would see a family.

"I suppose that makes us related too," Xander told his fellow Furies gravely.

As one, all three groaned and dropped their heads onto the table. He was already bossy just from being an Elder, let alone from being the oldest in their family!

Chapter Seventeen

After dinner, they adjourned for the night. Kelsey watched the way Jayda and Xander and Grecia and Roman walked with their heads together intimately, and suddenly felt immensely guilty as she went into her room with Solis. It just didn't seem fair that she be so early in her development that he had to wait for her. He had already waited *centuries*.

His arms wrapped around her waist and he buried his nose in her hair. "Kel," he said tenderly, "I wouldn't trade you for anyone else. I'm *proud* to be helping you through second puberty." He nuzzled her softly. "I won't say I'm not losing my mind and that not I'm exceedingly grateful for my Water patience, but I wouldn't change you at all."

She looked over her shoulder at him. "What was it like two thousand years ago? Did all Furies have to go through this? I mean . . . did Chronicles finish second puberty before meeting their Furies, or after?"

He frowned thoughtfully. "Those are very good questions, *ishke*. We've been so busy theorizing about why all of you are growing at such accelerated rates that it never occurred to us to question if it has always been this way. Xander should know."

"I think Jayda is a good example of what I'm wondering." She turned in his arms and lightly looped her own around his waist. "She had gone through second puberty but hadn't actually *gone* through it. And Roman was all but done. But their Furies are much older. And Dahlia's older than you, right?"

His brows lifted slowly. "I believe I see what you are inferring. The older the Fury is when their Chronicle is born, the more likely the Chronicle is to be at the end or close to the end of second puberty when they meet."

"It's that balance thing again. Opposites or identical." She took a breath and grabbed for her courage. "And on that note . . ." She firmly began to unlace his tunic. "You promised."

His heart began to beat harder and desire tightened his body. Unconsciously, he curled his power around her in a seductive call as ancient as time. Her power softly rose to curl around him, and his knees went weak with delight. "I suspect," he managed to say roughly as her hot hands softly spread across his bare chest, "I may be in the most trouble for reasons other than you being the youngest in development."

"Why's that?" The perfect line of his strong muscles was so tempting that she couldn't resist leaning forward and tasting it with the tip of her tongue. He was as pure and sweet as water in the desert. She loved the desert, and she loved the water. Her Fury was perfect for her.

"I think when you are fully grown, fully sure, you are going to be a force to be reckoned with."

The look she shot up at him from under ruby lashes was like seeing a promise of eternal, smoldering, passion. Her crystalline blue eyes were now more the eyes of a woman than a girl. "Does that scare you?"

His lips curved. "I'm shaking in my boots." When she pushed at his hips, he walked backward until the bed hit his knees and forced him to sit down. It took all of his considerable strength to keep from dragging her down onto his lap and teaching her the proper way to burn. He would have his turn later. They had forever.

There was something wildly thrilling at seeing the wonder in her eyes as she looked at him. "You're overdressed," he said huskily. "I thought you hated those clothes. Maybe you need to get rid of them." *Before he tore them off her body and ripped them into shreds for daring to hide her beauty.*

The hot lash of his thoughts no longer alarmed her.

She could feel that volatile third emotion inside her heart swelling and growing every minute, every second, and as it grew, it overshadowed any nerves. She wanted to feel his hunger for her, to know he desired her as terribly as she was beginning to desire him.

She started to reach for the edge of her shirt but paused as his mind curled around hers. Instead of simply yanking the shirt off, she slowly drew it up in a graceful motion and let the soft material caress her sensitive skin. When freed of it, she reached up to pull the ribbon out of her hair.

The feel of her own hair sliding over her body was as erotic to her as it was to him to watch it. Her sensitive skin had been such an annoyance that she had never thought to experiment with the other aspect. She slowly removed her leggings before stepping toward her lover.

He knew what she wanted and softly smoothed his hand down her long leg. The shiver that rippled through her body seemed to also move through her power where it touched him. "This," he said softly, "is what you should be feeling all the time. Stop thinking about the bad things. Just let yourself savor how it feels to live."

"Will it go away when I'm a true adult?"

"To some extent. But even after your body is used to the signals, some things will always be more wonderful. Like this. You're a Fire element. You will always be more passionate and sensual." He slowly smiled. "My reward for being a Water Fury."

She leaned down and pushed at his shoulders to make him fall over onto his back. It was more for his self-control than hers that she kept her bikini on. She felt it, that touch of nerves inside that warned her she was not yet ready. It was doubly frustrating with her body trying to insist she was *very* ready. She *burned* hotter than her power. She needed him to touch her, to hold her. There was something beyond the relentless pleasure, and she wanted it though she couldn't name it.

His soft laugh made her body heat and clench with longing. "I warned you."

"You're not miserable yet." She pinned his hands beside his head. "I need to change that. You're going to lie there and let me learn all about you." She freed her hands and slowly smoothed them across his powerful chest. She savored the tingle of power in his lines. *Her* power marked him.

There were little calluses on her hands from her years of work. Her power burned under her skin. He curled his hands into fists and his teeth clenched together as he struggled for control. Not yet miserable? He was dying. He was burning alive under her curious, questing fingertips.

She seemed to touch him anywhere and everywhere. She combed her hands through his hair, trailed over his face. She traced every line, followed every muscle. And when her hands were appeased, she began the journey with her lips. Her tongue teasingly flicked across a nipple and he couldn't bite back a groan.

For all her wild sensuality, her underlying uncertainty was obvious. Her hands never went below his waist, and her lips never went past his navel. Her eyes did, repeatedly, and with combination of curiosity, fascination, and trepidation in their blue depths.

He firmly caught her hand and pressed it to his aching erection trapped beneath his sturdy pants. "Don't be scared," he told her, his voice little more than a rumble as her heat seared him.

"I'm not." The flutter of her emotions made it a lie, but her fingers flexed cautiously. Curiosity and nerves fought for dominance until finally the nerves won and her hand instinctively tried to jerk away. He freed her hand and she sat back sadly. "I'm sorry."

"Don't be." Aching head to toe, he sat up to tug her

into his arms. "You'll put us out of our misery soon enough." His brows lifted as her arms wound around him and her lips feathered across his neck. "Kel?"

Her mouth closed over his skin hotly and sucked hard. The shock of it was as thrilling as the actual feel of her lips. His hands tightened on her waist without his control as he struggled not to return the favor.

She lifted her head and studied the little mark she had made. Something inside heated at the sight of it. "Grecia had one," she said huskily. "I wanted to see why."

He laughed, but it sounded strained. "I feel as if I should warn Dahlia. C.J. seems to be the type to see me and Grecia and become curious as well."

"He's further along than I am." She didn't feel the slightest bit embarrassed as his nimble fingers removed her bikini top. She was more comfortable being naked with him than him being naked with her. For now, at least. "He may have already tried it and we didn't see it. I could ask him."

He shook his head fondly. "There's no one else like you." He helped divest her of the rest of her clothes and then playfully tumbled her down onto the bed. He tucked her firmly against his chest and draped an arm over her waist. "There."

She snuggled back against him. "Solis, I really love you. It doesn't seem like the best word for how I feel, but it's the only one I have. I just wanted to say it."

He nuzzled her hair. "I love you too, *ishke*. Don't feel guilty. You wanted me to be miserable, and you succeeded. However, I am also very, very happy."

"How's that possible?"

"It's my body that aches, Kel. My heart and soul are jubilant." He pressed a kiss to her ear and nuzzled her untamed mass of red curls. She always smelled of rich and drugging smoke and mystery. "Go to sleep."

She forced herself to stop thinking and snuggled more

firmly into his arms. Her body ached, her mind was nervous, and her heart and soul felt a thrill at every new experience. The thought of having to endure this sort of thing for *months* was alarming. For the first time, she was grateful for her accelerated Chronicle growth. She would be close to insanity if she were normal.

The next morning, the Dragoon pairs met up for breakfast. The little knowing grins that Grecia and Xander shot at Solis made the Water Fury's cheeks turn slightly pink, but he gamely ignored them. He was well aware that the little mark was still visible on his neck. He saw Jayda whispering in Kelsey's ear, and his redheaded lover snickering softly, and he had a strong feeling he was indeed doomed.

It was as they finished breakfast that Daylar arrived. He flew in and landed gracefully on Dahlia's shoulder, and his lively face looked very serious. "Elder Juniper would like to speak with you, C.J. He would like to know more about what happened with Cole."

C.J. nodded slightly, his heart clenching with fear. It was only the soft caress of Dahlia's power and heart curling around him that kept him calm. "I'll go to him after breakfast, if you can show me where to go."

"Of course." The Faerie took a quick breath. "Tariah wrote back to me this morning. She and Dominic are grounded with Morgan and Jazz a few miles out from Prismatic. They landed to wait out a storm, but the storm is only getting worse. When I checked with some other Kin, they confirmed that the storm is spreading across Spectrum. Not moving, spreading."

"Those Flutterlies we saw," Jayda said to Xander. "They were flying unnaturally. Perhaps that is where they were going." She saw Kelsey frown and turned to look at her. "Did you see some as well?"

"I did. They were odd. I don't know how, but they were odd. They weren't off-direction, but they had a purpose. Solis and I thought they were going to storms on Mirah." She rubbed her hands over her arms to combat a chill her long sleeves couldn't block. "Storms are slowly covering the whole of Spectrum. Why?"

Xander rubbed his forehead as he encountered again the blank space in his memory. He felt Jayda moving through his mind, but she could not seek out what had been removed. "I am sure I've seen this before," he said softly, "though I can't remember where or when. It must be from the War."

"Your memories were removed of that time?" Dahlia looked at him in surprise. "You've never mentioned it before."

"It's never consciously on my mind. I only know I have memories that are missing because of moments like these. My mind looks and feels perfectly fine. There are no blank spots as was with our Chronicles."

"Like with the Elite," C.J. said. "Memories removed naturally." He looked at Dahlia and Roman equally. "Do you think either of you could help Xander? You are the element of Air, and it has power over minds, right?"

"It can't hurt to look," Xander admitted. "Feel free."

"I'm not sure I want to look inside a mind that old," Roman countered dryly.

"It's only a little dusty." Jayda's voice was impish.

Xander brought her wrist up to his lips and nipped at her skin lightly. When she squeaked, he leaned down to kiss her nose. "That's what you get for teasing a Dragon, *ishke*." He brushed a kiss across her lips with a smile. He cherished having someone tease him, and he knew she knew it. Too often he had been alone, even among his own kind.

He felt the sudden presence of both Dahlia and Roman in his mind, both of Air but very distinct with their own signature. They swept through his mind, and he felt entirely unsurprised when neither was able to find anything. As they pulled out, he said, "You have confirmed, again, my suspicions about Morgan and Tariah. What they do is not normal."

To his surprise, he suddenly felt Kelsey flit through his mind. He lifted a brow at her. "I believe our youngest fledgling is learning her Telepathy skill. And if she is developing that already, then the rest of us must surely have our skills growing as well."

"I can only assume I have Ultravision," Solis said. "When I noticed Kelsey's mind strengthening, I began testing the skills myself. I certainly am not Telepathic nor am I Telekinetic."

"What exactly are the skills?" Roman asked curiously.

"Telepathy allows a Dragoon to read most minds. Morgan and Tariah, however, can do *vastly* more than that. They can fully communicate with each other across any distance. Tariah once took control of the former Magi king's mind, and we all know what Morgan did even before his tertiary skill developed." Xander shook his head. "And then there was the Chronis Dragon."

"Maybe Morgan can do something about your memories," C.J. said.

"That is my hope."

"What's Ultravision?" Kelsey asked Solis.

"The ability to read history in an object. It evolves into Ghost Touch which allows communication with ghosts. Telepathy becomes Clairvoyance which allows for viewing events in another location." He glanced at Daylar. "Have Tariah and Morgan evolved?"

"They haven't said."

"Telekinesis," Dahlia offered, "is to move objects with your mind. It becomes Invisibility."

"That would be fun!" Roman decided.

"It's a good thing you think so." Grecia kissed his cheek. "You have Telekinesis. When you tugged me into your arms this morning, it wasn't with your hands. I felt it come from your mind." She shot a smirk at Xander as she blatantly poked at his mind so that he arched a brow at her. "And Telepathy is mine. Our Elder will have to stay on his toes."

"I would be more concerned," Xander said mildly, "for all of you." Rather pointedly, he touched all of their minds and watched all except Kelsey wince. She just grinned at him, but he had expected that. "It would seem your Elder has it too."

"I probably have Ultravision." Jayda tugged on his sleeve in a bid to make him behave. "I don't have Telekinesis or Telepathy. What about you, C.J.?"

"I don't know." He tried concentrating on her and felt nothing that indicated he was even close to peeking inside her mind. He focused instead on a cup of water. To his shock, it suddenly flew up into the air. He lost his concentration and the cup dropped back toward the table.

Thankfully, Roman and Jayda were quick. Roman caught the cup with his Telekinesis, and Jayda caught the water with her power. "That answers that," the Air Chronicle said dryly. "Please be more careful, Ceej." He glanced at Dahlia speculatively. "Do you know his full name?"

"Don't you dare!" C.J. muttered. "And those with Telepathy can stay out of my head! Especially you, Kelsey!" He sat back and crossed his arms. "When we find Cole, then I'll tell you. He's waited the longest to know, all right?"

Dahlia reached up to gently ruffle his hair. "I will protect you," she promised gravely. "I have Telepathy too." She looked at Xander. "Do you think we should go to meet Morgan and Tariah, rather than have them try to come to us?"

North.

All at the same time, the four Chronicles felt the sharp compulsion of their lines. It was so strong and fierce that it rippled into their Furies as well. Both Jayda and Roman, whose lines had partially darkened, felt it burning in the uncharted portion of their lines. Kelsey and C.J. felt it through all their lines. *North.* They had to go north.

"That answers that," Solis said quietly. "We go to Morgan and Tariah. If your journey is taking you north, it is taking you to them." He looked at Dahlia and C.J. "Go meet with Elder Juniper and then meet us at the beach. We can at least fly along the coast of Spectrum as far north as we can before the storms make us land."

"We won't want to go together," Xander said. "It might be too much power with the fragility of the land right now. Once we reach Spectrum, we will need to take different routes."

"I want to say goodbye to Etude," Kelsey told Solis firmly.

"Of course."

With breakfast done, and the Chronicles feeling their lines burning, there wasn't anything else to be done. Xander took care of paying Rumidia for the room and board for all of them, though she tried to turn down his money, while Kelsey and Solis went to find Etude. At the same time, Daylar led Dahlia and C.J. through the town toward where the Elder lived.

C.J. was fascinated by the forest. Admittedly, he disliked the covering clothing and he missed his desert sun, but there was something peaceful and beautiful about the trees and shade. Kindred was essentially a giant oasis in the desert of the world. The peace-loving nature of the Kin had seeped into the very land. Somehow he doubted the storms would ever reach this place.

Elder Juniper lived in a small house not far from the Healing Shelter. He was of average height for an Elf, a SunKin, and his golden tattoos glowed vivid against his pale skin. He looked fairly young to be an Elder, but his eyes spoke of many years. As the Dragoons approached, he touched his ears and bowed. "Greetings. I am Elder Juniper, Air secondary SunKin Elf."

C.J. made the gesture of respect even as Dahlia bowed. "C.J. Daragon, Soil Chronicle. This is my mate, Dahlia Stalker, Air Fury." He rubbed his hands over his arms to fight a chill. "You wished to speak with me about Cole?"

"Come in, young ones." He suddenly smiled. "Well, perhaps Dahlia is not that young compared to I. I am only a hundred years older, or so."

She smiled at him. "How much longer do you intend to live?" At five hundred, he was indeed old, even by Kin standards.

"I will not die until I finish my father's work," he said simply. "He fought for peace during the War. I wish to see that peace arrive." He gestured to a couch, and as soon as his guests had seated themselves, he sat down in another chair. "Now, C.J. Please talk to me of Cole."

"He's a Soil secondary SunKin Elf. About sixty years old. He's been my best friend for seven years." He couldn't keep the agitation out of his voice, and not even Dahlia's hand covering his could give him any comfort. "Why doesn't anyone know him? He came here for visits all the time."

"I did not say I didn't know him," Juniper said soothingly. "Please, tell me of what occurred."

"We were attacked by the Elite. One of them, Kappa, isn't our enemy. She's a good person, and Cole loved her. She loves him too, I think, and she loved me a little. She ended up helping us against Delta, and when Cole went to get Dahlia, she ran off. He went to follow after her. I just need to know he is all right."

"He has not checked in with me," Juniper said thoughtfully. "Which does not necessarily mean he is in trouble. Cole is a Second Born Kin, and he is much stronger than average."

"Second Born?" Dahlia asked curiously.

"It means that the soul and the body of Cole were not born together. The original soul within Cole's body died several years ago, at the same time that the body belonging to the current soul did. The two souls briefly touched, and it was agreed that the new soul would take Cole's body for his time was not yet up. It happens among the Kin not unlike you have Master Magi."

"He would know, wouldn't he?" C.J. asked. In a way, the knowledge didn't surprise him. There were many aspects about Cole that had never seemed normal, even by Kin standards. It also explained why he had always been fiercely protective of C.J. He had known what it meant to be different.

"Certainly he does. He brought in his memories of his old self and they combined with the memories of his new self so that he could use his new body comfortably. Bodies are little more than shells for our power and souls." He reached over to lightly touch C.J.'s knee. "I have Kin keeping an eye out for Cole. His family will let me know if they feel anything has happened to him."

"And you'll let me know?"

"As soon as I am able," the Elder promised.

"We might as yet meet him ourselves, *ishke*," Dahlia reminded C.J. gently. "If he has not caught Kappa, and she is as yet confused, she may be with the Elite and coming for us."

"Good." His chin set into a familiar stubborn line. "I don't care if she's older than I am. I'll box her ears!" He blinked, and a bemused smile crossed his face. "My mother used to say that. I didn't think I'd ever say it myself. Kindly don't tell her. I'll never live it down!"

Juniper chuckled softly. "Another sign of adulthood."

As they left the house a few moments later, Dahlia murmured, "Thank you, by the way, for keeping your curiosity where it can't be seen. For the time being, anyway.

Once we hit the desert, I'm sure it will be noticed."

He grinned unrepentantly. He felt absolutely no shame for his curiosity and rapidly growing hunger to know everything about his Fury's body. He had pointedly made the little mark on the curve of her breast just to see how she reacted. He hadn't been disappointed. "You weren't thanking me when I did it."

"I was *very* close to having my way with you," she grumbled. "Having you in the experimentation phase is maddening." Her breath caught in her chest as his power suddenly swirled around her hotly, his emotions colliding and tangling with hers. Her heart began to beat harder as she saw how very close that third emotion was to being as great as her own. "C.J."

"Next time," he said softly, almost shyly, "I don't think I'm going to want to stop. I won't make you wait any longer, Dahlia. You've waited long enough." He swung her into his arms and around in a quick circle, uncaring that the Kin watched with grins. "I guess it's a good thing that we're splitting up. I mean, I would hate to embarrass you in front of the others by seducing you nearby."

Her eyes lit with laughter and love. "I'd worry most for poor Solis. He would have the youngest Chronicle when she was Fire." Wildly happy, she threw her arms around her lover and held on. He had this way of making her feel wonderfully cherished, and she reveled in it. And yet, she loved the way he respected her strength and loved letting her protect and shelter him.

"You'll make me cry." He buried his face against her neck. "Damn it, Dahlia." He put her down and laced their fingers together. "We need to meet with the others. I feel a bit better after talking to Elder Juniper, and I'm glad to know why Cole was always different to me. I'm glad he was born again. I'd have had a very unhappy life without him."

"He would be to you what Daylar is to Tariah, just not

as formally," she murmured. "A Chronicle's power is too erratic to become an honorary Kin. Tariah got lucky because Daylar's power was erratic for a while."

"It doesn't have to be formal. It's there. That's enough for me." He grinned. "And you're going to be in trouble when we find Cole. He and I are terrible together, or so we've been warned. I can't help it. We bring out the worst in each other."

Or the best, as far as she was concerned. She could see his memories and knew the two males made a dangerous combination. "I'm terrified," she said drolly.

The beach where Xander had landed was where everyone else waited. The other three Chronicles wore packs with supplies, and Kelsey handed an extra one to C.J. "Here you are," she said. "And since we're going to a desert," she added hopefully, "can we *please*, *please* have desert clothes?"

He lifted a brow at her. "If you give me some sand, *Master* Kelsey."

"That's not fair," she told him. "I happened to see *someone's* tapestry hanging on a wall at the inn."

Roman kept his mouth shut because he wasn't about to defend either of them and get it pointed out by the other that he was also world-renowned for the glasswork he and Terina had made. He was much smarter than that.

Jayda smiled wryly up at Xander. "I am grateful that I am not an artist of any kind. I don't think I'd want to be known across the world. Well, more than I already was just for being a Master Magi."

"Now, kids," Grecia firmly stepped between C.J. and Kelsey, "let's play nice, shall we? Xander and Kelsey will make the sand, and I and C.J. will weave with it. If he will make cloaks to protect us from the sun, I will make clothes. We don't need much."

Kelsey stuck out her tongue at C.J. impishly and he returned the gesture before ruffling her hair. Not a single one of their friends doubted that even being full adults would stop them from sniping at each other. They had done it from childhood, and not even nine years had changed it. Nothing ever would.

C.J. used some of the plain sand under their feet to create two small bags, one for him and one for Grecia, so that they could carry the higher quality sand with them. Kelsey lifted her hands and billows of smoke swirled into the air. She had often made sand for weavers across the world. Many discarded hilts had become a beautiful piece of cloth somewhere.

To make sand, the creator first made smoke and then solidified it into glass. Glass could be formed either solid or liquid depending on its usage. The more intricate the work would be, the more likely the glass would need to be liquid. It could then be hardened further with fire or smoke. Roman had seen Terina make glass, and it fascinated him to watch Kelsey and Xander. He had never realized that making glass could be as unique as the maker.

Kelsey made liquid glass and solidified it to the state she wished before she dissolved it into sand by using her Smoke power. Xander made glass that was solid from the start and broke it down from there. Though both end results looked the same, it was still very obvious that they had been made by two different people.

Xander studied the bag of Kelsey's sand before smiling at her. "You are brilliant at your work, fledgling. I've had two and a half millennia to practice, and you're nearly as good as I am after less than a decade."

She flushed with pride. "I taught myself how when I realized what a waste it was to just get rid of my discarded glass."

"You know that tapestry you saw at the inn?" C.J. asked as he ran the sand over his fingers. "It ought to feel slightly familiar. It was made with some of your sand. Cole got the bag for me from Prismatic. I never realized it was yours until now. I suppose that's why it felt familiar. It was the best I've ever worked with. Expect me to nag you incessantly for a big supply once we're all settled on the Isle."

She grinned at him. "Only if you make me something for Solis' and my house."

"Deal." He straightened and gathered the sand in his hand. As Grecia formed clothing, he formed cloaks. It took no thought to know what he wanted to make. He made eight cloaks total, and all were pure white with the black chalice of the Black Magi in the back. The men's cloaks would fasten around their necks, and the women's would fasten around their shoulders.

Grecia made clothes in creams and tans since they would wear best in the desert. For the men, there were loose slacks and vests. For the women, she made shorts and tops that weren't much more than bikini tops as well, but much sturdier. As she handed clothes to Kelsey, she asked warmly, "Will this do?"

"Yes!" Kelsey clutched them close happily. "Forests are nice, but they're not for me!"

"I will need to get used to this again," Jayda said. "I've lived in Glacia for so long that I am acclimated to the cold. Xander hates the snow," she said gravely. "He wants to convert me fully into a desert girl."

"Can we compromise on the valley?" he asked hopefully.

She framed his face with her hands and went up to kiss him warmly, her power swirling teasingly around him. They both knew that he would willingly live in the mountains if it would make her happy, but she didn't mind meeting him halfway. "Compromise accepted," she said softly.

Since they wouldn't be wearing much beyond their bikinis anyway, the four females stripped off their forest clothes and put on their shorts and tops. The males, out of consideration for Kelsey who was still only partway through second puberty, decided to wait until they had all split up.

"I hate modesty," she grumbled. "Tell me it goes away. It shouldn't bother me to see a naked or mostly naked male. It didn't before!" It wasn't the same as with Solis; this was more an embarrassed feeling than a nervous feeling.

"It usually goes away eventually, Kel," Dahlia told her gently. Laughter lingered in her voice. "Especially for someone as outgoing as you."

"Back up," Xander warned with a smile. "Give me room to change form. Once I and Jayda take off, then someone else can change." Everyone cleared back and he called on his power to go back into his natural form. He felt no worry for how the other Chronicles might react; he doubted that much would unnerve them at this point.

Roman studied the immense Dragon now on the beach and then looked at Grecia and said solemnly, "You're right. He is much more intimidating than you."

Xander laughed as he helped Jayda up to her perch. He wrapped smoke around her to keep her held securely as he flew straight up into the air from where he stood. He flew out from the beach and hovered in place to wait for the others.

Dahlia changed next since she was the next largest and then helped C.J. onto her back. Once he was secure, she flew out to join Xander. Solis and then Grecia followed suit with their Chronicles, and when all four pairs were together, they began to head north across the ocean toward the land known as Spectrum. There was no worry that they would get lost.

Even at a day's flight away, they could see the darkness from the storms gathering on the horizon.

Chapter Eighteen

It was evening by the time the Dragoons approached the western shore of Spectrum. They had been forced to fly much farther north than intended, thanks to the storms spreading out from Mirah. Roman very carefully kept his worry for his best friend and parents hidden from all except Grecia. There was no hiding it from his lover.

The storms had begun to cover nearly every inch of Spectrum. There was only a small space between the ones moving north and the ones moving south. They pushed into the oceans and made the water seethe restlessly. Even if it had been midday, it would have been hard to see.

Among their supplies had been lanterns, and all four Chronicles carried them as they flew along the shore to find a place to land safely. They needed to land, split up, and camp soon so that their Furies could be fed. The long and fast flight had drained them all.

When they found a place secure enough, they all landed one by one. The four Furies turned back into Magi form, but even Xander found it difficult to remain on two feet. C.J. and Roman were able to lift their Furies off their feet easily enough, but Kelsey and Jayda could only brace Solis and Xander.

"It occurs to me," Jayda said warmly as she kept Xander's arm wrapped around her shoulders to support him, "that female Chronicles are at a slight disadvantage in moments like these."

"When we have a chance," Grecia said tiredly from Roman's arms, "then we will show you how to use our majiks to change into a Dragon form. It will increase your strength to a comparable level, and in emergencies, it will remove this problem."

"Is it hard to learn?" Kelsey asked curiously.

Xander suddenly smiled. "You'll have to ask Tariah about her first attempts." He carefully straightened and ignored the way his body protested his drained power. "C.J. and Roman can cover more ground right now than Jayda or Kelsey because of Solis and me. I suggest that the two of you move as far north and northeast as possible before camping. I still have reserves of power to draw on; Jayda and I will move as far as I can make it."

"I think we'll just stay here." Solis sat down on the sand with a wry smile. When Kelsey knelt beside him, he tugged her onto her lap so he could nuzzle his nose into her hair. He would never tease her for being the youngest of her friends simply because he was the youngest of his.

"We'll either meet up outside Prismatic, or wherever we find Morgan and Tariah," Roman said. "Maybe they can use their mind skills to reach out to anyone who doesn't make it to their side."

"I think that's a sound plan." Xander gathered his strength and let Jayda take some of his weight as they headed more east than north. Eventually they would turn and make their way north more than east, but they wanted some distance between themselves and the others to make their presence less conspicuous.

Roman and Grecia set out north, and C.J. and Dahlia headed northeast. In only a matter of minutes, Kelsey and Solis were left by themselves on the shore. He nuzzled her hair again and then trailed his lips to her neck. Her soft red aura lifted and made his mouth tingle with the anticipation for her taste.

Her lashes fluttered down as a shiver rippled through her body of sheer delight. His lips barely skimmed her sensitive skin, his breath cool against her heated flesh. It was a shocking contrast to where his hands rested on her back and hip. They burned hotly even through her cloak. She instinctively reached for him with her power, curling her emotions around him temptingly, trying to tell him what she wanted. What she needed.

He shuddered lightly and unfastened her cloak. Her breasts curved enticingly over the edge of her top and bikini, and he buried his nose there to taste her power. It was wild and spicy, sharp and sweet all at the same time. As strength poured back into his body, he tugged down her bikini so that her breasts were bared. Eagerly he closed his mouth over a taut nipple, thrilling to the soft whimper that she couldn't stop.

She buried her hands in his hair and pulled him closer. Her body was beginning to tremble with need. She burned hotter than her power. She could feel his emotions tangled to hers so that he could read everything she felt, and it had the effect of letting her feel what he did. For the first time, the volatile third emotion inside him did not scare her. She thrilled to it and reveled in being wanted that terribly. "Solis." It was little more than a pleading breath.

"If you intend to stop me," it was murmured huskily against her breast, "you had better do it now." She arched against him desperately, and his body throbbed painfully. Steam curled from both their bodies and made the air thick and sultry. He slowly slid his hand down her body and between her legs. Her skin was hot and soft and he wanted to taste her power everywhere from head to toe.

The feel of his touch on her inner thigh didn't frighten her this time. Her entire body twisted restlessly, begging for him to stop teasing her. She dragged his head up and kissed him wildly, and the feel of him as yet feeding on her power was erotic in a way it had never before felt. She could *feel* the strength pouring into her lover's body.

His knuckles brushed lightly against the sensitive flesh between her legs, and even with the layers of her clothing between them, the pleasure was sharp and terrifying. Her entire body instinctively tried to jerk back though she could not actually get away with his arm around her. Tears welled in her eyes as she burrowed against his chest. "Damn it!" Aching, needy, she quivered from head to toe. "That isn't fair to either of us!"

"If you're not ready, then you're not yet ready." His hands shook as he calmly stroked her arms and side, trying to soothe them both. He wanted her so badly that even his teeth ached, and his pants were far too tight on his arousal.

"How can you be this patient? This is torturing you." She wiped her eyes on his tunic.

"It is torture," he said softly, "but I don't find it that difficult to stop when you are afraid. That's why I let our emotions tangle as they did. I knew that feeling your fear would give me control." He tilted her chin up and gently kissed away her tears. "Anyone who could push beyond such a natural reaction is less than worthy of the gift of their lover's second puberty growth."

She took a long breath. "No more teasing me," she said firmly. "When you feed, keep your hands to yourself. Let me test my own emotions. I'll know when I'm ready. I'm sure I will." She framed his face and kissed him with all the love in her heart, letting him feel how terribly close to full bloom that third emotion was inside her.

He smoothed his fingers through her hair and savored how the curls clung to his skin as if they too would hold him. "Having you be mine fully," he said softly as he brushed her lips with his, "will make every minute of the wait worth it." His lips curved. "And it gives me an entirely new respect for my first lover. She was very patient with me as well."

Her lips curved in return. There was no jealousy in her heart for anyone in his past. There was no fear for anyone else in the future. She found it impossible to ever imagine him ever wanting or needing anyone else. That was the true miracle of the bond between Dragoons as far as she was concerned. That absolute confidence in each other, the surety in always knowing how the other would feel.

And her lover felt . . . hungry. His power was fed by feeding on her power, but his stomach had other needs. She grinned when he smiled sheepishly. "I'm getting hungry too. You find some fish and I'll put up the tent."

He reluctantly released her and got to his feet. If anything, the jump in the ocean might help cool him off. Steam still lifted from both their bodies.

She dug in her pack until she found the tiny little square box that the Kin had given her. She had been assured it was just like many other Kin inventions that could and would enlarge itself to proper size for whoever used it.

She held it out on the palm of her hand and waited for a few moments. Nothing happened. She poked the box with her other hand and it suddenly jumped into the air. She stifled a yelp as she fell back onto the sand and the box bounced away. With a sudden surge of power, it burst open and grew to a full sized tent that could easily hold both Kelsey and Solis comfortably.

Disgruntled, she turned her attention to making a small fire to cook whatever Solis managed to catch. It burned obediently on the sand, and she finally, belatedly, realized she was in a desert at last. She promptly fell over onto her face in the sand and spread her arms as if to hug the land. She had missed the desert something fierce! She loved the heat and the dusty ground. The taste and scent of the air. She wanted the world to have more plains and forests, certainly, because it would balance everything out, but she wouldn't want all of her deserts to go away for it!

Solis started laughing when he saw her. "I wondered how long it would take you to notice." Perfectly dry thanks to his power, he sat down beside the fire and began to efficiently clean the fish he had caught. Once that was done, he put them in the fire to cook. "And on a related note . . ." He pulled his desert clothes out of the pack. "I might as well change."

She sat up to watch unashamedly as he pulled off his clothes. She was no longer nervous with her Fury's body, and she watched with immense curiosity as he stripped naked. Only a day before, she had been afraid to confront the sight of his desire for her. Now, seeing the sight of his arousal blatantly declaring his need for her just made heat curl inside her body. Nerves did flutter, but they were not true fear. Just a slight trepidation.

He was utterly beautiful to her eyes. He seemed, to her, to be the ultimate in perfect beauty. And his complete lack of embarrassment or modesty allowed her the freedom to look her fill. If it hadn't been for those fluttery nerves, she would have tackled him down onto the sand to continue her exploration of his body. Watching him as she was, she could see the instant response of his body to the hot lash of her thoughts. It delighted her entirely. "You mean I don't have to actually touch you? I just have to think about it?"

He looked at her with eyes that smoldered. Rather than respond with words, he let his mind fill with everything and anything he wanted to do to her, with her. How he so desperately wanted to touch and taste her. He didn't censor a single image and gave her details he might have before hidden.

Her breath caught in her chest and her body instantly heated. It erased all of her efforts to cool down after the embrace. "Oh." It was about all she could think to say. If thoughts alone were going to do that to them, then they were going to have a very tempestuous relationship. Not that she was complaining, of course. Once she was an actual adult, she definitely wanted to explore those ideas in his mind.

A smile lit his face as he tugged on his vest. He walked over to where she sat and knelt down to kiss her softly.

"Never change," he told her softly. "You are perfect for me." He sat beside her and retrieved the fish from the fire. He divvied it between them, and a companionable silence remained as they ate.

She had never felt as perfectly at home as she did sitting in a desert with her Fury. And yet . . . she didn't feel entirely at home. She was far too conscious of being on Magi lands, too conscious of the fact that going near a city could be deadly.

"I don't think anyone would dare try to hurt us," he said softly, musingly. "General attitude seems to have been changing over the years, and the tentative truce between Magi and Dragons isn't about to be tested by any except the truly stupid. I think the Magi finally are beginning to realize that the danger is not from a Chronicle. It's from the Elite."

"Maybe we'll see the laws changed someday."

"Maybe so."

It was getting late, and they set up a protective shielding around their campsite so they could go to sleep. They removed the fire and shield in the morning as they let the tent collapse back down into its default state. When the area was as pristine as when they had found it, they set out across the desert.

Though it was morning, there wasn't much light. Kelsey carried their lantern as they walked. Solis had to be very careful not to expend even the slightest bit of power for fear of making the storms worse where they closed in overhead. The clouds of Flutterlies were more black than gray, and flickers of lightning were proof of the power they had already absorbed.

The air of the desert felt hot and humid. Both Dragoons could feel themselves sweating despite their respective powers. It didn't help any that partway into the afternoon, Kelsey's lines began to itch violently. Her power rioted under her skin. It burned into her lines and raised her agitation levels. She said nothing about it though Solis was well aware of it. Neither could figure out what would be causing it. It would make more sense for him to be agitated because of the storms, but he felt perfectly fine.

A short time later, she stopped walking entirely. "I can't stand it," she said fiercely. "Something's wrong, Solis. I can feel it. The last time I felt like this was when I was fighting Phi. It was as if I could sense the perversion of nature inside him."

His eyes sharpened and his nose flared as he smelled the air. Underneath the humidity of the storms, he could catch a whiff of tainted power. Without thinking twice, he gave her a sharp shove and sent her tumbling across the sand. He was barely in time. The blast of raw Soil power exploded the sand under his feet and flung him violently away. As he rolled to a stop, green blood began to flow from the wounds lining his legs and chest.

Kelsey scrambled up to her feet and rushed to his side. "Solis!" As she knelt beside him, her lines burned painfully. Her head jerked up and she looked to the side to see the familiar, and unwelcome, figure of Phi approaching. A low sound rumbled in her chest and her eyes flashed red warningly. "You."

Phi cackled at her. "We meet again, little Chronicle! Why don't you come to my side? We're going to destroy the Magi and make the world better! Don't you want to live peacefully? It'll be so much better when they're gone! You've got the potential we need to take command of the Lost Isle. Come on, Kelsey! Won't it be wonderful?"

Fire whipped up around her body and flew across the land at him before he could move. It slammed into his chest and flung him backwards through the air. "Attacking my Fury won't do anything except make me more determined to kill you!" she snarled.

Solis tried to lift himself to help, but a few of the wounds had gone to the bone. He didn't dare change into his natural form because of the storm, and Kelsey lacked the ability to heal with her power. "Xander." It was little more than a whisper. "Call Xander with your mind."

She had no idea if it would even work, but there was no reason not to try. With all the power she could muster, she sent out the mental cry toward Xander. Telepathy was supposed to be only for reading minds, but perhaps his being an Elder would let him feel her from a distance.

Phi had staggered back up to his feet, and yellow blood oozed from his wounds and stained his clothes. The scent was putrid and horrid in the humid atmosphere, and the clouds themselves seethed as if in protest. The land rumbled softly. It was unstable enough without the risk of battle.

He shot a tangle of vines at Kelsey and she reached out to grab onto them. The thorns bit into her flesh but she held on and sent fire whipping down the branches back toward him. He released the vines swiftly and instead began to agitate the quake until the ground started to roll and rock violently.

Kelsey held onto Solis tightly. She knew that if she left his side, then he would be an easy target. She couldn't risk losing him. Not Solis. He was the one thing she could never give up. If she lost him, then she would have nothing.

Phi was so busy trying to find an open shot that he didn't realize they were no longer alone until a massive fireball slammed into his back and sent him flying headfirst into the sand. When he managed to get free and scramble around, he saw Xander and Jayda approaching quickly.

While Xander went after Phi, Jayda ran over to Kelsey and Solis. She dropped down beside them with a soft curse as she saw the Fury's wounds. "Kel, shield me. Block the storm from getting my power so that I can heal these wounds."

Kelsey instantly surrounded them in a bubble of fire. Even if Jayda's power tried to escape, it would simply turn to steam. "Can you heal him with the quake?" she asked. It was a legitimate concern when the land still shook.

"I'm going to try." She formed a needle of ice and thread of water and got to work stitching the first of the truly terrible wounds. "He knew exactly what he was doing when he went after you here," she said grimly.

Phi barely spared the fire bubble a second look as he backed slowly away from Xander. The Fury Elder had fire swirling around his hands and feet, and his teeth bared in a soft snarl. "What are you doing here?" Phi demanded.

"You attacked my clan; what do you think I'm doing here?" was the retort. He shot another fireball at Phi and sent the Elite member scrambling. Almost lazily, he shot yet another fireball and had him dodging back the other way. "How does it feel to be on the receiving end for once?"

Phi managed to catch a breath only to lose it when the ground suddenly flung him straight into the air. When he landed painfully, he could feel at least one rib crack in the impact. His eyes jerked to the side and he saw the familiar form of C.J. and Dahlia. The male Chronicle's eyes were livid with an unexpected rage.

Immense thorns burst out of the ground and threatened to impale Phi entirely. "Don't forget us," Grecia warned as she and Roman joined Kelsey and Jayda. Both ducked into the bubble and knelt down. "Let me help," she said to Jayda. "I can use more power safely. Let me take over."

Dahlia, of no use with her Air power, went to aid the others with Solis. C.J., though not necessarily equipped for battle, joined Xander. Because Jayda had stopped using power, Kelsey took down the bubble and got to her feet to go join the males in battle. "You heard me," she said to Xander.

"I did." He ran a hand down her hair gently. "You scared me soundly, fledgling. Dragons are notoriously protective of their families." He rested his other hand on C.J.'s shoulder. "Cover us," he told the younger male. "If you think you can attack, then do it. Remember, your power is designed for art not combat."

Phi spit blood out of his mouth, either uncaring or unseeing when the yellow liquid burned the sand. "It takes this many to kill one measly Master Magi?" he taunted. "Maybe you aren't as powerful as you think you are. Don't you want a peaceful world without war-hungry Magi?"

"And you're any better?" C.J. demanded. He looked at Xander with a scowl. "Can't you just eat him?"

Xander bared his teeth as Phi went white. "I might get indigestion, but I'm willing to risk it." He started to glow as if to turn into his Dragon form.

Phi panicked and shot as big a blast of power as he could at the Elder. Death by being eaten was not only said to be extremely painful, but it was also the most humiliating way a Dragon could kill someone. It meant that they saw their victim as being of no more value than food, and to a race that valued life . . . that was a significant difference.

The Elite Magi was so busy trying to keep Xander away that he didn't even notice that Kelsey had moved out from behind the shield that C.J. had made. In fact, he only knew she wasn't there when he realized she stood right behind him. He went lethally still as her slender hand closed around the back of his neck.

"I don't hate you," she said quietly. "Perhaps the saddest thing is that I feel nothing for you at all." Her hand began to burn hotly as fire rippled across her lines and flowed down her arm. "Even Lucksphere has turned her back on you."

He opened his mouth but nothing emerged. The fire engulfed him without warning and the flames swept from head to toe. They burned hotter and hotter until the air quivered with heat waves. The smell of burning tainted blood filled the air and everyone gagged. Then, blessedly, he turned to ashes. The storms overhead began to rain viciously and poured down water that washed away the remains of the Elite.

The land stopped its shaking as Xander, Kelsey, and C.J. went to join the others. Solis was sitting upright while Grecia healed the last of his wounds. A few were still pink lines but rapidly healing as well. "Thanks," he said to Grecia and Jayda alike. When Kelsey knelt and threw her arms around him, he pulled her as close as he could. "I'm fine," he said into her hair. "I promise."

"Maybe splitting up was not the best of ideas," Roman admitted quietly as he sat down beside Grecia. "The way the elements fall, these storms prevent one half of us from being able to use our powers. And in our two Soil Elements' case, they aren't designed for battle. Grecia is a healer and C.J. is an artisan."

"Then at this point," Dahlia spoke up, "we need to stay together. It is a certainty that the rest of the Elite will be coming after us." The others glanced at her in agreement and immediately began to grin. She felt her cheeks slowly heating. "What?" she asked warily. It dawned on her and she hastily slapped a hand over her neck. Sure enough, she could feel the little abrasion. "C.J.!" she scolded. "You promised!"

He grinned mischievously. "I couldn't resist." He held out his hands and they could all see where a portion of his lines had significantly darkened. "I noticed this on Jayda and Roman and now me," he said to Xander. "Kelsey's lines aren't darker, and she and Solis aren't lovers. It's connected, isn't it?"

"It is an indication of a portion of your journey being done," he explained softly. "In the very old days, the final stage of your journey would be taking your lover, not the first. The final portion of your lines won't darken until you reach the Isle, if what happened to Tariah and Morgan holds true."

"Xander?" Kelsey suddenly asked. "Did Chronicles finish second puberty before finding their Fury in the old days?"

He frowned thoughtfully as he looked back to those years. "You know," he said slowly, "I don't think they did. Most, I believe, were like Jayda or Morgan. They had gone through the entire process—whether normal or accelerated I couldn't say—but they had never 'graduated' into being an adult. There might have been a few exceptions that I am unaware of, but I don't recall ever meeting a Chronicle who was fully an adult before they finished their journey and found their Fury."

"Lovers share power," Dahlia said softly. "Perhaps it is too uncomfortable for a Chronicle to share their power with any except their Fury." She took a soft breath, willing to admit her truth to help make sense of it all. "And some Furies are made that way as well."

"Oh, Dahlia." Grecia hugged her friend. "I had no idea. No wonder C.J. is perfect for you."

"So," Roman said slowly, studying his lines, "one portion of our journey is to take our Fury. Another portion is to find the Isle. What would the third portion be?"

"That," came an unexpected and yet familiar male voice, "we will simply have to wait and see."

Everyone turned sharply, and Kelsey took a swift breath as she recognized the four people standing just behind them. The two Chronicles were much shorter than average for Magi height and had matching auburn hair and silver eyes. They looked enough alike to be twins. The male Fury was of average Magi height, and the female Fury was much shorter, though not as short as the female Chronicle.

"Well, then," Xander said softly. "How long have you been standing there?"

Morgan grinned. "We followed the explosions. I knew Kelsey's temper would get the better of someone someday."

His smile softened as he looked at the young woman he had loved as if she were his daughter. All of his children had grown up. "Hey there, Soot."

She leapt to her feet and tackled him straight to the sand in a single bound. A sob caught in her throat as she clung onto him. "You promised us!" she almost wailed. "You *promised*, Morgan!"

It took less than a second for the other three Chronicles to scramble over to cling onto Morgan as well. All of them were taller than he was, except for Kelsey who was the same height, and it broke his heart that he had not gotten to see them grow up. "I'm so sorry," he whispered.

Tariah knelt down beside him. She had not gotten to know the four children the way he had, but it had not stopped her from loving them the minute she had met them for such a brief time those years before. "We were looking," she confessed. "We knew you had to be starting second puberty soon and that that could have an effect on what Morgan did. You can't stop a Chronicle from journeying."

Kelsey turned and hugged her fiercely but leaned back again with a bemused look on her face. "When did you get shorter than me?"

Morgan studied her lines, saw no darkened portions, and looked at Solis with a wry smile. "I'm sorry," he said dryly.

Solis grinned when Kelsey stuck her tongue out at Morgan. "I'm not."

"I think we need to camp here," Dominic said. "We have some things to discuss, and we're not going to get anywhere once it is fully night. The storm is getting worse." It was a legitimate concern since the pouring rain had removed any remaining ability to see more than fifty feet ahead.

And that alone was deeply concerning to all present. Deserts on Lucksphere were not known for rainstorms.

There was no knowing what sort of damage could be done to the cities scattered across the landscape. There was no protection from flooding. No protection from mudslides sweeping in from tall dunes. There was a tenuous balance in place that even the slightest vibration might upset.

At this rate, the Elite weren't going to need the Chronicles to help destroy the Magi. If just destroying Phi had done this to Spectrum, what would destroying the others do to the rest of the world?

Part Three

~Summer~

Chapter Nineteen

The storm was unrelenting with its fury. Kelsey dug out the tiny tent box from her pack and held it up. "Will it get big enough for all of us?"

"It should." C.J. grinned. "Morgan's short."

"Did they have to grow up?" Morgan complained to Tariah. "Now I'll have forever with them making fun of my height." Not that he truly minded, of course. Nothing could take away his happiness at having his children, though nearly all adults now, back together again. And it clenched his heart to see them all wearing the cloak of the Black Magi.

"It'll get old after a century or two," she assured him. "And as for the tent, I would assume it ought to get big enough. That's the whole point of Kin inventions. Daylar was showing off a new meal type to me recently that can become dinner for a whole family. They all have far too much time on their hands."

Kelsey tossed the box onto the ground a few feet away and it promptly grew into a full-size tent. As soon as everyone started ducking inside, it grew proportionately bigger. It allowed for enough room for everyone to sit or stand comfortably though several knees bumped. No one minded.

"How are your wounds?" Dominic asked Solis.

"Nearly gone. Grecia and Jayda took care of me." His face darkened with a frown. "Phi knew exactly what he was doing when he attacked me like he did. Whether he happened to find Kelsey and me first, or he was specifically looking for her, I don't know. But we are indeed at a disadvantage on Spectrum right now."

"There aren't many places we will have an advantage." Jazz kept an arm lightly around Morgan's waist.

She knew that his calm manner hid his guilt for not finding the four children sooner. "The storms are spreading into the oceans. Glacia is beginning to have full blizzards. Choral is dealing with desert tornados, and Carnelian is suffering like Spectrum."

"What about Kindred?" Kelsey asked swiftly, thinking of Etude and their other friends.

"Curiously," Tariah said, "it has been spared. The Isle of Dragons has been spared. It would seem that only Magi lands are under siege from nature. But that's to be expected, considering what the Elite have been doing. They deliberately tore up the balance of Magi lands."

"But they haven't found the Lost Isle," Dahlia murmured. "If they had, there wouldn't even be a world left."

"What isle?" Roman asked.

"When the massacre occurred," Xander began softly, "the Chronicles and Furies retreated to the isle they had called home. The genocide occurred there. The power from the battle seeped into the very land." His eyes closed. "I was there. But even now I don't remember what the land looked like or where it is. That entire time is sketchy in my mind, at best."

"That kind of power," whispered Jayda, "could tear apart anyone who tried to claim it!" She looked at Morgan and Tariah, saw the steadiness in their matching silver eyes, and felt her heart stop. "You can't intend to . . . to try to take command of it! It might kill you!"

"But it might not." Tariah and Morgan laced their fingers together. "It's something we've talked about for nine years," Tariah said quietly. "We're the strongest Chronicles here. We're not . . . normal Chronicles, somehow. And we . . . well, we made a promise. To end what was started a thousand years ago."

"Tariah, I have a question." C.J. sat forward to see her

better. "Would you say that it is perfectly normal for Chronicles to accelerate through second puberty when their Fury is there, but to take a regular amount of time if they aren't?"

She looked at Morgan. "You were normal, right?"

"Relatively speaking."

She looked at Jayda. "And you?"

"I believe so. It was several months from when I think it started to when I think it ended. I've thought it might be because of Xander's age that I was all but done with second puberty. It would be cruel to make him wait longer than he had to claim me." She slid her hand into his tenderly.

"I was thinking age might have something to do with it too," Kelsey put in. "The relative age of the Fury seems to have had a distinct impact on where in second puberty their Chronicle is when they meet. And Xander thinks that Chronicles never 'graduated' until meeting their Furies in the old days."

Tariah frowned thoughtfully, and Dominic smiled as he watched her mind move too quickly for even him to follow. After a moment, she said slowly, "What it really comes down to is that Lucksphere wants to survive above everything else. Chronicles were made to take in the excess power in the land and filter it through their Furies, whose Dragon birth gives them the capacity to process infinite power. But that dichotomy is dependent on the Fury and Chronicle being Dragoons."

Grecia's brows lifted. "You mean that we feed on our Chronicle's power more effectively when we're lovers?" She thought back, wondering if she had noticed any difference from the first time she had fed on Roman's power to the most recent time. An obvious difference was, of course, *how* she fed and from where, but his power *did* seem sweeter and more potent now that they were lovers. "I didn't think anything of it," she murmured. "I just assumed it was my emotions making it different."

"What about this?" Roman asked. "It crossed my mind when Grecia and I met that if Furies don't have infinite power, then how do they live so long without their Chronicle? Look at Xander."

Slowly, Tariah said, "A Fury knows when their Chronicle is born and when they die. That means there is a connection that exists before birth. That connection is what becomes a Chronicle's lines. So that connection is what sustains a Fury. And the older a Fury, the more effort the planet has needed to make to sustain them without a Chronicle. So their Chronicle is more likely to be ready to become a Dragoon."

"Again, it comes down to Lucksphere wanting to survive."

Xander suddenly frowned. There was something in his mind, something that he had forgotten. He was sure that it was critically important, but he simply could not call it up. It had to have been from that lost time. Were his missing memories another act of the planet in an effort to survive? Then why would they have all forgotten the Elite? That certainly wasn't helping anyone.

"Morgan," Jayda spoke up, "can you do anything for Xander? His entire memory of the final fight during the War is gone. He keeps thinking there was something important, that there's something we need to know, but it's simply not there. It's not like what you did for us by fragmenting our memories. They're not there at all."

"That's impossible," Morgan disagreed instantly. "Memories can't be fully erased. I've been thinking about it for nine years, and I think we do still have our memories of the Elite. They've been fragmented smaller than bits of sand, and our arrangement of memories were changed so that we didn't notice the lack."

"But could you or Tariah do something for him?" Dahlia asked. "Maybe, if anything, he can remember where the Lost Isle is."

"We can't do anything here and now." Tariah shook her head. "Not with the storms. Morgan is Air and I am Water. With our individual strength let alone our collective . . ."

"Then where do we go now? We can't go to the Isle, even if you could lead us," Xander noted. "Jayda, Kelsey, C.J., and Roman all must finish their journeys." He hesitated, then said slowly, "We can *guess* the location of the Lost Isle on the basis of where everything else is. And if you think about it, it might just make sense to you as well. Where is the one place no one can sail to?"

Jayda took a sharp breath. "South from Glacia. That huge expanse of ocean that no ship can pass through. Of course."

"We can't just sail into those storms and hope for the best," Solis pointed out reasonably. "We need to have directions or we're going to be stuck in there forever. What if we headed back to the ocean and went out to sea away from the storms here so that Morgan and Tariah can get into Xander's head?"

"That may be our best bet," Morgan agreed.

Because it was late, and everyone was tired, it was decided to keep camp where they were in the hopes of the rain passing. They stuck with the single giant tent and everyone dug out blankets. In a short amount of time, everyone settled down in pairs.

Kelsey couldn't sleep. There were too many thoughts rushing through her head in too many directions. Too many emotions inside her growing heart. She could only lie in Solis' arms and stare sightlessly at the wall of the tent. Softly, she heard Morgan ask, "What's wrong, Soot?"

Tears burned her eyes at the nickname. She shifted enough to turn her head and found him watching her over the top of Jazz's head. His Fury looked impossibly tiny next to him, but she held him no less fiercely than Solis held

Kelsey. "A lot of things," she finally said softly. "I'm just feeling overwhelmed."

"And rightfully so. Second puberty is a big enough upheaval without going through it in a matter of weeks while in the middle of fighting simply to survive. You ought to talk to Tariah about it. She went through the very same thing. But her Water element gives her more of a cool head than your Fire one gives you."

After a moment of silence, she whispered fiercely, "You promised me, Morgan. You promised to come find us. Why didn't you?"

"I tried," he said tiredly. The note in his voice broke her heart because it made him sound too much older than he was. "Tariah and I would take turns passing by cities, praying we might find one of you. We didn't dare ask anyone for fear of drawing attention to you."

"I was living as a Master Magi. I'm a Weaponsmith. You had to have heard about me. I couldn't get people to *not* talk about me." She took a soft breath. "Even not remembering, it hurt. I knew there was something I didn't remember, someone I cared so much about. And now I can't even tell Mom and Dad. Am I going to ever see them again?"

"You will," he promised. "I still see my parents. And if we can do what we intend to, can get rid of the Elite, maybe there will be a day not far in the future when we can go anywhere and do anything. The attitude is slowly changing, Soot. We can't undo things overnight. But we can start the efforts."

She sniffed and wiped at her eyes. "You still think you know everything."

He smiled. "I do know everything. I have eyes on the back of my head, remember?"

"You fibbed. I looked but I never found them." She suddenly smiled at the memories. "I caused you so much trouble, didn't I?"

"Of course. But there wasn't a day that my world wasn't better because you were in it. Each of you four . . . the moment I met you, I was wrapped around your fingers. But you were the worst of them all."

"I just wanted you to be proud of me," she whispered. "I think that even not remembering, that was all I ever wanted."

"I don't think anyone else could ever be more proud." His silver eyes softened. "I have every hope that if I have a daughter, you'll teach her all of your bad habits so that my life is never boring even when you're off living with Solis in a desert and raising tiny hellions to torment his uncle with."

"His uncle?"

He grinned. "One of the Council Elders. They're sort of fascinated and terrified of Tariah all at the same time. Something tells me that between the two of you, you'll have those stodgy old Dragons whipped into shape in no time." His smile softened. "Go to sleep, Soot. It'll be all right. We're all together, and we can't be stopped."

Just hearing him say it made it easier to believe. With a little sigh, she snuggled more firmly into Solis' arms and closed her eyes. Thinking about tormenting the Council Elders, she fell asleep smiling.

They shared breakfast in the morning. Tariah had brought enough to feed an army, and her family was more than happy for it. She could cook in a way that no one else ever could. C.J., who had grown up with an amazing cook for a mother, even had to admit Tariah was far better. "But don't tell her I said that," he pleaded.

The rain had become a very light drizzle though it was still no lighter out. Kelsey broke down the tent again and propped her hands on her hips. "It occurs to me that our plan is all fine and good, but we can't possibly fly north. We're going to need a boat or two. Are there any towns close enough that we could go to?"

"There's one further north along the coast," Dahlia

said. "It's not very big, but they might be willing to sell us a boat of some type." She grimaced. "Well, sell to Morgan and Tariah, anyway. No one yet knows anything about the rest of us except for the Kin."

"I'm not going to hide." Roman's voice was very soft. "I refuse to hide. I'm not going to be ashamed of what I am. If the Magi don't like it, that's their issue. We're the only ones who can stop the Elite, and unless the Magi really do want the world to be destroyed, they're going to know it."

"Then we'll go north." Tariah shrugged with a wry smile. "It'll be uncomfortable, but they won't really try anything." She jerked a thumb toward Xander. "Would you want to be on his bad side?"

"No," C.J. said with a grin.

"He's not that bad." Jayda rubbed her cheek against Xander's shoulder softly. As long as he was near, she no longer had to fear her sensitivity to people would tear her apart. His presence alone created a buffer for her. Though her friends didn't seem to affect her, the city would be another story entirely.

Uncaring of where they were or who they were with, he swung her up into his arms and kissed her soundly. She was more precious to him than anything in the world. Every lonely, terrifying minute of waiting had been worth it the instant she had smiled at him. He had known there had to be a reason why he survived so long. And here she was, her black eyes always filled with love for him.

"I think someone is wrapped around someone else's finger," Jazz told Dominic gravely.

He nodded sagely. "Quite so, Jazz. He's getting his just desserts for how he's always teased me about Tariah. There's no one more deserving."

Xander put Jayda down and distinctly ignored the younger Furies. He skimmed his fingers through his lover's hair with a smile. "You were going to tell Tariah something," he reminded her. "You might as well tell her now."

"That's right." She turned to smile at Tariah. "I'm a doctor," she offered. "A very good one. Xander says that you're pregnant, and I want to be the one who tends to you."

"You are?" Grecia brightened. "Tariah, that's wonderful! Oh, there hasn't been a Dragoon baby since well before the war!" Her eyes widened in shock as she realized. "Oh my," she said softly as she looked at Xander. "Wasn't the last one . . . ?"

"Yes," he said softly. "It was." When brows lifted, he said, "The last Dragoon children born before the war were a daughter to the female Chronis twin and a son to the male Chronis twin. I have every confidence that it is from those two that you are descended," he told Morgan and Tariah.

C.J. eyed Tariah and then Dominic and then back again. "So . . . which are you carrying? I would guess that a half-and-half baby isn't likely. Is it a Magi or a Dragon?"

"No Dragon!" Tariah muttered. "No eggs!"

Jayda wrapped an arm around her shoulders soothingly. "I will study with the Dragon doctors," she said warmly, "and I'll know exactly how to care for you if it happens that you're carrying a Dragon. The odds are more to be that it is a Magi because you are a Chronicle, but you never know what'll happen in the future."

"If it's you, Jayda," she conceded, "I guess it'll be okay." She smiled up at the taller girl. "Were you living as a Master Magi doctor? Where?"

"Glacia. Arctica to be precise. I lived outside of town because it was too painful to be near people." Without conceit, she said, "I was the best healer on Glacia. When the Elite attacked, I went into the mountains to save people from an avalanche and cave-in. That was how I found Xander." The look she shot her lover was teasing. "His head wasn't quite strong enough to fully handle a nosedive down the mountainside."

He nipped at her power with his in retaliation though he was smiling as well. Though more mature than her brothers and sister, she was still no less sassy, and he couldn't have been happier.

"What about the rest of you?" Jazz asked curiously. "You were living as Master Magi too, correct?"

"We were." Roman tucked his hands in his pockets. "I lived outside Mirah on a farm. I ran a windmill." Reluctantly, he admitted, "And I did some art with my best friend who is a Fire Magi. She would make glass figurines and I would etch them."

"I knew you were hiding something," C.J. grumbled. He grinned. "Though I'm one to talk. I was living outside Symphony. I'm a weaver. Some of my stuff is hanging in the Magi king's palace, though I think he'd be alarmed to learn his art was made by a Chronicle. Then again, maybe not. He's not exactly *pushing* the laws."

"I'm a Weaponsmith," Kelsey offered. "I got into this whole situation because the Militia wanted me to make them new weapons. Phi attacked us before I could head home, and Etude, my Kin partner, went to get Solis since we had seen him flying past. We didn't know he was a Fury until he awoke me." She thought of Ilian for a moment and her eyes darkened with sadness. It must have been a horrible shock to him. If they ever met again, what would he say? What would she say?

It was less than half a day of walking before they approached the town. It wasn't very large but its convenient location beside the ocean allowed for a decent enough trade and rate of visitors. Cruise ships would stop along the way, and in fact, there was one docked at that immediate moment.

There was also a Militia ship docked.

"Are we sure we want to go into town?" Roman

rubbed the side of his face where his lines rested. "I know I said I didn't want to hide, but I'm not sure I want to provoke the Militia either."

Grecia opened the bag of sand she wore and swiftly wove a hood to go on his cloak. She gave gloves to C.J. to cover his hands, and he, Kelsey, and Jayda closed their cloaks entirely. Once Roman pulled the hood far enough over his head, there was no noticing that they were Chronicles.

"Why are the Black Magi reforming?" Jayda asked the twins.

"To find other Master Magi to help stop the Elite," Tariah answered promptly. "To create a new sanctuary so they don't have to live as Jayda did, or Roman did. Most of you were thought to be dead when you disappeared, right? Well, obviously, that didn't happen. We managed to save all of you." She studied the four Furies. "And, clearly, Dragons are helping us for obvious reasons. No one knows the difference between Dragon and Fury without seeing their lines."

As the four Furies had already closed their cloaks, their lines were also hidden. It was possible someone might make the correct assumption based on the even number of males and females and the opposing elements, but few Magi truly knew anything about Chronicles.

"We can send letters to our parents to let them know we're alive, can't we?" C.J. asked hopefully.

"No need," Morgan said. "When Tariah wrote to Daylar the last time, she asked him to spread the word to Kin to have your parents retrieved and taken to Kindred for safety. By now, they should be there and away from danger." Something painful filled his eyes. "I don't want what nearly happened to my parents, and what did happen to Tariah's, to happen to them."

"And you'll give them back their memories too?" Kelsey asked pointedly.

He smiled. "Yes, Soot, I will."

The storm was over the town though it did not rain. People went about their normal lives with an undercurrent of tension. Militia soldiers walked around visibly armed as they made sure the people were protected. The upheaval in the land outside had turned normal creatures into monsters, and they crept close, just waiting for a chance to destroy anything in their way.

Many startled looks shot toward Morgan and Tariah as they were recognized, but no one outright said anything to them. Xander, not recognizable as a Fury, was nonetheless recognizable as a Dragon Elder, and the tentative truce was as fragile as the state of the world. Some people whispered, but not even sensitive Jayda could feel any true malice in the air.

While Morgan haggled with a boat maker for a good price on a decent enough boat that could carry them where they needed, the others wandered a few feet away to look at the wares on sale at the market. With no hood on her cloak, Kelsey's vibrant hair burned brightly in the desert air despite the gloomy light. It was as powerful as a beacon, unmistakable to anyone who had ever met her in the past. She only became aware of her distinction when a soft and familiar voice asked behind her, "Kelsey?"

She straightened and turned around swiftly to discover the familiar form of Argyle Ilian Deepforge behind her. His handsome face was filled with shock and hope mingled, and his eyes held a touch of fear. "Ilian," she said softly. She instinctively held her cloak more tightly closed.

His eyes lowered before moving to Solis, who had said nothing, and then to the others who wore the cloak of the true Black Magi. His gaze lingered on Morgan and Tariah, and then came back to Kelsey. "I am glad you escaped from Phi, Master Kelsey," he said formally. "When I reached the site of the battle, both of you were gone. We had feared for the worst. Yours is a gift the Magi couldn't stand to lose."

Solis softly rested his hand on the small of Kelsey's back. Her entire body trembled, and her emotions were a chaotic tangle of sadness and relief. "We Dragons," he said calmly, "were sent out by the Chronis twins to retrieve Master Magi and keep them safe from the Elite. I have been given the task of protecting Kelsey."

"So the Black Magi are reforming."

"We are." Kelsey found a smile. "I was always a Black Magi. Morgan sent me away for safety nine years ago but kept his promise to find me again. We want to stop the Elite." She shook her head. "We *will* stop the Elite."

Roman had only been listening with half an ear when he suddenly caught the scent of a familiar tainted power and his lines began to burn. His head jerked up. Grecia, reading his mind and emotions, was right beside him as they leapt for Solis and Kelsey. Grecia knocked Solis halfway down the street. Roman took Kelsey another direction and rolled with her in his arms safely. Only moments after they were safe, a massive lightning bolt struck the ground where they had been standing.

People screamed and scrambled for cover. The clouds tore open and started pouring rain. Ilian looked around sharply. "Stay calm and go inside!" he ordered. "Militia, escort any children and seniors to safety!"

Beta's strident cackle cut through the air. "You're wasting your breath, Argyle! I'm going to level this place!" She walked forward from the shadows, and her Elite cloak was a distinct mockery of the cloak worn by the others. "We meet again, Chronicle Roman!"

There was no denying it. In his effort to save Kelsey, his hood had fallen back to reveal his face. When he pulled Kelsey to her feet, her cloak also fell open to reveal the lines going down her arms and legs. "I'd have preferred never to see your face again," he retorted.

Grecia's eyes flickered with warning rage. "I claim

Fury Right," she said as she stepped forward. As Beta slowly paled, a cool smile touched her lips. "I see you understand what that means. Good."

"Fury Right," Solis explained softly for the new Chronicles and Ilian's benefit, "is the right to kill any who threatens the life of a Fury's Chronicle. Had Phi not gotten the jump on us, I would have claimed it against him."

Ilian remained silent for several moments. Fighting the Elite was supposed to be the matter of the Militia. His orders were very clear. Yet, very distinctly, he stepped back. "The Militia will bow to your right," he told Grecia. "We have trampled on the rights of Furies and Chronicles for long enough. I will not see it anymore."

"Nor will I."

Jayda's head swung around sharply at the familiar female voice. "Quinn!"

Argyle Quinn Flyer stepped forward from the other side of the street, her eyes dark and steady as she looked at Beta. The Elite fanatic had been caught in a crossfire of Magi, Furies, and Chronicles. "If there is any blight on the land," she said distinctly, "it is the Elite. I watched Jayda Lakemore risk her life and sanity to save others time and again. And I have told the king as much." She looked at Morgan and Tariah. "Morgan and Tariah Chronis. I bring an official declaration from the Magi king. He wishes to meet with you to discuss a formal treaty of peace. As of this moment, all Chronicles are welcome in Magi cities."

"Look at that, Beta," Roman said mockingly. "The Elite have done something good for the world. You helped the Magi see who the real threat is."

In a burst of furious power, she sent a tornado whipping down the middle of the street. It was aimed directly for Ilian, but ropes of Soil shot around his body and yanked him out of the way. He landed on his ass at C.J.'s feet, and the Chronicle winced. "Sorry about that. I didn't have time to aim."

"I won't complain. That I assure you."

The storm began to gather in violence as Beta whirled and lobbed another attack. The tainted touch of her power began to turn the dark clouds a sickening shade of yellow-gray, and the rain began to sting like acid. The land quivered warningly, and waves started rolling up from the sea and hitting the docks viciously.

We have to get out of the city! Morgan's voice rang in the minds of all Chronicles and Furies present.

Tariah followed him with her own order, *Roman, she wants you specifically. You must lure her out!*

Even Xander was slightly nonplussed that Morgan and Tariah had the ability to speak directly into the minds of others. He had never heard of such a thing before, though it wasn't the first time that the twins had done something beyond the normal realm of possibility. They were constantly defying the laws of power, as if Lucksphere herself blessed them.

Roman didn't question either of his leaders. He shot a taunting blast of lightning at Beta that deliberately missed her by inches. The power absorbed by the clouds promptly dissipated the ugly yellow tint, and the rain was purified. "If you want me, come and get me, Beta. Oh, that's right. You tried that once. You never stood a chance, old lady."

Her shriek seared the ears of those who heard it, and she went rushing after him as he turned and ran out of the city. Grecia was right on her heels, though Beta didn't know it. The Elite's eyes fully fixed on Roman. She wanted to wipe the smug look off his face and vent her wounded pride. What did that . . . *reptile* have that she didn't!?

When they were far enough out, he swiveled around and fired a tornado at her. It didn't seem to be making the storm worse, and it distinctly prevented the Elite's taint from spreading. Still, he was cautious. The land continued its violently shaking.

Just focus on destroying her, came Tariah's voice in his mind. *C.J. and Jazz are working on controlling the land in the city. Hurry, Roman!*

Breathing hard, Beta started at him malevolently. "Do you think you can destroy me?"

"I can," Grecia taunted from somewhere behind and above her.

Her dead heart froze in her chest as she realized there was only one way that Grecia's voice could be so far over her head and carry such a vibration of power. She carefully turned around and stopped breathing as she saw the Fury in Dragon form towering over her. All she could manage was a single squeal as Grecia's claw closed hard around her body. "Don't eat me!" she shrieked as she saw massive teeth looming close.

"And get indigestion? You jest." She hurled Beta through the air and didn't so much as flinch when the Magi bounced hard and painfully. Yellow blood oozed down Beta's side from where a cracked rib poked through her skin, and Grecia bared her teeth. "Lucksphere herself has turned against the Elite. Your yellow blood is proof of it."

Beta painfully began to gather all of her remaining power. "You won't win," she snarled raggedly. "I'm not going to let you walk away from this so easily!"

Realizing what she was about to do, Grecia grabbed Roman and flew backwards swiftly. Beta's power rose as she prepared to detonate herself, and the resulting shockwave was sure to tear apart the already fragile land. But just as she reached critical mass and her hair began to smoke, the area was lit by a blinding flash of light from a massive lightning bolt as big as Grecia. It struck Beta directly, as if it deliberately targeted her.

The sharp crack reverberated off the eerie silence a second later. There was nothing left of Beta. There wasn't even a sign of ashes as there had been with Phi. The lightning bolt had more than destroyed her. It had erased her entirely.

The land slowly began to stop trembling as the steadying waves from C.J. and Jazz were able to spread further. The storm lessened in its rage, softening to little more than a light drizzle yet again. The ocean continued to seethe angrily, but without its violence of only minutes before.

"Did she . . . she didn't detonate her power," Roman said softly.

Grecia's claws tightened protectively and possessively around him. "She didn't, no. But something or someone else certainly did." She went back into her Magi form, and her arms remained tight around his waist even though he was suddenly taller. "We better go back into the city and see what damage was done."

As they turned and walked, he glanced back over his shoulder to where Beta had stood. There wasn't even a burn mark. Whoever had used the storm's lightning had done so naturally. As naturally as the removed memories in everyone's minds.

Just what was really going on?

Chapter Twenty

The city was quiet and subdued. The Militia moved quickly to ensure that no one had been harmed. The shocking arrival of Beta and the resulting defense of the city by the Dragoons had thrown everyone off balance. More than even Quinn's proclamation.

"I don't understand," Jayda said quietly to Quinn as they stood with the others and Ilian. "Were you telling the truth, or was that just to get at Beta?"

"It was the truth, Jayda," she said. "I went right from Glacia to Prismatic. It was a risk. I knew it was a risk. But it was one I needed to take. I knew that in the worst-case scenario, people might know you were a Chronicle, but there are few who would dare try to harm you, especially with an Elder for your mate."

"You just walked into the throne room and told the king what was going on?" Tariah asked skeptically.

C.J. looked at Dahlia. "And you said I had no self-preservation."

His Fury snorted softly. "You don't."

Quinn shook her head. "Argyles are the highest rank of the Militia. We are given certain rights, and direct contact with the king is among them. I told him what I had witnessed without embellishing anything. I didn't have to. He wants to change the laws, but was hesitant to do so until the people could believe and the Elite might be less of a threat."

Xander studied her speculatively. "Why does he care so much?"

"He has a son," Grecia murmured. "Coming close to first puberty, isn't he? He fears his son being a Chronicle. He fears more that his son might be killed by a law he himself could have changed."

"But what about the people?" Solis asked.

"Chronicles."

They all turned and discovered that most of the people in the city had gathered. Instinctively, the Furies moved to protectively shelter their Chronicles. Xander also put himself in front of Ilian and Quinn, refusing to see them harmed for their compassion.

An older man stepped forward from the crowd with hands spread to show he was unarmed. "We Magi . . . we were wrong." The words were soft but clearly heard. "We can never make up for a thousand years of hate in a single night. It may be centuries before things are the way they should be. But we know we were wrong. These last nine years have shown us all. Our world has shown us."

A woman said, "If you weren't supposed to be here, then you wouldn't keep being born. And just now, we could all see it, that the storm was calmed by the younger Air Chronicle's power. You protected us from the Elite when you had no need to."

"You will always be welcome in Lumin," another man offered. "All of you."

"Should we go to the king?" Tariah asked Morgan. "Prismatic is days from here, and I don't think we have days. But we should at least send him a letter, or do something to acknowledge what he's said and done."

"There is no need." Quinn glanced toward the shadows of an alley between two buildings. "Am I still being demoted for shoving you out of the way?" she asked mildly.

A man stepped forward and pulled down the hood on the cloak he wore. He was unfamiliar to all the Dragoons, but he was certainly familiar to the Magi. There rose a collective gasp of shock, and many elbows bumped and collided as all the Magi hastily made the gesture of respect.

"I take it he's the king?" Jayda whispered to Xander.

He quirked a single brow. "Apparently so." He studied the shorter male intently. Plain in the face and overall average in height and frame, he was as yet slightly stronger than average in whatever power he possessed. There was an intelligence in his eyes that couldn't be hidden. "I'm surprised he journeyed this far."

"A king can't stay cooped up in his palace, no matter how badly his Argyles try to make him," the king noted reasonably. He made the gesture of respect to all those present. "I am Finus Clertain, Water Magi, and I am the king of Magi lands."

The Furies all bowed gracefully. "Xander Journe, Fire Fury Elder," the eldest said calmly. He gestured to his fellow Furies. "Grecia Laluna, Soil Fury; Dahlia Stalker, Air Fury; Jazz Eaglewind, Soil Fury; Dominic Whisperer, Fire Fury; and Solis T'mer, Water Fury."

To the surprise of all but Xander, Morgan and Tariah made a gesture that none but the Elder had seen before. The twins touched their left cheek with their right thumb, then their right cheek, then their left shoulder. If one had drawn a line between the points they touched, they would have drawn half the symbol of 'chron' for which the twins took their family name, and their race took its.

"Morgan Chronis, Air Chronicle," Morgan said calmly. "Black Magi leader."

"Tariah Chronis, Water Chronicle," his sister said. "Black Magi second." She gestured to the four beside her. "Jayda Lakemore, Water Chronicle. Roman Arequo, Air Chronicle. C.J. Daragon, Soil Chronicle. Kelsey Renaire, Fire Chronicle."

It seemed impossible somehow that four more Chronicles had managed to survive the laws, but there was no denying their presence. More still, all four names were very familiar to many people. If these four had lived as Master Magi successfully, then how could anyone doubt any longer that Chronicles were not the terror they had always been purported to be?

Finus sighed wearily. He was not very old, even by Magi standards, and only in his late thirties. He just *felt* much older than his physical age. The struggle he had made over the last few years to mend his broken people had taken its toll. "May I have the honor of an audience with you?" he asked the twins equally.

Well? Tariah asked it into her brother's mind.

We have nothing to lose, he answered wryly. "We would be honored to accept," he said out loud. "But we must be on our way swiftly."

"It will not take long." Finus rolled his eyes as Ilian and Quinn leapt to open the door to the inn for him. "Being king does not make me helpless," he scolded them. "Who was it who carted out those ridiculous statues from the palace?"

"And nearly broke his back in the process," Ilian retorted politely. "Kindly keep yourself healthy and safe so that your Argyles don't lose what is left of their sanity."

"I didn't promote you to be sane," Finus groused wryly as he walked into the building, letting Quinn pointedly go first.

Suddenly liking him a lot more than she had liked the last king, Tariah was smiling as she followed him with the others. The innkeeper was more than happy to show them into the dining room where there would be plenty of space. He felt slightly awed to have not just Chronicles and Furies present, but the king as well, and determined to give them the best service possible.

They found places to sit, and Finus studied the dynamic of those present with immense curiosity. He didn't need to ask to know who was mated with who. The Furies sat very close to their Chronicle, most touching in some way or another. Dominic held Tariah on his lap with his arm around her waist and his hand over her stomach in a familiar, universal, protective gesture.

It was also curious to note that Morgan and Tariah sat

slightly to the front of the others, even Xander. Despite their young ages, they were treated with the same reverence of an Elder as old as Xander. The twins also sat close enough that their bodies just barely touched. Finus knew they were not twins by birth, but he had trouble believing it. "Tell me what has been happening," he requested quietly. "From the beginning when the Black Magi formed fourteen years ago."

Without hesitation, Morgan laid it all bare. From his youth to his flight from Glacia, to his chance encounter with the Renaires and his determination to save his kind. The subsequent gathering of the other three, and the issues with Soh. Tariah offered her own tale of her restricted childhood and painful awakening with the death of her beloved Maxim.

They left no detail out, not even when Ilian flinched or Quinn looked away in shame. Not even when Finus seemed to age before their eyes as he listened to the litany of abuse and hate that the twins described in every city. He did not need to ask if what they spoke was true. Though welcome in all cities, neither Morgan nor Tariah had been seen more than a handful of times in nine years.

"The Elite are the fault of the Magi." He said it starkly. "If the laws had not been in place, if Chronicles had not been so hated, Phedo Emik would be alive and Soh Emik and Sistra of the Dragons would not have gone mad."

"I doubt that it would have made a difference for Soh," Morgan denied. "There was always something off about him before. But Sistra . . ."

"I do not believe she was bad inside," Jazz said firmly. "She would not have been made a Fury if she was not deserving of the gift of being a Dragoon. If we can find where she hides, where she recovers, we may as yet be able to reason with her. She might as yet be saved. Phedo must be lonely on the other side without her."

Hesitantly, Ilian asked, "A Fury cannot live without

their Chronicle?"

Dominic met his eyes unflinchingly. "Not once they feel the birth and death of their other half. A Fury feels the moment that their Chronicle is born. And they feel the moment that they die. They just . . . go away. They don't eat. They don't sleep. Every day that they live, they die a little more. The only respite for a Fury who has lost their Chronicle is a merciful death."

Quinn turned a sickly shade of green and rushed from the room. Ilian sat down hard, looking little better. Shakily, Finus asked, "Do you mean to say that every Chronicle we have killed over the millennia . . .?"

"Was the death of a Fury?" Xander asked bluntly. "Yes, we do. Dominic was forced to end his own brother's misery. I can't name all the Furies I have known and lost over the years. With every passing century, I grew more and more certain in my own destruction. When I felt Jayda take her first breath, I put my affairs in order." His eyes closed. "Then I met Tariah and Morgan. And I had final hope."

Jayda turned and burrowed against his chest, desperately curling her power and emotions around him, merging their minds, trying to crawl inside his soul to comfort, to give him the reassurance that she was there with him at last.

Finus closed his eyes. The idea of how much death and murder had occurred over the centuries was sickening. And it was murder. He saw that clearly. He couldn't even say why it had started. No one remembered any more. Magi lived an average of a hundred years, and the earliest records simply stated that Chronicles were vile, disgusting creatures who would destroy the world in their parasitic pact with Furies.

He did not see vile, disgusting creatures. He saw powerful, giving, and caring people. He did not see a parasitic relationship between Chronicle and Fury. He saw love, though he was hesitant to call the force by such a paltry word. And he did not see people who would destroy the world. He saw people who might just be the key to its salvation.

He straightened his back and looked every inch the king he had been made. "Is it true that you have the ability to sense other Chronicles?" he asked Morgan and Tariah equally.

"Seems so," Tariah admitted. "It was how Morgan found these four terrors."

"We grew out of being terrors," Roman promised her with a sudden grin.

"Some of us didn't," Kelsey said cheerfully.

Finus found a smile for the first time. Some things were truly not limited to one race. "Then I wish to ask a great favor of you, Dragoons of Chronis blood. Once a summer, I wish you to come to Prismatic. Your sanctuary will be rebuilt. There, families with children of questionable strength may bring their child to you to see if they are a Chronicle. Children who have already revealed themselves as Chronicles will come. You will teach them what they need to know of their own race, what they need to know to grow and be everything they are meant to be, so that they may live among the Magi as happily as possible."

"And none will stop them from journeying when they start second puberty?" Tariah asked quietly. "That journey is what will lead them to their Fury, what will define the reason for their birth."

"No Chronicle will ever be barred from any city. Wherever their lines lead, the Magi will be there to offer shelter, guidance, and friendship." His blue eyes abruptly glittered with painful tears. "My sister was a Chronicle," he admitted roughly. "Is there . . . is there any way of knowing who her Fury was? I want to have her grave moved to where her Fury rests."

Xander looked at Morgan and Tariah who nodded

slightly. "It can no doubt be determined," the Elder said after a moment. "You intend to make some sweeping changes."

The king smiled slightly. "They made me king. They can do as I damned well say."

Tariah decided she *really* liked him. "We will come visit you when this is done," she promised. "We will start what you ask of us, and we will meet your son as well." Her eyes began to sparkle merrily like silver coins. "I hope he is like you. You're a good person, Finus." With him in charge, there might just be hope for everyone.

"What do we do about the Elite?" Ilian asked Finus. "The only ones who can stop them sit before us right now."

Quinn had rejoined them, and though pale, she was composed. "They may take my ship," she said. "It is strong and sound. Wherever they need to go, it will take them there."

"Where are you intending to go?" Finus asked.

"We would rather not say," Morgan said softly. "As you said, opinion cannot change overnight, and, frankly, we do not trust Magi very much right now."

None of the Magi before him could find the will to argue with him. Neither Chronicle nor Fury had any reason to trust the Magi at all. Frankly, the Kin didn't have much reason either. For being the most populous race on the planet, the Magi had done a poor job of being a good neighbor to the other races and an even poorer job of being a child of Lucksphere.

"Can you tell me if you are chasing the Elite?" Finus asked instead.

"We are, and we aren't," Kelsey spoke up. "We're chasing something they want with the hopes of getting to it first." She frowned at Morgan. "Are we sure they haven't gotten there?" When the others eyed her, she shrugged. "The Elite aren't using normal power. They're doing things beyond what they should be able to. Beta wasn't naturally that strong, but she was acting like it."

"I had thought that before," Roman admitted.

"If they found it," Solis said, "then why is the world still standing? Why would they need a Chronicle to take control?" He frowned. "Unless that's the very problem. They can be affected by it, but they can't control it." He shook his head. "I still feel like there's something we don't know that we should. We need to get out to sea so that the twins can dust off Xander's brain."

Xander made a gesture with his right hand that looked similar to the Magi gesture of disrespect. It made both Argyles grin at each other. You had to admire anyone with the nerve to directly sass an Elder as old and powerful as Xander. "Watch it, whelp," Xander said mildly. "I'll clip your fins."

Kelsey stuck her tongue out at him. "You have to go through me first, old man."

Ilian looked at Quinn. "If you will escort them to your ship, I will start the journey back to Prismatic with Finus."

"I'm still here," the king complained.

Quinn hid a smile. "That will work. Swift journeys, Ilian." She got to her feet gracefully. "If you will come with me?" she asked the others graciously. As she led them out of the inn, she asked Jayda softly, "Are you happy?"

"Very happy." She was walking with her arms around one of Xander's, her head resting against his shoulder. Her need for his constant touch and presence was very obvious, as was her acceptance of her need. "I don't have words to describe it. I wish I did."

"You don't need words." Quinn smiled. "I have eyes." They walked onto the dock and she gestured to the ship anchored there. "Here we are. It is seaworthy and strong. It can stand most any storm that is thrown at it."

"How big of a storm?" Dahlia asked.

"Well, we sailed through a five-knocker, and it came

through fine."

Kelsey scowled. "Can someone say that in non-sea lingo for the desert dwellers?"

"My apologies, Kelsey." Quinn hid a smile. "A 'knocker' is a unit of storm measure used by sailors. It means that the wind knocks against the side of the ship five times in a second. They are the roughest storms that any ship can sail through. As a comparison, the storms south of Glacia are considered to be eight-knockers and therefore impassable." When there was silence, her stomach dipped. "I see."

"Can it handle it?" Grecia studied the ship intently. It certainly looked weather worthy, but eight-knockers were vicious beasts.

"I don't know," she admitted. "We came out of the five-knocker with no damage, so it's certainly possible. With the sort of Water and Air power you have present, you might fare better where others would fall far short." Hesitantly, she asked, "Are you sure you have to sail into those storms?"

North.

The burning pulse ripped through the lines of all Chronicles present . . . including Morgan and Tariah. The sharp compulsive urge was something they hadn't felt in nine years, and it shocked both so deeply that it ricocheted into Dominic and Jazz. Astonished, Dominic grabbed Tariah's shoulders. "Did you feel that?"

"That's impossible," Xander said instantly. "You finished your journeys."

"Did we?" Morgan asked softly. He pressed a hand to his chest as he felt the painful demand inside his soul. "I thought we had too, but I can *feel* it. My lines are burning. *North.* We have to go north."

Quinn didn't have a clue what they were talking about, but she was beginning to think that she could see why Tariah had insisted that Chronicles on their journey not be stifled. If it was their power driving them on, then stopping it could be devastating.

"It's a voice." C.J. shook his head. "I would swear it sounds like an actual voice speaking to me."

Tariah looked at Morgan sharply just as his head swung toward her. In the last phase of their journey, they had both been certain they heard an actual voice leading them to the Isle. It hadn't been just a feeling driving them a direction. It had been words, a soft feminine voice, urging them on.

"Curious," Xander muttered as he lifted Jayda onto the ship. "Let's go," he told the others. "We need to get out to sea as far as we can with the daylight we have left."

"There's daylight?" C.J. grumbled.

"Somewhere under the clouds, yes." Dahlia urged him onto the ship. "Come along, *ishke*." She nimbly hopped on board and then turned to help him the rest of the way onto the deck. Wisely, she hid a smile as he wobbled before he could find his balance. Desert dwellers were not often comfortable initially on boats.

"We could tow him behind the ship," Roman offered as he climbed up. "Use him as bait for dinner."

"And we could tie you to the sail to summon steady winds," was the retort. "There's space enough inside your head."

"Now, boys." Jazz, trying not to smile, pushed them apart. "Play nice or you're both going overboard. And don't think Dahlia and Grecia will stop me. They know better than that."

"We'll just go over after you," Dahlia promised solemnly.

The others climbed on board as well, with Solis and Kelsey last. As she was preparing to climb up, she sensed Ilian's approach. She turned toward him curiously. "I thought you were leaving," she said. "To escort the king safely home."

"I wanted to say goodbye." He took a deep breath and kept his voice lowered. He was well aware of the sharp ears of the brown-eyed Fury watching patiently. "I feel as if it will be the final goodbye, and I'm not sure why. When you finish your journey . . . you will live on the Isle of Dragons. By the time you will feel safe enough to walk freely in Magi lands, I will no doubt be long gone."

She lightly touched his arm. "Ilian," she said softly, "my parents will still live on Magi lands. I wouldn't cut myself off from them entirely. The Isle will be where Solis and I have our home, certainly. But I would visit my friends." She smiled. "And you're a friend. If Solis and I have a Linking ceremony, I want you to come see it."

"I wanted to love you," he admitted wistfully, "from the moment I met you. But I understand why Etude said you would never feel the same. Solis is a very lucky man." He hesitated before opening the pack he carried. He removed a small box that he held out to her. "Don't drop it," he warned. "And don't open it until you're out to sea."

Sensing his power inside the box, she held it protectively. "I won't."

He paused and then leaned forward to gently touch her lips with his in a bare kiss. "You are an amazing woman, Kelsey Renaire. Lucksphere knew exactly what she was doing when she made you one of her chosen children."

Somehow she managed to keep her tears hidden as he walked away. She kept them firmly held inside as she climbed onto the ship and saw the sympathetic looks on the others' faces. She even managed to hold onto them as they set out to sea away from the coast in an effort to get away from the spreading storms. But when she finally opened Ilian's gift, she couldn't hold onto them any longer.

Inside the box sat a pristine, brilliantly crafted, glass necklace. The chain was made of tiny flame links, each and every one different from the next. The pendant itself formed the symbol in all three languages that meant Chronicle, the one derived from the symbol 'chron' which was etched into the lines on Morgan and Tariah's right hands. 'Chron' itself had different meanings depending on the language of who spoke it. In Magi, it meant 'life.' In Kin, it meant 'strength.' And in Dragon, it meant 'heart's keeper.'

The glass of the pendant was the same crystalline, uncanny, blue color of Kelsey's eyes.

She carefully traced her finger across the symbol, trembling hard. "I couldn't love him," she whispered. "And . . . I didn't want to." Her eyes closed as tears spilled down her cheeks. "I didn't want to love him." The sob caught in her chest as Solis pulled her into his arms. "It's not fair that he would fall in love with me!"

He simply held her tighter and let her cry against his shoulder as if her heart was breaking. And though she hurt, he wouldn't have stopped it if he could. Painful though it was, it was another part of life, another part of second puberty. Hearts that could grow could also break. Hearts that could break were hearts that could feel every emotion life had to offer. In her despair for hurting a good man unintentionally, she was only moving farther down the road toward being an adult.

And that road was just as important as the one she took as a Chronicle. Perhaps they were the same in the end.

Chapter Twenty-One

The ship was well stocked for a long journey, and there was no worry for how far or how long they would sail. Rooms were plentiful enough that each Dragoon pair had their own, though Solis and Kelsey didn't need the privacy as badly as the others. Nothing was said to Solis about Kelsey's seemingly frozen growth. Her vibrant exterior hid a core as vulnerable as Jayda's, and in her unease and fear, she clung harder to the last vestiges of childhood. Solis was patient. He knew their day would come.

When they had sailed a day and a night, unease began to stir at last. They had not left the storms from Spectrum behind. There was no longer any blue sky to see. Storms covered every inch of the air with the Flutterlies in such thick and dense swarms that they made it impossible to tell day from night.

They had kept Spectrum as a line on the horizon, but after a few more days, even that disappeared at last. The waves grew rougher, more turbulent, as they began to sail beyond the scope of safety. With every passing mile, the wind knocked harder against the boat. Even with Roman and Morgan working in concert with Dahlia, it was hard to keep the winds steady.

Tariah and Jayda managed to keep the rain at bay, though many mornings they all woke to discover that at least some had fallen in the night. No one really knew where they were or where they were going, short of being sure that the worsening storms were a good sign.

They soon found themselves a week into their voyage and preparing themselves to sail into the very worst of storms where there would be no turning back. Passing time was filled with old stories and new study. Morgan and

Tariah had started developing their Clairvoyance, and the others as yet developed their newest skills.

It was mid-afternoon when Xander needed some air. He left Jayda with Tariah to discuss the latter's pregnancy and headed to the deck. There was no one steering at that moment and the anchor was dropped to keep them as stable as possible in the rolling waves. The untamed nature of the storm didn't concern him as he stood at the rail and looked into the murky distance. He had seen these storms before.

At the wayward thought, he went very still. It wasn't just any storm that he remembered. It was *these* storms. He could see it very clearly in his mind. The pattern of the Flutterlies that had seemed so familiar to him. When 'it' was happening. They broke pattern and flew to the heart of each city and spread outward. But *why*?

It's like scabbing over a wound that cannot be healed.

The voice whispered in his mind, sounding so much like Tariah that he immediately turned to find her, but she was not there. The voice in his mind wasn't Telepathy. It was in his memory. He struggled and fought, desperately reached for that voice. It merged with a familiar figure of his past and he went still.

Tarinah Chronis.

The memories slipped free further as he fought to gather them. She had been a healer. Her twin brother, Morignan Chronis, had been a powerful warrior. She had been a Water Chronicle, he an Air. As the end had slipped closer and closer, malice and hate rising in the land, Xander had stood with the twins on a brilliantly beautiful cliff that reminded him of home though it was not the Isle.

They had watched the Flutterlies flying with purpose, dragging a shield of storms that slowly began to encircle the island. *She is our Mother*, Tarinah had said, gesturing to the bits of puff in the sky. *They are Her tears. What the Magi do is killing Her. Killing Him. Our Mother and Father. But the Flutterlies . . . It's like scabbing over a wound that cannot be healed.* Her blue eyes had welled with tears as she pressed her hands to her very rounded belly. *My children will cry too.*

"Xander." Jayda pressed against his back and her arms encircled his waist. Tears slid down her cheeks and flowed through her heart. She had been there in his mind and seen those terrible moments. She surrounded him with her emotions and power, trying to soothe the wounds inside his heart and soul. The curse of an Elder: with age came strength but it also came with emotional sensitivity.

"We don't have a choice," he said grimly. "We have to find my memories now. We've delayed because of the unpredictable storms, but we can't delay any longer."

"It might very well destroy you."

He turned and lifted her off her feet to bury his face in her hair. She was as pure and sweet as the air of her home, and no matter how he complained, he had grown to truly love the scent of snow. "You'll hold me together," he said confidently. "I have complete faith in you and Morgan. I have to remember, *ishke*. There is no other option."

She knew he was right though she feared for him. Her beloved Fury was too gentle, too feeling, to suffer under the weight of his own past. A part of her couldn't help but wonder if that, more than any other reason, was why he had forgotten something that terrible.

Morgan was with Jazz in their room, and they had curled together on a chair to read a book. He glanced up automatically with a smile that faded as he saw the seriousness on Xander's face. "What is it?" He released Jazz so she could stand and then got to his feet as well. Automatically, he slipped his hand into hers for support.

"I had a memory. It was there and gone, but it was a real memory. I saw . . ." Xander fell silent for a moment. He wanted to say he saw Morgan's ancestors, but though it was true, it was not the full truth, though he wasn't sure how. Had never been sure how since the day he met Morgan and Tariah. "I saw . . . you."

Jazz said nothing. She simply held Morgan tighter. He took a long breath. "I have no answers," he admitted. "Tariah and I have discussed it, but we don't understand either. We simply . . . accept."

'It's easier to take it one day at a time.' The words were accompanied by a laughing grin from Morignan. 'And better for that old mind of yours, old friend.'

Xander shook his head swiftly. "Something's happening," he said. "Something has changed. Things you say are knocking memories free. The storm itself was knocking them free. You have to go into my mind, Morgan, and free the information we need."

The Chronicle said nothing for a moment, then finally murmured, "I will know all your memories, Xander. All of them."

Xander met his eyes unflinchingly. "You were there for fifteen hundred of them. The last thousand are not much to look at. Nothing but a hate for summer that all Furies who live long enough finally begin to feel. The most beautiful time of the year . . . hated by the ones who should love it most."

Tariah. Morgan called instantly to her. *Come to my side, little sister. I will need your strength and will if I am to do this. Jayda will keep Xander from breaking under the weight of those terrible days, but I will need you and Jazz to hold me together.*

When Tariah walked into the room, she wasn't alone. Everyone else had come as well. Xander looked at all those around him and felt staggered by a flash of déjà vu. A city sitting peacefully under the glowing sun. People laughed and played and worked. Children ran around underfoot, both Magi and Dragon alike. Nearly all adults had lines, though half had streaked hair marking them as Furies. "Sanguine." The word was breathed softly. "The City of Summer."

"What's going on?" Kelsey asked.

"There's something about where we are that is mending the missing memories in Xander's mind. And that makes me positive that I was correct about the memories not being *gone*." Morgan took a deep breath. "I've never done this. We will have to make it up as we go. With the storms outside, this room needs to be secure."

"The easiest way to do it," Grecia spoke up, "is to have those of us with Fire and Soil encase the room entirely. Layers. Chronicle, Fury, Chronicle, Fury. We'll have C.J. go last and put his on the inside." She grinned at the male in question. "Since he is so artistic."

"See if I make you any more blankets! Hrmph."

Dominic cocked his head. "Just Fire or Fire and Smoke?"

"One layer of each. We want this room to be *sealed*. I will go first." Power flowed up and around Grecia in a swirl of leaves and green color. She started with her Soil power and built up the walls, floor, and ceiling with plants and vines. Bits of bark swirled into her power as she used her Wood skills to build a lattice of planks and branches over the vines.

Kelsey went next, grateful to have a distraction. Over the layer of Wood, she built a layer of glass with her Smoke power. Only showing off a little, she made sure the glass was the same color of green as the vines it hid. She followed that with a layer of Fire that burned bright and fierce and did not harm.

Dominic followed with his own layer of Fire, and it was distinctly different from Kelsey's for it held the tinge of Dragon origins. The layer of Smoke glass that he built was not green but deep ruby. He couldn't let a fledgling show him up, could he?

C.J. built a wall of his own vines and branches over the last layer of glass and then built a layer of Wood. Since Grecia had pointedly challenged him, he opened the bag of sand he wore and used it to swiftly weave tapestries to hang down from the ceiling and cover the floor with comfortable padding. He used every color imaginable until the room was a whirl of color and life.

"I believe," Roman told his lover warmly, "you have been soundly power-slapped." The phrase was an oft-heard one in childhood. It meant that in a duel, the loser had never stood a chance of winning.

She smiled in bemusement. "Indeed." She lightly cuffed C.J. in the chin. "You are brilliant," she told him sincerely. "And I say it to you for the reason Xander once said it to Kelsey. You will have to decorate the Council's cave. Those stodgy old fuddy-duddies need to brighten that place up."

"Her grandfather is the Air Elder," Morgan told Roman politely, but with laughter in his voice. "Grecia is his favorite granddaughter, potentially because she's the only one who dares sass him to his face."

Roman winced. "How fun."

"He'll love you." She kissed his chin softly. "After all, you saved my life simply by being born."

"What do we do next?" asked Solis of Morgan. "The walls are a few feet thick with layers of shielding. I doubt even you, Tariah, or Xander could get your power through without doing it on purpose."

Morgan and Tariah looked at their right hands where the 'chron' symbol was etched. "This," they both said as one as they held out their hands.

'They finish each other's sentences,' the violet-eyed Fury said wryly. 'And talk at the same time, and in the same voice. It's so odd, but I think I love Tarinah almost as much as I love Morignan. They are critical to each other. Perhaps

another type of two halves of a whole.'

"Jazz?" Xander asked softly. "How do you feel for Tariah?"

Startled, the Soil Fury looked at her sister-kin. Though her first response was to, naturally, say that she loved her, she knew the question was meant seriously. And so she thought about it seriously. To her surprise, she discovered that there was a deep emotion for the shorter woman that went well beyond the scope of normal. "How odd," she murmured. "I never realized. I suppose I can say it best by saying that the only person I care for more than Tariah is Morgan." She looked at Dominic. "You?"

He slowly nodded. "I've often thought that way about Morgan. In the beginning, I was very jealous, which I don't deny. But it wasn't until the last year or so that I realized how important he was to me."

"Is that normal?" C.J. asked Xander.

"Not normal, exactly, but perfectly within the realm of reason for them. It coincides with another memory. And it confirms something that I have wondered for a long time. Morgan and Tariah couldn't live without each other in a way not dissimilar from what would happen if they lost Dominic or Jazz."

Because it was a fact of their nature, it was something both Furies had instinctively known and responded to without consciously understanding. It was also a dangerous caveat to their existence. If Tariah died, then she would take Dominic and Morgan with her, and therefore Jazz as well.

"You really do have a lot of important things in that dusty old mind," Kelsey said. She lifted her hands and fire flowed over her fingers. With her distinctive style of writing, she burned the chron symbol into the floor under their feet. "What next?"

"Xander needs to lay on the symbol. Everyone else form a circle. Be in pairs, but stagger the elements." Morgan fiercely pushed down his nerves. This wasn't the time for them. Too much rode on this. "I may only be able to do this a piece at a time," he told Xander as the Elder laid down.

"Then at the least get the location of the Lost Isle. That is the most important thing right now."

"Jay, kneel by his head. Jazz and Tariah, I need you beside me. Dominic, please kneel across from us on Xander's other side." Morgan took a steadying breath. "I've never done this, never tried to do this."

"You'll do it," Roman said confidently. He said it with absolute belief because he believed it absolutely. There was nothing that his father-kin and mother-kin couldn't do. Morgan had said he and Tariah were the children's brother and sister, but not a single former child believed it. The twins were their surrogate parents.

With a breath to brace himself, Morgan let himself go into Xander's mind. The complexity told him instantly that he would not be able to succeed alone. Without him even asking, Tariah was suddenly there with him. Their two energies fused into a single beam of pure soft light as they swept through Xander's mind.

Watching them, Kelsey knew the instant it happened. Neither moved but it was as if neither was there anymore. There was one consciousness between them. One will and one power. Small lines of pain edged the identical pairs of eyes as if whatever they saw hurt them as well.

A different painful struggle churned inside her mind and heart. Becoming an adult hurt. It meant hurting others and hurting herself. It meant feeling and thinking and experiencing on a level that was terrifying. Surrounded by the people she cared for most, she felt like nothing more than a nuisance. Some kid who was tagging along without being needed.

But scarier still was the thought of going back. Going back would mean losing Solis, and he was the only thing she had to hold on to. She was hurting him both physically and emotionally. There was no end of patience inside her mate, but she could see that it had strained to the limit. She wanted to be his, to be his lover as she was meant to be. Wanted him to be hers as was promised by their births. As long as she had Solis, then she didn't need to hide in the safety of childhood. In finally knowing it, accepting it, she knew the truth.

It was time to grow up.

Something thumped onto the deck of the ship over their heads. She looked up sharply and her nose flared as she caught the distinct scent of tainted power. Her lines began to burn and itch violently. "The Elite are here."

"They can't stop now," Dominic warned grimly. "They're buried too deeply inside Xander's mind. It's taking all of Jayda's will to hold Xander together. Jazz and I are fighting to keep Tariah and Morgan together as well."

"We can't all go," Dahlia said. "Some of us have to hold this circle together. And some of us are not meant for battle." She looked at her mate pointedly.

"I will go in his place," Grecia said. "I am a healer." She stood gracefully. "Solis, Dahlia, and I will take this battle."

Kelsey got to her feet swiftly. "I will go too." Her tone dared them to argue. "Dominic is Fire. He can hold our element for the circle just by being here. I am needed with you three. I'm not . . ." Her hands curled into fists at her sides. "I'm not going to sit back like a child anymore. I *have* to do this."

Solis softly curled his arms and emotions around her all at once and buried his face in her hair. There were no words he could find for how precious she was to him, how proud he was of her. If there was any emotion he felt for Ilian, it was sympathy. He could not blame the Magi for his love.

The easiest way to get out of the room without breaking it was to turn into their elements entirely and slip through the cracks. Kelsey had never tried such a thing in her life for it was a unique gift of the majiks that Dragon Lords used, but she could do it by drawing on Solis' own majiks. As he built the knowledge in her mind, she realized how very simple it was to do.

She reached for the majiks, bent them as he had shown her, and her physical body fell away as she dissolved into the flames of her own power. Actually moving in that form was much trickier, but all three Furies wrapped themselves around her and brought her along with them as they moved through the shields. She watched intently how they moved, read the skills inside Solis' mind, and determined to do it for herself next time.

They turned back as soon as they were outside the door. The smell of tainted power lingered even stronger in the hall, and the thumps from the deck sounded like someone staggering around in a stupor. "It sounds like someone had too much cactear juice," Kelsey muttered.

Grecia looked at her curiously. "Cactear juice induces intoxication?"

"If Magi drink too much of the distilled stuff, yeah. It affects Kin if it is mixed with something else, but Etude never said what that was. Does it work on Dragons?"

"We really don't even like the taste of distilled juice. Raw or pure, sure, but not distilled," Solis told her. He suddenly smiled as he felt her poking around inside his head. "I've only been intoxicated once, and I've avoided it ever since." The look he shot Grecia was sour. "And I've never trusted anything she gives me to drink since."

"It was an accident," she said in exasperation. "Get over it, whelp."

Ignoring them both, Dahlia led the way up the steps toward the deck. The storm was growing more and more agitated and the sea rocked the ship hard. Staggering around on the deck was a man in the Elite cloak, and though none present had met him before, they still knew he was bad news.

"You must be running out of members," Solis said calmly. "Since they seem to be destroying themselves as we go along."

The man looked at him with yellow eyes that seemed nearly feral. "We used to number hundreds. Thousands. Now we are a pitiful few, but we are not so powerless that we can't do what is needed. Those who remain are the elite of the Elite!" The rotting stench of decay lifted from his skin as he aimed a nearly gnarled finger at Kelsey. "Chronicle!"

She propped a hand on her hip. "*Poka!*" she retorted. It referenced a childhood insult. It implied the recipient was as stupid as a *pokagale* bird, known for breaking its own neck because it forgot it could fly. No one had any idea how they even managed to propagate at all. "Now that we're introduced, the name is Kelsey."

He bared rotting teeth in a smile. Whatever taint held him was one that had existed so long that it had gotten into his physical being. "Epsilon," he said. He made the Magi gesture of respect, but it looked distinctly mocking. "Come along with me, child."

Merged as he was with Kelsey, Solis saw the abrupt violent rage of her transition to adulthood long before it ever reached the surface. He leapt backward and dragged Dahlia and Grecia with him for safety. Though, technically, not yet an official adult until she took her first lover, Kelsey was no longer a child either.

"Don't call me a child!" The furious shout was accompanied by the biggest fireball that anyone on the deck had ever seen. It lit the area like the day as it shot through the air directly at Epsilon.

The Magi dove out of the way and clawed his way back up to his feet. Water power swirled around him as ice shards condensed. The storms overhead began to take a yellowish tint and rain began to fall with stinging drops. "If that's how you want it," he snarled, "then there are three others for me to take once you're gone!"

"Wait!" Solis grabbed Dahlia's arm when she would have lunged forward. "Let Grecia cover Kelsey in battle while you and I take control of these storms! I think I have an idea of what might have happened to Beta. We're going to invite it to happen again, if my hunch is correct."

Kelsey ducked one blast of ice and then dodged another. Her cloak felt restrictive suddenly and she let it drop to the deck. Small flames rippled down her now visible lines on their way to her hands. She wore desert clothes still, but she did not feel the cold. The pendant she wore seemed to pulse softly as if it radiated heat.

If Epsilon had any idea of what he had unleashed, it didn't show as he fired a barrage of attacks at her. When she either evaporated them or dodged them entirely, he clawed for the sword he wore on his hip. "Let's see how you like something more tangible!"

She took one look at the weapon in his hand and, shockingly, started laughing with real humor. "Go ahead and try!" she challenged. She walked forward with her arms held out. "Take your best shot, *poka*!"

Grecia's entire body tensed as she prepared to leap forward. Epsilon didn't notice her at all. He had forgotten the three Furies were even present. Snarling incomprehensible curses, he swung his sword with all his strength at Kelsey's head.

Inches from her red hair, the sword stopped itself in the air. He had thrown his full weight behind the swing, and though the sword stopped, he didn't. He went tumbling across the deck and smashed into the mast. Yellow blood dripped down the side of his face as he stared at the sword hovering in the air. "That's impossible!"

She reached up and took the sword from the air. With a casual strength that impressed Grecia, she swung the blade one-handed. At her touch, the corroded blade turned to bright silver and the glass hilt cleared from its clouded hue. She studied the blade for many moments, then said softly, "I'm so sorry you ended up in his hands."

She released the sword and it hovered in the air beside her. A cool and yet slightly savage smile touched her lips as she turned toward the fallen Elite. "Did you see the carvings at the base? The symbols 'kel' and 'ren'? Those would be my maker's mark."

Grecia looked at the way the two symbols flowed together and smiled to herself. When written as one symbol, the two characters formed a new word that, in Magi, was used interchangeably between 'fire' and 'adult' depending on the context. "Weapons forged by a Master such as Kelsey," she said calmly, "cannot harm the one who made them."

Epsilon staggered up to his feet and gathered his power with the familiar intent to detonate himself. Whether it was a choice or mental programming, all the Elite were clearly prepared to destroy themselves rather than lose. He had enough power that detonating himself would take out the ship and likely everyone on it.

Kelsey suddenly felt Solis in her mind and turned to jump at Grecia. She knocked the Fury down and away several feet just as Solis and Dahlia let go of the storms they had been controlling. The clouds broke into torrents of rain, and the taint washed away from the gray color. Blinding light flashed and an immense lightning bolt struck Epsilon in the head. As the crack reverberated off the air a moment later, there was nothing left.

"How did you do that?" Grecia asked Solis as she let Kelsey pull her up to her feet. There were a handful of minor wounds on the Fire Chronicle's arms and she swiftly set about mending them.

"We didn't," Dahlia said simply. "Solis was correct in his theory. We purified the clouds as the taint came in and kept them . . . protected, for want of a better word. When we pulled away, the Flutterlies were strong enough to fight back by themselves. *They* destroyed Beta and now Epsilon."

The sudden sensation of their ears popping told the four on deck that the shielding below had been lifted. The sea rocked with slightly less violence and the rain was onl6 a soft drizzle that caused steam to lift from Kelsey's still burning lines. Something triggered in her mind as she looked at the storms, and she whirled to run downstairs. "I need to talk to Tariah!"

In the cabin, she found Morgan and Tariah both resting wearily in their Fury's arms. They were pale and grief-stricken with tears fresh on both faces. It made her heart break to see shattered the two people she had always believed invincible. Xander looked little better where he rested in Jayda's arms.

"What happened?" Dahlia asked as she kneeled beside C.J. He felt as shaken as Kelsey looked, and so did Roman before he went into Grecia's arms. "*Ishke?*" She smoothed C.J.'s hair out of his face. He had always looked youthful, but he then seemed much older though physically he had not changed.

"The only way to get the location of the Lost Isle," Dominic said roughly, "was to go there in Xander's memories. The twins had to . . . had to become their past selves. They put themselves into Xander's memories to lure out the hiding pieces. I can't tell you how they did it. But the memories burned into Morgan and Tariah's own minds like an after-image. Xander managed to protect Jayda from experiencing the memories herself, but Jazz and I . . . we're not Telepaths. We could not do the same for our Chronicles."

Tariah stirred softly in his arms. "Dominic?" Her arms curled around him fearfully. "You're alive?"

"I'm alive. You're alive." His hand settled over her

stomach protectively. "Our daughter is alive." He had never before seen her this shaken except for that horrible moment nine years earlier when he had feared she would detonate herself. His lips curved as he sought to bring back her smile. "I think she might be a Dragon."

"No eggs!"

The mutter reassured everyone. Morgan's eyes opened slightly, and the silver color was dark and wet with tears. "We couldn't get all the memories," he said faintly. "Xander instinctively kicked us out of his head the minute he realized what we were doing. He was trying to protect us like he always does." His eyes closed again and he slumped against Jazz. "We know the location."

"Sleep." C.J. moved closer and covered his wrist with his hands. "Sleep, Morgan. You too, Tariah. We're going to be all right. Let us take care of you now."

"Tariah?" Kelsey asked softly. "Is it possible to *take* power out of a storm the way it is to put it in?"

Her dark lashes fluttered though they didn't lift, evidence that she was listening. Far too tired to use her voice, her words softly said into everyone's minds, *It doesn't seem impossible. We are Chronicles. We are here to take in the excess power for balance. If you have seen something that makes you think we can tame the storms, then believe in it. Being an adult means taking a risk.*

Almost at the same time, both her power and Morgan's went very still and could not be sensed any longer. The deep sleep was a good sign. It indicated that they would be able to rest and recover.

Instinctively, without intending to, Kelsey took immediate command of the situation. "Jay, are you feeling well enough to help us up top? We need your Water power. Tell me the truth, because if Xander needs you, then you stay."

"He is too deeply asleep to notice one way or another. He protected me from being imprinted by his memories, but I cannot escape entirely because I am inside his mind already." She took a very deep breath and wiped at the tears on her face. "He blanketed my heart and made himself vulnerable to his own pain. I will be fine."

Kelsey looked at C.J. "Weave the thickest, calmest, most damned *healing* blankets you can." As he instantly began to work, she turned toward Dahlia. "Do you know anything about boats? Solis doesn't."

Morgan had been their ship's captain, but he clearly would not be sailing anytime that day. Dahlia nodded quickly. "I do, actually." She kept a smile well-hidden where only C.J. would find it. Kelsey was a chip off her father-kin's block by automatically taking control when their two leaders were out of commission. Her newly found adulthood gave her a strength and surety as fierce as her fire.

"Then you're in charge of sailing." Kelsey got to her feet. "Grecia, can you stay with C.J. to aid with the healing process? I know minds and hearts aren't capable of being healed like a body, but I think there still have to be ways to help. You have Telepathy, and you're a healer. Maybe the two can be used together. Do we have anything to lose by trying?"

Grecia thought about it seriously, then said, "No, not particularly. At most, I might get kicked out of their minds if they sense I might encounter something painful to me." She moved closer to Xander, knowing he was the one in most dire need of comfort. "I'll take good care of him, Jayda," she promised.

"I know." Jayda gently put Xander down onto the thick pillow that C.J. had also made. With Grecia's help, she tucked the heavy blanket securely around his body. She could feel the pounding aches inside his body from his power being so low. She couldn't feed him until he woke, but Grecia might be able to make him rest easier.

She got to her feet and joined her brother and sister, and they with Solis and Dahlia headed up to the deck. While Dahlia went to take the controls of the ship, Jayda picked up Kelsey's cloak and helped fasten it around her shoulders once more. "Were you in a hurry?" she asked teasingly.

"It was odd." Kelsey studied her lines. "I just couldn't stand to have my lines covered that much."

"If I recall," Dahlia noted, "at the last fight with Sistra, neither Morgan nor Tariah could stand to be covered either. It must be a Chronicle thing." A smile touched her lips. "An *adult* Chronicle thing."

"I'm not an adult *yet*." Kelsey shot a look at her Fury that made her crystalline eyes smolder with desire and that powerful, fully grown, third emotion that marked Dragoons. "But it's a matter of time."

He curled his hands into fists before he yanked her into his arms and took the kiss he desperately needed. Before he touched her and tasted her from head to heel, fed on her power from any and everywhere. *His*. Finally, she was his for the taking, and the knowledge was heady. He had waited so long . . .

"How are we doing this?" Roman asked, breaking into his thoughts. "I've never tried to draw down a storm's power." He studied the sky and the clouds intently. "But I can't argue why you asked. Wasn't this a six-knocker earlier? It's barely a two now."

"Solis and Dahlia did it unintentionally." Kelsey shook her head. "It reminded me of the time I had a really bad injury from a blade I was making. The wound had gotten swollen and the healer lanced it to make it heal faster. That's what it seemed like happened here."

"A build-up of power with nowhere to drain." Jayda looked at the clouds. "Well, we have nothing to lose by trying, though I agree that I don't know how to do it." She looked at Dahlia. "Can you sail us into rougher waters?"

"Can? Yes. Want to? No." But she did anyway,

directing the ship to move past the calm two-knocker and toward the more deadly seven that tore up the waves barely a mile away. "Jay, do you have the directions from Xander's memories?"

"I do. Keep heading north and any time you see a dark wave, turn east for half a mile before going north again. It will pass us through the proper checkpoints and make the Isle reveal itself." She grabbed onto the mast for support as the winds picked up and began to pound against the ship.

Flashes of lightning crisscrossed the sky with their loud roars always arriving moments later. The gentle rain became a torrent, soaking even Jayda and Solis to the bone. Roman and Jayda moved to the center of the deck and started to lift their hands when lightning flashed right above them.

"Don't get fried!" Solis said swiftly. "Xander and Grecia would eat us for dinner!"

"We're fine," Roman assured him. "It just surprised us. Let's try this again, Jay."

She nodded slightly and they lifted their hands again as if asking for the storm to come for them. The lightning flashed again over Roman's head and then struck him directly. Kelsey would have yelped if Solis hadn't clapped a hand over her mouth hastily. Roman didn't even seem to notice he had been struck; his body absorbed the power easily.

The rain itself began to rush directly at Jayda and she absorbed it with the same ease. As the storms sensed the open outlet, they grew more and more violent. Stronger and more potent blasts of power were thrown at the two Chronicles. It seemed to go on for an eternity, the ship rocking so badly that it sent Solis and Kelsey tumbling across the surface.

But then . . . it stopped.

Legs trembling, Solis managed to get up once more.

He helped Kelsey stand as well and they looked out across the rocking waves. They were much calmer in force as they gently lifted the ship up and down. The rain had slowed to barely a drizzle, and the wind knocked only once or twice against the side of the ship.

"I can't believe it worked," Kelsey managed to say. "I was *guessing*." She walked carefully over to Roman and Jayda. "Are you all right?"

"If I move, I'm going to fall." Jayda's knees visibly trembled. "I feel well enough, but I'm a little shaky right now." She leaned gratefully against her sister as Kelsey wrapped an arm around her waist.

Solis moved to brace Roman and winced wryly as he felt the electric shock between them. "You certainly were hit by lightning. You're sparking into the air, Roman. We'll need Grecia to ground you. Literally."

The tame storm was spreading even faster than the untamed. When C.J. and Grecia came up to join them on the deck, there was no longer any fear that the ship would be torn apart. Dahlia held the ship on a steady direction following Jayda's instructions.

By the time it should have been evening, they could see a black line on the horizon that was potentially the worst storm any of them had ever seen. The good news was that it did not hover over the ocean and prevent passage. The bad news was that it hovered over a strip of land that was surely their destination.

"Drop anchor," Kelsey said softly, shivering even when Solis wrapped her in his arms and cloak. "We can't land like this. We'll let Morgan and Tariah and Xander recover and then land tomorrow morning. Tonight we prepare." She closed her eyes but could still see that broken island in the distance burned inside her mind. Something terrible had happened there. It could be seen even at a distance. Something terrible, something against the very laws of nature itself.

Something like the genocide of an entire race.

Chapter Twenty-Two

The easiest thing to do with the resting Dragoons was to leave them where they were, though Tariah got tucked into the bed because her pregnancy made her restless. C.J. and Grecia made sure that Dominic, Jazz, and Jayda had enough blankets to be comfortable since the nights had proven to be quite cold.

Those who were awake ate dinner together before they retired to their rooms for the night. Kelsey was all but vibrating with energy and emotion as untamed as her element and twice as unpredictable. Solis considered himself a very lucky man that he was inside her mind at all times and able, to some extent, to predict her movements.

Her cloak was still wet, and drops flew when she dropped it over the back of a chair. Her wet hair clung to her face, shoulders, and partway down her back with the curls slightly stretched out from the weight.

He couldn't hide his hunger for her and didn't bother to try. He stood in the middle of the room and watched her pace back and forth with chaotic energy, her long legs sleek and supple and her lush body moving in all of his favorite ways. "You were amazing, *ishke*," he said softly, sincerely. "You took command of the situation perfectly. Morgan and Tariah will be proud of you."

She stopped pacing and looked out the small window toward the darkened ocean. So many emotions swirled inside her heart that he couldn't identify them all. "I didn't even think about it."

"It's a part of who you are," her lover said simply. "When you chose to become an adult, then you were able to be that confident once more." Softer, he asked, "What changed your mind? Why did you stop being so afraid?"

"There were a lot of reasons. Fear was one of them. I

don't like hurting. I don't like hurting others. That scared me, so I pulled back. But there was a stronger fear. Fear of losing you." She turned around and her eyes glittered with every bit of her maturity. "You're mine. My Fury. I was given a *gift*. And I'm going to take it. I want everything. I want you. I want to be your lover. I want us to have a home, to have children." She smiled suddenly. "And unlike someone else around here, I don't care if I carry eggs."

A lump closed his throat with painful, overwhelming emotion. There were no words he could find. Instead, he wrapped her within his power and his heart, caressing her hotly so that her eyes darkened and a shiver rippled through her body. "*Ishke.*" It was all he could say. It was the only word that could say what he felt. There was nothing more precious to him than his beautiful Chronicle. His gift.

She paused for a moment and then pointedly unfastened the top she wore and threw it aside. Her shorts went next and left her in just her bikini. Her lines rippled like gold over her pale skin, as yet untouched by the sun because of the storms. As her fingers toyed with the tie to the bikini, she asked huskily, "Do you want to undress me?"

His brown eyes darkened. "You seem to be doing a fine job," he said just as huskily. "I might tear something. Imagine explaining that to the Soil elements. They might never stop laughing long enough to make you something new."

With a smile older than her power, she untied the top and let it fall to the floor. Not a single fear, not a single nerve, came to life as his eyes swept over her hotly. She could see and feel that nearly violent third emotion inside him and it called to what was inside her. It was so strong, so potent, that she didn't know how he had ever restrained himself.

She stepped toward him slowly and lifted her hands to push on his chest. He stepped back until the bed forced him to sit down. She slid onto his lap and linked her hands behind his neck. "Am I going to have to get tough with you, or are you going to touch me?"

He leaned forward and nipped teasingly at her shoulder. Her skin was sweet and spicy all at the same time, and a soft red aura instantly lifted to cover her. With a sound that was almost a tortured groan, he leaned forward to drink in her power. His mouth moved hotly down her strong arm, and his tongue traced any lines he found.

This time she could actually *feel* her power flowing into him and it sensitized her skin unbearably. His hair brushed against her and made her shiver. His hands curled around her waist strongly and the restrained strength was wildly erotic. She could feel him walking an edge, a thin edge, where patience met instinct and a gentle nature could not tame a primitive soul. What would an out of control Solis be like?

Wanting to know, needing to know, she let her mind and heart merge to his, let her emotions flutter up against his. She swirled her power around him this time with the deliberate intent to seduce. She was burning. He needed to burn with her.

Something much like a growl rumbled in his chest. Before she could catch her breath, he twisted and tumbled her onto the bed so that she was pinned beneath him. His hands and lips raced over her flesh a little wildly to find every nerve that would bring the most pleasure. There was always one spot, one place, that was the focal point of power on a body. When someone said a lover could push their buttons, it was that spot they referenced.

He knew when he found Kelsey's. It was buried in her golden lines directly over her right hip. He pressed his mouth there, and she cried out in shock and delight as her body arched reflexively. He lavished the area with kisses and nips of his teeth until she writhed underneath him, and the scent of her need mixed with the scent of her power intoxicatingly.

She gulped air to beg for him to stop tormenting her when he shifted and closed his mouth eagerly over her breast. The jolt of lust went through every nerve and gathered low in her belly with greedy knots. There was a throbbing between her legs that was maddening, never seeming to be appeased no matter what he did. "Solis!" It was almost a sob.

He muttered something wordless and fiercely stripped her bikini bottom off. He leaned back to survey her naked body with satisfaction, possessiveness in every line of his body and face. *His.* After the lonely years of waiting, the painful years of expecting to die . . . she was there with him at last. His immortal lover. "I'm not done," he said roughly, dipping his head to catch her mouth with his in a devouring kiss. How could she taste so *perfect*?

For the life of him, he couldn't get enough of her mouth. One hand curled around her neck to keep her as close as he could, and the other slid down her body in sweeping caresses. Without giving her a breath, without waiting to see if she would panic, his hand slid between her legs and pressed against where she ached so terribly. Even as she moaned into his kiss, a shudder tore through his body. She was hotter than her power, wetter than his. Steam lifted from both their bodies and filled the air with a sultry heat.

The teasing touch of his fingers did nothing to make the ache better. It only made it worse. She twisted against him desperately, curled her power around him, clutched at his shoulders wildly. When she encountered the vest he still wore, something seemed to break inside. She twisted and tumbled him off her with a lithe surge of seductive strength.

As he rose to his knees, she rose as well and yanked the vest down his arms. His lips, slightly swollen from their last kiss, were more than she could resist and she dragged his head down for another. She let her power well and called it to the surface until he could taste it in her mouth. His tongue tangled with hers hotly as he fought to get his vest off without breaking free.

Four hands went after the fastening to his slacks, and she laughed huskily. "You can't take them off if you're kneeling on them!"

"Someone distracted me." He nipped at her shoulder again and then soothed the sting with a kiss. He gave her a gentle push and she fell back against the blankets. Her hair spread around her like a breathing flame, and her blue eyes darkened to nearly black as she watched him. He brushed against her emotions, but there was no fear in her. She was sure of what she wanted even if she didn't yet know what to call it.

He rolled to his feet and almost ripped off his boots. As he fought with his stubborn pants, her sultry voice said teasingly, "Don't rip something."

He managed to get the pants off and pinned her to the bed bodily, a shudder rippling through them both as every curve and line fit together perfectly. "I think," he said thickly as he began to softly trail hungry kisses down her lines, "that it wouldn't be the first time they've seen something like it."

"Even C.J.?"

Her lover's laugh felt hot against her sensitive skin. "Didn't you notice Dahlia had a new top?" When she suddenly laughed, he buried his face against her belly. He wanted to see her carrying their child, to feel the life growing inside. How he envied Dominic! He wasn't sure he could wait nine years to start his family. Dragons *needed* family. They *needed* love. Was it any wonder they had been the chosen race to become Furies?

He slid lower and her breath caught in agonizing anticipation. The first touch of his lips on her sensitive flesh ripped a cry from her throat. The second scored her insides with sheer lust. There was a slippery precipice between pleasure and pain, and she *ached* for something she couldn't yet comprehend. "Tease!"

He nibbled at her thigh. "Your power is sweeter here." His voice was husky and loving all at the same time. "But spicy." She twisted beneath him wildly. "Not yet, *ishke*. I'm not done with you yet."

By the time he reached her ankles, she couldn't breathe anymore. There was no stopping her mate from his hunger to memorize her, to wring every cry he could, to find everywhere that brought her the most delight. If this was what an out of control Solis was like, then she was going to provoke him a *lot*.

"When do I get a turn?" she managed to ask as she struggled to catch her breath. His fingers brushed along her lines as he moved up her body and she stopped breathing entirely. "Solis!"

"Next time." He framed her face with his hands and kissed her wildly, the rough edge to his voice and embrace making hunger claw painfully inside her. "Any time. Every time. Let me have you now. *Ishke*."

She threw her arms around him fiercely and buried her face against his neck. "I'm holding you to that promise!" As his weight settled over her again, it was so welcoming and wonderful that tears burned her eyes. She curled her legs around his hips, instinctively needing to bind him. It left her open and vulnerable, but this was her Fury. He would *never* hurt her.

As his arousal slowly began to push into her body, she stopped breathing. He paused, his powerful body trembling, and she fiercely wrapped her emotions around him, needing him to know it was not pain. It was wonder. Pleasure. Joy. It was a wild and complex tangle of the three that no words could ever voice in any language. And as he surged forward, took her completely, tears slid down her cheeks. Finally she was complete. Finally he was hers as he had been born to be.

When he began to thrust into her slowly, then faster, it was that complex tangle that coiled tighter and tighter inside her body and her heart. That terrifying precipice loomed closer and closer, her body winding tighter and tighter until she couldn't even find her voice to cry out. His emotions tangled wildly with hers, seemed to fuse the two of them into one single being, and the tension broke in a searing wave of fire and ecstasy hot enough that her hair, for a moment, literally caught flame.

The sight was so erotic that he couldn't fight back his own release. He buried himself to the hilt and stayed there as his body shuddered with pleasure. He *felt* her. Felt her permanently engraved inside him. Live without her? He didn't even have a life without her.

He fell to his elbows and then simply collapsed into her arms. She didn't mind at all. They were both sweaty and hot, neither of their hearts yet able to beat a normal rhythm. He smelled wonderfully of male Fury and Water power, and the steam that curled from their bodies was almost a fog.

It was only when the steam began to dissipate and their bodies cool that she realized she felt a bit chilled. Even before the thought cleared her mind, her lover carefully levered himself up onto his arms and stared down at her face with wonder in his eyes. She traced his lips with her fingers tenderly. "Was it worth the wait?" she asked softly.

"Which wait?"

Her lips curved. "Either."

"I'd go through every minute again if I had to," he promised softly. He kissed her gently and lingeringly, then reluctantly pulled away and disentangled their bodies. He got out of bed to retrieve the stack of blankets, and when he turned around, he found her watching him with a combination of curiosity and appreciation in her eyes. "Like what you see?"

"Let me catch my breath and I'll start at your ears and work my way down. I mean, my eyes certainly like what I see, but I need to get *very* close to be sure." Her voice sounded impish and sultry all at the same time, and so perfectly her that it took his breath.

He spread out the blankets and then got underneath them with her. With a contented sigh, he tugged her into his arms where she belonged. "Weren't you supposed to throw me on the floor and ravish me?" he asked teasingly. "I seem to recall that being mentioned somewhere."

"The bed was closer." She flicked her tongue teasingly over his collarbone and it made heat happily curl inside her body as if she had never been satisfied to begin with. Still fused as they were, she could feel the answering surge inside his body. "Can I throw you on the floor this time?"

"We're already in bed, though."

"Good point." She nibbled at his chin. "I guess I'll have to ravish you here."

He laughed softly with anticipation. "Anytime, anywhere, and anyway you want, *ishke*. I'm all yours."

Her lips curved. "You certainly are."

They slept tangled together, one of her arms thrown across his chest as if she feared he would be taken away now that she had claimed him. When dawn came, it came with a gentle knock on the door. Sleepily, she lifted her head. "Yes?"

"Is it safe?" came Morgan's voice.

Heedless of her nudity, she leapt out of bed and rushed over to open the door. Fiercely she wrapped her arms around Morgan and held on. "You scared me!" she said into his shoulder. Though they were the same height, it was the first time she had ever truly noticed. How did he seem to stand so tall to her?

"*Ishke*." Solis' voice was warm. "Your father-kin is

staring at the ceiling."

She blinked and looked at Morgan to find him indeed watching the ceiling with a resigned look on his face. "Oh." She sighed and grabbed a blanket to swath it around her bare body. "Sorry, Morgan. I didn't think."

"You wouldn't be my Soot if you did." He cuffed her chin gently and ruffled her hair. "I suppose there are some things a father simply does not want to see or know, even after his little girl ran around naked when she was small."

She grinned impishly. "I'm really glad to know that my modesty was a byproduct of second puberty. Now that I'm secure in my emotions and know what they are, I'm not embarrassed anymore." She went over to sit on the side of the bed and smiled when Solis sat up to wrap his arms around her.

Morgan didn't need to ask to know that his little girl was, indeed, a full adult. A third of the lines, all of the ones going down her arms, had distinctly darkened. They flowed like molten gold over her skin as evidence that the first third of her journey, arguably the most important third, was completed.

"How are you feeling?" Solis asked him softly.

He took a deep breath. The imprint in his mind would never be removed. He would forever live with those memories. In a way, he did not want to remove them. It was not fair that Xander carry the burden alone. "Stable. I can't say I feel fine, because I don't. Tariah and I relived those memories with Xander. Rather literally. And because . . . because we were there to begin with, what we feel is not mere empathy."

"How is it even possible?" Kelsey asked softly.

"The body is secondary," Solis reminded her gently. "If Morgan and Tariah's power was never dispersed in their deaths, then there was no reason it couldn't take shape again. Dominic and Jazz are no doubt the same. I can't imagine Chronicles having two Furies."

"Tariah and I both feel it more strongly now than before," Morgan admitted, "that our Furies are not merely with us now but *again*. Their souls are not any newer than ours. They are far less sensitive, however, and other than what they see in our minds, they may never experience that painful past. And for that we are grateful."

Solis ran his fingers through Kelsey's hair softly and looked at Morgan. "Did the others tell you what Kelsey did?"

Pride filled Morgan's silver eyes. "They did. I'm very proud of her, as are Tariah and Xander. Now come join us for breakfast. We want to land as soon as we are able. There is no cover for us on the ocean, and we can't know how many Elite remain."

The door shut behind him as he left, and Kelsey's lower lip quivered. "He looked older."

"For all intents and purposes," her lover said into her hair as he drew her close, "he is. He and Tariah are . . . well, I suppose we might as well call them Elders now. Chronicle Elders. I am sure there must have been some once. Didn't you notice we always treated them as such anyway?"

"But he never *looked* it." She took a deep breath. "He's my hero, Solis. He and Tariah . . . I love them as much as I love my parents. Maybe . . . maybe more." She straightened her back and shook it off even as she shook off her blanket. It was not worth dwelling on what she could not change.

Once they were both dressed, they put on their cloaks and headed to the galley to have breakfast with the others. When they walked into the room, C.J. and Dominic promptly started clapping. The others either grinned or hid grins. Xander, also looking slightly older than even before, said, "Congratulations, Kelsey. And thank you for making Solis easier to live with."

She walked over and bent to hug him tightly. "Are you okay?" Since Jayda was her sister, that made him her brother. She didn't care how old he was, or how much power he had. He was family, and she was going to worry about him. It was just the way she was. She should have been a Dragon herself; her need for family was nearly as great.

Solis didn't think it was just Dragon blood, though he had no doubt that was why they had been chosen to become Furies. It was built into Chronicles as well.

"I will be fine, sister-kin." Xander covered her hands and kissed her cheek. "These memories are a part of me. They are part of what made me who I am. I wouldn't want to lose them again, even to make it hurt less." He looked across the table at Morgan and Tariah. "And there is something here that makes it easier to bear."

"Does that technically make you older than Xander?" Roman asked the twins.

The look Tariah shot Xander was teasing even though there was still something painful in her much older eyes. And here, on her face in particular, was the proof it was no illusion: the twenty-nine-year-old had suddenly gained the three little lines at the corner of her eyes that she should not have had for another year. "I suppose it does. I guess I shouldn't feel bad about hitting you with a pillow that time." At the lifted brows, she smiled. "He walked into Dominic's and my room, and I was naked. It was reflex!"

There was little further talking while they ate. No one wanted to stay in one spot. Epsilon had already proven that that could be dangerous. When refueled, they all went up to the deck and Morgan took control of the ship once more to direct them toward the broken island ahead.

Within the last five hundred feet from shore, they realized that docking was out of the question. Jagged spikes of rock littered the ocean, and the waves threatened to smash anyone crazy enough to navigate through.

The island itself did not look very big, and it was one of several small pieces of land that dotted the ocean. There was a bigger landmass in the middle, but immense whirlpools surrounded it and the storm was focused directly over it.

A sort of cry seemed to drift on the wind, as if someone wept uncontrollably. And if the wind was not weeping, it screamed a shriek of anger and retribution. Chills raced over Morgan's arms, and he clamped his hands over his ears desperately to shut out those terrible sounds of unbearable agony.

Tariah, too, could hear them. And she could hear even more. She could hear in the waves the sounds of hundreds, thousands, of voices at war. The deadly cacophony tore across her soul with razor claws until it was as if she could see the bloody battles that had been fought.

Tears ran ceaselessly down Jayda and Kelsey's faces. They could not hear the voices but they assuredly felt the echoes left in the air. Xander was pale but struggled to hold himself together for Jayda's sake. If he let himself buckle, then she would have nothing to hold onto for her own sanity.

"We have to land." Grecia's voice was soft from where she stood in the circle of Roman's arms. "You have to be strong. Let us help you. Share the pain among us. I know we can. Dragons do it. Kin do it. Magi, if they wanted, could do it. Therefore we can do it."

The instinctive refusal to do so was written across all five faces for a moment before they all exchanged a long look. Reluctantly, they let their power well into the air. The others lifted their power as well, and when they touched, the pain instantly dispersed among those present, dividing on the basis of who could handle the most.

In the end, it was Roman and Solis who carried the heaviest weight for theirs were the strongest hearts that would only bend under the hardest of trials. Those who carried the lightest weight were Jayda, Xander, and Tariah.

Though Tariah had a strong heart, all feared for her unborn child who might absorb the pain herself if her power was strong enough.

Able to breathe again, Morgan anchored the boat. "We will have to fly." His voice was a little rougher than usual, but it was steady. "Can you navigate through these winds?" he asked the Furies in general.

"If Xander goes first," Grecia said. "He is the biggest and flying behind him will shelter us. Jazz needs to be last because she is the smallest."

"Not that I doubt you," C.J. said to Xander, "but how can you change form on the boat? You're bigger than it is!"

Xander lifted an amused brow at him. "So little faith." The teasing was new to him and yet entirely enjoyed. Too often he had been handled gingerly because he was a Fury, and an Elder with it. Finally, he had his own clan to be himself with.

Much to the absolute fascination of all except the other Furies, he partially shifted and allowed for his wings to reform and open. He leapt backward off the rail of the boat and flew up into the air. When he was clear enough, he glowed brightly and transformed the rest of the way back to his natural shape.

"I didn't know Furies could do that!" Kelsey exclaimed.

Jazz's voice warmed. "Only fourth tier Dragon Lords can, and it takes at least two centuries of practice." She ruffled Jayda's hair affectionately. "I will carry you up to him as he cannot fly closer without capsizing us."

Jayda smiled. "Thank you."

Solis and Dahlia opted to dive overboard and swim far enough away to change shape. Dominic, Grecia, and Jazz were just small enough to be able to, one at a time, change form where they were. Dominic was only ten feet long while Jazz was eight.

As Grecia hovered close enough for Roman to climb

up onto her back, she said teasingly, "Isn't Dominic cute? He's average enough in Magi form, but he's actually quite small for a Dragon."

Dominic flicked his tail at her and snorted smoke out his nose in a distinctly rude response. He had once lamented his size, certainly, but having found Tariah, he thought he was perfect for her. She was so small that she needed a smaller Fury if she was to ride on his back.

Jazz gently picked up Jayda in her claws and flew up to where Xander waited. Jayda nimbly climbed up to her spot near his horn and held on securely. Wonder dazzled her as she looked around the air and saw the pairs of Dragoons. She couldn't even be sure if it was her emotions or Xander's. She had never imagined such a thing, and he hadn't thought to ever see it again.

He started flying toward the closest bit of land with the others falling into line behind him from biggest to smallest to provide the best protection against the terrible winds. And they were terrible. They grew stronger and more vicious the closer they got to the land. The tiny piece of land was only a few square miles big, and its edges had no shores. They were torn and jagged cliffs.

Flying past the piece of land was potentially deadly for the winds kicked into what could only be called a ten-knocker the instant the outer edge was reached. Instead, Xander circled down and landed near what might have once been a forest but was now blackened and decayed stumps. They dotted the land like broken teeth.

Once they had all landed, the Furies, except for Xander, went back to Magi form. He turned slowly, critically studying the landscape around them. He had a perfect view from where he stood to across several isles. It almost seemed as if they were connected together somehow, creating a pathway on land toward the center where the worst waited.

He turned to Magi form as well. "I suspect we can make our way there on foot, but I can't promise that for sure. There's so much vegetation and destroyed land that I don't recognize where we are in relation to my memories."

"Are we sure this is the Lost Isle of Chronicles?" Roman asked.

The answer came in an unexpected form. It came as a sudden geyser of power that opened directly under the twins' feet and engulfed them both. Neither was harmed at all, though Dominic and Jazz leapt forward to brace them when they staggered. "Oooh." Tariah stared at Dominic woozily. "I feel funny."

Morgan held up a hand. "Who spiked the power with cactear?"

"Are you . . . intoxicated?" Kelsey had to cover her mouth to hide a grin. "From power?"

"It was some first class power." He shook his head but the fuzziness would not clear. Gratefully, he leaned on Jazz for balance. He had an absurd urge to laugh but bit it back as hard as he could. Unfortunately, when he looked at Tariah, she had the same look on her face. It set them both off.

"Oh my." Jayda bit her lip to, unsuccessfully, hide her own smile. "Well, with a potency such as that, and a reaction like this, I would have to say we must be on the Lost Isle. And that it is clearly declaring Morgan and Tariah as its . . ." She sought the word she wanted. "Its heirs."

Dominic just sighed and lifted Tariah into his arms. He firmly wrapped his emotions around hers and merged her mind to his so that he could hopefully diminish the effects. "They won't be of any use to us for a while," he said dryly. "We might as well start walking."

Jazz sighed and turned into her Fury form again. She could, technically, carry Morgan in her Magi form since she retained her strength, and she more than once had hauled him around under her arm. She preferred not to this time, wanting him to stay upright until his head cleared. She firmly picked him up in her claws and merged to him in the same way Dominic had to Tariah. It wasn't just the giggles, which had faded. It was the distinct wooziness and fuzzy thinking that was the most detrimental.

They made their way carefully through the broken forest toward what Xander hoped was a pathway to the next isle. Knowing the danger of them, they carefully avoided any geysers they found. They seemed to just spew up into the air from out of nowhere, but after a short time, C.J. and Grecia could predict where they would pop up.

"There aren't any quakes though," Dahlia noted. "Perhaps the geysers prevent it from occurring. I've never seen this many in one place. You can *feel* the instability." She let out a soft breath. "And I think we now know what happened to the Elite."

"No wonder Epsilon and Gamma seemed intoxicated," Jayda murmured. "They are very lucky they were not torn apart. I wonder why they weren't."

The sudden acrid scent of tainted power touched them all at the same time. Without even thinking about it, they all moved to close ranks around Tariah and Morgan. Nothing happened, though the scent did not go away. It simply grew stronger. The clouds overhead began to turn slightly yellowish.

All Chronicles felt their lines begin to burn. It was so sharp and strong that it rippled into their mates. Speculatively, Xander studied each in turn. They all felt their lines burn when they were in proximity to not just the Elite but danger in general as well. Were their lines an early warning system as well as a map? If so . . . who was sending the message?

The storm clouds began to pour rain just as five figures approached from the distance. Two were female and three were male. All wore the cloak of the Elite, and all except one carried the stench of decaying power.

C.J. stopped breathing as he recognized the woman at the end. "Kappa!" He would have rushed forward if Dahlia hadn't grabbed him. "Kappa!" he shouted. "Come fight with us! Come fight on our side! You're not like the Elite! Where's Cole? You must have seen him!"

Kappa said nothing as she looked away. Pain lined her face and eyes. The male at the other end of the line laughed nastily. "Don't waste your breath, Chronicle. Kappa knows just who she is beholden to for her very life. You're on our territory now, so why don't you come along quietly?"

If we were on 'their territory', came Tariah's still slightly slurred voice, *then they wouldn't need us to go along quietly.*

Kelsey and C.J. exchanged a look. As one, they made the rude gesture of the Magi with their left hands. The other female of the Elite looked so horrified that it nearly amused the Dragoons. Really, she should have been used to seeing it by then. The Elite weren't exactly *welcome* by anyone.

"Since you won't come along quietly," the male said with a sneer, "then I suppose we will have to take you by force."

No one got a chance to respond. No one needed to. The very land began to rumble softly as if to protest more war upon its surface. It was evidenced when geysers of power opened up in a circle around the Dragoons, forming a protective wall that could be deadly to pass through if you weren't a Chronicle. In this battle, the Lost Isle itself would be a combatant, and that swung the battle in the Dragoons' favor.

And at that moment, even the Elite knew it.

Chapter Twenty-Three

There was no question the fight would be bloody. It was also not one that could be fought as a group. Too much danger came from the geysers. It didn't help that the two strongest Chronicles were incapacitated, and C.J. was not designed for battle of either healing or combat orientation.

In a very soft voice, Kelsey said, "Ceej, you have to go after Kappa. She won't attack you. You have to get her on our side! Dahlia will protect you. The rest of us need to split up and get rid of the others. Xander and Jayda should go after the two males with the black hair; I think they're Soil power. Roman and Grecia can handle the other female; she seems to be Fire." Her eyes narrowed slightly. "Solis and I will take care of the one with the big mouth."

That left Dominic and Jazz to defend Morgan and Tariah, but if all the Elite were distracted, it wouldn't be that bad. Both twins had started to recover rapidly as they focused all their effort on repelling the effects of the power they had absorbed.

The four Chronicles still standing exchanged a long look. All unfastened their cloaks and let them drop. As fast as her power, Kelsey suddenly shot across the landscape toward the blond who had been such a smug bastard. She wanted to rearrange his face purely on principle.

He fell back in shock and swiftly dodged the fireball that shot for his head. His allies didn't even have a chance to help him. The others struck as well, forcing them all to scatter apart. Kappa saw C.J. coming toward her and desperately scrambled back. "No!" she shouted. "C.J., please! Don't make me fight you!"

The blond had recovered and he threw back the hood on his cloak to stare at Kelsey and Solis malevolently. "I am the highest class of Elite," he said icily. "My name is Zeta."

"Highest class? Or the highest class that's *left*?" Solis began to gather his power, and water swirled around his feet with bits of ice mixed inside. "I wouldn't brag about how strong you are when we've been taking out those who were stronger than you."

"Oh there's still one stronger. But don't think she would ever fall to you! And I will not either!" Zeta hurled an immense tornado through the air and the yellow taint cut through the land. The ground was so saturated from the storms and sea that the gouge in the soil made water well. In the dim light, it looked as if the land bled.

Kelsey gracefully dodged the tornado and returned the favor with a powerful stream of fire. Where Magi could only fire in staccato bursts, the fire poured from her hands in a steady blast that she had more than enough time to aim. It left a trail as she pursued Zeta.

Even though he outran her fire, there was Solis to deal with. The Fury was lethally accurate with the shards of ice he threw from his fingertips. When the two powers of the mates happened to cross, they did not cancel each other out. They merged seamlessly into a blinding force that was not dissimilar from the Kin power over Light. When it streaked past Zeta, narrowly missing him, just the heat of it burned his arm to the bone.

The other female of the Elite had once been an attractive enough Magi, but her face now looked worn and haggard with the skin sagging on her bones. When she saw Grecia and Roman rushing toward her, she instantly began to shoot bursts of Fire power at them. From the corner of her eye, she could see Kelsey's pure stream and was bitterly envious. Couldn't these foolish Chronicles see that the Elite were trying to make them a world to live in!?

"Before we turn you into dinner," Grecia said pleasantly enough, "why don't you tell us who you are?"

"Lambda." Her green eyes narrowed to slits. "You're nothing but a healer, Fury. What makes you think you can even hope to compete with me?"

She went white as a surge of power turned Grecia into her natural form. The Fury bared her teeth in a mockery of a smile. "I might be a healer, but I'm also a whole lot bigger than you."

Lambda was smarter than that. She turned and ran back across the field to put distance between them. Roman immediately swung up onto Grecia's back and held on with his legs as he lifted his hands to call his power. If Lambda wanted to make this a round of target practice, then he was happy to oblige.

The two males with black hair that Xander and Jayda went after were identical twins. Both were of the element of Soil, which was not uncommon among twins. Morgan and Tariah were, as was their way, different yet again from the normal course of things. It couldn't even be blamed on the fact that they were not, technically, twins in this life. It was the last that counted for it was then that their power had been born.

Jayda was a healer and more so than even Grecia. It did not make her any less accurate as she hurled a blast of snow directly into one of the twin's face. As he swiped at his eyes so that he could see, she shot a stream of water into his stomach and sent him flipping backwards across the ground.

His brother rushed to his side and snarled at Jayda, "Is that the best you can do, Chronicle? Mu and I will tear you apart!" At Xander's arched brow, the Elite offered haughtily, "I am Nu."

A mocking smirk touched Xander's lips. "How fitting. If I were to write your names in Draconic, it would form a word meaning 'the worthless.'" At Jayda's surprise in his mind, he mentally showed her the written characters in Magi and then compared them to Draconic. The similarity was amusingly close.

Mu scrambled to his feet and hurled a blast of small rocks at Jayda. Xander calmly stepped in front of her and swung his hand through the air. In his wake, a ribbon of fire appeared that melted the bits of stone. They became encased in smoke as they turned to glass shrapnel and reversed their course.

The twins managed to put up a soil wall as a barrier, but more than one of the tiny projectiles went clean through and narrowly missed them both. They'd had no idea that an Elder could do such a thing. "Just surrender," Nu bluffed, "and we won't have to get tough with you!"

There was no immediate retort, but a heated air swept over them and they both slowly looked up to see an immense black Dragon leaning over the wall. His breath was close enough that they could smell the fire in his power. "Get tough with who?" he asked softly, his voice a dangerous rumble.

When C.J. did not divert from chasing her, Kappa turned and fled. Tears choked her throat and ran down her face as she scrambled across the landscape to get away. She couldn't do this! She couldn't fight C.J.!

He moved over and around obstacles as nimbly as if he was on the dunes of his homeland. With every stride, his long legs gained on her lead. "Kappa!" he shouted. "Just stop running! You can fight with us! I know you're not tainted! I *believe* in you!"

Pain ripped her in two. Over her shoulder she shouted, "You don't know what I've done!"

"I don't care!" Panic fluttered in his stomach as he saw how dangerously close they were to the cliffs. "Kappa, stop! Please! You can make anything right if you just try!" He felt as if he was fighting not just for her life but Cole's as well. If she was alive, then so was he. C.J. was somehow sure of it, and he was sure that losing one meant losing the other as if they were Linked. He couldn't bear the idea of losing either of them for good.

The land gave way suddenly to a cliff. Kappa tried to skid to a stop but she had been running too fast and the grass was too slippery. She pitched forward over the side, and she couldn't even be upset over it. She had been on borrowed time anyway. Perhaps, in her death, she could atone.

Dahlia didn't hesitate. She threw her majiks into C.J. and shoved the knowledge into his mind. She believed in her Chronicle. His lead of several hundred feet would give him those precious seconds that might save Kappa's life.

He dove over the side of the cliff and grabbed onto the majiks to bend them sharply. A bright green glow engulfed him and changed him into a Dragon shape. Because he was of average Magi height, he became a Dragon of average length at roughly eighteen feet long. That added size was just enough. His claws closed around Kappa, his wings arched, and they sailed back up into the air mere feet before hitting the ragged rocks below.

Her eyes flew wide in shock and she stared at his draconic face. She hadn't seen the change, but she would have known him anywhere. His eyes were still the same as when she had first seen them in a boy's face. They were now the eyes of a man, and quite livid with it. Her gentle weaver was *furious.*

He landed more gracefully than one would expect from someone new to the form, but Dahlia had shoved *all* of her knowledge in his mind. He put Kappa down and firmly rooted her with vines before releasing the majiks and going back to normal. He could feel the sharp drain on Dahlia's power and pulled her into his arms to keep her steady. As soon as the battle was done, all the Furies would need to feed.

Kappa tugged at her binds, but found herself very firmly caught. "What are you going to do with me?"

He sat down on the grass and crossed his arms. "Right

now, I'm going to bite my tongue before I yell at you. When everyone else joins us, I'll yell at you then." He blew out a hard breath and then suddenly seemed to realize what had happened. He boggled at Dahlia. "I turned into a Dragon."

Inexplicably, Kappa found herself smiling. Maybe he hadn't changed that much after all.

Mu and Nu, despite their combined strength, were no match for a fifty-foot Fury. Xander took care of Mu by flinging him into the violent storm clouds. Lightning flashed across the darkened sky, and the Elite never came back down. Nu, sensing his own demise, turned to go after Jayda.

She stood silently as he approached and she neither ran nor dodged. Just as he lunged for her, she lifted her hands. A giant ice spear instantly formed. He was moving far too fast to stop and impaled himself on it. Yellow blood welled nauseatingly, and his shocked eyes met hers. "I might be a doctor," she said softly, "but there's another side to that. To know how to heal even mortal wounds, you often need to know how they were caused."

The ice shard surged outward and froze him solid. A sharp strike from Xander's tail shattered him into millions of fragments. The stench of rotten power dissipated.

Lambda could only run. There was no stopping to catch a breath, not when there was a mounted Dragoon pair behind her. Roman was shockingly accurate with his wind pellets, and many struck her flesh before she could evade. Blood oozed down her arms and legs and stained her cloak. Pellets that missed her and struck the land did not do damage. They were simply absorbed.

When she found herself running into a large wall of cliffs, she knew she was done. There had been no cliffs there before the fight. The Isle itself had decreed her death sentence. Her mouth bitter, she turned to face the pair hovering in the air behind her. All she had wanted to do was get rid of the war-mongering, hate-filled Magi. What was so bad about that?

Zeta was by far faster and stronger than his brethren, but he was outclassed by Kelsey and Solis. The simple fact was that his power was not infinite. Kelsey's was, and she deliberately forced him to use more and more power, her every blast growing stronger and stronger with no clear effects to her. "I can go on for days," she told him as she hurled a spear of fire at him. "How about you?"

His body had begun to ache and burn, his muscles locking and knotting painfully. He reached desperately for his final reserves of power, and instead of attacking, he let it well inside. He would destroy himself before he ever gave them the satisfaction! Could the Isle handle a detonation? He didn't know. He didn't care.

"Get back!" Solis grabbed Kelsey and dragged her as far back as he could before they encountered the line of dead trees.

Zeta's body began to glow brightly when an immense shard of ice wrapped in lightning shot out of nowhere and slammed into his chest. It expanded to encase him just as he detonated. Trapped inside the ice, the power that blasted outward was purified as it passed through. By the time it reached the air, there was nothing it could damage.

Kelsey shot a fireball at the ice and blew it into tiny fragments to leave no trace of him behind. Heart pounding, she looked to where Morgan and Tariah now stood with Dominic and Jazz. Both twins looked lucid and alert, and power still swirled around their hands. "Are you sane again, or should I be glad you hit what you aimed at?"

Morgan had to grin. "My aim was never good to begin with, so count your blessings, Soot." His smile faded quickly as he looked around the scene. There should have never been another battle on these broken lands. It was like pouring salt into an open wound. "Is everyone all right?"

"We're fine." Xander kept an arm around Jayda's waist. "Tired, though. C.J. and Dahlia have Kappa captured."

Though all Furies needed to be fed, they were not at a critical level just yet. They could wait until camping, if camping was a possibility. To find that out, they needed to talk to Kappa. Morgan and Tariah led everyone to where C.J. and Dahlia waited.

There was something eerily familiar about Kappa to both twins, but if she had been at the last battle in Bergia, that was hardly surprising. Those missing memories had slowly started slipping free inside everyone.

"Well done." Morgan sat down next to C.J. and ruffled his hair. "We knew we could count on you." He turned toward Kappa and studied her critically. No taint clung to her power. It was as clean and fresh as the air around them. She still looked as lovely as she had always been.

Zeta's words danced in their minds. No one asked why she would be beholden to the Elite for her life, but they all wondered. Tariah asked only, "How many are left?"

"Two, if you include me. The strongest, Alpha, is farther from here. She can't come to you. You would have to go to her." Her lips twisted into a bitter smile. "None of us answer to our own names anymore. You already know Alpha by another name. My true name has been forsaken to me."

"How did all of this happen, Kappa?" Dahlia asked gently. She could not help but care for this other woman. She could see C.J.'s memories and feel his emotions. It broke her heart.

Kappa took a deep breath. "Years ago, Sistra appeared before Soh Emik. He was . . . broken. His mind was broken. Sistra wanted revenge and wanted to destroy the Magi for destroying her happiness. Maybe, in her own way, she wanted to save other Furies. There's no knowing now.

"When that fight happened back then, Sistra translocated everyone far away. I woke up in the middle of a desert. It was like being born again and very disorienting. Years later, we all suddenly got contacted out of nowhere by Sistra. She had found the Lost Isle and showed us how to get here. The geysers made everyone stronger, but it . . . twisted them further. I did not go near them. I didn't . . . I didn't even really want to be here."

She closed her eyes for long moments and then looked at C.J. "I don't know where Cole is. I've felt him following me, but I haven't seen him. The two of you . . . broke my heart. I wanted to die, yet something about the two of you made me want to live."

"I think that you already have your answer," Xander said softly. "Your power is true, Kappa. You were with the Elite, but you were never one of them. Lucksphere still loves you, still forgives you anything."

She looked at him in shock for a moment, then looked away. "I don't know how it could."

"Don't ask why." Kelsey's blue eyes were fierce. "Just accept it. Just go forward from today. Learn from your mistakes. Isn't that what adults do?"

"Most of them do," Solis murmured. "The smart ones, anyway. And I think Kappa is a smart lady." He rubbed a hand slowly over Kelsey's back. "Why cause the disruptions, Kappa? Was it to destroy Magi, or was there some other reason?"

"It was that and it was a hope of forcing more Chronicles to be born. Or to lure out the ones who still lived." Her breath came sad and long. "I don't know anything about the storms. We didn't do that. They just started forming when we were upsetting the lands. The storms here have been here for a millennia."

It only proved their theory that the storms were the world's attempt to heal. Grecia looked toward the center island where it seemed dark and malevolent. It was sickening to think of how severe the wound must be to produce such a storm. "What is at the center?" As soon as she said it, she knew. "Sistra is your 'Alpha', isn't she? She is the one you are beholden to for your life."

"If we can reason with her," Jazz said, "then we can free Kappa. I don't believe Sistra is bad. She was chosen to be a Fury. She knows she belongs with her Chronicle."

Tears slid down Kappa's cheeks. "How I envy you all."

"You'll have Cole." C.J. freed her from the vines and moved closer to hug her tightly. "It won't be the same, no, but it'll be wonderful for you. You need each other. I know Magi and Kin don't usually become permanent mates, but if you two love each other, then you can't say it isn't right."

"Is it safe to camp here?" Tariah asked.

Kappa nodded. "As I said, I am the only walking Elite member left." She studied Morgan and Tariah. "How did you shrug off the intoxication? The Elite never could."

"They weren't Chronicles," Morgan said simply. "We are designed to absorb power. And we think the Lost Isle has . . . has selected Tariah and me to take control. The power was potent, and that gave us the intoxication. Now that we're used to it, we should not be in any danger. The Elite are very lucky they weren't simply torn apart."

Tents were dug out of bags and put up. Kappa didn't have one, but she did not mind sleeping outside. There were enough meals packed for at least one more night of camping, and C.J. forced Kappa to take one of his extras. If Cole was his brother, then she was his sister. It was that simple.

By the time what should have been morning came around, everyone was fully recharged. The Furies had been fed, and unexpected geysers during the night had affected all the Chronicles and not just the twins. It made them all much more powerful than before. It also did something else.

The four Chronicles still on their journey discovered that the next third of their lines had darkened. That left no doubt in anyone's mind any longer that this was where they were supposed to be and what they were supposed to be doing. Once they were able to fix what was wrong, finding the Isle of Dragons would likely be their final step. Luckily, the four older Dragoons still remembered how to get there. It would not be hard.

Kappa was gone when they emerged from their tents, and it did not truly surprise anyone. What did surprise them was the fact that she had left a distinct trail for them to follow. She was breaking down and opening the path that would lead them toward the center island where Sistra hid.

They wasted no time in following the route. It was not easy. The further they went, the closer they got to the center, the worse the storms became. It was only when they were able to look across the divide and realize for the second time that they could see where they had come from that Xander realized why the shape had looked odd. "It's a spiral. The islands form a spiral chain leading toward the center."

'Do you see that, Xander?' There was laughter in Tarinah's voice as she perched gracefully on her Fury's back. They hovered in the sky over Sanguine with Xander beside them. 'Our city is surrounded by a spiral of mountains!' She held out her hand where the chron symbol was etched into her lines. One half of the symbol seemed to form a similar spiral. 'Just like in our name.'

Jayda's hands flew up to cover her mouth as tears welled in her eyes. "What is it?" Kelsey asked as she hugged her taller sister tightly.

"In Xander's memory." She closed her eyes helplessly. "We walk on what . . . what were once mountains. The mountains were the spiral leading to Sanguine."

"How big was this land once?" Roman asked softly.

"Roughly the size of Choral." Xander took a long, steadying breath. "We must keep walking. I will be fine. And stay out of my head," he scolded Morgan and Tariah. "You have endured enough!"

At one point along the path, they found themselves at a point higher than the quickly approaching center island. It looked slightly sunken with an immense crater situated in the very center that looked as if it might go into Lucksphere itself. There was a figure of some sort in the middle that might have been a Dragon . . . or Fury.

It seemed as if there were shadows moving across the center island without stop, but that made little sense when there was almost no light to be had. It was only when they heard the rumble on the wind that they realized what they saw.

Monsters.

Hundreds of monsters.

"There was nothing to mutate," Dominic said. "They must have . . . have somehow been *born* this way." He took a long breath. "We will have to fight our way through. C.J. . . . I'm sorry. You're going to have to make your power do something it was never intended to do."

"You can do it," Dahlia said softly to her mate. She framed his face with her hand and her heart and power swirled around him soothingly. "You wouldn't be here if you weren't important. You're good with vines and quakes. Use them."

He nodded slightly. He was scared. He would have been lying to say he wasn't. But he wasn't going to leave. He had to do this. Kappa and Cole were counting on him, and so was his family. He would never shame Dahlia or Morgan and Tariah.

It felt like hours passed before they were actually underneath the terrible storm clouds. There was no longer any path to follow. No grass and no growth of any kind. They had to pick their way over broken rocks and jagged cliffs as they steadily made their way down toward the crater. The wind screamed and cried and begged for mercy.

Miraculously, it did not rain. The lightning flashed so often, so strongly, that it was easy enough to see where they were going and what they were doing. As they reached the edge of the five hundred foot crater, they distinctly saw Sistra hovering in the center.

She was blue in color with white spots, roughly around Dominic's size, and there was something more terrifying than beautiful about her face. In the last battle, she had lost an arm and a wing. The wing had re-grown but the arm had not. Even after nine years, the wound remained open. It did not bleed, yet it was nothing remotely resembling healed.

She looked worn and haggard with every one of her years weighing heavily. She, too, was an Elder. A Fury Elder. She was only a thousand years younger than Xander. She had endured the massacre destroying her dreams. She had endured the millennia of waiting. But she had not been as lucky as the rest. Her Chronicle had been killed by Magi law. It broke the hearts of those who looked at her. How could they hate her?

C.J. spotted Kappa standing not far away on the edge of the crater. Tears ran down her face without stop, and in a flash of lightning she looked almost as tired and worn as Sistra. This madness had to end before more lives were destroyed.

Painfully, Sistra lifted her head. Her green eyes were in turns dull and bright, and sane and insane. "Dragoons." It was little more than a sibilant hiss echoed by the monsters that crawled over the crater, always moving close but not attacking. Not yet. "Do you see what has become of our rightful home? Help me destroy the Magi. Make them suffer as they made us suffer."

"The Magi are changing, Sistra," Morgan called. "The laws are revoked. Chronicles are to be protected, to be sheltered. They will not be murdered anymore. No more Furies will suffer as you did. You *succeeded*. You saved them."

"It is not enough." Her head slowly turned toward Kappa. "Attack them!"

"I can't." Her voice sounded thin. "You know I can't."

"And just who do you think gave you life?" The words that spewed into the air were as vicious as the storms. "I gave you that form and flesh. I gave you your second life. You served me already. I could have erased you, but I let you live. I will not release you! Do my bidding if you wish to ever be free!"

Painfully, slowly, she turned toward the Dragoons. Her refusal was written all over her face. "Kill me." Her voice came out so faint that it was almost impossible to hear. "Please, C.J. I beg of you to free me of this curse."

On a violent oath, he turned toward Sistra. "Is this what you want?" he shouted. "This destruction of people who just don't know any better? How is destroying the Magi going to make right all the wrongs? It can't! Is this what Phedo would have wanted?"

"No," came an unexpected male voice. "It is not what I want."

They all turned sharply and discovered the form of a SunKin Elf standing on a large rock nearby. Only C.J. and Dahlia recognized him, and Dahlia had to grab C.J. before he leapt forward. "Cole!" he shouted. His friend's words sank in and his eyes widened in shock. "Wait, what do you mean it's not what *you* want?"

A surge of power rippled over Cole's body and the golden tattoos suddenly connected and changed shape. Morgan stopped breathing entirely as he recognized the shape and form. A Chronicle's lines were unique to each individual. No two would ever be alike. "You're a Second Born Kin," he said softly. "You're Phedo."

Chapter Twenty-Four

Cole looked at Morgan for a moment and then said softly, "I never hated you, Morgan. I never hated anyone. If you have felt guilty for not finding me sooner, then stop. This was a path set before me long before you ever arrived." He looked at Tariah. "For what my father did to Daylar . . . I am sorry."

"Is it . . . is it possible?" Kelsey whispered to Xander.

He slowly shook his head. "I have never seen a Second Born Kin that was not twice a Kin, but that does not mean it is not possible."

"Help us!" Jazz called to Cole. "Please, help us talk some sense into your Fury!"

Cole looked directly at Kappa. "The sense is there. She's just too afraid of it." He leapt down off the rock and walked toward her purposefully. "She couldn't even see me when we met. She wasn't looking with her heart. But I saw her heart. I knew."

"Stay back!" She held up her hands to hold him off, her eyes blind with terror and tears. "You can't be . . . it can't be . . ."

He brushed aside her hands and pulled her into his arms. "I am." He buried his face in her hair and let his power well. He reached for her with his emotions and his power, let her see and sense what was inside. That wellspring of desperate emotion that the Dragons called *ishke*. The emotion that marked only a Chronicle or Fury. "Kappa."

She collapsed against him on a sob, her hands beating at his shoulders wildly, and her cream-colored hair suddenly streaked with golden yellow in evidence of her true power. "You were dead!" she sobbed into his shoulder. "Why couldn't I die to find you?! Why did I turn to hate?!"

He held her closer. "It doesn't matter anymore. It's done." He looked over her head to where the shocked Dragoons stood. "I don't know the 'how', I'm sorry. But I knew when I met Kappa that she was a Second Born as well, and I knew she was my Sistra. When I died . . . I just knew I couldn't. I met the original Cole halfway to the Underrealm. His body was alive, but his soul was not. We traded to give me the time I needed to find my Fury."

It dawned on C.J. at last. "That's why . . . that's why she was drawn to me. I'm a Soil Chronicle, and you and I had been together so long that your presence was a part of me. It sent out a confusing signal."

"Then what happened to Sistra and Kappa?" Kelsey demanded.

"Me." The one who held Sistra's body stared at all of them malevolently. "I wanted this body. I forced her to live again to do what I could not."

"That's why you wanted to die," Tariah said softly to Kappa. "You were trying to return to Phedo. You didn't know he was still alive." She took a deep breath. "Why did you change your mind? You were so determined to destroy the Magi!"

"That . . . other being was inside me." She shuddered. "Her rage, my rage, her grief, my grief . . . it was one terrible force. I couldn't fight it. But when I saw you and Morgan become the Chronis Dragon . . . I could see the hope for future Furies. It gave me the strength to die though she would not let me. All these years . . . I did as she bid, praying someone would destroy me at last."

"Then just who is in your other body? You said she was there all along?" Morgan stared at Sistra, trying to determine why she still seemed so very familiar even without the proper soul and power inside.

"I don't know." Her voice was weary and she rested heavily against Cole. "I don't. I don't even know how to live anymore . . ."

"I do." He tilted her head back and met her eyes. "I do. Whatever we do from now on, we do together."

Sistra hissed at them all. "So be it!" She roared furiously and the sound reverberated off the rocks and crater, bounced down from the clouds. "I will destroy all of you, then all of the rest, and we will start over from scratch!"

The monsters lunged up out of the crater with claws and fangs bared. Destroying them was no easy feat, and for every one destroyed there were two more to take its place. All Furies went into their natural form to fight more efficiently, but even Xander had his claws full. The monsters just kept pouring out of the crater.

To make matters worse, Sistra began to attack as well. She did not throw merely the tornados and lightning of her Air element. She threw them all. She caused quakes and hurricanes; she threw fireballs and shards of ice. She sent blasts of Light at Cole and Kappa that the Second Born Kin was forced to block and repel. She even threw blasts of Dark, regenerating the monsters when they were down but not dead. She used every element. She *was* every element.

'Xander?' Morignan was sitting on a cliff outside Sanguine where they could watch the sunset. 'Did you know our island is alive? Tarinah and I can hear it breathe. I would daresay it is the very heart of this world. We live in the heart of the world. It is no wonder we exist on love.'

A sickening feeling swept through Xander as he stared at Sistra. "She's the Isle," he said softly. "She's possessed by the Isle of Chronicles!"

"Close but not quite it, fledgling." Sistra blew ice at him that he had to block with his wing. "I am not the heart of this world. I *am* this world. I *am* Lucksphere. And I am going to erase it all and begin again!"

Something rang false in her words though Tariah could not figure out what. Her sharp eyes could see quite plainly that there was at least some truth. Every time the land took damage, a matching wound appeared on Sistra's body. The storm was surely the manifestation of her torn arm. Destroying her would, at the very least, destroy whatever was left of the isle.

But there was something else odd. Though Sistra attacked them, she did not leave her crater. Tariah stared harder and could not see anything. She turned and swiftly located Cole. He was a Chronicle, but he had inherited Kin power. *Cole! Fire some light under Sistra! I need to see what she is hiding!*

He immediately sent a ball of power whipping down into the crater. She watched intently, and the light illuminated a distinct hole in the crater that led even deeper into the ground. Whatever was in there was what Sistra defended. *Morgan! We have to go down there! We have to see what she is hiding!*

"Go!" Jazz clawed apart another monster. "We will cover for you. Just go! You're the only ones who can do this!"

Morgan and Tariah sprinted for the edge of the crater, and the others began to cover them with attacks. Cole and Kappa went after Sistra directly, forcing her to focus on them and not the twins. The monsters barely noticed the twins going past; they were too focused on the battle at hand. When one did notice, it was C.J.'s perfect aim with his vines that kept it from following.

The hole in the crater was several feet wide and so deep that it was pitch dark. Morgan called up a bubble of air and wrapped himself and his sister within it. There was no telling how far into the land the hole went.

They seemed to descend forever. When Tariah looked up, she could see the entrance becoming a dim and distant memory. The hole at the top was little more than a pinpoint by the time they actually landed. It felt bitterly cold and it was gut-wrenchingly dark. The twins took a hesitant step forward, and light suddenly flooded the area and blinded them. When they could see again, Tariah could barely stifle a cry of horror.

The place at the center of the world was a swamp. It was a putrid, oozing mess. Rivers and pools of mud and filthy water stood motionless. Some dripped from the thorn covered walls. Vines that might have once held flowers now held dead bulbs. Everything was covered in a pale and sickly cast, and the air smelled of rotting vegetation. Hard dirt covered where there wasn't sludge, and cracks crossed it like scars.

None of that was as truly horrifying as what stood in the very center. Bound within more of those vicious thorny vines were the figures of a man and a woman. The thorns bit into their skin, and their faces were lined with pain and fatigue. On first glance, the man seemed to be dead for he did not breathe and he did not move, but when Tariah cautiously stepped closer, she could feel the faintest of power inside him still.

The woman stirred slightly, her lashes lifting to reveal eyes that were half white and half blue. Old eyes. Ancient eyes. Eyes that had seen far too much and suffered far too long. "My children?" Her voice was thin, almost non-existent, but it was very, *very* familiar.

"It was you," Morgan whispered. "You led us on our journeys." His throat closed painfully as tears welled in his eyes. "Who . . . who are you?"

"I have no real name." Her eyes closed for a moment and then opened again. "You might call me Sphera. I am one half of this world. Air, Water, and Light are born from me." She took a ragged breath as if speaking was simply too much for her to endure. "My Luck . . . does he live? Have I lost everything?"

Tariah bit back a cry, her fingers tangling desperately with Morgan's. "He lives. There is power in him, so he must live."

Sphera's lips tried to smile, but they were dry. They cracked in places and golden blood welled. "If he dies, I will have no will to hold on. I have carried the weight alone for so long . . . If we die, there will be no Lucksphere. I am sorry."

Tariah moved closer and tore a piece of cloth from the one wrapped around her hips. She wet it with her Water power and tenderly wiped at Sphera's lips and face. "What has happened?" she asked softly. "Tell us how we can make it right."

Her sigh was long. "Our garden . . . see what it has become. The Magi . . . the Magi began to kill our garden as they killed the balance. We let our gardens bloom with flowers, let the flowers be born on land. Our beautiful Dragoons. Our precious children." Shimmering love filled her eyes as she looked at Morgan and Tariah. "How we loved you! All that lives is our child, but . . . Chronicles. . . you are our flesh and blood.

"We chose our most beautiful, our most precious flowers to become our first Chronicles. But we could not ask you to do things alone. We looked at our other children, and we saw the beautiful love inside Dragons. Oh, how they love everything! We made them our Furies." Tears slid down her cheeks. "You are happy? Tell me you are happy."

"Our Furies make us whole. We are strong because of them." Morgan's voice broke and then steadied again. "They waited patiently for us, Sphera. They loved us before we were ever there. You chose them perfectly. And Xander . . . look at him to see just how well you chose."

"I'm glad." She smiled though it trembled.

"What happened to Luck?" Tariah gently touched his face and found it cool to her fingers. He was a handsome man and Sphera's perfect opposite. She knew, was sure, his eyes would be half green and half red. His hair was silver where Sphera's was gold. His skin was dark where hers was pale. The father of all that lived.

"The massacre." A sob tangled in Sphera's chest. "The Magi came. They tore apart our heart. Our children were destroyed. It . . . broke Luck. In all the years, I have tried to bloom our flowers again and again. But they were always killed. Our beloved Furies were mercifully killed before their love turned them . . ."

"Into you." Morgan stepped forward and touched her hand where it was caught between two horrid thorns. "We came back," he said softly. "We came back as we promised. We're here, and we can make it better."

"When I saw your flowers blooming in the middle of our dead garden . . . I felt hope again." Her hand stirred, her fingers brushing his. "Blooming again. Morgan, Tariah. Your flowers were so strong that they came back to us to be born again."

"Then tell us what to do to make it right." Tariah gently touched Luck's face and then Sphera's. "I've lost one set of parents. I can't lose another. Tell us how to defeat Sistra. How to help you."

"Sistra . . . my pain, my rage, my fear, my grief . . . even my hate. It took shape. In my worst moment, I hated my Magi children. And my hate doomed them all. It met Sistra's grief and found an easy outlet." Her eyes closed. "I'm sorry."

The sudden feeling of their mates calling urgently had Morgan and Tariah looking up sharply. The others needed them. "It's getting worse."

"Go," Sphera urged softly. "Please. No more death."

The twins turned and ran out of the swamp, and Morgan carried them swiftly up toward the surface. The fight was not going well. The Furies were starting to run low on power, and there wasn't a single person who was left unwounded. The monsters finally diminished in number, but not quick enough. Sistra seemed slightly weaker, but still impossibly strong.

Morgan rushed over to Jazz in time to shield her from an unexpected attack. He forcefully poured his power into her and gave her enough to change into Magi form. As she collapsed into his arms, his power rose to cover him in a white aura. "Feed," he told her sharply. *Cole! Kappa! You still have reserves! Cover us so we may feed our Furies!*

Cole and Kappa ran down to join them from where they had been fighting and they worked swiftly to distract the enemy. The Chronicles followed Morgan's lead in forcing their Furies to change form so they could feed as well. They couldn't go on like this any longer!

It's Luck! Tariah spoke directly to Morgan's mind. *We have to restore Luck. It's the only way Sphera's grief will lift!*

My children. Sphera's voice softly whispered across all of their minds. *The only way to restore Luck is to restore the balance. Our garden must bloom again.*

"We'll go." Cole straightened his back. "Kappa and I will make the garden bloom."

Phedo, Sphera's voice warned gently, *you know what that means.*

He smiled at Kappa who smiled back tremulously. "We know. But . . . we were on borrowed time anyway." He walked over to C.J. and knelt down beside his friend. "I love you," he said softly. "You're my brother in every way that counts. I wish we could have flown the skies with our Furies. The one thing I cannot regret in my second life is getting to meet you."

Tears slid down C.J.'s cheeks. "You're saying goodbye."

"Who knows? Maybe my flower will bloom again."

C.J. took a deep breath and leaned over to whisper softly in Cole's ear. He eased back and somehow smiled. "I promised, right?"

His Kin brother smiled as well, and it was a genuine smile. "I think your name *does* suit you, C.J. Your parents knew more than we did. Don't look at it in Magi language.

Look it up in the Kin. You'll see what I mean. Our many more characters bring beauty to mundane things." He gently touched Dahlia's hand. "Take care of my brother."

Her lips curved. Her strength was pouring back in now that she had fed on her Chronicle's power. "You'll have to come back," she told him, "and make sure that I am doing a good job."

He got to his feet and walked over to Kappa. Their hands linked and they leapt down into the crater. The monsters started to go after them, but the Furies were back to full strength from those precious few minutes. They joined forces with their mates, and the combined strength of the Dragoons formed a thick shield to protect them all. They needed to buy time for Cole and Kappa.

Kappa used her power to take herself and Cole down to the swamp, and they walked with their hands linked to where Sphera and Luck were trapped. Her throat tight, Kappa said, "I'm so sorry for what I did."

"You are not to blame." Sphera's eyes opened slightly. "You must never believe that. You were chosen, Sistra. You are one of our chosen ones. Jazz was right about you all along. C.J. was right. The love in you is true."

"Are you ready?" Cole asked his mate softly.

She looked at him with shimmering eyes filled with her emotions, the greatest of which was that wonderful third Dragoon emotion. That gift of their mother and father. The gift of their world. "I'm with you," she said simply.

He pulled her close and kissed her tenderly, and lines that matched his swirled down her body. He let his power, both born and born again, well in the air around them. Her power, born and born again, rose to meet his. They both began to glow brightly, brilliantly, as if they were going to detonate themselves. At the very moment when they would have been destroyed, they instead turned into pure light. They flew into Luck, merged into his body . . . and his eyes opened.

He drew a deep breath. It was the first he'd had in a millennia. Strength and power poured into him from the unconditional gift of life. "Sphera." He reached for her with his mind and his power and wrapped her within his love. It burned as bright as any Dragoon's. "I am here."

The thorns began to change, began to fall away from the vines, as she moved her hand toward his. Their fingers met, meshed, and a sob slipped past her lips. "I've missed you!"

Power flooded from their joined hands and tore through the swamp. The cracked ground pulled together and bloomed with lush green grass. The deadened vines bloomed again with desert roses. The filthy water evaporated, and fresh, pure, water cascaded down the walls to fill the pools and rivers. The vines encasing Sphera and Luck lost their thorns and bloomed with flowers as they fell away. And as Luck drew Sphera into his arms, the garden began to glow softly, strongly. Beautiful once more.

On the surface, Sistra screamed in pain. Morgan and Tariah felt the rumble within the land and leapt to their feet. The barrier came down as they rushed toward the edge of the crater, and they threw themselves out over the top. Within the first two feet, they had become Dragons. Within the next two, they fused.

The immense Dragon was twice the size of Xander and covered in silver scales the same color as its eyes. Four wings held it aloft and fins extended from its starkly beautiful face. The Chronis Dragon, as it had been named, had only been seen twice before. Perhaps this would be the last time it was ever needed.

There was nowhere for Sistra to move. Nowhere for her to retreat. The Chronis slammed into her and tore her from her perch over the crater. She did not fight or resist as the Chronis hurled her up through the air. She did not open her wings to fly away. She simply waited for the end.

Finally, it had come.

From one claw, the Chronis hurled a stream of raw ice at her that encased her fully. From the other claw, lightning flew and shattered her into millions of pieces. The abrupt destruction caused a shockwave to be released and the entire island went ballistic. Geysers spewed into the air as the ground shook violently.

Without hesitation, the Chronis Dragon began to draw it all in. It pulled in every geyser and loose tendril of power. It hovered over the center of the crater and began to glow blindingly bright. No one could look close yet no one could look away. The Chronis threw back its head and, with a roar that shook the world, released the power.

The shockwave ripped across the land and sea and tore across the sky. The storms were dissipated instantly and released the Flutterlies to their proper duty.

The Lost Isle began to shake violently and then rose swiftly through the air as the ocean receded and pulled back. In minutes, the spiral isles had become the top of the spiral mountains once more. They rose high enough into the air that it was certain to snow when cooler weather returned.

The crater filled and healed with green grass rushing to cover it. The hole down to the secret garden disappeared entirely, safely protected within its heart once more. Across the world, the storms dissipated and lands stopped shaking. The small islands of Kindred found their shores expanding as the ocean pulled back. Other lands were as yet born new. Some were forested. Others were beautiful flat fields of grass and flowers. One even had mountains not yet covered in snow.

As the last of the power left, the Chronis Dragon circled the spiral mountains before landing gracefully in the center where its city had once laid. With a glow, the Chronis became the Dragon forms of Morgan and Tariah. Another glow returned them to their normal Chronicle forms.

The shockwave had healed and replenished all the Chronicles and Furies. They made their way down the mountains by air and rushed across the plains toward where Morgan and Tariah laid. Both were perfectly fine though they were deeply asleep. When Dominic lifted Tariah into his arms, shock stole his voice entirely. "Jay," he said hoarsely. "The baby."

She lightly rested her hands over Tariah's belly and her eyes went wide. Her lips trembled as she saw the miracle that had occurred. "A Chronicle. She's carrying a Chronicle. The garden is in bloom."

Deep below the surface in the immortal garden of life, Luck and Sphera stood together looking at the beauty surrounding them. They were not healed fully, not yet. More Chronicles and Furies would need to be born to truly restore the balance.

Luck softly opened his hands, and on his palms rested two seeds. He released them into the garden and smiled. "When you bloom," he said softly, "then we will know we are healed. Until that day, sleep well, little ones."

His arm slid around Sphera, and she turned into his embrace. Finally, she was alive. She was not alone any longer. Their children would laugh. They would play. They would love and they would live. No one would ever cry again.

Chapter Twenty-Five

Kelsey awoke one morning a few days later and realized that her lines were pulsing. She sat upright in shock, dislodging Solis, and stared at her arms. Her lines were darkening. The darkness slowly flowed down her skin and marked the last of her journey.

It had been days since the resurrection of the Lost Isle. None of the Chronicles or Furies had left yet. They had been camping in the valley and savoring how it felt to be somewhere they belonged. And they did belong. None had ever felt more at home.

They had built small homes of wood and stone and glass to rest within, but most of the time they were flying over the mountains and valleys to see and learn. To Kelsey's absolute delight, the western side of the land, just past that side of the mountains, was a wonderfully hot and beautiful desert. She had made everyone laugh by diving into the sand happily.

They had known the journey was not yet over, though they hadn't felt any urge to go anywhere. Perhaps Sphera had been recovering still. No one, not even Tariah, had been able to guess. But as Kelsey saw her lines darkening, she felt the stirring inside of that urge telling her where to go.

South.

The voice whispered softly across her soul welcomingly. "How far south?" she asked suspiciously of the air. "After what we went through, you could be more specific!"

Soft laughter filled her soul with joy. *Go south to the end of our heart. Your journey ends there.*

She scrambled out of bed and jerked on her clothes. When Solis didn't move, she scowled and went over to shake him. "Wake up, you lazy Fury! We have to go south to the end of the island!" She blinked. "Well, it's not really an island anymore, is it? It's more of a continent finally. We need a name for it."

He opened one eye. "You kept me up all night."

"You're the one with all those fascinating ideas in your mind. I was just trying them out." She tugged on his hand, so vibrantly alive that he couldn't tear his eyes away. "Solis! We have to go! My journey is almost over!"

He got out of bed with a smile and pulled on his clothes. How would he ever say no to her about anything?

She wasn't the only one who had felt the call. By the time they got outside, the other three who were still on their journey had also gathered. C.J. looked much older than he ever had before, but he was healing as well. He clung onto the hope that Phedo could be reborn again, and even if not, that he and Sistra were happy in the Underrealm where souls went when they were done.

"Elder Tariah!" Roman called teasingly toward her home. "Elder Morgan! You need to come with us, too!"

The twins were only reluctantly resigned to the fact that they were Elders, which made it all the more fun to tease them about it. For that reason, Tariah was pulling a face as she and Dominic left their home to join their clan. "You can't call me that for another thousand years," she scolded.

"Deal," Roman answered promptly. "I'm holding you to that."

"When do we get to know your name?" Kelsey demanded of C.J. "You told Phedo, so you have to tell us."

"No." He smiled. "I'm going to wait to tell you until he's with us again. You'll just have to be patient, Kel." He rubbed his cheek against Dahlia's hair as she slid her arms around him. "But I don't mind my name that much anymore. Dahlia knows Kin, and she told me what it meant in that language. Phedo was right. He usually was."

When Morgan had joined them as well, the Furies

went into their natural form and their Chronicles climbed to where they belonged. Together, they flew over the mountains and made their way toward the distant ocean. It was not a long trip by flight; it was only an hour or two. A Fury with a Chronicle could cover the entire continent within a day. By foot it would be a week. Big, but not too big. It was perfect.

They landed on the southern shore, and they were still not entirely sure what they sought. Despite that, their lines steadily continued mapping their journeys. Just as they fully darkened, Kelsey saw something on the horizon. "Ships!" she exclaimed. "I see ships!" Her eyes slowly widened. "A lot of ships . . ."

It was an entire armada and all bore the flag of the Magi king. It was also not the only thing on the horizon. A darkened line moved in as well, and within minutes it was recognizable as a fleet of Dragons. There were at least a hundred of them, and at the front were the four Dragons on the Council of Elders.

Grecia studied the ground and then the sky. When Roman arched a brow, she said, "I'm making sure we really did win and the world is not ending. I thought nothing less would get those old fuddy-duddies off the Isle!"

As the ships grew closer, it became obvious that they carried not just Magi. There were dozens of Kin on board as well, including Elder Juniper. There were no docks to land at, so the ships dropped anchor and sent in smaller boats that could land on shore. Riding in the first one came Finus and Juniper, and they had a few other familiar faces with them.

"Kelsey!" Etude nearly wailed it as she shot through the air and hugged her friend around the neck. "I missed you! You're okay! Oh, I knew you'd do it!"

"Etude!" Kelsey hugged her happily. "I missed you too!"

Sparkle and Daylar were also on board, and flew over to hug Tariah in the same way. The others didn't get a chance to feel left out. The boats also carried all of their parents.

"Mom." C.J. rushed forward and scooped her up off her feet. "I can't believe it! Why are you here? Do you . . . remember?"

Ferris smiled through her tears as she studied him. "When that shockwave came through, it put our memories back together." She scowled at Morgan. "And you, young man, have some explaining to do!"

He winced wryly. After meeting Sphera, he had suspected she was the one who had erased the other memories. He was sure of it now. It still didn't make him any less guilty of the same! "Yes'm."

The boats continued to carry out more people as Finus and Juniper walked toward where the Dragoons stood. The clan moved automatically to put Tariah and Morgan at the front as their leaders. The Dragons had begun to land, and those who were Dragon Lords turned to other forms to make more room. The four Elders were Lords, and they took a Magi form. It shocked the Furies even more because they had *never* done it in the past.

"We have come to make amends," Finus told the twins. "We bring supplies and artisans to help you build your city. I am offering a formal treaty of peace with you all. Dragoon, Dragon, and Kin. There will be no more war."

"We accept your offer, gladly," Morgan said softly. "There's been too much hate for too long." He made the Dragoon gesture of respect. "We would like you to stay with us, Finus. And learn about us."

"I would like that as well." He took a deep breath and turned. "Elen." As a young boy ran forward, he put a hand on his shoulder. "This is my son, Elen. He has twelve summers."

At one look, Tariah and Morgan knew what they saw.

The power in the boy bloomed bright and true. They knelt and offered their hands, and Elen took them with a smile. He liked how their silver eyes were warm. He felt safe near them.

The jolt went up through the twins' arms, and they looked up at Finus. Without hesitation, Morgan said, "Your son is a Chronicle."

There was a long silence before Finus scooped up Elen and tossed him in the air with a smile. "I suppose we need to celebrate, don't we?" As he caught his son in a fierce hug, everyone began to clap and cheer. The world needed Chronicles. They were the keepers of their beautiful Lucksphere.

Kelsey barely noticed when the Dragon Elders started talking with Finus about trade and possibly restarting the air service that had existed a millennia before. Instead, her eyes fixed to where Ilian and Quinn stood with members of the Militia. No one was in uniform, but it was obvious who and what they were.

She lightly touched the pendant she wore as she walked over to where Ilian stood. "Ilian." She smiled at him. "Thank you for your gift. It's beautiful." She felt Solis' arms around her waist and leaned back against him. "There is a Dragoon ceremony that is our version of a Linking one. I want you to attend."

"I would be honored." He smiled at her. She was, as he had always known she would be, a beautiful and confident adult. Solis suited her perfectly. "I'm glad you're happy. And that you aren't upset with me."

"Why would I be?" She studied him, then studied Quinn, then him again. "You know," she said, "maybe you've got the perfect match too. Maybe you just haven't noticed yet. Promise me that if you notice, you won't hesitate."

"I promise," he assured her, but inside he was amused. What woman in her right mind would want to be a mate to an Argyle who was always on the road?

The ceremony was held a week later in the half built city of Sanguine. People from all over the world were coming through, and a small port city was being built as well. People of all three races wanted to live on this peaceful land, and Morgan and Tariah had made it clear that the shores were open to all. They would have a festival every summer, and children could come to see if they were chosen as well.

After much bickering among the Council of Elders about who would preside over the ceremony, they finally decided to make Finus do it. He felt humbled and honored to be given the duty, and he made sure to memorize the ceremony to the last detail. It was more beautiful than he had imagined.

The four Dragoon pairs stood before him in the formal clothes of their homelands. For C.J., Roman, and Kelsey, that meant clothing of the desert. Kelsey had grown up in a forest, but she was a desert girl at heart. For Jayda, that meant the clothing of the snowy mountains.

Their Furies would have normally been in their natural form, but there wasn't enough room. Instead, they wore clothing that best suited the area of the Isle of Dragons where they had lived the longest. They also wore sashes in the color of their element to denote which clan they came from. All of the clothing had been woven by C.J. for he was the best the world had to offer.

"This ceremony," Finus began, "is an old one. It is steeped in heritage and history. Furies, will you dedicate your lives to protecting your Chronicles? Will you always support them, and give them the wings to fly across the skies as Dragoons?"

"We will," the Furies said as one.

"Chronicles, will you dedicate your lives to protecting your Furies? Will you always support them, and walk beside them when they wish to see the land as Dragoons?"

"We will," the Chronicles responded.

"Then it is with honor that I name you all full Dragoons and confer upon you the full privileges associated with such a position. I also declare you to be Linked by Magi standards, Bonded by Kin, and United by Dragon. You will stand as one, you will live as one, and you will die as one. For eternity."

"For eternity," said all those who were in the crowd.

He grinned. "Let us see our Dragoons take their first flight together on their new paths." He felt Elen hug him around the waist and lightly rested a hand on his shoulder. He couldn't wait to see the day that his son was able to start his journey and find the Fury meant for him.

Everyone moved back as much as possible so that there was room enough for all four Furies to change form. Many Magi felt nonplussed at the sight of Xander's fifty-foot size, but the tenderness in the way he lifted Jayda up to his back made his face more beautiful than terrifying.

As the pairs lifted to the sky and began to fly around the city, a cheer rose on the air. Sanguine was stable. It was the beating heart of the world. No Dragon or Fury would ever fear flying over it. Perhaps, someday, they would never fear flying over any city.

"How do you feel?" Solis asked Kelsey as he did a playful loop-de-loop in the sky.

She stretched her arms high and laughed as she got an armful of Flutterlies. They looked fat and happy as she released them to continue their peaceful journey. If they stormed again, it would be a normal storm. It would not be a portent of devastation. How long had it been since anyone had seen a storm and been unafraid? "I feel wonderful." She leaned down to wrap her arms around his neck. "And I saw my father talking to you very seriously. What was he going on about this time?"

Her mate chuckled softly. "He was giving me some of the finer points on how to raise a daughter just like you."

"Oh, are we planning on having one?"

"I was considering it."

She smiled and let her emotions swirl around him hotly and powerfully. His rose to meet hers and they flowed back and forth in an endless loop of infinity. "When do you want to start trying? Who knows. We might not take nine years like someone else we know."

His laughter rolled across the skies. "I could be persuaded to start trying now, if you promise you'll do your best to give me a blue-eyed daughter."

Her eyes filled with tears. She had never imagined she could ever be that happy and complete. Her wait, though shorter, had been no less sweet. "Then take me home," she said softly.

As he angled down toward the desert, they could see the setting sun in the distance illuminating their beautiful continent. It was called Esteria. In the language of the Magi, it meant 'peace.' In the language of the Kin, it meant 'heart.' In the language of the Dragons, it meant 'home.'

Esteria, the peaceful home of the world's heart. The place where a garden could bloom forever.

Epilogue

Dear Reader,

Summer is the most beautiful time on Lucksphere. In the thousand years I have walked this world, I have never seen anything as beautiful as this time.

There used to be a festival in Esteria every summer. We would welcome to our land the children who might be Chronicles. There were always at least a handful. We would guide them, tell them of what to expect, and wait for that summer in the future when they would begin their journey. No matter where it led, at the end was a Fury who had waited patiently to love them.

But that was how it was long ago. With every passing century, the number of Chronicles and Furies being born has diminished more and more. Furies stopped being born four centuries ago. The last one that was born is a female Air element. Do you know who she is? We did as soon as we saw her.

This summer was the most wonderful yet. On the ship coming in from the other lands was a young boy of thirteen summers. When his feet touched the soil, his first puberty began and familiar, wonderfully familiar, lines traversed his body. Our last Chronicle. Many cheered. Others wept for joy.

This summer heralds in a new time for Lucksphere. Our world is healed at last. The garden is in full bloom. In six or seven years, we will get to celebrate the last Dragoon ceremony. To know it is the last, to know that our world is healed . . . there are no words.

Oh, but I suppose there are a few words. C.J. was forced to keep his promise and tell us just what his name is. Prepare yourself. It is Chrisanthedel Jiordan. When you break down the characters of his name, the closest Magi equivalent is 'festival chaser.' But when you break it down in Kin . . . it becomes 'weaver of the heart.' I suppose the best parents, in the end, really do know their children better than anyone else.

And this is where we say goodbye, gentle reader. When the summer is warm, the sun shines bright, and you see flowers blooming, remember our story. Remember our laughter and our life. Remember our love.

May it never end.

Elder Tariah M. Chronis

Author Notes

I hope you enjoyed reading CHRONICLE OF SUMMER and coming along on this epic journey! It was an adventure to write, and I promise that I laughed every laugh and cried every tear along with you. If I've left an imprint on your heart, then I've done my job right.

If you loved this story, leave me a review on Amazon.com (http://amzn.to/1ODDYw3). I love hearing from fans just what touched them most about my stories, and reviews help more readers find me.

Want to keep up-to-date on what I'm writing or taking photos of? You can follow me on Facebook (www.facebook.com/stacyjgarrett) or Twitter (@stacyjgarrett). You can also sign up for my mailing list (http://eepurl.com/bNafOD) and hear first about new releases and get background info not shared anywhere else.

Never stop believing in a wonderful future, readers. Even in the darkest time, a small light can shine enough to bring back hope.

Stacy J Garrett

About the Author

Stacy J. Garrett (S. J. Garrett) was made in England but born in Sacramento, California, and like the redwoods of the state, her roots have dug deep. Her destiny as a bard was somewhat inevitable. Little else can explain how she constantly told her mother tall tales so outlandish that she couldn't even get grounded for them. Her mother and grandmother had her reading by age three, and that love of a good story propelled her through so many books that Scholastic Books gave her a medal. At the age of twelve, she picked up a point-and-shoot camera, and her love of telling a story took itself on a new journey as she starting taking photographs no one believed an untrained child could. She entered junior college by age fifteen to study photography, and in the same year, she wrote her first story. She has never looked back.

Stacy has seen both good and evil in her life, and her works, like life, have no half measures. Even in fantasy worlds of dragons and faeries, she knows that the constants of real emotion never change. Whether shooting photographs in stark straight black and white or brilliant digital color, or turning out fantastical novels of over a hundred thousand words, she shows an ability to move hearts, engage minds, and take people beyond the borders of reality into another world entirely.

Her current haunt is a comfy house in her beloved Sacramento where she wrangles four feline fur-kids and consumes peppermints like mana in order to balance a calendar filled with more creative venues than a sane person should realistically undertake. She considers herself extremely blessed to be surrounded by a group of amazing friends and associates who never hesitate to volunteer to do something a little strange for the sake of art, whether it is getting almost naked in a park or dressing up for a steampunk tea party.

She holds an Associate of Arts Degree in Fine Arts Photography, as well as a Bachelors of Fine Arts in Photography.

www.ingramcontent.com/pod-product-compliance
Lightning Source LLC
Chambersburg PA
CBHW070737190726
48292CB00002B/314